Better Off Dead

Sean Watkin was born and raised in Liverpool and studied a BA and MA in Creative Writing at Liverpool John Moores University. He has been shortlisted for Fresher Writing Award, Book a Break Prize and Bristol Short Story Prize. His writing has been featured in *The Gay UK* magazine, and *The Content Wolf* e-zine, as well as other LGBT+ publications. Sean lives in Liverpool with his partner and two dogs.

Also by Sean Watkin

DCI de Silva Crime Thrillers

Black Water Rising
Better Off Dead

SEAN WATKIN
BETTER OFF DEAD

First published in the United Kingdom in 2026 by

Canelo Crime, an imprint of
Canelo Digital Publishing Limited,
20 Vauxhall Bridge Road,
London SW1V 2SA
United Kingdom

A Penguin Random House Company
The authorised representative in the EEA is Dorling Kindersley Verlag GmbH.
Arnulfstr. 124, 80636 Munich, Germany

Copyright © Sean Watkin 2026

The moral right of Sean Watkin to be identified as the creator of this work has been asserted in accordance with the Copyright, Designs and Patents Act, 1988.
All rights reserved. No part of this publication may be reproduced or transmitted in any form or by any means, electronic or mechanical, including photocopy, recording, or any information storage and retrieval system, without permission in writing from the publisher.
No part of this book may be used or reproduced in any manner for the purpose of training artificial intelligence technologies or systems. In accordance with Article 4(3) of the DSM Directive 2019/790, Canelo expressly reserves this work from the text and data mining exception.

A CIP catalogue record for this book is available from the British Library.

Print ISBN 978 1 83598 132 0
Ebook ISBN 978 1 83598 133 7

This book is a work of fiction. Names, characters, businesses, organizations, places and events are either the product of the author's imagination or are used fictitiously. Any resemblance to actual persons, living or dead, events or locales is entirely coincidental.

Cover design by Andrew Smith

Cover images © Shutterstock

Printed and bound in Great Britain by Clays Ltd, Elcograf S.p.A.

Look for more great books at
www.canelo.co | www.dk.com

This book is for my mum and dad, who taught me hard work pays off.

One

Monday 15 August, 2022

The heat had been searing all month, but on that day it rained. DCI Winifred de Silva drove onto the carpark; stones and loose gravel pinged against the doors of her Ford Kuga, which was in desperate need of a clean. She took an umbrella from the boot, pressed the button and its skinny fingers spread open.

The entrance to the Freshfield squirrel reserve had been blocked again after her by Police Community Support Officers in raincoats, and she supposed they'd cordoned off the access points to the beach, too. She'd have to check.

A PCSO stood at the cordon where a path opened up into the woods. The white and blue police tape flapped like wet washing. A uniformed bobby was there, speaking with a man and a woman. The man's face was stone: grey and hard. The woman, she supposed his wife or girlfriend, clung to her tiny dog and cried into its fur. A Pomeranian, de Silva noted. It shivered in her hands as though it were cold, or frightened.

Her dad had always said, 'If it's small enough to kick over a fence, it's not a dog.' She hid her smile at the memory, bit her lip and flashed her warrant card to the PCSO. Her phone buzzed in her pocket and she smiled again as she looked at the screen. Crosby calling. He would have to wait until later.

De Silva hadn't been to these woods since she was a child, since those long summer days spent walking between the trees with Laney, or on the nearby beach with food and blankets when the sun went down over the Irish Sea. Those days were gone. Her dad dead, her mum's mind decaying in a care home and she hadn't spoken to her sister in months. The promise of those days when the sun was fat and orange, the hope there, had amounted to nothing. Her family was all but gone.

Still, she had Ritchie. There was once hope there too. Once promise. But the doctors had put an end to those dreams years ago.

Up ahead, a white tent had been pitched against a broken fence. Someone in a white crime scene suit waved at her. From the way they towered above the other officers, and the hulk of his shoulders, de Silva guessed it was Detective Sergeant Ben Barclay. She nodded from the shadow of her umbrella.

The clouds that had sprung up despite the weather man's promise had turned the sky slate grey and a team had already started on the lighting rig.

She ducked under the tent's tarpaulin and set her umbrella down. Crime scene photographers picked up their cameras, wrapped in plastic to protect them from the rain and walked off into the woods. In their white suits, they looked like they could have come straight from a horror film. Ghosts. Wisps of the people they once were, out among the trees. Among the dead.

De Silva grabbed herself a suit in a clear package, tore it open and began to dress. She pulled on the blue shoe coverings and said, 'So, what have we got?'

'Witnesses, Edward and Karrie Bradley, were out walking their dog.' Barclay pulled the white hood over his close-cropped dark hair. 'He ran off into the woods. Wouldn't come back, but they heard him barking from the path here and went to find him. That's when they found the body. They ran straight back to the carpark, where they managed to get some signal, and called 999.'

'I bet if I asked for the dog's name you'd know.'

'Bear.'

She laughed. He was thorough, she'd give him that.

'The husband described the body as "badly rotted". At first, he thought it was some type of woodland animal.'

De Silva had heard that so many times before. Witnesses would think it was an animal, a bin bag full of rubbish, or someone who'd been drunk and fallen asleep.

She put on the plastic safety specs, standard for any crime scene, and pulled up the suit's hood over her hair net. 'You ready?' She took a step out from under the tent. 'Show me the way.' De Silva had to be quick to keep up with Barclay, two steps for each one of his.

He led them down between the stand of trees, where rain dripped and made the parched ground sodden. De Silva knew that Scientific Support would have to move quickly. Photograph everything, gather as much evidence as they could and move the body before the weather got any worse. With each moment that passed, there was an increasing chance that a vital piece of evidence could be washed away in a stream of rainwater.

'Who's the Area Forensics Manager?'

'Brennan,' Barclay said.

De Silva nodded. 'That's good.' She respected Brennan. He had a dedication to the victim that she'd first seen in him when she was a fresh-faced detective.

Another tent was sitting in the wood, white against the brown and green. It made her think of the house in Hansel and Gretel, the one where the witch lived. *But this place isn't made of gingerbread or sweet things.*

A shallow grave had been dug in the earth. Scientific Support had edged the lines of it with boards so muck and debris wouldn't fall back in. Scene-of-crime officers were on their knees wiping away dirt and soil, like archaeologists on some great discovery of historical importance.

The work was slow, the officers meticulous in their efforts and de Silva knew that it could take hours.

'Oh good, you're here.' Brennan's voice. He was over the opposite side of the open grave, putting samples away in a cooler bag.

'You know I never like to miss a party.'

'Well no, and it wouldn't be the same without you.' He chuckled.

'So, what have you got for me?'

'There are still some samples I need to take once we unearth the whole body, but look here.' He knelt down and de Silva was sure she heard his knee pop. 'It's a male. You can tell that by what's left, plus the pelvis is narrow. I'd have to liaise with some colleagues in entomology, but I'd say this guy's been here for decades. Twenty, thirty years is my guess.'

'Entomology?' Barclay had knelt down beside de Silva, his eyes all over the remains.

'To see how much has been eaten, over what period of time, all that stuff.' De Silva turned her attention back to the body. She agreed with Brennan's estimation of how long the body had been here. She'd seen bodies like this less than a handful of times in her career, but they'd stuck with her. 'How certain are you that he's been here that long?'

'As I said, there's testing I'd need to do. Send some samples off for analysis. It's a guess at this point.' He stood up and moved to what remained of the man's head. Mostly skeleton now, but some skin clung to the bones: dark and thin, like wet paper. 'See here.' He leaned in again. The skull was turned, facing the opposite way, the back of it exposed. Brennan pointed out a hole in the bone. 'Likely the cause of death.'

She closed her eyes, steadied her breath. In her mind, she felt this man's pain as something hit him on the back of the head. She felt his knees buckle, his ankles give way, his body hit the floor. She imagined him being dragged down the path, covered with pine needles, to this spot. *How premeditated was this? Was the grave dug before or after?*

'Someone hit him over the head, let him die and buried him here.' De Silva said it to no one in particular, but let the words sit on the warm, wet air between them.

Brennan had been watching her: she could feel his and Barclay's eyes on her. He continued, 'Tracks here. Probably from the people who found the body. There's some tiny paw prints.'

'They have a dog,' Barclay said. 'He's the one who found the body.'

'We'll ask them to bring their footwear in for printing,' de Silva said.

'There's one thing. Unusual, I'd say.' Brennan moved to the skeletal remains of the man's right hand. 'His middle finger. It's missing.'

De Silva took that in. *Why? Why the finger?* A trophy, perhaps. 'When can we expect your preliminary?'

'I'll be here a few hours.' Brennan looked about him, at the organised chaos of the crime scene. 'Tomorrow morning, maybe?'

'That'll do us. I'll speak to you later?'

'Yeah, see you.'

They reached the tent on the muddy path and quickly pulled off their protective gear. 'Get those shoes off that couple who found the body. We'll give them a lift home if we have to. And you might want to call Nick,' de Silva said. 'It's going to be a late one.'

'Will do.'

'How do you feel about taking the lead?'

'What? Are you joking?'

'No, I'm not joking. I'll offer guidance, some advice. But this is yours. Where are you starting?'

Barclay took a long breath. 'A victim from that long ago, and given Brennan's estimation, I'd say we start with missing persons from the local area between 1990 and 2000.'

'That's a decent place to start. A lot of work. A lot of sifting and reading and shortlisting.'

'Shortlisting?'

'Potential vics.'

'I never heard anyone call it that before.'

'Something my dad used to say.'

They walked in silence to the carpark. De Silva could feel Barclay thinking: it pulsed out of him like blood from an open vein.

—

The last two days had taken their toll on de Silva. The air con had broken in the entire building and the incident room was a sauna. Interviews, discussions, theories, a press conference Barclay suggested she did instead of him. She was exhausted and wanted nothing more than a long, cool shower, to eat something that didn't come in a plastic container and to get into bed.

Crosby had called her when she was just minutes away from home: she hated cutting it so fine. There was always a risk that he'd call as she set foot in the home she shared with her husband, always the chance that Ritchie would overhear them, suspect something.

'I can't talk,' she said. The smile had been wide across her face. 'I'm almost home, Ritchie'll be in.'

'Ann's away at her mum's.' His voice was breathy; he slurred his words. 'I need to see you. There's so much I—'

'I can't, sorry.' She turned into her road, where all of the windows in every house had lights in them. Number three had the big light on in the living room. Number four sat on their couch, their blinds open, the telly illuminating their laughing faces. But as de Silva turned up the drive of number one, she noticed that her house was in darkness.

'I have to go,' she said. 'I'll call you later.' She didn't wait for him to respond.

The curtains at the front of the house were pulled back, the slats of the white Venetians she'd insisted on having installed in summer were open. Through the window, she could see the living room was black, lifeless, like the cavity of a rotten tooth.

She parked behind Ritchie's van, thick with dirt. Someone had written 'clean me please' and drawn a crying face in the filth. He went everywhere in the van, he even drove it to the corner shop, but to de Silva, it looked as though Ritchie wasn't home.

Something shifted in her stomach, a weight that she couldn't quite place or name rolled over itself and sank in the pit of her belly.

Something's wrong.

Every step along the driveway, she felt the weight sink a little lower. She fished her keys from the pocket of her jacket and unlocked the front door. She daren't step into the hall.

Ritchie's feet and knees at her eye-level. She looked up. His dirty work trousers, thick with whatever messy stuff he used for plumbing. His massive hands and his waist. His chest, still, not moving, under a dirty polo-neck T-shirt. 'De Silva Plumbing' embroidered on it in white letters.

She looked at his face for just a moment. The bulge of his eyes, the grimace of his lips, the paleness of his skin. He was, she thought, unrecognisable. For as long as she lived, she would never forget that at first, for just a split second, she thought he was laughing at her.

Two

Seven months later

Barclay had managed just a few hours' sleep before his alarm went off at seven. The single bed had been uncomfortable the last week and a half. The mattress springs jabbed into his back and shoulders, and the pillow was a lumpy bag of stones. He'd thought about ordering a double bed at least, but even that wouldn't fit in the tiny bedroom he'd spent so many hours in as a kid.

The wallpaper, blue and white stripes because his dad had supported Everton, peeled away from the wall in the corner above the door. His mum had kept it as it was when he left for the navy for reasons he couldn't understand. It had been the same since before he met Nick, since before they adopted Sarah. Before he'd messed all of that up and had to come back to his childhood home, suitcase in hand.

His mum had welcomed him with open arms, of course, and had turned to her big book of family recipes to console her only child. She'd never been good at using her words to express her emotions; she cooked instead, using the recipes her own mother had taught her: scouse made with lamb, curries made from a block of Maysan, home-made pies and chips. The stuff that had comforted him as a child; the stuff he'd worked hard to put behind him, to eat healthier.

She'll have you chubby again.

Barclay pulled at the thin royal-blue curtains and peered out at the morning sky. Over the houses at the back, he saw the pale pink of sunrise and knew that Nick would be up with Sarah soon. They'd sit down to breakfast at the kitchen table together. Toast with jam or chocolate spread, or cereal with too much milk on it. She had one of those bowls with the straw in, and loved to slurp up the milk after she'd finished with the cereal; sometimes before too, and the loops or flakes would be a sloppy mess she'd refuse to eat. He wondered whether Sarah told Nick that she missed Barclay. He felt an instant stab of guilt.

What kind of person would want their child to be upset, to miss someone they can't see every morning?

He crawled out of his bed and felt the cold of the room instantly. Not the iciness of winter, but the chill of early spring. He pulled on some clean underwear, adjusted himself, dragged open the chest of drawers and white paint flaked to the floor. He found his gym gear and shoved it into a bag: he'd have to go later, after work. It was his turn to take Sarah to school.

The bedroom door opened and his mum bustled in, arms full of clean washing, her dark hair combed straight. He covered himself, embarrassed. 'Knock, Mum!'

'Oh behave, I've wiped your shitty arse before now, so stop clutching your pearls.'

He rolled his eyes, determined that tonight he'd dedicate some time to finding himself a flat somewhere. He loved his mum, but she was difficult. Hard to reason with, and above all, she had a habit of entering his bedroom without knocking. One time, she'd almost caught him on X Net. Thank God he'd had his earphones in.

'You home for dinner?' She busied herself, putting clothes away in the drawers.

'I'll be home tonight, yeah.'

'What time?'

'I don't know. I'll be going the gym after work.'

'Well I can't have your dinner ready if I don't know a time.'

'I'll sort myself out, don't worry.'

She huffed and turned to the bed, lifted the duvet into the air and let it fall down again, swiped out any creases. 'I'll leave some in the oven.'

'Well don't go to any trouble,' he said. 'I'm going to grab a shower.'

'You taking Sarah to school today?'

'Yeah. Did you want to come?'

'No,' she said. Her voice hard as stone. 'If I see that lad, I don't know what I'd do or say.'

'You wouldn't say or do anything. This is the agreement we made. And his name's Nick.'

'He kicked you out. Of your own home. And you just took it.'

'I'm not having this conversation with you again.' He went to the bathroom and closed the door. There never had been a lock on it for as long as he could remember. He showered quickly, brushed his teeth with the awful toothpaste his mum had in, the one that tastes like powder. He made a mental note to get some of his own.

—

'I want you to come home,' Sarah said. Her little mouth downturned, her bottom lip quivered. Her dark brown hair was pulled back into a high, tight ponytail, and tears brimmed at her copper-coloured eyes.

They'd sat in an awkward silence since Barclay had picked her up outside the house. Nick had waited at the gate, her school bag and lunch box already prepared. The message had been clear: you're not welcome inside.

'It's you,' Nick had said the night before Barclay left. 'You bring it into our home. Where our daughter lives. The misery, the upset, everything from your work. It's on you and it stinks.' He'd cried himself to sleep while Barclay sat propped up against the headboard. He knew it was coming. He felt it resting in the bed between him and his husband: an awful understanding. It watched him with its eyes open and whispered to him, *Your marriage is over*.

Since Barclay's case last year, where a threat had been made specifically to Sarah, and he'd had to have her put in a safe house in Cheshire, things had changed between them. It wasn't Barclay's fault. It was his work, and that, according to arguments they'd had in the past, was enough.

'I want to come home, too.' Barclay felt his own bottom lip quiver. He and Nick had always said it was best to be honest with Sarah. Some parents decorate the truth with paint and glitter, but that hadn't been their way. 'But Dad needs some time to himself at the moment.'

'But why? Were you naughty?'

That question weighed heavy on him and he couldn't quite understand why. He didn't really have an answer to his daughter's question: there had been no further discussion between him and Nick. On that morning, when Nick woke up, his eyes red and puffed, there seemed to be an understanding between the two of them. Barclay would pack his things and go before Sarah got out of bed. He'd regretted that these past weeks. He'd not said goodbye to her, not explained what was happening, and Nick had said later: 'I told her we're unhappy. I'm unhappy. That we can't be together until we're both happy.'

Barclay had wanted to say that happiness was something that needed to be worked at, something that took time to cultivate after years together. With the pressures of life and work and a child, Barclay had wondered whether their happiness was like the dying plant in the bathroom he'd insisted on keeping. It was clearly struggling in its environment, but it clung on, roots and all, and Barclay wouldn't ever admit it was going to die. They'd moved it a few times, but it just got worse.

'Daddy?'

'Hmm?' He swerved a pothole in the road. 'No, I wasn't naughty.' He forced light-heartedness into his voice, but instead it cracked under the weight of his feelings. 'Dad's already told you, hasn't he? There are things we need to work on.'

'Your happy.'

'Yes, that's right. Our happy.'

'But why are you not happy? Was I naughty?'

His heart cracked. 'No, Sarah. You weren't naughty. We love you lots and lots and lots.' He reached over and squeezed her leg lightly and she giggled. 'Sometimes two grown-ups spend so much time together that the feelings they have for each other get a bit... lost. Or muddled. But you're our special girl and we love you.'

Sarah nodded and looked out of the window. Barclay couldn't know if she understood, or if he'd confused her even more than she was before. As they rolled up to the school, he had to hope that he'd done his best.

'Okay,' he said. 'Grab your lunch box, and I'll carry your backpack.'

He climbed out and walked around to her side of the car, unclipped her seatbelt and lifted her out. 'I think I know what makes Dad not happy.'

'Oh yeah?' He slung her backpack over his shoulder as best he could and locked the car. 'What's that then?'

'When you're not around,' she said. 'When your phone rings and you have to go.'

He barely breathed. She knew as much as Nick and Barclay did – that his work was, and probably always would be, the problem. He held her hand, walked through the school gates and smiled politely at the other parents.

'Why don't you show me around your classroom before school starts? I've not seen your painting on the Art Wall yet.'

'Okay!' She ran ahead and he felt something he couldn't quite name as her hand slipped out of his. In his pocket, his phone buzzed.

He took it out and saw on the screen: De Silva calling.

Three

De Silva put her mobile into her pocket and picked up her reusable coffee cup: rose gold from Starbucks. She needed a fresh drink, something strong, not the piss water they served in the small canteen or the vending machines. She was exhausted and hadn't slept the night before: she'd had dreams, nightmares, about Ritchie. They were still frequent, despite the therapy she had been ordered to undergo before returning to work.

Last night, in her dream, she'd sat on the bottom step of the stairs at her old house, the one where she'd found him hanged over the banister. He was sitting next to her, except he was just a little boy, and above them, the adult Ritchie hung, sobbing. Then, the banging on the front door. She'd woken up, her chest pounding.

The open-plan office was busy, detectives tapping at keyboards or talking into their desk phones about missing persons, requesting CCTV footage from key locations, or liaising with other departments. The leg work she'd completed for so much of her career.

She'd cringed when Barclay had explained it was his turn to take Sarah to school. She could have kicked herself. Dead things can wait, it was the living that was important. De Silva knew that more than most.

As she pushed through the double doors out into the quiet corridor, an email pinged on her work phone, whose screen was cracked. A repair she'd promised herself long before she took her leave of absence after Ritchie's death. From Murphy, Shannon (DSI): *Please could you come to my office.*

De Silva shook her head. *What now?* The new Detective Superintendent had been brought in from the Met when O'Brien had tendered his resignation with immediate effect. De Silva hadn't seen it coming. Attrition at Merseyside Police was low, and short-notice resignations were rare. Even rarer was someone being brought in from the Met. When she'd heard the news, de Silva had gone to O'Brien's straight from work.

'It's Kath.' He'd shown her upstairs. His wife lay on a hospital bed, tubes in her nose, her bald head pale and grey. Her breath rasped in her chest and throat. She wasn't conscious, wasn't aware that de Silva, or her own husband, were there. 'I have to say goodbye,' he'd said.

The funeral had been agony. It had snowed when they lowered Kath into her grave; it came in sideways on the wind, and threatened to cover the mourners' black clothes with white.

O'Brien had laughed at first, at the absurdity of it, de Silva supposed, until finally he wailed. She had gone to him, put an arm around him and held him as close as she could – the way Ritchie had held her close at her dad's funeral. She didn't care which of her peers saw, or what they'd say about it. He was her mentor, her friend and he was in pain. A pain de Silva recognised, an old adversary – and, in some ways, an old comfort.

In that moment, she'd hoped that his grief would be quick, would be straightforward at least. She wished that for him with everything in her.

Murphy arrived less than a week later, her hair and skin shining in the northern winter gloom. When de Silva first met her, she knew they wouldn't get along, though couldn't say why. Just a feeling, something in her gut. As a detective, she relied on her gut. Trusted it. *But sometimes*, she thought, *sometimes it can be wrong*.

De Silva went back into the open-plan office and took the harness from the back of her chair, complete with PAVA spray and extendable baton. Since last year, when she'd been seriously hurt by Lewis Lamond, the perpetrator in a local murder case where teenage girls were brutally killed, she'd not gone anywhere without it under her jacket. Not even to see the DSI.

They'd arrested Lamond, charged him, but while awaiting trial, he was found hanged in his cell. The CCTV cameras on his landing had malfunctioned, and there was no way to see who went in or out. He was dead.

She reached O'Brien's old office and saw that his name had been removed and replaced with Murphy's. She huffed. She needed that coffee more than ever then, but it would have to wait. She knocked lightly and pushed open the door, not waiting for a response.

The old office looked new. It had been painted white and the spring sun blasted through the windows now that the yellowed office blinds had been taken down. The smell of cigarettes and air freshener had gone, replaced by lavender and something de Silva couldn't place.

Murphy locked her computer screen and gestured that de Silva should sit down in the chair opposite, her perfect platinum bob bouncing. 'Thank you for coming,' Murphy said. One of those southern accents that could cut glass.

Glars, de Silva imagined Murphy saying.

De Silva wanted to say that she hadn't been given a choice, but instead said, 'No worries. Ma'am.' De Silva hated being called that herself, but Murphy seemed to revel in it.

'I have some concerns.' She paused, steepled her fingers in front of her. 'About Barclay.'

De Silva had half expected this. 'I see.'

Murphy stood and went to the window, looked out as if she was looking at some perfect view of a Welsh valley or from atop some mountain, instead of at a rooftop and carpark. She turned to de Silva and perched on the window ledge. 'His personal life, what's going on there?'

De Silva felt the hairs on her arms stand on end, bristle against the cotton of her blouse. She shrugged. 'He's doing okay, considering. The ins and outs, not really my business. I've made him aware of the support available.'

'Bloody hell, de Silva, I'm asking about *him*. I have concerns about his well-being, not his ability to do the job. Though one feeds the other, I suppose.'

'He's lost his family, ma'am: how do you think he should be acting?'

'But should he be here, in work?'

De Silva took a deep breath and let it out sharply. 'I've not noticed any lapse in concentration, no distraction.' She was lying to her superior officer, but what Barclay needed most was time. 'He has other things to contend with now, like shared care of Sar— his kid, but that's it. Is someone feeding you something? If you want to give me their names, I'll make sure they're well informed.'

Murphy smiled, but de Silva couldn't read it. The look of someone amused or a sneer? She couldn't tell, but doubted it mattered too much. 'Yes, I'm sure you would,'

Murphy said. 'But no, no one is feeding me information. It was an observation of my own.'

De Silva stood up. 'Will that be everything, ma'am?'

'No,' she said. 'I'm afraid not.' She turned her hand, palm up, indicating de Silva should take a seat again. Murphy joined her, leaned in slightly. 'This case. This app you're focusing on, the death of Lewis Lamond. The disappearance of DCI Crosby. I'm going to have to ask you to leave it alone.'

The app. It was called The Woulds, and they'd detected it first last year, on the mobile phone of one of Lamond's victims. It was housed, hosted, or whatever, somewhere on the Dark Web, and their digital teams were unable to find out any more about it.

'Not a chance.' De Silva's stomach flipped over itself. She wanted to get up. Leave. Not look back and keep pushing through the case despite Murphy's instruction.

'I've allowed you some indulgence in it, de Silva, but I'm afraid we're just not seeing any results.'

'We?'

'Chief Constable Bradshaw has been contacted by investigators from the National Crime Agency.'

De Silva crossed her legs. 'Why would the NCA be interested?'

'Read between the lines, de Silva.'

De Silva opened her mouth to speak, but thought better of it. She pushed the anger, the injustice of it, aside and let the information sink in. If she was being asked to leave it alone and the NCA were involved, it meant this was all something far bigger than she'd originally thought. Well beyond Liverpool and Merseyside.

It was bigger than the abuse Lamond reported he'd endured during his time at Rainford Lane School for

Boys. The same school, she'd found not too long ago, her own husband had once attended. Her Ritchie.

A lump formed in her throat and she cleared it away with a light cough. 'And if I don't leave it alone?'

'This isn't a suggestion, de Silva. It's an order I expect you to follow.' There was a silence where Murphy let those words sit on the varnished maple desk between them. 'I'm insisting.'

For God's sake. She could have screamed in Murphy's face. The frustration bubbled under her skin and burned like lava. Any minute, she'd explode if she didn't get a handle on it. All of those hours researching, the worry, the wondering about what Ritchie might have gone through… all that evidence she'd amassed, would all be passed along to the NC – fucking – A.

De Silva took a breath. 'So what will I be doing with my time? Waiting until another dead body drops somewhere?'

'There's no need to wait.' Murphy opened her desk drawer and dropped a thin file onto the desk, barely three pages by de Silva's estimation. 'This is what you'll be working on.'

De Silva glared at Murphy, didn't take her eyes off her as she slid the file across the desk and flipped it open. Then she scanned it quickly. *Great*. 'This case has already been worked on.'

'Yes,' Murphy said. 'By you and Barclay initially.' She took a breath and let it out through her nose. 'It's unsolved still, and you'll be returning to lead a team on this.'

'There were others on this last year.'

'I see. Who?'

De Silva scanned the pages again. 'These are just the preliminary reports from me and Barclay, and the autopsy report, such as it is. Where's the rest of it? The investigation, the reports from the detectives put on the case after…?'

Murphy stood up again, came around to de Silva's side of the desk, perched on it with folded arms. 'My predecessor—'

'O'Brien,' de Silva interrupted.

'Former-DSI O'Brien assigned two detective constables to this case. Neither of whom are with the force any longer. No reports were filed. This case has been cold since the day you began your leave of absence last year.'

De Silva sensed there was more to the story, something else that Murphy didn't want to say yet. She felt as though they were circling each other, waiting for the other to make a move. To react, to say something.

'That's everything, de Silva. An officer from the NCA will be in touch to ask some questions of you and Barclay. Separately, of course.'

'Are you telling me we're going to be interrogated?'

'That's certainly a choice word to describe inter-organisational co-operation.'

'It's certainly a choice thing to interview two detectives separately when it's just co-operation.'

Murphy returned to her desk and unlocked her computer, with what de Silva could tell was a very short password. Probably a pet's name, or a child's. She couldn't imagine Murphy as a mother, or a dog person for that matter. 'They'll let you know when you're required. In the meantime, if you could jump back into this case. We'll catch up again soon to review any progress you and Barclay make.'

De Silva stood to leave. 'Yes, ma'am.'

'And if you notice anything,' she said, 'about Barclay, do come and see me.'

'Look, I'd trust Barclay with my life.'

'Let's not put that to the test,' Murphy said. 'Again.'

De Silva didn't know how to respond. Of course, she'd expected Murphy to read up on her new team. She'd be more concerned if Murphy hadn't. De Silva needed to figure out who'd been talking behind Barclay's back, have it out with them and set it all right before Barclay ever found out.

'I'd best get on, ma'am,' de Silva said. 'I'll need an incident room. I know it's not a fresh case, but I can't focus out there.'

'Permission granted.'

De Silva hadn't been asking. 'Yes, ma'am.' She pulled open the office door and wanted to slam it behind her. To hear the windows rattle in their frames, the crack of splintered wood. She closed it softly instead.

Why would Murphy be so concerned about Barclay or his performance all of a sudden? She knew it could be her paranoia over-riding her common sense. But either way, it was information best kept to herself. If Barclay thought for a second that Murphy had concerns, it could be the straw that broke the camel's back.

Four

De Silva's text told Barclay to meet her in the basement room, and he winced at the thought. They'd not been down there since the Lamond case. Their current investigation had operated from their desks upstairs in CID; and with the new setting, he reasoned that something had changed.

Great. Someone else is missing or dead.

In the lift, he did his best to shake off the emotional weight of his morning with Sarah: how she'd painted a house, a pretty front garden with blooming flowers, the sun beaming down from the top left corner. Inside the front window, a little girl in between her two dads. One dark-haired, one blond. His heart had ached for a memory he didn't actually have. They'd never stood at the front window together and looked out onto the flower beds. But they had spent so much time together in that room. There had been love there once, he and Nick had cherished each other, and the daughter they'd adopted.

Focus, he told himself. *Focus on the now*. That's what his therapist had told him to do. Don't obsess over the past, don't worry about the future, ground yourself in the now. It was easier said than done. Every so often, those memories from his time aboard the HMS *Iron Duke* came back like a rising tide, and sometimes, just sometimes… he wished it would pull him out to sea.

The lift pinged as the doors slid open onto the dark, cold basement corridor he'd walked down so many times. A light spilled out into the gloom from a room up ahead, and from it he could smell the warm bitterness of filtered coffee.

He pushed open the door. 'Morning.'

De Silva looked up from her computer and stood immediately, handed him the thin casefile. Her blue eyes were fenced in by dark circles, her curly auburn hair as wild as ever. 'We've been pulled from our case. NCA are taking over. We're back on this one. I think you're up to speed now.'

'What? Why?' Barclay didn't bother opening the file, but threw it onto the desk opposite de Silva's.

'Her upstairs.' She was almost shouting. 'NCA are muscling in, they'll probably tell us nothing, and she's letting it all happen.'

'I'm sure she doesn't have much choice if they're involved though.'

De Silva's brow furrowed, her eyes narrow, like she was trying to decide what she was looking at. 'Whose side are you on?'

Barclay laughed. De Silva laughed.

'I'm sorry.' She shook her head. 'Just pissed off. We've worked on this for months.'

'And are no closer to any answers,' Barclay said. 'Couldn't find anything on The Woulds app, the CCTV cameras around Lamond's cell had malfunctioned—'

'Allegedly.'

'Yes, allegedly. And the only man alive who could offer us any sort of answers has pulled a Houdini.'

Crosby's disappearance had been of great interest to Merseyside Police, and had sparked a nation-wide manhunt for him that, but in recent weeks, that interest seemed to have dwindled. The public lose interest quickly, and she had the feeling that the force was losing interest, too. He and de Silva had been close, but Barclay knew it was more than that. Everyone knew.

When they'd finally tracked down Lewis Lamond last year, they were disturbed, shocked, to find that Crosby had been involved this whole time. There were questions they needed to ask there, and Crosby needed to answer for his crimes.

'We'll find him,' de Silva said.

'Or maybe we won't.' Barclay hated being the voice of reason, the one to shatter anyone's illusions, but that's what this all was. They'd not found a way forward in months. All the time and effort they'd put in had come to nothing. He sat down on the chair opposite de Silva's desk and exhaled. 'I'm just saying. Maybe it's not a bad thing NCA are involved. Maybe they know something we don't.'

'Which is what bothers me. How? What do they know? Why wouldn't they share it?'

'Because they don't have to,' he said. 'If they're involved this is huge. Bigger than us.' De Silva nodded without looking at him, and he knew that she'd already considered this. 'It's out of our hands now.'

'Do you remember O'Brien telling us that he'd assigned someone to work on this case? This man in the woods, I mean.'

Barclay had a fuzzy memory of de Silva telling him what O'Brien had said when she had asked him about the case. 'I'm not sure, not one hundred per cent. But I think so.'

'Scale of one to under oath?'

'Five?' he said. 'A solid five. Couldn't be sure.'

De Silva huffed. 'Yeah, me too. We're supposed to be the sharpest minds, Barclay, and look at us.'

'A lot was going on back then. The girls. Lamond. Crosby.'

'Yeah.'

Barclay flipped open the file on the desk in front of him and sighed. 'Where do we even begin?'

'I don't know.' She shrugged. 'I feel so removed from it, you know. Like it was a lifetime ago.'

In some ways it was. In some ways, it was a lifetime they might never get back to. In de Silva's case, might not want to; in his own, he was desperate to return to it.

'Shall we get out of here?' she said. 'Sometimes when I need to connect with something, I'll go to the place where it happened. Months ago, I know. Decades ago for the victim, but it might help.' She was already holding her jacket. 'I read about it once, it's called contextual-binding theory, it's—'

'Sure,' Barclay interrupted. 'Let's get out of here.'

'Great, we can grab some breakfast on the way.'

In truth, he felt too ill to eat. He'd left the smoothie he'd made in the car on purpose, so that he didn't have to look at it and feel guilty for not eating. 'Yeah,' he said. 'That's fine.'

The car ride had been peaceful. Barclay was thankful that de Silva seemed so lost in thought that she'd barely spoken. It gave him time to breathe. To think, even though everything came back to Nick. Even this case they'd been put back on had almost broken their relationship the first time, and he'd only been on it for two days then.

He'd known Nick ever since they were young, had always wanted him, but then Barclay went away with the navy for three years. When he returned home after being discharged, they'd met once again at a mutual friend's party.

Barclay and Nick had started to date. Few drinks here and there, dinners out, the cinema. It had taken months before Barclay finally felt comfortable enough to have sex, and whenever Nick asked why he'd left the navy, he'd never been able to answer.

'One day,' Barclay would tell Nick. 'I'll tell you everything one day, I promise.'

That had only pacified Nick for so long.

The McDonald's on Altcar Road was busy, the line for the drive-through stretched around the side of the building and into the carpark. De Silva pulled up in an empty space and said, 'We'll eat in. Don't know about you, but eating on the go has started giving me really bad heartburn.'

'Can't say I've noticed. Must be an age thing.'

De Silva unfastened her belt, let it slip over her shoulder, as she stared at Barclay. 'If you're looking for a black eye, you're going the right way about it.'

He laughed. 'My mum used to say that.'

De Silva smacked his arm hard and it stung. He rubbed at it.

'You see, not too old now, am I?'

They climbed out of the car into a bright spring day. There were clouds in the sky, the colour of cotton wool and far away. The sun was yellow, almost a light watercolour, and Barclay wondered whether that meant rain was coming.

Inside was mayhem. Workmen laughed like barking sealions, somewhere a baby screamed, a toddler threw a tantrum and all Barclay could think about was the quiet of the car journey.

'What're you having?' De Silva stood at the self-serve console, already tapping in her order. 'I'm starving.'

'Just porridge.'

De Silva's lip curled back. 'Now who's old?' She tapped in his order, regardless, pulled her ticket from the printer. 'Go take a seat,' she said. 'Rest those weary old bones. I'll get your porridge and your slippers, okay?'

Barclay picked a small table near the window that his legs barely fitted under. These places were always cramped, not built for someone his size at all. He stared out of the window, at people in the drive-through queue, a woman singing along to a song he couldn't make out.

'You all right?' De Silva sat down with a tray. She handed Barclay his steaming porridge and tucked into one of her hashbrowns.

'I'm fine,' he lied. *Chill out, lad. This is all just getting to you*. Nick, Sarah, being back at his mum's. The case they'd lost to NCA. He stuck his cardboard spoon into the porridge and stirred it. Steam rose into his face and eyes.

'Tell your face that then, it might have—'

'It's definitely forgotten,' he interrupted her for the second time that day. He pushed the porridge away. 'I'm sorry, I'm like the grim reaper sat here.'

'It's fine.' She touched his hand. 'You'll be all right, you know. No matter what happens next.'

He wondered whether she was right. 'What do I do in the meantime?'

'Your best.'

Barclay wondered whether de Silva was ever haunted by her own living ghosts. Faces she'd see in the crowd – or whether, half-asleep, she'd hear Ritchie call her name from upstairs. He wondered whether that was why she'd moved. He wondered how many times she'd seen former-DCI Crosby when out taking a walk. Barclay knew that Crosby was the man she'd loved. His betrayal must have felt personal to her.

'Do you ever think about Crosby?' he asked. 'Ever think you see him? Hear him?'

She chewed slowly. 'Yeah,' she said. 'I think I've seen him a few times. Followed him, just to find it's someone else. Just the brain playing tricks.'

'Why?'

'Why what?'

'Why do you think it plays tricks?'

'Maybe it makes us see what we want to see,' she said. 'Do you ever think you've seen him?' De Silva wiped at her mouth with a napkin.

'Me? No,' he said. 'I've never experienced anything like that.'

De Silva nodded at him, slowly, taking him all in. She'd know he was lying and there was nothing he could do about it. Right then, he just didn't care enough.

Barclay sat in silence while de Silva finished her breakfast and took a sip from her coffee. She winced at the taste and left it on the table when they left.

Formby Point and the woods at Freshfields were just a few minutes away, and the rain Barclay feared would come patted against the windscreen in small spots. De Silva turned on the radio and hummed along to a song Barclay had heard a handful of times.

He wanted, so desperately, for the day to be over. To go to bed. But even there, his nights were sleepless, dreamless – just shadows moving across the tiny back bedroom in his childhood home.

Five

The walk in the woods hadn't helped. They'd taken the long way around from the carpark, down toward the beach and turned left at the sand dunes and back on themselves past the old asparagus fields and onto the woodland path.

Dogs ran ahead of their owners, relishing the freedom from their lead. A cold breeze blew in from the Irish Sea and over the dunes, and seagulls turned in circles above. But still, that thing that de Silva was looking for, that shock of inspiration, that fire in her gut, eluded her.

She'd been searching for some connection, some link between the location and her instinct. Instead, she felt even more distant from the body in the woods than before she'd arrived. Judging by the way Barclay walked a few paces behind her, his head down, she knew he felt the same.

'Last year, did you get far with missing persons?' she asked.

'Shortlisting? No. I'd started it and then Lynsey Renshaw went missing.'

The first girl in the Lamond case. Kidnapped. Brutally raped and murdered. Body dumped. De Silva had watched the first two victims being found on the news from the safe dark of her living room, where the curtains were drawn and the air stank of her own body, smelled of her own despair. By the time the third girl went missing,

Kelly Stack, de Silva knew she should expect a call from O'Brien. The call came the morning her body was found, pearl-white in the moonlight, at Canning Dock.

De Silva stopped to let Barclay catch up. 'It's like starting over then.' *Not for the victim. Not for their family and loved ones.* Still, she reasoned, they'd already waited twenty to thirty years, according to Brennan's initial analysis. She'd seen him accurately determine times of death in so many cases, but in this instance, she knew there was no guarantee.

Depending on the soil type, the weather over the years, whether the area had flooded or experienced drought, whether there were worms or other insects present, the estimation could be years off.

Somewhere out in the woods, a branch snapped and Barclay flinched.

'It's just a squirrel or something,' de Silva said.

'What's that thing people say? If you feel like you're being watched, you probably are?'

'Who says that?'

'You know... it's on Insta Reels and stuff.'

'I see.'

'Could be someone out there.'

De Silva frowned. 'Or it could be a squirrel. Or a ghost. Should we ring Yvette Fielding, or are you going to get a grip of yourself?'

'What's crawled up your arse?' He'd stopped to look at her, brow creased, lips curled back over his perfect white teeth, and then she noticed his usually bright eyes seemed dull. Muddy. 'You've been grumpy since we got in the car.'

'I'm surprised you've even noticed.' She faced him now, tried to keep her voice even and flat. If she raised it out here, it would echo in the expanse of trees.

Barclay's face changed. Softer somehow and he looked down at his shoes, caked in filth and pine needles.

They stood in silence for what felt like minutes. De Silva's mind raced ahead, already having conversations with him, explaining that Murphy was asking questions, that he was on her radar. She had already imagined, reviewed and resolved possible scenarios. 'Look.' She put a hand on his shoulder. 'I know you're going through a lot at the moment. But Murphy's watching us both. We can't afford to get distracted now.'

'I'm not—'

'I haven't said you are. I'm telling you that we can't.' She sighed. 'I don't want to be on this cold case any more than you do, not after the things we've seen and heard. But here we are, Barclay. No choice.' She wanted to add that there was a family out there waiting for answers about their loved one who'd gone missing decades ago. She wanted to say that they needed him too. 'We have to just move forward now. This is what we're working on, and I'm going to need you.'

The wind blew through the tree branches and as they shook, de Silva thought of how much they sounded like the sea. The echoes from inside a seashell.

'I'm sorry,' Barclay said. 'I'm trying my best, I really am.'

'I know,' she said. 'So just keep at it.' She sighed again, exasperated, and said, 'Right, so shall we get out of here, because this hasn't gone to plan at all.' De Silva walked on, dodging a small pile of dog shit.

'I don't know what you expected to get from being here.'

'I'm not sure myself, to be honest.'

She laughed it off, and they headed back toward the car in silence. Inside her, something stirred. Some small agony had begun to form on the drive out here that she couldn't quite name. She'd thought it was resentment from her time in Murphy's office, from being booted off the case they'd worked so hard on. But that wasn't it.

Places hold memories, she'd known that when she put the house up for sale. Felt the weight of it lift when it sold and she moved all of her stuff out. It was the reason she'd bought a four-bedroom new-build in Prescot, near the Tesco. She didn't need the room, but it was the last one left in the area. Closer to her mum than before. *New-builds don't hold memories*, she'd thought when she signed her contract. *The bricks are new, the cement just mixed*.

Sometimes, when she lay in the bath late at night, with lavender-scented candles burning, she'd get in too deep. A rabbit hole, they called it. She thought how the walls may not hold memories, but the ground might. That everything comes from something else, and who's to say whose memories were stuck in the garden soil, in the blades of grass, in the dust that mixed the cement, in the water that came through the tap.

Memory and memories are everywhere. Even if they're half-formed, made foggy by time, as distant as the oil rigs from Formby beach, the emotions they carry are fresh. Like sand, they get in everywhere. Cutting. Coarse.

These woods held memories too, trapped between the stand of trees, caught up in the highest branches like some living, breathing dream catcher. Walks with dogs long-since dead, first dates, family trips. She and Ritchie had spent time here, held hands as they walked under the canopy of trees and tried to spot elusive red squirrels. Mixed with her own memories, there'd be love, laughter, tears.

This case. The man buried in the cold ground. These trees, unchanged by the years, may have been the last thing he saw. They may have been the last thing to hear his voice, if trees could hear. His cries. His screams. And, like the people who left him there, they were unmoved.

But there was more than that here, de Silva knew. That little agony in the centre of her chest grew and throbbed as she circled it, knowing its name, realising its nature. The last time she'd stood in these woods, looking down into a ditch where a dead man lay, she'd had something to anchor her.

Someone.

Ritchie.

Her Ritchie.

She'd been a wife, a friend, a confidant. And on that day when he took his own life, all of those things ceased to be. Except out here, in the woods, where those memories were trapped or held, so close she could almost reach out and touch them, or breathe them in.

Maybe that was what she'd expected to find in the Freshfields woods.

The things she'd lost.

Six

The basement room was hot and Barclay switched on the air con. He put his oat-milk latte down on his desk and threw his coat onto a spare chair. De Silva sat opposite him, logged onto her computer and seemed to get to work.

She'd been distant since the woods and he knew it was because of him. Because of how he'd been toward her, his approach to work. In truth, he'd stopped caring.

They'd pushed and pushed and came up with nothing in the case they'd worked on before. Digital Forensics hadn't been able to find anything on The Woulds app they'd found on one of the victims' phones. Former-DCI Mike Crosby was on the run, missing since they'd discovered he was somehow involved in the murders. The CCTV footage that could have proved or disproved Lamond's suicide in custody was non-existent. A system issue had caused the cameras in that wing to fail.

They had nothing. And, when he thought about it, Barclay himself had nothing too. His husband hated him and he hardly saw his daughter except on those days he got to take her to school, and every other weekend. He'd lost so much, and in truth, he had nothing left in him to give: not a single fuck could be mustered for the whereabouts of Crosby, the origins of The Woulds, or the death of a serial rapist and killer of children.

No, the body in the woods was a welcome change of pace. A chance to start over, push through a case to its conclusion. That's what he craved, to see something through from beginning to end. The completion of it. The sense of satisfaction. The post-case closure drinks with the team.

A team. We need a team. Researchers, people to do the leg work. They should put in a request for PC Lawrence. Barclay liked her: she got stuff done, and she was still fresh to it. No ego there, just a sense that she was doing the right thing. The good work. Barclay remembered when he'd had that outlook, though it seemed like a lifetime ago.

'I'll pull some people together from other non-urgent cases,' de Silva said, seeming to read his mind. 'We don't know what year we're looking at, but I suggest we start with 1990 to 1995? What do you think?'

'Based on what I remember from Brennan's estimations, that sounds like a plan.' Barclay nodded. 'I'll check over his full report. Dig out the post-mortem too, see if there's a narrower window there?'

'Who performed it?'

Barclay opened the casefile on the desk in front of him. 'Carey.'

De Silva nodded. 'Good. But it might be best if she could talk us through it.'

Barclay understood. Sometimes in conversation, you could pick up on things you couldn't get from a report: a slight inflection on certain words or phrases that cast doubt or reaffirmed beliefs and theories, and Carey spoke with her hands. Barclay had watched her demonstrate how a victim might have been tied to a bedpost or a radiator.

How the knife had gone in, and the force required to get through the flesh, to fracture bone, to perforate organs.

'I've emailed a request for Lawrence to Her Royal Highness upstairs,' de Silva said.

Barclay felt a smirk spread across his mouth. 'She's not all that bad.' Murphy was formal, a lot more than O'Brien was, but she was focused and dedicated. She paid attention to rank and hierarchy and structure, and Barclay found that appealing. Knowing where he fitted into everything had always made him feel secure.

De Silva rolled her eyes as Barclay logged onto the computer in front of him. The wheel turned slowly on the screen and pulsed like a heartbeat. He couldn't turn his eyes away from it, and his mind wandered away from the basement, from the dead man in the woods, and back to his own life.

The muggy, cramped bedroom in need of decorating at his mum's house, the shambles he'd made of his relationship with Nick, and Sarah. *No. Focus.* He willed himself to leave all that at home. But Barclay didn't have a home. Not really. His things were spread over two houses, but his heart belonged to the home he'd shared with Nick and Sarah. The one he'd helped to build.

Focus!

The screen blinked and his desktop appeared, files and folders all organised neatly by name. His emails loaded automatically and new ones bounced into his inbox. Quickly he flicked through and moved them into a separate folder labelled 'Outstanding'. He'd pick them up soon.

He typed Carey's name into the search bar and located an email from her, opened it and found her office number in the signature at the bottom. He picked up the desk phone and dialled. It rang for a few moments but she didn't answer. He left a voicemail asking her to call him back when she could.

'I'll try again later if she hasn't gotten back to us.' The phone on his desk rang. 'Oh this'll be her. Barclay speaking.'

'You're required in Meeting Room One.' Murphy's voice was cold and distant. 'Are you able to make it now?'

'Erm…' He tried to get de Silva's attention, but her face was illuminated by her computer screen. 'Yes, ma'am.'

De Silva looked at him then, her shoulders dropped an inch or two and she breathed through flared nostrils.

'I'll be right up,' he said. The phone went dead, and Barclay put it back on the receiver. 'Bye to you, too.'

'See… she's fucking awful. What kind of person doesn't say goodbye? A psychopath, that's who.'

It was true. He used to watch his mum say 'bye' or 'terrah' over and over until her face practically touched the phone's hook. He chuckled at the memory. De Silva's lips pouted, she shook her head slowly and her auburn curls bounced.

'I'd give anything to be back on that case, de Silva,' Barclay said. 'But here we are. It's not our case any more and we have to co-operate. You said it yourself. And anyway, as long as someone gets the bad guy, it's a win, isn't it?'

He knew even as he said it that that wasn't entirely true. Getting the bad guy was good, but de Silva thrived on the how and why, the investigation. The painstaking research, the witness interviews, the full understanding of why the perpetrator did what they did. Barclay loved that aspect of it, too. Needed it.

But rules are rules.

He pulled on his jacket and headed for the door. 'It's just us telling them what we know. They'll be finished with us in a few days.'

Meeting Room One was a comfortable temperature. Glass jugs on a plastic tray sat on top of the varnished table, beaded with condensation. The two NCA officers sat opposite Barclay, in impeccably tailored suits. Barclay clocked the man's shoes, highly polished Oxfords with broguing in tan leather.

'My name is Robert Ayris, but please call me Rob.' His teeth were wide but perfectly straight, and he had those sharp-looking incisors that always reminded Barclay of vampire TV shows from years ago. 'This is Fitzgerald.' Ayris's accent was soft, but definitely Scottish, his green eyes shining. Barclay had loved it up there when he'd visited with Nick.

'And what should I call you?' Barclay said, nodding to Fitzgerald, half joking.

'Fitzgerald.' Her face was expressionless and Barclay doubted it would move even if she had to sneeze. Her skin was flawless, but had the sheen people get from too much Botox. There was no warmth to her, no way that Barclay could read her. 'Please, take a seat. Benjamin is it, or Ben?'

'Detective Sergeant Barclay,' he said.

Ayris smirked. 'Please take a seat.' He adjusted his tie, a paisley print in shades of blue, and opened a small notebook in front of him. 'Would you like a drink?'

'No, thank you.'

'I hope that by now DSI Murphy has informed you about the Agency's involvement?'

'Involvement.' Barclay twisted the wedding ring on his left hand and noticed that the skin was dry. 'I thought you came in to take over?'

The Fitzgerald woman made notes on an iPad with a black stylus that clacked against the glass. Ayris gave her a look, and something passed between them that Barclay couldn't quite read.

'I think there may be some confusion here, DS Barclay.' Ayris clasped his hands together in front of him, massive things covered in scars and cuts. Barclay wondered if he played rugby. 'We very much want to work with you and DCI, erm…' He quickly scanned his notebook.

'DCI de Silva.' *Jesus, they've taken her case and don't even know her name.*

Ayris smiled. 'Yes, that's right. Apologies. I'm still getting up to speed.'

You were saying… 'That's okay.'

'Well…' Ayris took a pause here, a dramatic flair that Barclay didn't appreciate. 'We wanted to work with you and DCI de Silva on this. Sure, we'd take the lead, but we appreciate the work you've put into this. We value your insight.'

'So why aren't you? Working with us, I mean?'

'We were informed that you'd moved on to something new.'

'I don't know what you've been told, but—'

'I think we're getting off topic here,' Fitzgerald said. 'Let's get back to it. Please.'

Ayris nodded. 'You're right.' He looked at Barclay. 'She keeps me on it, can you tell?'

Fitzgerald's eyes were on Barclay and he swallowed hard. There was something in her way, her manner, the way she projected herself, that made Barclay uneasy.

Good cop, bad cop. That old trick.

'The Woulds app,' Ayris said. 'You first came across it when?'

'It's all there in the files,' Barclay said. 'I have a case I should be working on.'

'We appreciate your co-operation here.' Ayris turned a page in his notebook. 'When did you first come across it?'

'Our Digital Forensics team found it on the phone of one of the victims in the Lamond murders in November last year.' Barclay swallowed hard. 'Kelly Stack.'

'Tell us more about the case. She was the third victim, right?'

'Three out of five, yes,' Barclay said. 'All of them were between thirteen and fifteen years of age. Most taken and held for days on end. Subjected to rape, severe beatings and strangled. Bodies dumped along the river.'

'Most?'

'One he took and… disposed of quickly. He was frantic, losing control.'

'I see. And why do you think he chose the river?'

'We're not entirely sure. We can't get answers from the suspect. Lewis Lamond was found hanged in his cell while in custody just weeks after we got him. After that, all we have are our own theories. De Silva proposed that it was some sort of way of purifying them. Cleansing them in the water and in doing so, maybe cleansing himself.'

'I read about Lamond's suicide.' Ayris turned pages in his notes. 'CCTV was out in that wing, wasn't it?'

Allegedly. 'Yes.'

'Any thoughts on that?'

'We were looking into it,' he said. 'Brick wall after brick wall. But if you're asking me if I think Lamond killed himself, then the answer is no. I don't.'

'You think he was murdered?'

'Yes.'

'Why do you think that?' Fitzgerald didn't look up from her notes.

'As I say, we were looking into it. We have nothing solid.'

'Your reports made mention that a former police officer, DCI Michael Crosby from your Protecting Vulnerable People, or PVP unit, was somehow involved in the murders?'

'We're not sure about the extent of his involvement, but he was there. We found a footprint at the suspect's home address which matched Crosby's shoe size and a pair of police standard-issue boots which are given to all police constables. He must have kept them all these years. And he was there at the end. At the school. Rainford Lane School for Boys, or what's left of it. He attacked us, de Silva and me. Lamond confirmed his involvement. It's in the recording of that first interview. He didn't give us much, just that they knew each other. From school. That Crosby had always looked after Lamond in some way. But he wouldn't talk about it after the first interview.'

'And the app you found on the Stack girl's phone. You didn't find it on the mobile or smart devices of any other victim?'

'No.' He drew a breath, about to continue, but thought better of it. *Let them do the work*.

'Why did you think it was important enough to warrant further investigation?'

'It was an app that wasn't available on any app store easily accessible by the everyday internet user.'

'Go on...'

Barclay knew Ayris and Fitzgerald already had this information. Sometimes, in his own interviews, he circled back to information over and over again. A lot of people believe that innocence is shown when a story doesn't change. In fact, any interviewer should expect some micro changes to any witness or suspect's story. Whether they were remembering something new or their brain was filling in the gaps, sometimes something important would come out of it.

'Holden,' he said, 'who heads up our Digital Forensics team, found that the app led to the Dark Web. The site was shut down. Or moved. Deleted, maybe.' And Lamond. They'd questioned him about the app when they'd apprehended him. There was something in the way he said *No, I've never heard of an app called The Woulds.* It would be there in the interview recording and transcript if they looked.

'Have you ever heard of an app called In2Web?' Fitzgerald's cold, clear voice cut through the silence in the room, cut through Barclay's thoughts like a knife.

'No, I've not.'

Fitzgerald nodded.

'Should I have heard of it?'

A pause. Barclay looked from Fitzgerald to Ayris.

'What can you tell us about the relationship between DCIs Crosby and de Silva?'

'What do you mean?'

Fitzgerald interjected again. 'What was the nature of their relationship?'

'They were colleagues,' Barclay said. 'They'd worked together for years, long before my time.'

'There was nothing more?' Ayris looked down at his notepad.

'If there's a specific question you want me to answer, then you're going to have to ask.'

'Were DCIs Crosby and de Silva having a sexual relationship?' Fitzgerald asked without hesitation.

'I don't know where you got your information from, but I don't concern myself with office gossip.' He knew the truth, everyone knew. But if they wanted to know de Silva's personal business, they were going to have to ask her themselves.

'A detective who doesn't listen to gossip.' Fitzgerald's lips pouted, her chin flexed. She was mocking him.

'I didn't say I don't listen. I said I don't concern myself with it. It's none of my business.' He glared at her until she looked down and wrote on her iPad. 'I know Crosby was involved with Lamond, but I can't see the connection between him and the app. Or is there another reason you're asking about de Silva?' A rage built in him. Ayris and Fitzgerald were crossing a line. 'Can I ask you a question?'

Fitzgerald nodded. Ayris said, 'Of course.'

'Are you wanting to discredit her? De Silva, I mean.'

'Why would you think that?' Fitzgerald held her stylus poised over her tablet.

'You're asking personal questions unrelated to the case. Unrelated to the app. Are you suggesting that because Mike Crosby was involved that somehow de Silva was too?'

Fitzgerald looked to Ayris, and her lips parted just slightly as though she was about to say something, but thought better of it. She turned back to Barclay and said, 'I think we're done for now. We'll be in touch again soon.'

'I'd like an answer to the questions I've asked, thank you.'

Fitzgerald shot a look at Ayris, and he said, 'Look. We're not here to discredit anyone. And no, I don't think de Silva had prior knowledge of Crosby's involvement in that case, or that she was in some way involved herself. We want to get to the bottom of this. We have to ask these questions and sometimes we're not at liberty to say why. We can't discuss an active case so openly with you. Not right now. We're in the early stages of our own investigation: I'm sure you can appreciate that.'

Barclay nodded, even though he wasn't in any way happy with the response. He asked, 'Shall I send de Silva up?'

'She's already with our colleagues.' Fitzgerald smiled politely, almost a smirk. *Smug.*

Barclay left the meeting room, his head buzzing. He tried to piece it all together but couldn't. Their line of questioning seemed to be confused. First the app, then the case, Lamond and Crosby, then de Silva's personal life.

They'd gotten nothing from Barclay that they couldn't have taken from the casefiles, the reports, the interview recordings. His stomach churned, completely unsettled. There was only one reason Barclay could think of: they were feeling him out, trying to understand him. The interview had meant nothing, not really. He wondered what they'd learned about him.

He took out his phone and his thumb hovered over de Silva's name. If her phone went off mid-interview, it could throw everything for her. He thought better of it. It was after six p.m. already.

If he hurried, he'd be able to get a steam in after the gym.

Seven

De Silva thought about calling Barclay on the drive home. She'd gone down to the basement to get her bag and coat and found that he'd already gone. She knew he'd likely be at the gym so thought better of it. She needed someone to call, to rage at, but who would pick up the phone? Who'd want to listen?

When Ritchie had died, she'd gone into herself, ignored her friends' calls and texts and concerns. Her world had been colourful, vibrant, until he died. Until he had found out about Crosby. As she stood in that doorway beneath him, his shadow stretched across her, beyond her and out onto the path, she'd felt like her whole world had become just that. Shadows.

Even now, months after his death – the love, the laughter, the early days when things were perfect, now just memories – things hadn't gotten any easier. Sure, the drink was gone, but she'd learned to live with his absence because a person never stops grieving.

She'd planned to leave it all behind. The crime scenes, the victims found dead, their bodies destroyed, the interview rooms where information was a commodity, a power that shifted and thinned out until the closest thing to truth surfaced.

The decision had tortured her. Who was she if not a detective? Would she be letting her dad down by giving up? Giving in? She'd worked so hard to rise through the ranks as quickly as she had done. Late nights, early mornings, over and above her male counterparts just to get half of the recognition for it.

After everything with Lamond, she'd not made any plans for her future beyond leaving Merseyside Police, and that had been fine with her. Her future was a path no one else had trodden, and that had exhilarated her. Revived her. Until she began to sort through Ritchie's paperwork. The folded bits of his life, which had yellowed across the decades, that had lived in her home the entire time they were together; they held a truth that Win de Silva hadn't known about, hadn't guessed. Facts that would, if she left the police, haunt her forever.

That was why she stayed. That was her drive. To know the truth. To work the case until she uncovered everything, and then, finally, when the suspects were apprehended, when the trial was due to begin, she could leave. She could walk the path no one else had yet set foot on. Her own prospects. Her own fortune.

Or, her own doom.

With the NCA investigation, that was all gone. Any hope of finding out the truth for herself gone with it. She was glad, initially, that she'd not mentioned what she'd found in Ritchie's old paperwork to Barclay. Hadn't put it in any record or report. Hadn't turned it over as evidence. She'd felt it was hers to uncover. To put right.

These two NCA officers would never know anything about it from her: a missing piece of the puzzle that she knew, one day, they might come across anyway.

Earlier that day, she had sat at the table in Meeting Room Four across from the two investigators, two women, and had wanted to blurt it all out. To get it off her chest. Finally.

'This might be painful to talk about,' the younger one had said. She'd been all smiles and shining eyes, and introduced herself as Rachel Gray. 'We can take a break at any time.'

De Silva nodded.

'We have to ask about your relationship with Detective Chief Inspector Michael Crosby from your PVP unit.'

'I've known Crosby my entire career. We trained together. Learned a lot under O'Brien's leadership. Back when he was a DCI himself.'

'Former-Detective Superintendent Thomas O'Brien you mean?' The older one. Chris Summers, she'd said her name was. She wore the job on her face: the late nights had puffed her eyes, and there were lines around her mouth. A smoker. De Silva could smell it, and it stuck in her throat.

'Yes,' de Silva said.

'There was more to it.'

'Are you asking me a question?'

'Was there more to it?' Gray's face hardened now. The smile gone.

'We were friends. Him and his wife, me and my husband: we had dinner together a lot. Drinks. We were close.' She knew what they were getting at, what they were circling around. She took a deep breath. 'We were fucking. Having an affair, whatever you want to call it.'

Gray swallowed and her throat clicked, as though she needed a drink of water. 'Purely a sexual relationship?'

'Not just sexual,' she said. 'I lo— I was in love with him. I don't know if he felt the same, if it was anything more than sex for him. I couldn't answer that, if you wanted to know.'

Gray nodded. 'I understand.'

'During your time together, did Crosby ever talk about his childhood? About Rainford Lane School for Boys? His time there?'

'No.' She shook her head. 'We never spoke about his childhood. I had always assumed it was the same as mine. Working class. Our parents struggling for money in the eighties and early nineties. But otherwise normal. I assumed.'

'There was never any mention of abuse?' Summers clasped her hands together.

'We didn't talk about his childhood, as I've said.'

'He never mentioned the relationship between himself and Lewis Lamond?'

De Silva stared for a moment. 'I know you're trying your best to make sure that nothing was missed. That I didn't drop the ball on this case. But you're speaking to me like you don't trust me, which, in turn, makes me not want to trust you.' She forced a smile. 'If there was something else to add, I'd have told you.' Even as she said it, she felt her stomach churn. She didn't know anything more about Crosby's involvement with Lamond, but she did know *something else*.

She knew about her dead husband's link to that school, and maybe to Crosby and Lamond.

'I've been here almost an hour and you haven't asked a single question about the app we found,' de Silva said. 'The Woulds? I assumed that's what your involvement would be mostly about.'

'What do you think the app was?'

'I don't know,' de Silva sighed. 'We couldn't find anything on it. But anything connected to the Dark Web can't be good, can it?' *There's only one reason they wouldn't have asked about the app during an interview*, she thought. *If they already knew all they needed to know about it.* 'Do you know what it is?'

Gray looked at Summer, who cleared her throat.

'I think that'll be all for now, thank you.' Gray stood up and motioned toward the door. 'We'll be in touch again soon.'

De Silva nodded, as much to herself as to Gray. They knew. As she left the room and stepped out into the warm corridor, she wondered how much they did know about it. Its purpose. It was important, she knew that. But how it all fitted together, she couldn't guess.

That's all she would be able to do now. Guess. The case had been taken from them, and she had to focus her attentions on the cold case Murphy had assigned. It wasn't the case she wanted to be working on, but it was the one she had. She wondered whether it was reason enough to stay.

The scream of a car's horn brought her back to herself. She'd drifted into the righthand lane of the roundabout. An angry driver flashed his lights at her. She considered stopping and pulling them over. Asking for his licence. She flipped him the middle finger in the rear-view instead.

She turned off the roundabout and onto Huyton Lane, then Carr Lane and on to home. Her detached house was at the edge of the new-build orange-brick estate, and she was thankful she had no immediate neighbours she could bump into as they got out of their cars with their kids or shopping bags.

She pulled up onto the drive a little after seven. The sun had already set, and somewhere behind the roofs, it had blushed the sky the colour of grapefruit skin, but all around it the night crept in, ink-blue, and soon it would all be dark.

She fumbled in her coat pocket for the door keys. Dropped them, and dropped them again. They chinged like fallen pennies. She had set the heating to turn on before she left the station, and the house was a cosy warm.

'Alexa, turn on the lights,' she said. Lamps in the living room and dining room came on, warm white. In the kitchen, the spotlights sprang to life, the clinical white of a hospital or mortuary. She wanted to call Barclay, to see if Dr Carey had gotten back to him about the post-mortem results on the man in the woods.

She decided that it could wait until tomorrow. One more day after twenty-odd years lying in the ground was nothing.

She went straight up the stairs and into the bathroom. Turned on the taps and waited until steam rose out of the water: it spread in the air like clouds and de Silva watched for shapes.

Her phone vibrated on the edge of the sink and slid down into the basin. Two drops of water fell on it from the tap: she'd have to get the spanner out and tighten it again. Laney calling.

She took a deep breath and stared at her sister's name on the screen. They'd never been close, even when they were kids. In fact, the last time they'd seen each other was last year when their mum was in hospital with a broken hip. And it hadn't ended well then, either. She pressed the green button. 'Hello, Laney,' she said finally.

'Are you at work?'

'No, I'm at home. I was just about to have a bath.'
Silence.

De Silva waited a few more moments before she asked, 'Are you still there?'

'Yeah,' she said. 'I'm sorry.'

Laney never apologised for anything. De Silva was certain she could hear something in her voice, there was a thickness to it. She'd been crying, de Silva decided. 'What's wrong, Laney?' Her sister had never rung her when she was upset before, they'd not had that kind of relationship for years, even as kids.

'You know, you're the last person I'd think to call on like this.'

De Silva pursed her lips. 'What's wrong?'

'Can I come over?'

De Silva's heart almost stopped in her chest. 'Erm…'

'If it's a problem, I—'

'It's not,' she said. 'But I've moved since you were last around.'

'Oh.' There was something else in her voice now, but de Silva couldn't quite make it out. A sense of loss, maybe, or was that de Silva's own hope?

'1 Amber Mews.'

'I'll be about forty minutes.' She hung up the phone.

Great. De Silva climbed into the bath and closed her eyes. She could think of nothing worse than company right then, especially with Laney. An upset Laney.

Forty minutes. She'd have time for a quick nap.

Eight

The red circle on Barclay's watch showed that he had met his six-hundred-calorie-burn target for the day. The spin room had been stifling, and the music had vibrated through the frame of his bike; above the noise, the instructor had shouted commands at the class. But Barclay hadn't heard any of it.

Sweat had dripped from the tip of his nose and onto the rubber-tiled floor and he was lost in the motion of his legs turning and pushing. When his thoughts drifted beyond the room, to Nick and Sarah, he'd pedalled harder, let the burn in his legs singe the edges of his hopes, his dreams. Since he'd left their home, he and Nick hadn't spoken much about the future. It was as though Nick didn't want him back, and the thought of that hurt.

Now, as he stood under the shower, thick and foamy suds slipping down his toned body to the cold tiles, he was glad he'd got a workout in before the office, just as much as he was glad it was over.

Barclay used the same locker every day, number one hundred, because it was one of the few that had a pole for a coat hanger left in it. Over the years, the others had snapped or vanished, and he liked his top to be freshly ironed, not a single crease in it. He entered the combination to his padlock – 1809, Sarah's birthday – and pulled his bag out.

'Your phone's been going nuts in there. Probably that de Silva one.'

A familiar voice, but changed somehow. Barclay turned around to find former-DSI O'Brien standing there, a towel wrapped around his bulking waist, his thinning hair messy and wet. Barclay forced a smile. 'Sir! What're you doing here?'

O'Brien looked around. 'Easy, Barclay, for God's sake. It's just O'Brien now. Thomas. Tom if you're lucky. I didn't know you went here.'

Barclay nodded, spraying deodorant onto his underarms. 'Almost ten years now, I think.'

'I knew you went to the gym, I mean look at you.' He slapped Barclay's upper arm and for the first time, Barclay noticed the tattoo of some colourful bird, a swallow maybe, on O'Brien's forearm, faded by the years. The name of his wife under it in swirling letters that almost wrapped around themselves: Kath. 'Thought I'd check out what all the fuss was about,' he said.

'Well yeah, now you've got the time on your hands.' Barclay winced at his own insensitivity. 'I'm sorry, I didn't mean…'

'It's fine.' O'Brien wriggled into some M&S underwear, awkwardly without removing his towel. 'It's true, I do have time on my hands. And with my Kath gone, well… she was my life. I suppose I have to see what life is without her.'

That hit Barclay hard. He sat down on the bench and pulled on his fresh, plain white Vivienne Westwood T-shirt, the famous Orb logo embroidered small on the left of his chest.

He hadn't ever considered life without Nick. This whole mess had been a misunderstanding. A misstep on the road of their marriage, something which they could recover from. Make amends for.

'What else have you been up to?' Barclay asked, to fill the awkward silence.

'Well I took up fishing,' O'Brien said. 'Dreadfully boring pastime. I'm not sure what people get from it, Barclay, are you? All that time sat with your rod in the water hoping for a bite. And if by chance you're lucky enough to catch one of the things, you put it right back and start again. I don't see the point.'

'Surely there's more to it?'

'Not that I could see. But you'll have to come with me some time. It'll be nice.'

Barclay tried to keep the abject fear from his face. He pulled on his black Armani jeans. 'I'm not sure it's my thing.' In truth, he couldn't think of anything worse than sitting still for that length of time.

'No, I don't suppose it is.' O'Brien shook his head. 'You got time for a coffee?'

Barclay looked at his watch. He did have time. 'I'm sorry, not this morning.'

'Big case going on?' O'Brien's smile was soft and spread to his eyes. 'How's all that going? I was sorry to have left in the middle of it all.'

'You had a lot going on, si— O'Brien?' He tried it on for size, and it felt strange. Too stiff and tight, but Thomas or Tom felt too informal. He wished someone else would come along and join the conversation.

'That I did. So... how's it going? The case?'

'I can't really talk about it, you know—'

'Yes, yes. I know. I should know better. Old habits die hard and all that. The new DSI, I heard she came up from the Met. Big promotion for her, as if there was no one up here capable of doing it.'

'You left big shoes to fill.'

O'Brien beamed. 'You flatterer. How is she?'

'She's fine, I suppose.' Barclay rubbed a hyaluronic acid serum into his face. 'Thorough. Careful. Considered.'

'Are you describing the new DSI or a prostate exam?'

Barclay laughed out loud and rubbed in a vitamin C cream. 'She's not so bad.'

'De Silva hates her, doesn't she?'

'Of course she hates her,' Barclay said. 'She's not you.'

'That's uplifting to hear.' O'Brien pulled on his trousers, navy-blue chinos, and fastened his brown belt. Looked down at his naked, hairy feet. 'Would you do me a favour?'

'Yeah, what is it?' Barclay pulled on a black and white checked shacket with sherpa collar.

'Ask her to visit?'

Barclay felt a small crack split his heart. He didn't know the reasons de Silva had distanced herself from O'Brien. It was none of his business. But O'Brien was clearly in pain and needed de Silva.

'Or call at least,' O'Brien added.

'I'll ask her, sir. I promise.'

O'Brien nodded and Barclay thought he saw his bottom lip tremble for just a second. 'Well then.' He pushed his feet into some pumps, shoved his dirty gym stuff into his bag and lifted it onto his shoulder. 'I'll see you, Barclay.'

'See you.'

'In tomorrow?'

'Maybe,' Barclay said. 'You know what it's like…'

'I remember.' He chuckled. 'See you around. And don't let the new one grind you down.'

—

Barclay stepped out of the lift just before nine a.m. Traffic had been particularly bad down Speke Boulevard.

The light in the incident room was already on, and he heard the rumble of the coffee percolator.

'Put one on for me,' he called.

PC Lawrence came to the door. 'Morning, sir.'

'Lawrence, I'm so sorry. I thought you were de Silva.'

'It's fine.' She smiled broadly. 'Sugar?'

'Sweetener. There's some in my top drawer. Thanks. Did Murphy send you?'

'Yeah. De Silva organised the rest. Milk?'

'Please.'

'I'm glad the DSI asked me,' Lawrence said. 'I've been trying to catch you for ages.' There was a softness to her hazel eyes, amber flecks that seemed to reflect the light.

'Oh yeah?' Barclay sat down at his desk and logged on. He took his work mobile out of his pocket. Dead. He put it on charge. 'What's up?'

'I'm putting in for my detective exam.'

'That's fantastic, Lawrence. You'll make a great detective. CID?'

'Or Major Incidents, I'm not sure.'

Barclay nodded. 'We'd be lucky to have you. I mean that.'

His phone came to life and pinged instantly. An email from the Coroner's Office. Dr Carey could see them today at ten thirty for half an hour. 'Forget that coffee,' he said. 'Has de Silva been in yet?'

'Here I am.' De Silva looked tired. Puffy eyes, hair scraped back into a low-maintenance messy pony.

'Carey can see us this morning. In about half an hour. Grab a coffee on the way?'

'I could do with one. A strong one. I had no sleep last night.'

'Yeah. Looks like it.'

Lawrence snorted, the glass coffee jug clattering against her mug. 'Sorry,' she said.

'Watch yourself, Lawrence. De Silva on no sleep is like a viper. Coiled and ready to attack.'

'No, *you* watch yourself,' de Silva snapped back. 'Or you'll be wearing Lawrence's coffee jug like a hat.' She looked to Lawrence now. 'I told O'Connor, Braxton and the others to get here for nine. Any sign?'

'I've seen them around. They're just doing handovers they said. Resource is pretty thin,' Lawrence said.

Barclay rolled his eyes at de Silva. *Nothing new there.* 'Who did you get?'

'O'Connor and Braxton, like Lawrence said, but I also asked for McLachlan and Harris to join us.'

Barclay nodded. 'That's good.'

De Silva looked to Barclay, who was still in his seat. 'Come on, let's go.'

She didn't wait for Barclay, she was already out the door as soon as she'd finished speaking.

Barclay smiled politely at Lawrence and said, 'We need lists of missing persons between 1990 and 1995. Male victims. I want to speak to Carey again before we determine an age, so I'll be in touch soon as we've spoken with her, all right?'

Lawrence nodded. 'Anything else?'

'Chase the rest of the team,' he said. 'We need them on this now.' Barclay closed the door behind him and half-jogged toward the lift, where de Silva waited impatiently, her finger on the button to keep the doors open. 'I'm guessing your meeting with NCA didn't go so well then?'

'I don't even want to talk about it,' she said. Her voice had a low timbre to it. She was angry or upset. Probably both. The NCA agents had grilled Barclay on de Silva's relationship with Crosby and he could only imagine the things they'd asked her.

Nine

De Silva couldn't stop thinking about Laney. It was all that occupied her mind, more than her interview with the NCA. She'd expected that, knew it was coming, had time to prepare. But nothing prepares a person for their estranged sister showing up on their doorstep, bag in hand, split-lipped and black-eyed, with her crying daughter in tow.

She had to push it out of her mind. Had to keep her focus on the day, on the case. The man in the woods, she told herself, he was the priority. The only comfort she could find in this scenario was that Laney's husband, David, didn't know where de Silva's new house was.

De Silva had never been one of those people that could turn work on and off at the incident room. It had always followed her home, always slept in her bed, always showered with her in the morning and ate dinner next to her.

Her dad had been the same and her mum had called him obsessive. De Silva had watched her dad's work ruin family holidays, events, parties, and still she always knew she wanted to do what he did.

'Do you want to talk about it?' Barclay asked.

'No.' De Silva gripped the steering wheel tighter. 'I don't.'

'Well I'm going to, because I need to.' Barclay cleared his throat. 'They asked me about your relationship with Crosby.'

He paused here. Was de Silva supposed to say something? Offer some verbal cue that Barclay should continue?

'I said nothing,' he said. 'Well, I told them if they wanted to know about your personal life that they should ask you.'

'And they did,' de Silva said. 'But they gave me this impression that—'

'That Crosby was somehow connected with The Woulds app?'

De Silva hit the steering wheel, one sharp slap. 'Yes! Their questioning was transparent.' They'd found no connection between the app and Rainford Lane School for Boys in their original investigation, but still, something about it bothered de Silva.

'Unless that's what they want us to think? To see if we knew more than we're letting on. You know, obstructing their investigation?'

De Silva glanced across at Barclay. That hadn't occurred to her at all. 'I mean, it's possible. I'm sure they'll have us in again.' She paused here, her breath held tight in her chest, unsure whether she should tell him what she'd done before she went to sleep last night, when both Laney and her niece, Bonnie, were settled.

'I know that look, de Silva.'

'What look?'

'That look! What have you done?'

'I haven't done anything!' She he put her palm flat to her chest, over her heart, as though swearing some oath on every pulse, every beat.

'No, you've done something.'

'Well, I mean, it's nothing…'

'Your version of nothing and mine are two different things.' His smile was wide, but de Silva could see in his eyes that he was panicked. Worried.

'I just contacted Holden, that's all.'

'What for?'

'Well, I mentioned his name in there, so wanted to give him the heads up that they'd come knocking on his door.'

'His name is all over those files. He's the one that kicked the app up to his contact in the NCA in the first place. They know all about him, so why did you pick up the phone?'

'Courtesy, honestly.'

Barclay said nothing more, but stared at her, his thick, heavy eyebrow arched.

'Fine, it was just a little request.' De Silva coughed, not to clear her throat but to scramble for time. A way to put the words she needed to say in an order that would do the least damage. 'I just asked him to look again into the app.'

'De Silva…'

'I know what you're going to say.' She mimicked his gruff voice: 'This isn't our case any more. The NCA are handling it and we should leave them to it, follow our orders from the Grand High Witch and keep our noses out of it and our arses clean.'

'Well I wouldn't have put it quite like that, but the Grand High Witch is an excellent reference.' He sighed. 'You didn't think to ring me before you contacted Holden and asked him to put his career on the line? Again.'

'He's not doing anything bad. He's just looking at it.'

'Looking at and looking into are two different things, and we both know it. If Murphy finds out…'

'She'll turn me into a mouse, I know.'

'I'm going to pretend we haven't had this conversation. My arse is clean, de Silva.'

'Okay, I get it.'

'I'm just going to say—'

'Oh, here we go…'

'I'm just going to say that you put Holden's career at risk last year when you asked him to hack into Crosby's emails. Your own career for that matter.'

'I remember.'

'Well I'm just reminding you.'

'I said I remember.'

'Good.'

De Silva rolled her eyes. Barclay was insufferable sometimes. Rigid to the point of snapping, but his heart was in the right place. He was loyal, professional, always had his eye on procedure. Protocol.

Nothing like de Silva.

The rest of their journey passed in a silence, not the awkward kind where you don't know what to say, but the easy type of quiet where everything has already been said and that is just fine. De Silva focused on the road ahead, and Barclay watched the world through the window.

Dr Carey's office was bright, the walls a brilliant white, and on them were photographs of trips she'd taken with what de Silva assumed was her partner. He stood in front of a waterfall, bundled up in a thick red coat and woollen hat and scarf. His arms stretched above his head, as though celebrating. Another showed them on safari, a pride of lions in the background watched on, no regard for the presence of the visitors. Another on a canal, Venice by the looks of it, not that de Silva had ever been, then inside a helicopter, a massive canyon in the background.

De Silva wondered how long they'd been together. How long they'd been able to stay happy. Stay faithful. Remain in love.

'Sorry to have kept you waiting.' Dr Carey had a warm fragrance about her, not floral but something sweeter, stronger. Almost like honey. Her skin was sun-kissed, somewhere between red and brown. 'Please, take a seat.'

De Silva sat down, and Barclay hovered a moment then sat. 'I was admiring your photographs,' she said.

'Ah yes.' Carey smiled, but there was a sadness in there. De Silva didn't recognise it at first. 'We tried to get away as much as we could. All those holidays were everything he'd ever wanted to see and do. They call it a bucket list.'

De Silva's chest swelled, a lump turned to stone in her throat. 'I'm sorry for your loss.'

'We all lose people we love.'

Barclay shifted in his seat, crossed his legs, and de Silva wanted to say, *Yes, we do*, but she stayed silent.

'So,' Carey said. 'I'm sorry, I'm not sure there's anything more I could tell you beyond what's in the report. It was a long time ago, and in that time...' She spread her hands in front of her, an indication of the nothingness in the months since the body's discovery, de Silva thought.

'No, we get it,' Barclay said. 'But anything you can tell us will be useful.'

'Well, the remains belonged to a male over the age of twenty-one. The bones were all fully developed. There was, as you know, a fracture on the right radius.' Here she pointed about halfway up the inside of her forearm.

'Could that have been caused by osteoporosis?' de Silva asked.

Carey smiled. 'I get your thinking. Tests showed high bone density, so no, I wouldn't say osteoporosis was the cause.'

'How common is osteoporosis?'

'In men over the age of fifty, one in four, one in five, I think.'

Barclay sat back in his seat. 'So we can't safely say that he was under fifty, with odds like that.'

De Silva wasn't sure if he was saying it to her or to himself. 'I understand you had the body analysed by an entomologist?'

'No, your Area Forensics Manager did that,' Carey said. 'Brennan, is it? I did receive a copy of the report though.' Carey turned to her computer and loaded it up. She put on the perfectly round glasses hanging from the pocket of her blazer and they reflected the computer screen. 'Let me just get my notes up.' She cleared her throat and took a few minutes. 'Again, I'm not sure this will tell you anything. There was evidence of insect activity. Maggots, flies. There was some rodent activity too. Squirrels maybe. Rats.' Carey moved her index and middle finger together, tapped her thumb, like pincers or teeth.

'How long would it take for maggots to move in?' Barclay asked.

'Larvae can move in quickly and eat away at most of the body within a week, but underground, it's difficult to say. They found evidence of gnawing at the bones. Not large enough to be a rodent. The entomologist concluded, one second, ah yes, they concluded it was due to beetles.'

Barclay winced and Carey chuckled, clasped her hands together. 'Death isn't pretty,' she said.

For the second time today, Carey had hit de Silva where it hurt. In her heart, in the memories of her husband. In the swollen bulge that grew ever bigger in her chest, the thing her therapist called PTSD.

'Look, none of this is going to tell you anything about the post-mortem interval.' She locked her computer and turned to face them both, removed her glasses. 'The body was buried in sandy soil. Typically, that type of soil advances the rapidity of decomposition. It can move fluids away from the body due to its drainage properties. It's aerated, so oxygen can get to the body even if it's buried. Microbial activity, obviously, and the animal activity I mentioned earlier. Sandy soil is more accessible to animals.'

'So what you're saying is…'

'That there's no way we could easily determine how long the body was in the ground. I understand Brennan indicated it could have been there for decades. I'm likely to concur, but there's no certainty. For the reasons I've mentioned, a body buried for five years in this type of environment could look the same as a body buried for twenty years.'

De Silva sighed. 'Do you have any good news for us?'

'It's all in the report.'

De Silva had the feeling that they were wasting Carey's time. She felt bad for that. Everyone was feeling the agony of doing more with less. 'I'm sorry. I know you're busy. I read in the report that there was some evidence of hesitation around the wound where the middle finger was removed?'

'That's right.' Carey looked at her watch. 'There was evidence of cutting through the bone, clearly. But next to that there were other cuts, lines, some deep.' She mimicked cutting through her middle finger. 'Variations in pressure. As though they'd started cutting then had to stop and come back to finish it. Maybe they started in a slightly different place on the digit.'

'Or maybe it took more than one person to finish the job,' Barclay said.

De Silva looked across to him and felt her mind lift out of Carey's office and enter the woods, shift back through the seasons where leaves drifted to the ground and rotted, where snow blew through the naked tree trunks and covered everything in white, where the sun turned morning dew to mist and from beneath it, green shoots pushed through the earth. Where the sun set beyond the Irish Sea and the night came on cold.

She imagined the body of a man, faceless to her then, carried through the woods, his head hanging back at some unnatural angle, blood oozing from a wound in his head. Pine needles and cones stuck to his hair. Two other faceless men, because in her experience they were always men, one at the dead man's feet the other had hold of his arms. Moments later, he was in the ground and they cut at his finger. One of them stopped and cried or vomited, and the other continued. Their instruments were shadows to her, things that didn't catch the glint of the crescent moon.

'Detective?' Carey said.

De Silva snapped back to the present, to the stuffy office. 'Thank for your time,' she said. 'We appreciate it.'

As they made their way to the car, Barclay stayed silent. She wondered whether he knew her mind was racing, whether he wanted to give her the space to think, or whether his own mind had whirred into action and began building a narrative.

'More than one person,' he'd said. She hadn't considered that before this meeting. The removal of the finger was important, it meant something to the suspect, or as the evidence suggested, suspects.

But why?

Ten

His flat was stuffy, he knew that. Any smells from cooking or his bathroom movements lingered in the air for hours, sometimes days. He couldn't remember when he last opened the windows: even in the blistering heat of the last summer, he'd had them closed. There was just one night, when he'd lain down on the cold tiles of the bathroom floor, the only place he could find some respite from the heat, where he'd panicked and wondered whether he would be cooked alive. That someone would come to his flat and find his body roasted like a cut of pork belly.

He hadn't slept the whole of that night.

Now, he sat at his desk, tiredness like weights under his eyes, and unfastened two more buttons on his checked shirt, ironed with almost military precision.

He knew that he was nearing the end, slowly after all the years of trying to get it out of him. His story. His sorrow. The torture he'd experienced, the truth of his childhood and the revenge he so badly wanted.

The truth was that he knew no one would believe him. It was all too surreal. People had a way of not seeing the horrors that were right in front of them. They were distracted by deadly viruses, the war in Ukraine, another Tory in Downing Street. Diversions to keep the blind people blind, the sheeple grazing at the grass while the truth seekers, the enlightened, burned the skies above their heads.

They had no idea.

Online they called him a conspiracy theorist for his ideas about Covid-19, a freak for understanding that he had been born into a world where those in power, the Cabal, used up and spat out people like him. Or tried to. They'd called him sick for talking about police corruption, their involvement in covering up the activities of predators of children: the police, judges, lords and ladies, even the royal family.

His stomach growled like an angry dog. He hadn't eaten since yesterday morning, but he knew he'd need to break his fast. Tomorrow, he'd try to go for longer. Two full days maybe. He followed someone on Instagram who'd once fasted for over a week. He'd get there, he knew. It would just take time. Patience on his behalf. Discipline.

He pressed print and watched as each slip of paper came out of the printer, his own words, his own truth, there for all to – one day – read. When it was done, he put the pages with the rest in the top drawer of his desk.

A shiver crept up his spine despite the heat in the flat. He pressed the save icon and shut down his computer. When it had finished, he flicked the switch under the desk and the standby light blinked and turned black.

From the top drawer of his desk, he took a disinfectant wipe and cleaned the keyboard, the computer screen and his mouse. He threw it into the pedal bin in the kitchenette, and turned to the sink where he cleaned his hands with alcohol gel. It smelled strong and stung at his nostrils. The only good thing to come from Covid-times was the fact that more people got into the habit of cleaning their hands.

He chopped some summer berries and spinach and popped them into a blender, watched it spin and obliterate the fruit until finally all that was left was a thick, wet, red mess. It tasted good. Strawberries and cherries were sweet but they left a bitter tang at the back of his throat.

As he drank, he moved to the far wall. He stood there, free hand on his hip and looked. There were maps of the UK, some were nation-wide, and some more local. Pins in various areas, all red. Headlines carefully cut out of newspapers so that the edges were straight.

Amongst the scraps of paper, yellowed over time, was one that he paid particular interest to. When he'd cut it out of the *Liverpool Journal* last year, he'd left massive wet blots all over the paper from the tears that had fallen. From the fear that had revisited him from decades ago.

The guilt. The shame. The truth.

The headline said: *Unidentified man's body found in local woods.*

Revenge, he thought.

Eleven

By three p.m., Barclay felt the weight of the day on his back and across his shoulders. He'd spent the afternoon hunched over the Police National Computer, pulling off databases that matched his search criteria.

The men reported missing from 1990-1995 were already being handled by Lawrence, Braxton and the others. He took the timeline forward, and pulled them across both of his screens. Around 160,000 men went missing in the UK every year, though most were found after a few days on a bender. Still, with around 90,000 people missing and never found per year, the numbers were alarming.

He narrowed that down to missing men from Merseyside, and still there were over a thousand. It was a start. *The only sensible place to start.* After all, just because the body was buried in Merseyside didn't mean he was reported missing here.

This could take days.

De Silva sat opposite, light from the computer screen illuminating her face blue, but she was somewhere else. Her mind adrift some place away from the basement incident room. He'd seen the same look on her face back in Carey's office. She'd be playing out what she knew about the case, the victim, letting it run through her head until something clicked. Barclay knew that because he'd seen it so many times before.

'You want to take a break for lunch?' she asked without looking at him, without breaking her apparent trance.

'Do you? You look like you're deep in thought there.'

'Nothing I can't come back to.' She looked at him then, blinked until her eyes focused and turned on her swivel chair. 'Lunch, everyone. Back in an hour.'

The small team leapt at the opportunity to get away from lists and databases and cross-referencing, and grabbed their jackets.

'Chins up, ladies and gents,' de Silva said. 'It's slow, I know, but it's essential. You're doing great work.'

They said nothing as they filed out of the incident room.

'So.' She turned back to Barclay. 'I fancy something a dietitian would frown at, how about you?'

—

Chop Chop was a small Korean place on Fenwick Street near the courts. It was always worth the short drive into the city, but lunchtimes were packed, and as de Silva and Barclay sat on cold metal chairs, he watched the line of patient people through the window, waiting to get in and place their orders.

The place smelled like fried meats, soy sauce and spices. It smelled of warmth. Comfort.

As the man in a white apron called out their order from the counter, de Silva sprang up to get it, and Barclay knew he'd have to put in some extra work at the gym later. A spin class after his training session maybe. He quickly checked the app for availability. Class full. *Great*.

He rolled his eyes and thought of the swimming pool instead. After seven p.m., it was always dead.

'Here.' De Silva put the tray down in the middle of their small table. Two clear plastic take-away boxes filled with noodles, chicken and vegetables. 'Mega chicken noodles, Barclay. You'll die, I promise.'

'Well any food with the word "mega" in the title has to be good, I suppose.'

De Silva dived straight in, deftly working her chopsticks. Barclay tried to pinch some yellow bell pepper with the sticks, but it slipped out time and again.

'I've been trying to picture it, you know? Trying to see how it was done. How the killer may have felt about it.'

'Go on...' Barclay didn't look at her, too focused on handling the chopsticks in his massive, untrained fingers.

De Silva lowered her voice. 'Mutilating another human being highlights a lack of empathy: there's no emotional attachment there. They didn't see him as a person. If we asked the killer how it felt to do what he did, he probably wouldn't know.'

'Why?' He skewered a piece of chicken with the chopstick, not caring how it looked.

De Silva's mouth fell open at the sight and she shook her head, but she pushed on. 'It would feel like something he did every day. Like brushing his teeth or frying an egg. There's no emotion to any of it. He can't feel.'

'But taking the finger is different to the mutilation, isn't it? Is the cutting it off serving a different purpose than taking it?'

'A trophy. Has to be. Why else would he do it? And I keep coming back to those hesitation marks, and said that there could be more than one person involved.'

'One second.' He went to the counter and grabbed a wooden fork.

'Something to keep in mind for now, but with no physical evidence, it's just theory.' She fell silent again as her eyes stared past Barclay. Through him. Absently popping food into her mouth and chewing slowly.

'What would he do with a trophy? And why?'

De Silva shrugged. 'He could keep it in a pickle jar,' she said. 'In the airing cupboard with his towels, or in his top drawer with his undies. I don't know. He could look at it every day, try to relive the high.'

'And what happens when he can't relive the high?'

De Silva looked at Barclay and for a moment their eyes caught each other and they both knew exactly what would happen when he couldn't relive the high. The killer would have killed again.

'Thirty years is a long time to try to recapture a high. There'd be others, wouldn't there?' Barclay wrapped noodles around his fork as though it were his mum's spag bol.

'Cross-referencing similar cold cases in the PNC should be easy.'

About the only thing that is easy with the Police National Computer. Barclay shook his head as he chewed. 'That thing needs a good update.'

'Needs lashing in the bin.' De Silva put down her chopsticks but Barclay was nowhere near finished. 'Let's get back,' she said. 'Get on it right away.'

Barclay's phone pinged, a message from a number he didn't recognise: *Hi this is Cora from Liver Lettings. Just a heads up that I'll be calling you later today to discuss your lettings criteria. Looking forward to speaking with you.*

He was unsure how he felt. Pleased he'd be able to move out of his mum's? Maybe. He just needed something short term, a flexible lease. This thing with Nick wouldn't last forever, and soon he'd be back in their bedroom with Sarah sleeping peacefully next door.

But still, underneath that certainty of how things would work out, there was a sense of something cold, like water. *What if...*

'You ready?' De Silva was already on her feet, pulling on her coat.

'Yeah,' he said.

Barclay dropped his half-full container into the bin and was hit with instant guilt. He was raised not to waste food, not only because they couldn't really afford it as kids, but his mum had always said, 'There are starving kids all over the world who would kill for that.' He heard her voice in his mind then as he walked the few yards down Fenwick Street to where de Silva had parked.

His phone rang out, an unknown caller. He buttoned it.

'You're popular today.'

'The letting agency.' He stooped to get into the car without hitting his head. 'I can't stay at my mum's any longer. She's driving me nuts.'

'Yeah, my sister's with me at the moment,' de Silva said, her mouth a straight line, her eyes on the steering wheel as she started the engine.

'Laney?' Barclay tried to keep the pitch of disbelief from his voice. 'I thought—'

'Same.' She pulled away from the kerb. 'I'm not sure what's going on there, but I'll get to the bottom of it.'

Barclay didn't doubt that for a second.

When they arrived back in the incident room, the other detectives and Lawrence were already back from lunch and hunched over their computers.

'Okay,' de Silva said loudly. 'I need you all, please.'

They rolled their chairs into the centre of the room, away from their desks. Lawrence sat with a notebook on her lap, a pen hovered above the page ready to go.

'You'll understand that what we're about to discuss is conjecture at this point. Pure theory.' De Silva had their attention, all eyes on her.

Barclay watched Lawrence, already writing even though de Silva hadn't shared anything. He had just been like her, so eager to absorb anything he could: every moment an opportunity to learn something new. To push the boundaries of what you're capable of as an officer.

De Silva told them all of it. The possibility that there could be more than one person involved, the trophy theory, the fact that they could be dealing with a suspect, or suspects, with a lack of empathy for their victim. The idea that they may have killed again since. They took it all in, Lawrence scribbling quickly on her pad.

'So,' de Silva said. 'Keep at it. I need one of you with me. Harris, you'll do.' Barclay felt bad for her overlooking Lawrence, when this opportunity would have been a positive one for her. He wondered whether de Silva had had a female role model to look up to herself when she was stepping out of uniform. Or whether, like Barclay, she'd cut her teeth in the straight-white-male-dominated CID and Major Incidents Teams of the time. It had moulded him, prepared him for what it would be like when he passed that detective exam.

'Yes, ma'am.' Harris stood from his seat, pulled his trousers higher on his hips, his chest puffed out. De Silva winced at the word 'ma'am'. She'd always hated it for reasons only known to her. He knew she'd have a word with Harris about it.

'Don't get too excited, Detective, you're back on the PNC looking for similar cases in the Merseyside area.'

Harris cleared his throat, a rattling sound that came with years of smoking. 'Because you think he may have killed again since?'

'We can't rule anything out,' de Silva said. 'If we can believe Brennan's timeline that this body has been in the ground for decades, then it's likely the killer will have killed again. Let's not let it catch us by surprise later on. Cover all the bases we can.'

Harris nodded. 'I'll get started, ma'am.' He headed back to his computer and got stuck in.

'Okay.' De Silva clapped her hands together. 'Let's get back to it.'

Twelve

Progress had been as slow as de Silva had expected it to be. For the first full day of an investigation, especially a cold case, there was nothing else she could expect. Before she'd finished for the day, de Silva made a request from the lab to run the DNA gathered when the body had been found last year. It should tell them more: the man's race, his age maybe. Anything they could find that would narrow the search parameters.

Last year, when O'Brien had put these two detective constables in charge, they'd not even requested a DNA report from the lab and she couldn't understand why the original detectives hadn't gotten this far. After she'd gone on her extended leave, Barclay had been put onto the Lamond murders, and this cold case had been given to more junior detective constables. O'Brien hadn't elaborated any more than that. She needed to speak with him.

He'd texted and called her, but everything had been a million miles an hour since he'd resigned. There were other things to focus on. Work. Crosby on the run, the death of Lamond in custody, the new DSI. But they were just excuses.

For now, as she climbed into her car, the sun about to set, she needed to focus on her sister. Laney needed her. Finally, when she got home, maybe she'd get some answers. Last night had been too awkward. They'd not seen each other in months, and Laney had been exhausted. She'd bathed Bonnie and put her to bed, showered herself and gone straight to her room. Door closed. She still hadn't been awake when de Silva left that morning. Or hadn't come out of her room at least.

De Silva's eyes were tired from staring at her computer all day, from focusing on lines of potentially comparative cases. They'd come up with nothing by the time she'd left, and Harris had said he'd stay after hours and complete the search. De Silva told him not to, but she'd appreciated his insistence.

She started the engine, scrolled through the contacts on the dashboard screen and found O'Brien's number. *No time like the present.* It rang out and she almost ended the call, and then—

'Well, well, well. Winifred de Silva.' His voice was warm and it made her smile straight away.

'Hello, old man.'

'Never mind "old man". Remembered I'm alive, have you?'

'I'm sorry.' As soon as she heard his voice, she realised how sorry she was. She'd intended to give him space after Kath, but as the weeks went on, some sort of distance was created. That feeling that she could put it off another day.

She never should have.

'As if I could get rid of you that easily.'

'Cheeky as ever. Tell me.' He coughed. 'Sorry, I've had this cough for months now. Since that bloody Covid jab I've not been the same.'

'Just a coincidence, Tom. You've not turned into a conspiracy theorist since you've retired, have you?'

'Got to pass the time somehow, Win. You know how it is. It only comes on me every so often. Anyway. Tell me. How's everything going? What're you working on? I saw Barclay earlier, did he say?'

'He mentioned it, yeah.'

'Ah, he's a good lad, that one. Built like a bloody unit; have you seen him without his top on? No, I don't suppose you have.'

That made de Silva uncomfortable. She had never thought of Barclay that way. 'You know what it's like, same old, same old. Listen, I wanted to ask you something.'

'So that's why you called.' A hint of teasing in his voice. 'Not to check on your old boss.'

'Give me a break, will you? I'll come and see you soon as this is all over.'

'Could be months, de Silva. You know that as well as I do.'

She rolled her eyes, but she knew he was right. 'Fine, fine. I'll pop in at the end of the week. We'll have a nice cup of tea, a scone and a natter.'

'Don't take the piss, de Silva.' He used the voice he'd used so many times in his office when she'd done something wrong. 'Come on then, out with it. What can I do for you?'

'The man found in the woods. That last case I worked on before... before I went on leave. You said you'd put some detectives on it?'

There was a silence, where all de Silva heard was the rumble of her tyres on the tarmac. She had to check the line was still connected.

'Hello?'

'Yes, I'm just thinking.' O'Brien coughed again. 'I just don't remember, I'm sorry. So much has happened since. Anyway, it should all be on record.'

'The detectives you put on it have both left the force since,' she said. 'I'm having a hard time tracking them down, so I thought you might know.'

'Might know what?'

'Why they never requested DNA testing on the remains?'

'I couldn't tell you. It wasn't my main priority at the time. We weren't on it long before we had to switch our focus onto the girls.' He took a breath. 'Onto Lamond. So, anything on Crosby yet?'

'Nothing,' she said. 'I just find it unusual that—'

'Look, Win, I can't help you. I've moved on from that life. Forgot most of it. God, at my age I'm forgetting to eat some days.'

She sighed. Sometimes she forgot about his age because he'd always seemed so sharp to her, all over any case he was involved in. But, ultimately, he was right. In his late sixties now, and her dad would have been even older than that.

'You're right,' she said. 'I'm sorry. Look, I'll definitely come and see you Friday. Unless something extraordinary comes up.'

'Don't worry, I know you're busy. Look, I'd best go. I'm meeting a friend for a walk around Speke Hall. See you Friday maybe.'

He didn't wait for a reply before he hung up, which was unlike him.

She thought about popping in on her mum, but she didn't have the energy. It had all become such hard work. Marie had all but forgotten who de Silva was, and that made every visit an exercise in agony.

She'd turn on her smile as soon as she walked through that room her mum now spent most of her time in. Marie would always be asleep in the chair and de Silva had begun to feel as though her mum had already died. The woman who inhabited her body now was not de Silva's kind, lovely, sharp-tongued mum. She was someone de Silva didn't know, someone who didn't know de Silva.

Not tonight.

As she pulled up onto her drive behind Laney's grey Range Rover, de Silva could see the glow from the lamp in the living room slipping out onto the fence at the back of the garden.

Laney met her at the front door, the bruise around her eye still dark and terrible. It seemed to have gotten worse, especially now that her eye was bloodshot.

De Silva could smell her own floral shampoo on her sister, the one that was scented like bluebells.

'I started dinner,' Laney said as they walked into the kitchen.

'Oh. I'm not very hungry.'

Laney rubbed her hands together, her shoulders lowered a few inches. 'Oh, well no worries. Sure you could take some to work tomorrow?'

'What is it?'

'Nan's Chinese curry.'

De Silva smiled. She'd not had that in so long, she couldn't even remember the last time. Nan would cook it from scratch with herbs and spices from the Chinese market on the dock road.

'With the raisins?'

'Of course I've put the raisins in.'

'Where's Bonnie?'

'She had a bath, I hope you don't mind, and I put her to bed.'

'Of course I don't mind.'

De Silva felt awkward in her own home. This whole conversation was strange to her. They'd not been civil with each other for years, well before their dad had died, and his death had been the icing on the cake. 'Anyway, do us a bowl.'

'You sure? I won't be offended.'

'Yeah, of course. I'll just run and have a quick shower.' She slipped out of her ankle boots and hung her jacket up on the hook next to the door, where Bonnie's backpack was, pink and sparkling.

She'd just put her foot on the first stair when Laney moved toward her. 'Win.'

'Yeah?'

'Tomorrow, will you come back home with me? To pick up some more clothes, a few school bits for Bonnie? I don't really want to go on my own.'

'You're taking Bonnie to school still?'

'I've called and explained the situation,' Laney said. 'It's just for a while. I don't know where we'll go or what we'll do next, but she needs some normalcy.'

'What if he's there?'

'I'm not taking her to school in the car, I'm using a taxi service,' Laney said. 'The school have arranged a secure pick-up and drop-off. Not sure what that means.'

'Do you want me to come with you?'

'Every morning? God no, you can't commit to that, Win. Just come back home with me.'

De Silva smiled softly. 'Yeah, of course. We'll go first thing. I can be a bit late for work. But let's have a chat over dinner. You need to tell me what's been going on.'

De Silva felt that she already knew. She'd assumed last year that Laney was ending her marriage when she'd gone back to using her maiden name.

Maybe you don't know the half of it.

As de Silva closed the bathroom door and turned on the shower, an email pinged through from Harris. He could find no similar cases in the Merseyside area and he was calling it a night.

Great. She knew then that they'd have to widen the search. There was no way that this was the only time this person or persons had killed. She knew that somewhere there'd be another victim just like the man in the woods.

She just had to find them.

Thirteen

Barclay had offered to do the coffee run on his way in that morning. If he was completely honest with himself, it was less about keeping the team on-side, and more about having some time to himself.

He knew that he was becoming obsessed with his own misery. The case, as gruesome as it was, was slow and boring. Not the distraction he had hoped for at all.

'Hello?' The young guy behind the counter at Starbucks wore one of those looks on his face. The pained yet concerned look Barclay usually reserved for old or confused people. 'What can I get you?'

Barclay didn't even look at him. He flicked open the Notes app on his phone and found the list of drinks. 'Probably easier if I just show you it. I'm not with it this morning.' He shook his head and tried to smile, showing his phone to the young man who couldn't have been more than nineteen years old.

'You and me both,' he said as he typed the order into the till.

Barclay looked at him then. Pale, sagging skin under red eyes. He looked awful. 'Put an extra shot of your strongest stuff on there for yourself. You look like you need it more than I do.'

The guy looked around, nervous. Barclay spotted his nametag then. Steve. 'Yeah, er, thanks, mate. I shouldn't, but...'

'No worries.'

'Your drinks will be at the end, can I take your name for the order?'

'Ben.'

'Nice one, Ben.'

Barclay smiled. He supposed that it was his good deed for the day. His nan had always said you should do something for someone else that makes them smile at least once a day. 'And if you can't do that,' she'd said, 'you're a miserable old sod.'

By the time he got to the Operational Command Centre, it was almost ten, and there was a buzz about the incident room. He handed out the drinks one by one.

'Thanks, sir.' O'Connor sat with his hands on top of his paunch. Barclay's own personal nightmare was to let his body go like that. But still, O'Connor seemed a decent guy. Quiet for a detective, unassuming.

'What's going on?' Barclay asked.

'We completed the list,' Lawrence answered.

'Oh yeah, which one?' Barclay kept his voice light.

'Missing males in Merseyside between 1990 and 1999.'

Barclay knew there was no use getting excited. There was still a lot of work to be done and he was eager to get on with it. Still, it seemed to have reinvigorated Lawrence, O'Connor and the others.

'Where's de Silva?'

'Okay, listen up.' De Silva came in, her face red and flushed. She took a paper cup from Barclay – her steaming hot Americano with hot milk – and nodded a thanks. 'Don't get too excited about this list: we've got miles to go. It's for a nine-year window, so we're by no means in the clear yet.'

'What's next?' Lawrence had her pen ready over a clean page in her notebook.

'What do you think?'

A little test. Barclay held his breath, suddenly nervous for her. If she got it right, the men would sit up and pay attention to her. If she got it wrong, he hoped they'd swoop in and talk her through it.

'The broken arm,' she said. 'We know the victim had a broken right radius. We start searching through this list for men who had a broken arm before they were reported missing.'

Barclay jumped in. 'The arm could have been broken at any time. Maybe even during the murder itself. We'd never know. Medical records take time. But we're lucky this is a cold case. We've got the time.'

'So I'll start there then?'

'It's as good a place to start as any. O'Connor, how about you work with Lawrence on that one?' de Silva said. 'Braxton, McLachlan, I still want to be sure. I want to keep pushing on with extending the dates. Carey said we can't be certain of the time of death because of the ground the victim was found in. Let's move forward. 2000 to 2005. It's another broad window, I know.'

'What about me, ma— de Silva?' Harris asked.

Barclay smirked. De Silva had already had a word with him about calling her 'ma'am'. He remembered the talk well.

'I'm not your ma'am, I'm not your mate, I'm not your mother. It's de Silva, Detective, or DCI,' she'd said to Barclay.

A knock at the incident room door. A uniformed officer stood there, chewing at her bottom lip, her thumbs hooked around her harness. 'Can I come in?' She had that lovely lilt to her voice found only in Welsh accents.

De Silva looked her up and down. 'Yes.'

'I'd like to have a word with you, if you don't mind?'

'With me?'

The PC nodded. 'That's right, and DS Barclay if it's not too much trouble.'

De Silva shot Barclay a look, but was already walking toward the corridor. Barclay moved in behind her and closed the door as they left the room.

'I'm PC Jones,' she said. 'I know we've not met. I've not been with Merseyside Police very long. I came over from North Wales Police last year when you were on leave.'

De Silva nodded. 'I'm de Silva. What is it I can do for you? Are you looking to help out?'

Jones laughed, not an absurd laugh, but soft. 'No, not for me, all of that, if you don't mind. I don't know how you do it. All those dead bodies.'

Barclay wondered whether he knew how they did it either. It seemed to have become instinctual since last year with Lamond and his victims. The rage and violence had opened Barclay up to a whole world he'd never expected to find, and it was the blackest place, filled with fear and anger.

'What can we do for you? Only, we're in the middle of something.'

'I know, I am sorry to disturb you, like, but I had to come.' She unhooked her thumbs for the first time and let her arms hang by her sides. She looked de Silva dead in the eye. 'I know a little something about this case. To be honest when I heard it was open again and you were working on it, I half expected you to ask to see me.'

'Why would we do that?' Barclay's brain fired up. She'd piqued his interest for sure.

'Well, on account of what I said last year.' She looked from de Silva to Barclay and must have read their blank expressions. 'To DSI O'Brien, like.'

'I'm really sorry,' de Silva said. 'I don't know what you're referring to.'

Barclay bit his lip, wished she would just come out with it.

'You mean he didn't tell you? Well I suppose he wouldn't now, would he? Now he doesn't work here any more. But I did tell him.'

'Tell him what?' De Silva's mouth was a thin line, her eyebrows arched into a frown. 'PC Jones, can you cut to the chase?'

'It's just that I told DSI O'Brien last year, ma'am, and he said he'd tell it to the detectives that were working the case and that they'd be in touch. They weren't. In touch, I mean. So I just supposed that they'd looked into it and it was nothing.'

'Into what?'

'Three years ago, when I was working with North Wales Police, I was called out to an incident in Beddgelert, you know in Eryri, er, Snowdonia. Oh it's a lovely place, if you've not been. So picturesque and—'

'I'll take it under advisement, Jones. What was the incident?'

'All sorts of people visit. Hikers. Families. Dog walkers. Anyway, a hiker had come down from the hills and into the village, called 999 from the gift shop, Beddgelert Woodcraft. His phone had ran out of battery, you see.

Said he'd found a body at the base of the hills. Less than a mile or so from the River Glaslyn.'

De Silva looked to Barclay and he found himself frowning along with her. He knew what PC Jones was going to say before she said it.

'I arrived on the scene first. The guy walked me out to where he'd found the body and I cordoned it off. Called for backup. Oh it was a terrible mess. They don't warn you, do they? And while I was waiting for help, I spotted it. The middle finger on the right hand was missing. Just like the victim you found in the woods out there in Formby.'

De Silva took a second to process it all. Barclay could almost hear her mind buzzing. 'Okay, this is really great information, Jones. I want to thank you for coming down and speaking with us.'

Barclay spoke up: 'Will you be available if we have any more questions?'

'I'll make myself available.' She smiled broadly with crooked teeth.

'Right.' De Silva pulled Barclay's shoulder so he moved closer to her. She lowered her voice, though he wasn't sure why. Habit, maybe. 'We need to look up this cold case out there in Beddgelert.'

'Oh no,' PC Jones said. 'Sorry, I think I gave you the wrong idea. This wasn't a cold case. I mean, the body wasn't decades old like your man in the woods. No,' PC Jones said. 'This was a fresh one. And, there's something else.'

How could there possibly be any more to this?

'The body,' Jones said. 'The woman. She'd been... hacked at, I suppose.'

'Dismembered?' de Silva asked, the tone of incredulousness in her voice was apparent.

PC Jones nodded. 'That's right,' she said. 'Who would do something like that?'

Fourteen

De Silva thought about it. About jumping in her car and heading down the M53 into North Wales and onward to Colwyn Bay, where the North Wales Police HQ was. Or even further in, to Beddgelert so that she could feel the place around her. To understand, or try to understand, why there. Why that place?

Why the woods in Formby potentially decades ago, and why a small village in Wales years later? She imagined that Beddgelert wasn't the place you could shift a body round in the middle of the day, or the type of place where the sound of a van or large car went unnoticed in the middle of the night. But, in truth, she'd never been. She couldn't know for sure. She'd looked it up online and knew that two rivers ran through it. Could the noise of the rushing water hide the sound of an engine? Could rain on windows and roofs cover tyres on tarmac, the squeak of a handbrake, the shuffling of a man dragging a body, or body parts, from a boot?

The first victim only had his middle finger taken, so why had the killer changed their MO? Why go from something so small to a larger-scale dismemberment? She knew then that her original theory about the killer having no feeling whatsoever toward his victims was right, that he, or they, had a complete lack of empathy.

And, moreover, had the woman been alive when the killers started to cut?

She shook her head. She was getting ahead of herself as usual, her mind racing.

Someone had left the air con on in the video conference room, and the place was like ice. De Silva felt the hairs on her arms stand on end as soon as she and Barclay walked in.

They'd found the name of the lead officer in the case and had emailed to ask if she had the time to join a call about it. She'd replied within fifteen minutes.

DCI Cordina Awbry joined the video call just as de Silva and Barclay sat down in the new swivel chairs. 'Afternoon,' she said. Awbry was a pretty woman in her mid-fifties, de Silva guessed.

'Thanks for jumping on.' De Silva forced brightness into her voice. 'I'm hoping we won't keep you long.'

Awbry shook her head. 'It's no problem. Not every day we get a call from Merseyside. Your email said something about a body in Beddgelert?'

'Yes. A colleague you may remember worked in North Wales at the time. PC Jones. She's here now, and we believe there are some similarities between our cases. She said you were the lead detective. Do you remember the case?'

'Remember it?' Awbry chuckled, her teeth stained from years of coffee or wine. 'I've worked with North Wales Police for thirty years. There's only one body we found out there.' She paused and de Silva let the silence linger in the room. 'I remember it.'

'The victim was dismembered, is that right?'

Awbry looked down at something in front of her. 'The victim was a woman.' She was reading from her notes.

'Yes, she was dismembered. Arms, legs.' She swallowed hard. 'Head.'

Barclay sat forward, writing notes in a jotter. 'Did you find out who the victim was?'

'Yes, a Margaret Finch.' Awbry looked down again. 'Fifty-seven years old, originally from Conwy. She'd moved out of the area in 1992, lived up near your way in Wirral.'

'Where on the Wirral?' Barclay got there before de Silva.

'A place beginning with B.' She looked down at her notes.

'Birkenhead?' de Silva offered.

'No.'

'Bebington?' Barclay asked.

'That's right.'

De Silva knew the area. A nice place to live, mostly middle-class families.

Awbry continued, 'She came back to Wales in 2016. Opened up a campsite in Caernarfon, right on the coast there.'

'Did you send officers out to the site?'

'We did. Bookings were low at the time. Just two small families and three friends. They all confirmed they saw no one else on the site. But you know, it's right on the beach, so... people can come and go.'

De Silva knew instantly that there would be no way to track someone coming or going in the night. 'Who was the last person to see her?'

'Her partner, Lucille Rogers. She put in a missing persons' report less than twenty-four hours before the body was discovered.'

'Was there any CCTV on the site?'

Awbry nodded. 'Cameras up at the main house, outside the shower block, one on the front of the barn. Footage shows Ms Finch on her phone, leaving the house through the patio doors, crossing the small lane that separates the house from the camping fields. The shower block picks her up a few seconds later heading out toward the beach, around the back of the fields.'

'What about the finger?' Barclay asked. 'What were your thoughts?'

'We thought it was some weird memento for the killer.'

De Silva nodded. Her theory precisely.

'That is until it showed up in the post three days later.'

'What?' De Silva's eyes went wide, her mind scrambling to make sense of this new piece of information. 'Whose post?'

'Finch's partner.'

She thought about what that would do to the partner, to Lucille. What level of shock, disgust, horror, she must have felt to open up a package and find her partner's finger inside. She imagined them holding hands sitting in front of a crackling fire in the middle of winter. She imagined the tears, the snot bubbling at Lucille's nose, as the finger slipped out of a padded envelope onto the breakfast table.

Just when she'd thought the horror was over, it arrived in her home where she ate her toast and poached her eggs.

There was a significance to the middle finger. Specifically that finger, de Silva knew. A "fuck you"? Maybe, but for now, she'd have to push it out of her mind. 'Did you have any suspects?'

'Not to speak of, no.'

'Not to speak of,' de Silva repeated. 'What do you mean?'

'A hunch, you know. A feeling in my gut. There was a man, helpful at first, offered to come out and help talk to the locals. We told him no, of course. Civilian interference is – well, I don't need to tell you, do I? But I had a feeling about him. He was almost… too insistent, if you like. Too eager. Called the station for updates every few hours.'

De Silva imagined him, a faceless dark figure for now, but there nonetheless, reaching out for the crime scene, for the body of Margaret Finch. So many serial killers tried to integrate themselves, attempted to manoeuvre themselves into police investigations. Out of curiosity, amusement, fear maybe. 'Did you find anything on him?'

'He arrived at the crime scene just after the body was removed. We'd been there just a few hours with our scene-of-crime team. Four hours at the most. We looked into him, and he'd checked into one of the local hotels in the village that morning.'

Barclay scribbled down notes, trying to keep up with Awbry's quick delivery. 'Any record of him staying in any other hotels in the area?'

'We checked the whole of North Wales. Nothing. We tracked his car down the motorway from Wirral into Wales. He wasn't here when Ms Finch was murdered.'

De Silva shifted her weight, sat forward. Her mind racing. 'He lived on the Wirral too?'

'Yeah. That other place you mentioned beginning with B. Birkenhead?'

De Silva nodded. 'I know it. Do you have a name for him?'

'I have a whole file on him.' Awbry's face tightened. 'That feeling I had about him never went away, I can tell you that. The guy... well, there was something about him. I'll send you everything I have, but his name was Jacob Meeks.'

Fifteen

Barclay tried to keep his head in the game. There was much to focus on and now, finally, they had a potential lead in Jacob Meeks. But still, his troubled marriage was at the back of his mind, niggling away, trying to creep forward. He wondered what Nick was thinking, whether he too lay awake at night and longed to be next to his husband.

He felt useless. A failure. He thought that Nick would know that about him, too. That he would laugh about Barclay with his friends. That Nick knew – had always known – that Barclay was not good enough.

'Barclay.' De Silva snapped her fingers in front of his face. 'You all right?'

'Yeah,' he said. 'Sorry, yeah I'm fine.'

'Million miles away?'

Barclay took a breath and lowered his voice. 'Do you ever feel that, sometimes, you know, there are things you've never really confronted?'

De Silva looked over her shoulder, and Barclay knew she was checking that none of the team were listening. She lowered her voice now too. 'All the time.'

'Like they're out there, these things, watching you from a distance. Ready to make you feel them again. Live them.'

'If you want to talk about Nick' – she looked at her watch – 'we can take fifteen and go grab a coffee?'

'It's not about Nick.' Barclay shook his head. 'Not about Sarah. I'm just asking you a question. Whether you feel like that.'

'Yes, I do.' De Silva looked at her hands, pale with deep lines across her knuckles. 'I felt it in the woods. Like it could be watching us. Memory, I mean. *Memories*. Like shadows out there between the pine trees.' De Silva took a breath, and Barclay was sure he saw her shiver. 'Is there something you want to talk about?'

Barclay considered it. The old saying was that a problem shared was a problem halved.

'It's nothing I can't handle.' He turned back to his computer and felt de Silva's warm hand on his shoulder. 'Thank you, though.'

When de Silva's husband had killed himself, Barclay had felt her pull away. Felt her lock him out of her life, and he'd resented her for it. His fear was that, in losing Nick, he would do the same to her; and in that understanding he realised something. *Our histories are our own, our grief is private and how we choose to cope with it is an individual choice.*

Barclay's email pinged on his phone first and then his laptop. It was from DCI Awbry, an attachment of the file she'd had on Jacob Meeks. 'Got the file,' he said. 'I'll get to work on it.'

De Silva nodded.

He wondered whether he should ask Lawrence to help, even though he didn't need it. He liked her, wanted to see her succeed, wanted her to have a broad experience. He shrugged it off. It wouldn't take him long to read through the file, to check Meeks's address was still valid. To cross-check his name in the Police National Computer. It would be quicker to work alone, to leave Lawrence to her task at hand.

He opened the file and sent it to the printer, heard it whir into life across the room. As he moved to collect it, he noticed a flicker on his laptop screen. *Bloody thing.* He'd have to get someone from IT to look at it.

As he brought the slim sheaf of paper back to his desk, the screen glitched again. 'Anyone else having problems with—' A message appeared on screen, announcing that he had been disconnected from the server.

De Silva backed away from her own computer, looked around. Confused faces everywhere.

Internet and server access was down for the entire incident room.

De Silva's phone rang out among the baffled chatter. 'Holden, what's going on?'

'Need to see you and Barclay right away.' He sounded breathless, like he was walking quickly. 'Murphy's office.'

The line went dead.

De Silva looked at Barclay, nodded toward the door. He knew she needed him to follow her. 'We'll be right back,' she said. 'Touch nothing. Lock your screens.'

Barclay followed her out to the lift. He could read in her that something was very wrong. 'What's going on?'

'Not a clue. Murphy wants to see us. Holden, too.'

Barclay had been inside the office less than a handful of times since Murphy made it her own. She was on her feet, her blonde bob tied back into a short pony. She was adjusting the gold watch on her wrist when she turned to face Barclay and de Silva.

'Ma'am.' De Silva inclined her head.

'Take a seat.'

Barclay could hear Holden's laboured breathing somewhere outside on the corridor, the thud of his heavy feet as he half-ran into the office. 'I came... as fast...' He didn't bother finishing his sentence, but slumped down into a seat near Murphy's desk.

'What's this about, ma'am?' De Silva said. 'I've got an active incident room to handle.'

'We've had to shut down access to our internal servers for a short time, so your incident room is inactive for the time being.' No emotion in her voice.

'What's happened?' Barclay scrambled for some sense. If the server was shut down, that could only mean—

'In layman's terms, there's been an attack on our computer servers.' Holden scratched at the skin behind his ear and his neck wobbled. 'A cyberattack.'

Murphy looked at Holden, finally letting her watch settle on her wrist. 'How long until we're on the backup server?'

'We're just doing some testing with it, ensuring it's safe.'

'And how long until we have the regular server back online?'

'We're running some testing on that too, but we hope inside of the hour.'

'Pull your team from whatever they're doing. Do we know if this is localised, or is it a national breach?'

'Local. Just Merseyside Police.'

'See if you can borrow resource from Manchester and Cheshire. Get this fixed. Now.'

Holden took out his phone and made a quick phone call to one of his team about requesting resource.

Barclay looked at de Silva. Her mouth opened slightly, a frown on her brow. She was just as confused as he was.

'I'm sorry, ma'am,' de Silva said. 'I'm not sure why we're here.'

Murphy looked down at her desk, took a deep breath then looked up at de Silva and Barclay. 'The hack was detected, but only after certain files were accessed.'

'What files?' Barclay's voice was almost a whisper, fearful of what was about to come out of Murphy's mouth.

'Your personnel files.' The words hit like three bullets. 'Both of yours. But I don't want you to panic. None of your personal information is stored there. Not your home addresses or your personal phone numbers. Your work phones, though. Well, we can work on getting you some new numbers.'

'Can we be sure nothing else was accessed?' de Silva asked.

'We're still checking. But the person knew what they were looking for. Straight to your files. The truth is, we may not know for hours what else they accessed.'

'Can we, erm, trace them? Like a phone call?' Barclay asked.

'Hackers are complex,' Holden said, his phone to his ear. 'They'll have used a VPN at least, bounced their signal around. We could be chasing it anywhere on the planet.'

Barclay had grown to distrust the internet. He'd spoken to Nick about the possibility of restricting Sarah's access to it, and she was only ever allowed to use it for an hour after dinner and for half an hour in the morning.

Can't protect her forever.

'But yes,' Holden said. 'We're going to try. I've got a team running a trace, another looking into whether there are other areas of our systems this guy accessed.'

'You'll bring it straight to me,' Murphy said.

'I've already reported it to the North-West Regional Organised Crime Unit. They'll liaise with other forces in the region, and other ROCUs in the country.'

'Let me know if there have been similar attacks,' Murphy said. 'And get us back up and running as soon as you can.' She inclined her head toward the door, and Holden heaved himself up from the chair. He knew he'd been dismissed.

When the door closed behind him, Murphy spoke again. 'We'll get to the bottom of this, detectives. I promise.' A beep from her computer. She bent down to look at it. 'Backup server is on.' She nodded. 'I'll let you know what I know when I know it. For now, keep this confidential. Us and Holden's team. That's it.'

'But ma'am,' De Silva said. 'Why would anyone want to look into us two specifically?'

It was the same question that burned in Barclay's mind.

Sixteen

He printed off the last of his manuscript and put it with the rest. He'd bought a binding machine from eBay, still in the box and stored on top of his wardrobe, and he fetched it and bound the whole thing together. Tomorrow, he would read over it all and do his best to remove any typos, grammatical issues, or expand on points that needed further clarification.

His history demanded it.

He would read through it tomorrow.

When the manuscript was bound, he put it into the top drawer of his desk, switched off his computer, making sure all of the files were successfully saved and closed down first. He didn't take chances, not with his story. Not with his life.

He lifted a book he'd been reading earlier, *Pizza Parties and the Cabal*, from the coffee table and put it back into its slot on the shelf, arranged in alphabetical order. The only way to organise things of note.

In the coming weeks, he would further spread the truth for all the world to see. His work, his story: he would show everyone, finally, what a cesspit the world is. How we're all pawns in a big game orchestrated by the rich, famous and powerful. The elite.

But knowledge is power. Truth is knowledge. And he knew the truth. Yes indeed, Jacob Meeks knew it all. And when the time came—

A notification on his watch vibrated at his wrist. It told him that someone was at the door. He searched around for his smartphone, quickly turned off the flight mode, waited for it to connect to his WiFi, switched on the VPN app then loaded up the doorbell.

'H-hello?' His voice cracked. He'd not spoken to anyone in days, not since he'd had to go out for some bottled water from the corner shop. There was no way he was drinking tap water again. It tasted too metallic, and he didn't like to think what was in it.

'Mr Meeks?' a woman asked. She was short, ginger hair like wire wool. She stood next to a man, tall and broad. 'Jacob Meeks?'

He swallowed hard. He knew that they were police because he recognised their faces instantly. How had they found out? How did they know? He glanced across at his computer, now completely shut down; he could see himself in the reflection on the blank screen, hazy and undefined.

'Who's asking?' As if he didn't already know.

'Detective Chief Inspector de Silva,' she said. 'This is my colleague Detective Sergeant Barclay. May we come in?'

'Hold up your warrant cards to the camera.' He watched as they exchanged a look. 'One at a time, hold them close so I can see them.' He screenshotted each one on his phone. 'What do you want to talk to me about?'

'I think it's better that we come inside.'

'Do you have a warrant?'

The big one spoke up now, his voice coarse and low. 'We don't need a warrant to have a conversation with you, but if you'd prefer us to make this more formal...'

He didn't finish. He'd half expected DS Barclay to make some sort of threat. He looked the type. He turned and took in his flat. There was nothing around that was incriminating. *Besides, they'd need a warrant to really look, right?*

He thought about opening the windows, letting some air into the heat of the room. He shrugged the thought away.

'You can come up,' he said. 'For five minutes. I'm very busy.' He moved to his wall and pressed the door release button, watched on his phone as they headed inside.

He was unsure how he felt about someone coming to his flat. His office, his own little sanctuary away from the bullshit.

He considered the corkboard. They'd be outside his door at any moment. Photographs, sketches, newspaper articles, pinned by golden tacks, lines of thread leading from one thing to the next. The other consuming passion in Meeks's life. His other truth.

He lifted it carefully and slid it underneath the couch. As two sharp knocks came from his front door, he hoped that nothing on the board had shifted. If it had, he knew, he'd be able to put it back in place easily. The whole thing had been imprinted on his mind.

He took one last look around the place, tidy as always. Then pulled open the front door. He always thought it best to look people in their face, even if they made him feel uncomfortable. It was the best way to show no fear.

He said, 'Come in.'

The man stepped in first, Barclay, and she followed. Smelling like flowers and fruit.

'Shall we sit down?' she asked.

There was something about de Silva's eyes, Meeks decided. A dullness there, like a shadow over the blue colour of them. A sadness was in her, and he wondered whether she'd ever get over it.

Losing your partner must be difficult, he assumed. But that wasn't information he'd managed to get online. It was something else, and he wondered whether she knew. *No*, he reasoned with himself, *how could she?*

'If you have to,' he said. He closed the front door gently so that it didn't make a sound, then hovered there. He shoved his hands in his pockets so that his nerves didn't get the better of him. He watched as de Silva and Barclay sat down on the couch. He'd have to clean it when they were gone. 'What's this about?'

'Why don't you sit down?' Barclay said, gesturing toward the armchair.

'I'm fine here.' He knew why they were there. What he didn't know was why they were alone. Why they'd come in so softly and not broken down the door. But maybe they weren't alone. Maybe there was a SWAT team and backup outside ready to pounce, somewhere out there?

'We've come to ask you about some time you spent in Beddgelert,' de Silva said, plainly.

He hadn't expected this. His shoulders dropped and he breathed out his relief, thought better of it and tried to mask it with a cough. If he showed any sign that something was wrong, they'd be all over him in an instant.

He tried to focus on their faces and not look at the strand of white string that was sticking out from under the couch. They were sitting on top of it all and if they looked down, they'd know everything.

'That was all ages ago,' he said.

'What were you there for?'

They know. 'I told the police everything I knew back then. It's all done and dusted.'

'Yeah.' De Silva tried to keep her voice light and even. 'We spoke to the DCI in charge of that case. Awbry, do you remember her?'

He shrugged. 'Why would I?'

De Silva looked down at her knees, snorted a laugh through her nose. 'You tried to help out, didn't you? You were in touch quite a bit, Awbry says.'

Fear formed in his throat, a great, hard stone. He swallowed it down. He felt them circling him like predators on a David Attenborough programme. Now was the time to give them just enough to get them off his back.

'This is what I do in my spare time,' he said. He relaxed his shoulders and finally sat down on the armchair next to him. 'I look into unsolved murders. I'm planning on writing a second book about them one day.' He glanced at his computer.

'A second book?' Barclay asked. 'What's your first about?'

'My childhood,' Meeks said.

'So you look into unsolved murders. Local police told us you seemed interested, maybe invested is more accurate, in the murder of Margaret Finch?' De Silva cocked her head. 'Why her?'

He shrugged. 'Not too far away from where I lived at the time. I suppose it piqued my interest.'

'How did you hear about it?' Barclay again.

He was clever, Meeks would give him that. Barclay knew that the murder had not yet made national news when Meeks had left his house, and was probably pinged on CCTV somewhere along his route. 'There was a network of us back then.' It wasn't a lie. 'A friend of mine lived in North Wales, right near Beddgelert. She started a thread on it.'

'A thread?' De Silva asked.

'Online. On a message board. It's where I pick the cases I'm interested in.'

'Could you show us the thread?'

'The site that hosted the message board doesn't exist any more.' Also not a lie. 'The host, well he erm… he had cancer. He closed it down before he…'

'So what now?' de Silva asked. 'How do you get your tips? The cases you're interested in?'

'Does that matter?'

'No,' she said. 'I suppose not. Unless you plan on trying to integrate yourself in any cases now you live in Liverpool.'

'Is there anything else I can help with? I've got things I need to do.'

'So, you investigate these cases yourself,' Barclay said. 'What did you find out about Margaret Finch?'

He'd walked right into that one, it was all his own doing. He felt the passion for it all surge inside him; his heart galloped under his ribcage. He fought the urge to drag the board out and describe it all. Take it all back to the dirty, disgusting start of it. But even then, after all of the years, his work wasn't finished.

'She was murdered. Dismembered. Her middle finger removed specifically. It arrived in the post to her lesbian life partner three days later. Detectives found a partial fingerprint on the nail. The killer had done a crap job of tidying it up. As far as I know, it didn't match anyone on their databases at the time.'

Barclay sat back and laughed. 'Well, I'd say you found out quite a bit. Maybe our work here is done. You want a job?'

'I don't think so. Wouldn't put myself through that again.' He shrugged. Very few opportunities presented themselves in Meeks's life where he could educate those who should know the truth, those who protect it without even knowing they do. He wondered about these two detectives, about how much they knew of the true purpose of the police institution: to protect the rich, to protect those in power.

'Mr Meeks,' de Silva said. 'I'm sorry, I can't get this right in my mind. I'm going to need your help with this. A woman who lived in North Wales was murdered, and you go there to try to help. To form your own investigation alongside the police. And you've not once mentioned that the victim lived just five minutes from your address in the Wirral before she moved to Wales.'

She stopped talking, stared with eyes that seemed to have hardened now, had somehow become sharp.

She went on, 'Did you know Margaret Finch before you heard from your online friend that she'd died?'

Awbry had asked the same question that hot day at the police station, when sweat dripped down his back and between his bum cheeks. He couldn't tell whether it was the heat of summer or the fact that he felt Awbry's suspicions at his back.

He'd lied then like he'd lie now. Still, he was thankful she didn't pursue it any further. It would take some digging to unearth the paper trail that led from Margaret Finch to him. So long ago it was almost a past life.

'No,' he said. 'I've already told you, I found out about her on the message board.'

'The now-defunct message board,' Barclay added. He glared at Meeks, the usual tactic police used on him. Intimidation. It never had worked before, and Meeks would be damned if it worked now.

'Yeah, that's right. Look, I can't help you any more than I already have.'

De Silva got to her feet and Barclay followed. Meeks could have breathed out a sigh of relief, but he kept his composure. 'Mr Meeks,' de Silva said. 'Thanks for your assistance. There's just one more thing.' Her body visibly tensed. She was ready to make a move should she have to.

He made an mm-hmm sound, and hoped it sounded as confident as such a thing could.

'Last year, a body was found in the woods in Formby, did you know that?'

'I remember.' His heart raced.

'How did you hear about it? From the message boards?'

'No.' There was a tone to his voice, completely intended, slippery with spite. 'It was all over the news.'

'Was that case on your watch-list?' Barclay asked.

'Yes,' he confessed. 'It was. There was a similarity to the Finch case, of course I was all over it.'

'What did you uncover?'

'Nothing much. Same as you, probably.'

'Mr Meeks, have you found any other similar cases from anywhere in the UK that relate to these cases?'

'No.' A lie. He wasn't about to help them. They'd have to work for it, like he'd had to work for everything in his life. Including these cases.

'Okay,' de Silva said. 'We'll be in touch if we need to talk to you again.' She headed for the door, Barclay in tow. 'Oh, Mr Meeks. The middle finger taken from both victims. What were your thoughts?'

'It's a "fuck you",' he said.

De Silva's eyes flicked to the left, she paused and then looked back at him with a smile. She seemed to have already considered this. 'To whom, do you think?'

'Well,' Meeks said. 'That's the question, isn't it?'

Seventeen

The red light seemed so offensive, so insulting. Barclay braked, but in his mind, he'd run through it, hurtling on toward the OCC, to the incident room. O'Connor had called while they were on the stairwell of Meeks's building, and Barclay was champing at the bit to get back.

'We think we've found our vic,' O'Connor had said.

De Silva had told him they were already on their way back, but since then they'd hit every red light. De Silva seemed unbothered, but the anxiety broiled under Barclay's skin. He needed to be there. Needed something to focus on other than worrying about his own life. He'd have to talk about this hyper-focus in his next therapy session.

'What did you think of Meeks?' De Silva didn't look up from her work phone. She squinted at the cracked screen, and despite Barclay telling her so many times to have the device replaced, she'd ignored him. It came from a time before she'd taken her leave of absence, before she found Ritchie, and he wondered whether that brought her some level of comfort.

Barclay shook his head. 'He's not exactly a shining example of convention, is he? Couldn't decide if he wanted to keep the heat in or was worried about some government mind-reading radio waves. But then, speaking to him… he seemed quite… normal. Average.'

'Yeah, and that's what concerns me.'

'Go on.' The light flashed amber then green and Barclay put his foot down.

She shrugged and looked up at him. 'I had the feeling that he was trying hard to come off as normal. Like an innocent bystander in all of this, when really we know that he fought hard to involve himself in the Finch investigation.'

'Wouldn't he have done the same with the body in Formby?'

'I don't remember seeing his face,' de Silva said. 'Do you?'

'No. And if we'd have spoken, I'd remember a conversation with someone like that.'

De Silva laughed. 'Yeah. These detectives who took over the case after you were reassigned… they've left since, we know that, but can we track them down maybe? Awbry seemed concerned about Meeks. Maybe we should be too.'

'I'll get one of the team to look into it.'

'Good.'

'God, these fucking lights.' He banged at the steering wheel. Nick had told him he'd started doing that more and more in the weeks following the Lamond case. Everything that happened there, when Nick and Sarah had had to be shipped out to some safe house in Cheshire… another of Barclay's failings as a husband. As a father.

The creeping cold of anxiety crawled across his back and shoulders, swept through his chest until it tightened, then down into his arms and hands, and he flexed his fingers. He glanced sideways at de Silva. She was staring out of the window, watching the world zip past in blurs of lamp posts, shrubs and people at bus stops.

He took in a deep breath through his nose, gently. Exhaled it, long and slow through his mouth. Again. And again. The anxiety rolled back, his chest loosened until finally he felt confident enough to breathe as normal. This was new. Something else he'd have to talk about in his next appointment. He'd have to start keeping a list on his phone.

When he walked through the door of the incident room, the place was loud, everyone talking.

O'Connor was slow to rise, but despite that was first on his feet. Barclay assumed, by looking at him, that he was just a few years away from retirement. He'd be holding on, going through the motions until finally he could retire. Not that the pension was worth it.

'Think we've got him,' he said.

'Great.' There was something about de Silva that commanded whatever room she was in. The others fell silent and she threw her jacket onto the back of her chair. 'Talk me through it.'

'Robert Thomas Turner.' O'Connor drew their attention to the mostly blank evidence boards at the far end of the room.

There was a poor-quality photo of a young man in his late twenties, Barclay thought, but he knew that everyone looked older in the 1990s than they did today. He lowered his estimation to early-to-mid-twenties.

'He went missing in 2002 from the Kensington area. His girlfriend reported him missing after he failed to return from a night out with his friends at the 051 club on Mount Pleasant. Friends remember seeing him leave the club with a woman, but by the time they caught up with him, he was gone. Obviously, CCTV being what it was back then... there wasn't much to go on. Camera outside the Adelphi saw him get into a taxi with a woman. Then that was it. Last he was seen.'

De Silva stared at the man's face and said, 'What makes you think this is our vic?'

'We tracked down his then girlfriend,' McLachlan said, the first time Barclay had heard him speak since he arrived. 'She's married now. Two kids. I asked if there were ever any accidents involving his arm breaking and she confirmed there was. We're awaiting medical records.'

Lawrence asked, 'Will they still have records from then?'

De Silva shrugged. 'They might.'

Barclay spoke up. 'Did you check the PNC for any other incidents involving Turner's girlfriend?'

O'Connor blinked at him. 'Like what?'

'Well, we know now that in one of the previous cases, a family member had the victim's middle finger posted to them,' he said. 'Did the girlfriend report anything like that?'

'She never mentioned it,' O'Connor said. 'Didn't find anything on the PNC.'

Lawrence was already typing away at her computer. 'There are a few reports here. A domestic dispute where an ex-boyfriend was arrested. Fifteen years ago, well after Turner was reported missing. A caution for being drunk and disorderly. That's it.' Lawrence looked back at them. 'No middle finger.'

'It's not our man,' Barclay said.

O'Connor almost growled, deflated.

'Listen, you did good work, O'Connor. That's as close as we've got so far.' De Silva smiled at him. 'But let's keep this line open, okay? Let me know when those medical records come back, we'll take a look at any reports. If the break is in the same place, I think we keep Turner in mind.'

'It's not our man,' Barclay repeated.

De Silva shot him a look, but spoke to O'Connor. 'We're not sure of anything just yet.' She took a breath. 'Good work though, O'Connor. Could you take Lawrence and run through the PNC for any reports of body parts being mailed to people? National. Fingers, toes, a strand of hair. Anything.'

O'Connor nodded to de Silva, and inclined his head to Lawrence, a signal that she should join him at his desk.

The room had become tense. There was an excitement that builds in any incident room when there's a break in a case. A lift in morale, an upswing in momentum. And, conversely, when that lead turns into a dead-end, all of that reverses. The mood flattens, the spirits lower and temperaments begin to fray. And in moments like that, there's usually only one thing to do.

'Come on, guys, we've got a few hours left of the day,' de Silva said. 'Pending anything urgent, we'll wrap at half four. Drinks are on Barclay.' She gave him that look, the one where he knew he'd fucked up. He couldn't meet her glare. 'Can we have a word outside?'

He followed her out into the corridor and closed the door behind him. 'I know what you're going to say.'

'Well I'm still going to say it, Barclay. So listen up.' There were times when de Silva seemed tall, larger than her five foot four stature should allow for. This was one of those moments. 'They're busting their guts out in there. You may have forgotten how hard that manual work is, how mind-numbing it can be. We don't have fancy systems that do all of this for us, we rely on those men and women to do a good job. Look at me, Barclay.'

His eyes snapped to her face. He hadn't realised they'd drifted down to the floor.

'Some encouragement. That's all that's needed. We don't know that this Turner isn't our man.'

Yes we do.

'We keep every line of investigation open until we have something concrete, then we close down each avenue one by one.'

The doors to the lift slid open, but Barclay didn't look away from her. 'I feel like we're wasting our time on it,' he said.

'The work's already done and we're moving on.' De Silva glanced down the corridor, then lowered her voice. 'O'Connor did what was asked of him. They all have. So tonight, when you're at the bar getting the round, you'll tell him how much of a good job him and the team have done.'

Barclay didn't like the thought of hand-holding a grown man, and was surprised that de Silva felt the need to. He knew he was a hypocrite, knew that the thing he couldn't give to O'Connor was the exact thing he craved himself.

'Yes, ma'am.'

De Silva frowned. 'Are you trying to piss me off?'

'No!' He held his hands up in submission to her. 'Just a slip of the tongue.' *Yes I am trying to piss you off.*

'Oh ho!' Holden's voice boomed through the corridor as he approached, wearing a far-too-tight *Mighty Morphin Power Rangers* T-shirt. 'Am I interrupting an undressing here? What's Boy Wonder done now?'

'Will you shut up, Holden,' de Silva said. Her voice light, but the intent behind it heavy and clear. 'And it's a dressing-down, not an undressing.'

'Well I did come with some news, but I can go back to my desk and open those Krispy Kremes if I'm not wanted.' He took two steps backward.

'Behave yourself and get in there.' De Silva inclined her head to the incident room. 'I'll be in in a second.'

Holden pushed past them both. 'Well, forgive me for daring to bring some lols.'

It had been some time since Barclay had seen de Silva like this. Back in charge. Sharp. A leader.

'Go on in,' de Silva said to Barclay. 'Let's see what the Pink Ranger has to say.'

The office was quiet, and Barclay felt what de Silva had spoken about. The atmosphere was flat. He'd drained it of any energy, any buzz it had had before. He'd had no intentions of going out for a drink with anyone after work. He needed to get to the gym, but that would have to wait. He owed it to the team.

'So what's the news?' De Silva stood in front of the evidence board, where she wrote *HACK?* in red block capitals and ringed it twice. 'Caught the bastard?'

'No,' he said. 'I don't think we will. They used a VPN, like I said. We can't trace it.'

Barclay cleared his throat, tossed his guilt aside. 'And what now? Is everything safe?'

'We've put some additional firewalls in place on our main server, so we'll be switching back over to it from the backup in the next half hour or so. You might notice some disruption during the switch,' Holden said. 'Nothing to worry about.'

De Silva sighed.

Lawrence called out, 'So we know that this person tried to access two detectives' files…'

Holden threw a look at de Silva.

'I've told the team,' she said.

Barclay shook his head. Murphy had asked her specifically to keep it private, and she hadn't done. She'd said they needed to know. Deserved to know. But Barclay couldn't escape the fact that she'd gone against what was asked of her.

This isn't new. This is who she is.

Lawrence pressed on, 'Do we think this hack is in some way related to the case we're working on?'

Barclay felt de Silva's eyes on him, and he knew that she'd been thinking the same thing as Lawrence. He had thought it himself. It was obvious. The only natural conclusion.

Holden shrugged. 'You lot are the detectives.'

O'Connor sighed. 'I just got the X-rays back on Turner.'

Holden excused himself, promised he'd be back if his team had any other developments.

'It's not our man,' O'Connor said. 'Break's in the wrong place.'

Great. Square one.

Eighteen

The gym was quiet. Just a few people on the equipment, one guy on the free weights. The booming music of group classes that reverberated through the floor had stopped ages ago.

The place was quiet. Just how Barclay liked it.

He strapped his heart monitor around his chest, set up the app and stepped onto the cycle. Watched his calorie burn climb into double figures as he pushed hard.

It wasn't that he'd been keeping an eye on de Silva. But he did notice that she'd only ordered orange juice all night, while the others sank pint after pint. Guinness for Braxton, whisky and Coke for Lawrence and pints for the others. Barclay had ordered lemonades for himself, and now as he rocked on the bike, he regretted his choice. The bubbles burned in his gut, and he felt like he needed to burp.

De Silva had been right. It was nice to spend time with the team outside of the incident room, to see them as they were when they weren't being detectives. When they don't have their heads in the game. To see them how their friends saw them, their families maybe.

The pub hadn't been Barclay's first choice, but O'Connor had insisted. The carpet was sticky, the table-tops ringed years ago from pint glasses decades old. A constant rumble of chatter competing with the too-loud nineties Britpop.

The last time music was good.

He glanced at his watch. Ten thirty already. He'd have to make it a short one and head home before his mum started calling to ask where he was. She'd have made him some dinner even though Barclay hadn't asked her to. Something with chips, or a stew probably.

He'd eat it, of course, to be polite and because it was late and he didn't want to argue. But really, he craved a salad or some salmon and greens.

He pedalled harder.

One by one, the other people in the gym left and the lights turned off. He waved an arm and they burst back to life. That was the thing about these 24/7 gyms. They were great to access any time of the day, but when you were left there all alone, it felt a bit weird.

That old feeling where the body has gone into hyper-arousal, suddenly and unyieldingly aware of everything around. He heard a clatter from somewhere, and took out one of his earphones, stopped pedalling and listened. Every little sound amplified.

Nothing.

He looked at his watch again. Four hundred calories burned. That would have to do for the day. He promised himself he'd come back early in the morning, maybe do a body combat style class. He usually burned about six or seven hundred in those.

The changing rooms reminded him of school locker rooms in high school PE. The smell of must and sweaty things. The place where he knew he had to avert his gaze from the other boys as they got themselves dressed. As they wrapped and unwrapped their towels, combed their hair into place and talked about girls. Barclay had always kept quiet, got dried and out of the changing rooms first. It was best for everyone, to save any embarrassment.

He pulled his holdall out of his locker, took out his washbag and left the rest on the bench. The steaming hot water in the shower felt calming on his skin as it sank deep into his muscles. There was something transformative about a shower, Barclay thought.

He dabbed himself dry, wrapped the towel around his waist. The lights in the main changing area had gone out, and as he walked toward the bench, they came back on.

Another man was there, his towel on the bench, and he was naked. Some men were unashamed of walking around without clothes on in the gym changing rooms, of starting full-blown conversations while in the buff. But Barclay wasn't like that, it had always made him uncomfortable.

'All right, mate,' the man said. 'Didn't realise anyone else was in.' He put his leg up on the bench and dried himself.

Barclay moved to his holdall and slipped into his underwear first. 'Yeah, late one for me,' he said. He kept his eyes averted, away from the man. But it was too late, he'd already taken him all in. The hulk at his shoulders and arms. The tightness of his stomach and the leanness of his legs.

'Seen you around a few times,' the man said. 'Looking good, bro. You've been here loads lately.'

'Yeah,' he said. Unsure of what else he could say.

'Late one for me, too,' he said. 'Was on it last night and couldn't face the place this morning. Needed to work off some tension. Know what I mean?'

'Yeah, the gym's good for that.'

The man laughed. 'Not what I meant.' He took a breath and faced him full on. 'It's quiet in here at night, isn't it? You could get up to all kinds and no one would know.'

Barclay knew where this was going. The realisation of it washed over him and made his hairs stand on end. He thought of Nick. He'd forgotten what his husband's skin felt like, the smell of his hair, the feeling as Barclay...

'You game?'

Barclay thought about it. Imagined them in the shower, the water running, the steam rising, their eager mouths all over each other's bodies. He felt movement down there and pulled on his jeans quickly. 'I'm married,' he said.

'Me too. No one needs to know, do they?'

'I love my husband,' Barclay said. It was the truth, and he hoped the end to this whole exchange.

'Come on, lad.' The man grabbed himself and squeezed. 'I'm gagging.'

'Leave me alone!' Barclay's voice echoed in the changing room for no one else to hear but the two of them.

'Woah, be easy, bro. It's sound.'

Barclay pulled on his top, grabbed his bag and headed for the door. He knew, as he walked toward his car, that it wasn't sound. It wasn't okay. Because, just for a split second, he'd have fucked that stranger in the changing rooms just to feel something other than the cold he'd felt since he'd left the house he shared with his family.

He knew, if that man ever asked him again, he'd probably do it. He knew then that he'd be a failure again. He'd let himself down, his husband, their daughter, and for what? For sex.

Some things, he knew, meant more than a fumble in a changing room with a hot guy. He still believed that his marriage could work. Would work.

Nineteen

The call came in the early morning from the man Meeks only half-expected to hear from. You go digging around in the past, and surely it's only a matter of time before someone notices.

He'd been marking up his manuscript, and made notes on how he could clarify key moments from his childhood. But when the call came, he put it back into the top drawer of his desk and left it there. It wasn't ready for anyone to read, or, as he preferred to think of it – to *witness* it. He couldn't leave it lying around.

Meeks had deep-cleaned the entire place. Most people hated scrubbing the bathroom, getting elbow deep in the toilet bowl, but Meeks enjoyed it. Knew he'd worked hard when his knuckles were scraped and his skin was red.

He'd taken every book from the shelf, polished it, made sure the top was dusted and quickly checked the pages for any damage. There was none. Not a dog-eared page or notes in any margin. He always made sure not to break the spine of his books like other people did. There was nothing more unsightly than those lines down the spine of a book, like exposed veins. They put Meeks's teeth on edge.

The cleaning didn't take him long: the flat was small. Just everything he needed, and not much of what he wanted. Spartan, his mum had described it as once. He'd wondered whether that was where the word 'sparse' came from.

He didn't bother to look it up, but he did see himself as a hero. A warrior of the truth, unlike so many people out there. The sheeple didn't know anything other than what was fed to them, and they opened their mouths and swallowed it all. The lies. The corruption.

They vilified and ridiculed people like him. In the beginning it had hurt, but after years his skin had thickened. He didn't care what they thought. But those police detectives... that de Silva and Barclay. He'd only met them once, but knew them instantly. It was no wonder people were sick, depressed, addicted to drugs and alcohol. Nearly eight billion people just looking for the easiest way out.

They were his opposition, the lions to his gladiator. But in the end, they would uncover it all in his manuscript. The truth of the things Meeks had seen and heard and researched. They'd find that it was him who'd tried to hack the police network. That it was him who recognised de Silva's name and said nothing. They would come for him.

That's why he was so surprised when his landline rang. He answered it, expecting it to be one of the detectives. The voice he recognised spoke quickly and told Meeks that he had information about the cases Meeks had been looking into.

'Like what?' He had grown accustomed to people reaching out with information, only for it to turn out he already knew it, or that they were making it all up.

'I know you've been speaking to de Silva and the other one,' he'd said. There was an edge to his voice, just like on that awful, freezing night when they were kids. 'I know it's been a while, but we need to talk. Today.'

'Why now? Shouldn't you be being careful, with the police knocking around?'

A pause. 'Necessity,' the man said. 'I can meet you, but it will need to be tonight. When it's dark. I don't want anyone seeing me. Okay?'

'Okay.' He checked his watch. Night time was hours away.

'I'll be seeing you.' The line had gone dead.

Meeks had taken a lemon-scented antibacterial wipe from a drawer and cleaned down the handset. That was when he'd set about cleaning the whole place. He washed and dried two glasses for water, left them on the draining board ready.

He'd made sure to put the bottles of water from the corner shop in the fridge so that they were cold, so there wasn't any awkward need for tap water.

He wondered whether his old friend was still a seeker of the truth, or had he become one of them? A liar. Part of the corruption that pervaded society and warped minds? Meeks would know soon.

He sat on his couch for hours, until finally he peeked out the window and saw the sun setting. He hid the evidence board back under the couch.

When the buzzer sounded, Meeks pressed the intercom without saying anything into the mic. He knew who it was and he had no other visitors. Only the detectives, and they wouldn't be back so soon.

He poured water from the bottles into the glasses he'd already prepared, and set them on the coffee table on top of two coasters made from slate, a gift he'd bought himself in Beddgelert.

Then the knock came at the front door. His friend looked so changed. Skinnier. Paler. Ill. He tried to control his breath as he invited the man in. 'I prepared some water.'

'I'm not thirsty,' his friend said.

He sat down on the couch opposite Meeks, his black hoody pulled up to cover as much of his face as possible, but still Meeks recognised that chin, and the tip of his nose.

'What did you come to talk about?'

'A few things,' he said.

'Oh,' Meeks said. 'Like what?'

Twenty

Clouds had moved in, covered the stars and the sliver of moon, as de Silva parked in her driveway and turned off the engine. A light was on in the living room. Laney would still be awake, drinking a bottle of wine she'd bought from the local Tesco, probably.

As de Silva pushed open the front door, she found her sister sitting on the stairs, a half-empty glass of red gripped in her pale fingers, as she sobbed into her free hand. She looked up when de Silva came in.

'What's happened?' De Silva wanted to go to her, throw her arms around her, despite all the things that had been said and done in the years since they were kids. Instead, she sat on the step beneath her sister. 'Laney?'

'I'm sorry.' She wiped her tears away. 'I shouldn't be here and behaving like this.'

'Where's Bonnie?'

'She's in bed.'

De Silva was thankful for that. 'You can't let her see you like this, you know? She'll worry.'

'I know, Win, for God's sake. I know!'

De Silva let it go. Nodded instead of reacting. 'I know you know. I'm sorry. I just meant that... so much has happened already.' She took a few breaths, listened to her sister's sniffles. 'Do you want to talk about it?'

There was a long pause where neither she nor Laney seemed to breathe. Talking about it had been their problem since they were young. It had been the thing that had driven a wedge between them, the thing that prevented them from fixing whatever had gone wrong all those years ago.

They'd never been close, and de Silva regretted that. They chose different lives for themselves. But since their dad died of cancer four years ago, they never spoke. Didn't see each other. Except for that time last year when their mum was in hospital.

'Okay.' Laney's voice sounded like it was made from glass, like it could break or shatter at any moment.

They moved into the kitchen and sat at the island de Silva had had put in when she bought the house. Laney poured herself another glass of wine, while de Silva held a steaming cup of tea between her cold hands.

'What do you want to know?' Laney asked.

'You've not told me anything, Laney. You and Bonnie show up here, and you're welcome, of course you are. But you've not told me exactly what happened. We were supposed to talk last night, and you clammed up. We went back to your house and got clothes, and you said nothing. But you were on edge, Laney. More than just not wanting to run into David. Like you were scared to see him.'

'I was,' she said. 'I am.' She burst into tears. 'Oh God, Win, the things Bonnie must have seen.'

De Silva touched her sister's hand and found it hot and clammy. 'Just start from the beginning. What's been going on?'

Laney nodded and wiped tears from her eyes and cheeks. She took a few deep breaths. 'It all started during Covid,' she said. 'Work stopped. David was sitting at home. Bored out of his mind. Started drinking. Gambling. Going to one of the neighbours' for all-day parties on the downlow.'

Tory behaviour, de Silva thought.

It was just like David to disregard the rules with his buddies. He'd always thought himself above others. De Silva had the distinct impression that he looked down on Laney's family.

'He got into it bad. He started to get agitated. Frustrated.' She took a chug of her wine. 'He'd shout and swear and rage at me. It all started small, really. We had to turn off the pool to save money. "Just for a while", he said. Then Bonnie's live-in child minder had to go. He sold some of my jewellery. His car disappeared. Next thing I know, the house is re-mortgaged.'

De Silva listened in silence. She'd heard this story so many times before as a PC in uniform. She knew it so well that she knew where this was all going.

'The first time he hit me was at his brother's barbeque. It was Linda's birthday, his brother's wife, and we were meeting just as the lockdown lifted. He got drunk on the free bar. I asked him to take it easy, we had to be up early the next day for Bonnie's dance class. He told me he'd already cancelled them. I asked why he hadn't spoken to me about it. And then—' She looked down at her glass, as if the memories of that night swam in her Pinot Noir.

'Fuck, Laney,' she said. 'I'm sorry.'

She shook her head. 'It's not your fault. Things escalated from there. He did it that night and I left. I can't remember how many times I've left. Went to a friend's house. The shame of it all. Everyone knew. People stopped speaking to me, stopped offering me and Bonnie a place to run to. So I had no choice but to stay.'

'You'll always have a place here. You and Bonnie.'

'I've been awful to you,' she said. 'Too awful, I couldn't show my face here.'

'Why did you? Finally contact me, I mean.'

Laney looked anywhere but at her sister. De Silva wondered whether that was from shame, guilt, or something else. 'Three nights ago, he came home. He'd been out all day. Doing God knows what since he's been out of work. He called me all kinds of things, and I told him to wait until I'd put Bonnie to bed. I didn't want her to hear the things he was saying. But he kept on. Said, "She should hear what a useless bitch her mother is".'

De Silva's fists clenched. She hid them under the breakfast bar. 'Laney, did he hurt Bonnie?'

'No,' Laney said. 'He grabbed her arm, but I managed to get him off. I slapped him so hard I thought I heard his teeth snap together.'

'Good.'

'He got hold of me, and I told Bonnie to go to her room and to lock the door. Then he just laid into me. When he was finished, he walked away, made himself a drink, came back and—'

'You don't need to tell me any more. I get it.'

'No, you don't.' Laney shook her head. 'He really hurt me, Win. Down there.'

De Silva felt sick, felt the need to get into her car and go to David's house and show him that women can hit back. To make him hurt like he'd hurt her sister.

'When he finally fell asleep, I packed some stuff and got into the car. Called you when we were heading for the tunnel.'

'Laney, I know you're not going to want to hear this,' de Silva said. 'I think we should get a kit done.'

'Not a chance.' Laney's voice was loud. 'You think I'm going to what? Take this to court? Sit across from him and have his lawyer tear me to shreds? Not a fucking chance.'

De Silva understood. The justice system had a habit of making women in rape and domestic violence cases feel like liars, like they were somehow to blame, like their whole life – and their sexual history – was on trial.

'I'm glad you came,' de Silva said, finally. 'Have you got any idea where he is now?'

'No. Why? I'm not pressing charges, Win, if that's what you're getting at?'

'We don't need your consent to press charges. The Crown Prosecution Service can proceed without it.'

'No, Win. Please.'

'Laney, look at you! Look what he's done to you.'

'This will all heal.'

'Not all of it.' De Silva had seen so many women, and men, struggle with the psychological damage caused by an abusive partner. 'Some of that will take real work to heal. He deserves to be locked up.'

Laney shook her head. 'I didn't come to you for this, Win. I came to you so that we could feel safe.'

De Silva wanted to insist. Wanted to offer statistics of re-offending, of how many abusive exes turn stalker. But Laney was right, she'd not come to her sister for that. All de Silva could do was make her home safe for them.

Laney went to bed after midnight, drunk and a little unstable on her feet. De Silva got a quick shower and climbed into her own bed. In the dark, as her eyes adjusted, she thought of the things she'd do to David if she ever got her hands on him.

Somewhere in the night, when her rage had subsided and her eyes had closed, she felt a rhythmic vibration through her bed. Through her body. When she opened her eyes, a light shone on the ceiling. The vibration again.

Her phone.

She sat up right and reached for her phone. Wicked Witch of the North-West Calling.

'Ma'am?'

'De Silva.' Her voice was breathy. 'Where are you?' She sounded as though she was driving.

'Well, I was asleep.'

'I tried Barclay when I couldn't get hold of you. He's not answering either.'

De Silva's brain kicked in. 'He might have his daughter tonight,' she lied. 'I'm not sure. What's going on?'

'I had a call from a friend in West Lancashire Police. How quickly can you get to Pendle?'

'Pendle? As in the hill?'

'I'm heading to a police station near there, in Nelson. I want you to head straight to the crime scene in Pendle, then report to me in Nelson.'

'Where am I heading?'

'There's a base set up at the carpark on Barley Lane: you should be able to find it on Google Maps. You'll need sturdy boots: it's a bit of a walk from there.'

'Our suspect?'

'From what I've heard of the victim, it certainly looks that way. My friend there called me as soon as they had the particulars on the body.'

'I'm leaving in ten minutes.'

'Try to wake Barclay.' The line went dead.

The maps told her that she would arrive at Pendle around three thirty. She'd quickly dressed, brushed her hair and shoved some chewing gum into her pocket before she left.

She'd tried to call Barclay from the car, but there was no answer. But in reality, she knew he didn't need to be called out. She'd leave him to rest. God knew he looked like he needed it lately.

The country lanes leading out to Pendle from the motorway were almost black. Every so often there was a lamp post near a solo house or small row of terraces, fronting onto the road. She drove most of the way with her full beams on, keeping an eye for any approaching cars.

There were none.

Pendle itself was a different matter. Neighbours were out in dressing gowns, or pulling on shoes and boots on their doorsteps, ready to go and ask local police what was going on. De Silva knew their small community would rarely experience such a police presence, if at all.

She showed her warrant card at the cordon, told them that DSI Murphy had asked her to come along and that she was to be expected. The PCSO let her through straight away, and gave her some quick parking instructions that de Silva didn't quite catch.

The night air was cold, like a chill had rolled down from Pendle Hill. Ritchie had taken her there a few times throughout the years, especially in the summer when his need to get out in nature was insatiable. He liked to hike, to keep fit. For a few weeks in the warmer weather, de Silva had come to like it too.

He'd told her how, centuries ago, accused women were walked over the hill to stand trial as a witch. Shoeless, up and down paths that were not what they are today. Wild and untrodden, sharp stones would cut at their feet, or they'd slip in the wet.

She had wondered what had gone through their minds as they walked toward what was, very likely, an execution. How easily their lives were turned upside down if they did something the town, their neighbours, or the Church disapproved of. Something men disapproved of.

She remembered thinking that not much had changed.

Up ahead, floodlights had been set up across from the carpark, on the main road and on through what looked like public footpaths. She followed their white glare, hoping to bump into someone on the way who could offer some direction.

Crime scene photographers and the West Lancs. equivalent of Scientific Support headed back to their vehicles with metal cases, probably filled with evidence and samples. A police van sat nearby. Empty.

She scanned the area for Meeks. She could see nothing in the dark beyond the carpark. No person anyway. She quickened her pace.

'De Silva!' A voice she didn't recognise. A man's gruff and hoarse voice came out of the night. 'DCI de Silva!'

De Silva looked about for the source, and spotted a tall, slender man with white hair coming from the carpark, waving in her direction. She stopped and waited for him to catch up with her. She gave him the once-over. Walking boots, already caked in mud. A trench coat with a belt, thick with a nice paisley lining. In his hand, two torches. He had a devastatingly handsome type of face that de Silva may have fallen for in her younger years.

But not now.

'Hello there,' he said. 'Thought I was going to have to break into a run. This time of the morning, nobody needs that, do they?' He showed her his warrant card. 'DCI Lennox, West Lancs. Police. Your DSI knows my DSI. They asked me to come join you.'

'Thanks. I appreciate it.' She began walking again, and he followed. 'What've we got here? Do you mind if we walk and talk?'

'Not at all.' He gestured that she should take the first step, like de Silva had seen in those old movies about romance and chivalry and corsets. 'Hikers found a body out there at the base of the hill.' He handed her a torch and pocketed his own. 'We only rigged the lights so far, you'll need this soon.'

She did the same. 'What time?'

'About three hours ago,' he said. When she looked at him with an arched eyebrow, he continued. 'I know, we get all kinds out here. Ghost hunters. History groups. They like to walk on the hill at night. See what they can see.'

'This is the second conversation about ghosts I'm having this week.'

'Oh?'

'Sorry. They found a body. In what state?'

'Dismembered.' His face seemed to pinch around his mouth, his eyes narrow. 'That's why they called you in, isn't it?'

'Sorry, I got that.' De Silva squared her shoulders. 'Is the body fresh?'

'Oh.' His voice quivered. Embarrassed by his misunderstanding, maybe. Even in the dark of the countryside, de Silva was certain DCI Lennox blushed. 'He's a fresh one all right.'

'Any ID?'

'No ID on the body.' His voice regained its strength. 'But we know who he is. Pending an official ID from his daughter, of course.'

'Go on…'

'Charles James Heaton was reported missing two days ago by his daughter. He lives not too far from here, but she's up in Scotland. Some research facility. Said she'd not been able to reach her dad all week and they usually spoke every day.'

They reached a stile which led onto a path across a brook, but here the light rigs ended. They turned on their torches. Lennox held out his hand to help de Silva up onto the step. She ignored him and stepped over unaided. 'You searched his house?'

'Yeah.' Lennox's long legs made quick work of the stile. 'There was no sign of forced entry, nothing seemed to be missing. We found suitcases and weekend bags in cupboards, so we assumed he'd not gone far.'

'But he lived here,' de Silva said. 'Not like he'd have gone out walking and got lost.'

'No, I suppose not.' Lennox laughed. 'Not these days. Always a phone in our pocket, and never too far away from a road.'

'You sound sad about that.'

'Well, I am a bit. This place has changed a lot since I was a kid. New roads. New houses. New people. The world's getting smaller, and I get claustrophobic.'

De Silva considered this for a moment. She thought about Pendle, Lennox's Pendle, and about the memories held in any place. She wondered what memories his home-town held for Lennox, and whether he felt them watching him from far away, like the shadows in the pines she'd felt at Freshfields.

'Anyway, he lived here. But he's not from here. He moved about twenty, twenty-five years ago, maybe. From St Helens. That's down your way, isn't it?'

'Well, it's close enough.'

A pause. That awkward silence that comes after a joke someone doesn't understand. Lennox said, 'We're not too far away now.'

De Silva looked ahead down the small track, pockmarked with potholes and grey puddles. It had rained here sometime recently. Beyond the path, a shaft from the floodlights on a rise, and to her vision, it was all encompassed in a yellow-white circle of light.

It still looked a fair way off, and de Silva did her best to breathe quietly through her nose. She'd been meaning to get back into her running regime, but hadn't found the time.

She thought about this victim being from St Helens, another of the victims who had been local to Liverpool and then moved away years before they were murdered.

Is there something in that?

'And hikers found him,' de Silva repeated, eager to fill the silence between them. Her phone rang out. 'Excuse me.' She stopped and he took a few steps ahead. He could obviously still hear her conversation, but at least he was being polite. 'Barclay,' she said.

'Sorry I missed your call.' His throat sounded hoarse. 'What's up?'

'It's fine, I'm on it,' she said.

'On what?'

'I'm out in Pendle,' she said. 'West Lancs. There's another body, Barclay. Just like our victim in the woods. And just like Finch.'

'You're kidding.' His voice was flat.

'You should get back to sleep,' de Silva said. 'I've got this. Hopefully I'll be back before the afternoon. I can catch you up then.'

'I've not slept.' She could hear him moving about. 'I'll be an hour or so.'

'Barclay, don't—'

'See you soon.' The line went dead.

'Everything okay?'

'All good,' she said. She didn't sound convinced of her own words and she knew it. Barclay had sounded off. Not himself. Sure, it was early hours and he should have been asleep, but she'd woken him up at all hours before. This was different. Something was wrong.

The crime scene was quiet, not as hectic as de Silva was used to. She'd seen the photographers leave as she arrived, but even then, there'd be other SOCOs, a forensic team. One man stood just outside of the lights of the crime scene. He'd slipped the top of his white suit off, tied it by the arms around his waist, his mouth twisted into a long, howling yawn.

'Morning, Stan,' Lennox said. 'Your team done here?'

'I sent them back for more equipment. Some samples they wanted to take. A boot print, they think.'

'This is DCI de Silva from Merseyside Police.'

'Morning,' de Silva said.

'Oh, a Scouser. Best watch our pockets, 'ey, Lennox.' Stan laughed at his own joke.

De Silva glared. Some people had these little prejudices about others. The Scottish were angry piss heads, the Irish also piss heads, people from Birmingham were boring or slow and Scousers... well, they were thieves. A hangover from reporting on the Hillsborough Disaster in that rag of a paper no one in Liverpool would even wipe their arses with.

'This is...' Lennox was clearly embarrassed. 'This is Stan Bruce. Area Forensics.'

De Silva nodded. 'You just stand there, Stan. See if you can manage to find your dick through your pocket while I get on with some work, okay?'

Lennox's mouth fell open while Stan fumbled for words he couldn't quite find.

De Silva fished in her coat for a new packet of latex gloves and pulled them on, didn't look in Stan's direction again. Finally, Stan trudged off somewhere and Lennox's shoulders dropped a few inches.

'Sorry about him,' Lennox said. 'He's known for thinking he's funny.'

'Don't worry, there's one in every force. Quite a few in mine, actually.' She nodded toward the body. 'Do you mind?'

'Go ahead.'

De Silva squatted above a shallow grave. Earth had been piled at the sides, mixed with shards of grass. The killer hadn't taken the time to dig a grave like they had done in the woods at Formby. The Finch crime scene was the same, according to the report. He'd been hasty. Uncaring.

She imagined the killer here, scraping out the earth with their hands or a rock. Had he been disturbed? Had something spooked him and he'd abandoned the hopes of burying his victim so that they weren't found for months? Years maybe. In that time, he'd be long gone.

The body was a mess of parts, all dismembered from the torso. Charles James Heaton had been stripped of everything, except for his underwear. Once white briefs that had been dyed red, in patches, by his own blood.

In her mind, she imagined the killer instructing Heaton to strip. He'd be standing watching with a weapon of some kind, perhaps even the tool he'd eventually use to dismember his victim. Heaton would cry, beg for his captor to let him go. He'd plead that he had kids. A family.

'He didn't have a wife?'

'No,' Lennox said from somewhere behind her. 'He lived here alone. I think he did have an ex-wife back in St Helens.'

De Silva scanned the body parts, torch in hand, painfully aware she didn't want to touch anything, but all too eager to get stuck in and find what she was looking for. She wasn't sure how far into their work the forensics team were.

'Do you think that's important?'

'If I can get a name, I can speak to her when I get back. See if she knows anything?'

'I can get the name for you no problem.' He cleared his throat. 'What're you looking for?'

'In previous cases, the middle finger on the right hand was removed. A kind of calling card.'

'I read about this,' he said. 'A woman in Wales, and then an unidentified male in your neck of the woods.'

'Yeah.' She held the torchlight still. Her heart raced. Then, there it was. Sticking out from underneath Charles Heaton's thigh was his right hand.

'Well,' Lennox started. 'Is it your suspect?'

De Silva took a breath, and wondered whether she could catch Barclay in the car to stay put in Liverpool. To drive out to St Helens and find Heaton's ex-wife. In her experience, de Silva had come to understand that families sometimes knew things about cases without realising.

'Yeah,' she said. 'Looks like his MO for sure.'

Twenty-One

De Silva's call came as Barclay had approached the last Warrington junction on the M62. 'Stay there,' she'd said. 'I need you to visit Josephine Houston, formerly Heaton. She's living in St Helens, I'll send you the address. She's the ex-wife of the victim up here, Charles James Heaton. Ask a few questions, get a statement. Anything you get, copy for the attention of DCI Lennox up here in West Lancs.'

'Got it,' he'd said. He pulled off the M62 and took the streets toward St Helens. There was no point in going back home now, and he'd only wake his mum up again. She'd have more questions, and he didn't have the brain power for that.

Not with how he felt about last night at the gym. Confused. Aroused. Disgusted in himself.

He found a Starbucks near to the Houston residence, which he was thankful was open at this early hour. One of those twenty-four-hour places. He ordered an oat milk latte and sat in the carpark.

De Silva had said she'd be back before midday and ended the call without a goodbye, which was unlike her. *She's busy*, he told himself. *Probably eager to learn what she can and get back to it.*

He pushed it all aside. There were bigger things for him to think about.

The Houston residence was a red-brick end-terrace on Wilbur Street in the Junction area of St Helens. A white-framed porch on the front, and a rusted gate with black, flaking paint. Barclay managed to park right outside the house. There was a disability parking sign on the wall with stickers for local clubs and bars covering it, and someone had scrawled their name on it. *Jess 2K1*.

Despite the sign, there was no disabled parking bay sprayed onto the road, so he took the opportunity to leave his car there. He double checked his watch. 8:03 a.m. He'd timed it so that it was late enough for them to be up, but early enough that she may not have left for work yet.

There was no doorbell, and the letter box creaked as he lifted it, and clattered against itself as it fell back into place. Barclay looked around, aware the noise may have caused some neighbours to come to their windows, covered in yellowed office blinds or pristine white net curtains. The type his nan used to have. She'd put them in the wash at least once a month and clean her windows with screwed-up pages from the *Liverpool Journal* and white vinegar. The house stank but she was always so proud of how gleaming her windows were.

His phone rang. Nick calling. Even though he ached to answer it and the need to speak to Nick pulled at his chest, he turned the phone to silent mode and buttoned the call.

Finally, the inside door opened, and a woman appeared. Her loose skin was heavily lined and gave her face the look of someone who wore the weight of the world on their back. Her eyes looked full and wet, and tissues had burned the skin around them pink. He knew that she'd already heard the news. De Silva had mentioned that a daughter had raised the alarm over Heaton's disappearance. Maybe she'd already called her mum to tell her.

'Josephine Houston?'

She wiped at her nose with well-worn tissue paper. 'Yes. Come in, I've been expecting you.'

The living room was hot. Much hotter than outside, and in the corner a small neon-green glass lamp was switched on. A grey couch sat against the wall, L-shaped, and the cushions were plump and inviting.

'Sit down,' she said. 'Would you like a drink? Tea?'

Barclay knew he might be there a while. These things could take time. 'That would be lovely. I can help?'

She looked at him with a blank expression, as though not really seeing him. 'Yeah. Okay.' She walked through to the kitchen without another word, and Barclay followed her.

The kitchen was dark, and his shoes squeaked as he crossed the lino. He watched her fill the kettle up and dig a cup out.

'Go on, then,' she said. 'I know you're here about Charlie. I know they found his body up in Pendle.'

'Do you want to sit down?'

'I've known this day was coming for years,' she said. 'But, you know, it's still a shock, isn't it? To be married to someone for so long and then for them to just—'

Barclay knew what she meant. There was a gap in Barclay's own life since Nick asked him to leave, something he knew he'd never be able to fill again. Even when they fixed things, when the plasters came off, there'd still be a scar. It was inevitable. He wondered whether they'd ever really heal.

But Josephine's gap was different. He wondered how close she was to her daughter, and how the child she'd had with Charles Heaton had a life that was emptier now. That little bit colder. Barclay wondered whether Josephine felt the same. Clearly she'd been crying, so he must have still meant something to her.

'I know you're upset, Mrs Houston. Maybe we should sit down.'

She handed him a steaming cup of tea. It smelled amazing. Warm and sweet. 'I'm not upset,' she said. 'I'm relieved.'

Barclay looked at her, searching her face for an answer to the question that bubbled at the back of his throat. He took a sip to give his mind a moment to process. 'You're relieved he's dead, or am I misunderstanding?'

Josephine nodded. 'God forgive me.'

'Would you like to sit down?'

'You keep saying that,' she snapped. 'No. I'm fine.'

'Can you tell me why you're relieved?' His mind raced to abuse, to coercive control, to a messy and ugly divorce and a young girl caught in the middle of it all.

Josephine chewed at her bottom lip for a moment, then said, 'You don't know anything about him, do you?'

Barclay put the mug down on the countertop, piled with folded laundry and brown envelopes. 'Is there something specific you want to tell me about?'

She shook her head. 'He got away with it, then. He legged it up there, and it didn't follow him. I was so worried, you know. About our girl. My Amy. She was so young when it happened, just five years old. Didn't understand why her dad had to leave. And I couldn't tell her. How could I?'

Had to leave?

'There were... accusations,' Josephine continued without looking at Barclay. 'You see, he used to volunteer at local schools. Some after-school football club for girls. He was going to be a pro when he was younger, you know. Snapped his ankle on a night out and his career was over just like that.'

Barclay knew what she was about to say. He heard so many stories start this way. Accusations. Schools. He nodded, a signal that she should continue. 'What were the accusations?'

'A few of the parents had reported things to the schools that Charlie volunteered at. Things their daughters had said. You see, he'd recorded their practices so that he could show them their own performance. So they could improve. So that he could highlight what was working. What wasn't, you know? He had full consent from the school, from the parents. I suppose everyone just wanted their kids to do well. At least... that's how it started.'

Josephine looked away from him, out the window at her concrete-flagged yard, where washing hung from a line and flapped in the breeze.

'One of the girls found a camera in the changing rooms. Another came out shortly after, saying he'd tried to kiss her. Another that he'd tried to undress her.'

Barclay swallowed. He thought of his daughter, of how he'd feel if this were her. 'What happened?'

'The police were involved, of course. He was questioned. They released him. No evidence.'

'What about the camera?'

She shrugged. 'I don't know.' She shook her head. 'I told him to leave that day. He took his stuff and I've not seen him since.'

'He wasn't prosecuted?'

'No.'

The kitchen turned cold in the silence then. Somewhere in the house, a clock ticked the seconds away and Barclay's tea stopped steaming. His phone vibrated in his coat pocket. Nick again.

'You can answer it,' Josephine said.

He buttoned the call again. 'Your daughter...'

'No,' she said. 'I know what you're thinking. But no. I had that conversation with her. But no, he didn't touch her.'

Barclay wondered whether she could ever be sure. Really, truly sure.

'They were close,' Josephine said, as though reading Barclay's mind. 'She always said that the things he was accused of weren't true. That her dad wouldn't do that. But me... well, I always felt...'

She stopped herself. Stared at the lino.

'Felt what?'

'I don't know how to put words to it. But I felt, after Amy was born, when I became a mum, that something was wrong with him. I thought it was all in my mind.'

Barclay had read about these signals our bodies can send to our mind in instances where a person may have crossed paths with a murderer, a rapist, some other suspect character. These signals were warning signs that something was off about them. How this fear was important for our survival. Something evolutionary. The reason we say we don't get good vibes from someone, or about a particular place.

He nodded.

'Thank you,' he said. 'You've told me some really important information here.' He took one last sip of his lukewarm tea. 'I'd say I'm sorry for your loss...'

'Yeah. I wouldn't bother. I've wasted enough tears over that man.'

Barclay climbed into his car and as he drove away, he processed everything that had been said. Knew he'd need to look further into Charles James Heaton. His phone rang through the speakers.

'Nick, I'm at work.'

'I need to see you. We need to talk.'

'What's happened? Is Sarah okay?'

'She's fine. It's not about her. Could you come the house?'

He closed his eyes and breathed out his relief. 'Nick, I'm working... what's this about?'

'Just come. Please.'

The house looked like home, maybe a few things were moved, or a new plant added into a corner. Nick was obsessed by a shop he'd found in South Liverpool, Chandler's. 'It sells the best house plants,' he'd said. But something had changed. It felt different, and Barclay found it difficult to realise that things had continued on in his absence.

Every house had its own scent: air fresheners, deodorants, washing detergent. Each one its own unique blend, and he thought he knew what his home had smelled like. But as he stepped inside, it smelled so different. So unlike it did when he had left. He couldn't put his finger on it.

When Nick opened the door, he wasn't smiling. He couldn't remember the last time he'd seen his partner's eyes light up in happiness, the last time a smile bounded across his face, or his his eyes crease up with laughter. He wondered whether that had changed too.

'Nick, I can't just come around in the middle of the day when I'm working.'

'I know and I'm sorry,' Nick said. He led Barclay through to the kitchen and invited him to sit down at the table they'd picked out together. There were fresh flowers in a vase on top of it. Lilies. Nick's favourite. Barclay had always thought they smelled like soap.

'What's going on?'

'We need to talk about what we're going to do next, Ben. With us. With Sarah.'

'What do you mean? It sounds like you don't want to... fix this?'

'There's nothing left to fix, I don't think,' Nick said. 'We're in different places. Different spaces. I'm back at work at the gallery now and when I come home it's peaceful here. It's relaxing. Even when Sarah's having a mad hour.'

'You don't miss me then?'

Quiet. Nick stared at him, and for the first time Barclay felt like those eyes were cold. Unloving. Distant. 'I miss you,' Nick said, finally. 'But not enough. Not like I thought I would.'

That hurt. 'You called me out of work for this?' His voice was thick with agony, and he felt tears building. This was it. The moment that Barclay had dreaded the most. The awful, heart-breaking ending to their marriage.

Nick moved to him, and held him close. 'I know this is going to be difficult.'

'You're the love of my life, Nick. I can't see myself without you. Without our family.'

Barclay held back his tears, breathed in long and hard and caught the smell of Nick. Sweet and warm. Like the house. It had felt like years since he'd last held his husband.

There was a new strength in Nick that Barclay hadn't felt before. Something in the way he held himself. In how he moved. A type of confidence.

'You'll be okay,' Nick said. He moved away from Barclay now. His T-shirt had risen when he hugged Barclay, and he pulled it back down. 'Is there anything I can do?'

There was so much Barclay wanted to say, wanted to ask. Help, support: yes. But his love. His kisses. Their bed with Nick asleep next to him. He swallowed down the words. 'No. I don't think so. But… could I maybe come for dinner one night this week, with you both?'

Nick smiled. 'Yeah. Sarah would love that.'

Me too.

Barclay struggled against the waves of his emotions, and sobbed.

Nick moved in again and enfolded him.

Barclay's skin prickled, his eyes wet, his heart filled and swollen with feelings he couldn't name. Didn't care to. 'I miss you so much, Nick.'

A moment of quiet, where he felt the hot wet of tears seep through his cotton T-shirt. He ignored it and held on to his husband. When finally they looked at each other, Nick closed his eyes and kissed Barclay.

He didn't have the time for this. There were things to do. But somewhere on those lips he'd ached for, he laid down his worries, his duties, and surrendered.

Later, after a shower in the en suite, while Nick slept, his face pink and flushed, Barclay felt promise for the first time since he'd left their family home. The plant that he'd loved, which was once near death, now flourished on the window ledge. It had even started to flower. Barclay didn't know it could do that. There was a new hope in him that he hadn't expected to find just yet. In the future maybe, weeks down the line. There were things to work out: Nick would have to take back his words, his certainty that they were over, and finally they could move forward.

Nick used a particular scented shower gel. Flora Luminare from Molton Brown. Barclay rubbed it into his body, his hair, and hoped that he would be able to smell it on him for the rest of the day.

He sneaked out while Nick slept on and left a note on the kitchen table, reminding Nick about dinner later that week, and how much he'd loved being with him again. He'd written the note three times, certain that whatever he said about the sex they'd just had sounded ridiculous. Obvious. Somehow creepy.

He crumpled up the first two drafts and put them in his pocket. He'd throw them into the confidential waste bin when he got back to the office.

As he walked down the stairs and toward the front door, he realised why the place seemed so different, why it no longer smelled like his home.

It was him, or rather the absence of him.

His aftershave. His shower gel. His body. He wasn't there any more.

Everything inside, on the air, against the walls, was Nick and Sarah.

When he stepped outside into the afternoon, the clouds had cleared and the sky emerged the exact shade of the paint Barclay and Nick had picked for the downstairs loo. It had been dark in there and needed brightening up.

When he drove away from the house, Barclay had felt so certain that things were about to change. That something was on the verge of manifesting itself. The hope he'd felt, that someday very soon, he and Nick would be back together.

Where they belonged.

As he got nearer to the OCC, that hope began to weaken, started to dull. He pushed it aside. Tried to hone in on the work, on investigating Charles Heaton.

On his potential connection with the other victims.

Twenty-Two

The drive had tired de Silva out, and the seemingly unnecessary traffic on the motorway had made her grumpy, and she'd stopped once to use the toilet. She'd met Murphy in Nelson to update her, and was on the road later than she'd planned, and the coffee Lennox got her from the station kitchen was strong and bitter. She liked it so much, she asked for another, knowing full well it would cause her to stop on the drive home.

Once he'd wrapped everything up in Pendle, he'd offered to come down to Liverpool to help out. She'd refused, naturally. She didn't need his help, and she'd make that very clear when she spoke to Murphy face-to-face.

Before she left, she mentioned Meeks to him. 'He tried to force himself into that case in Wales we spoke about. Just, you know, if he shows up. Let me know.'

He'd smiled those perfect teeth. 'Of course,' he said. He was attractive. There was no getting away from that.

She pulled up into a parking space outside the OCC and headed inside. It was just after one in the afternoon, but she felt the need to go home to bed already. But Laney was at home. She'd maybe want to talk over things again, begin to make sense of what had happened to her. De Silva would sit and listen, of course she would, but she needed rest. Needed to close her eyes from the things happening around her.

The basement incident room was loud with chatter that de Silva couldn't quite discern as she stepped out of the lift. 'Too much chatting in here, not enough work,' she joked.

'There are more.' Barclay sprang out of his chair when he saw her. The smile wide on his face. 'There's more of them, look.'

He led her across to the evidence boards, where Braxton and McLachlan were sticking up photographs and making notes. 'What am I looking at?' she asked.

'Three of them,' McLachlan said. 'All missing middle fingers. All previously lived in or close to Merseyside and then moved away. Moved to Scotland, Yorkshire, Somerset.'

The information was coming fast, and de Silva's head was still swimming from the drive, from the crime scene in Pendle. *Six of them*, she thought. *So far*. 'What about their fingers? Posted to loved ones?'

'We're working on it,' Barclay said. 'We're still trying to find anything on the PNC and the national database about anyone local receiving a finger in the post.'

'It's in there.' De Silva was sure of it. 'Might just need to work on the search parameters.' She'd found that some keywords didn't match exactly with what was written in reports. Spelling mistakes, usually, but sometimes the officer who wrote the report had used slightly different, or even out-dated, terminology. She'd made a case for standardised language, but O'Brien had always felt that it was too constrictive. She'd dropped it. It was times like this, as she stood in the warm incident room with a machine that was supposed to make searching archive records easier, that she wished she hadn't dropped it. Another thing to speak to Murphy about.

'Who are they?' she asked.

'Sharon McEntire. Previously lived in Liverpool city centre, but moved to a village in Scotland called Killin in 1996. Found dead in 2001,' Barclay said.

'John Abbot, formerly of Rainhill, moved to Bradford in '97, body found 2009,' McLachlan added.

O'Connor said, 'And Terry Peters, used to live in Speke. He left for Chard in Somerset in '95, his body was found in 2010.'

'What was the timeline between the murder and the bodies being found, do we know?'

'Days,' Barclay said. 'Nothing like our vic in the woods. All of them were dismembered. *Except* our original vic.'

De Silva frowned, the tension focused her mind. 'You see it written down like that. Coupled with the body potentially from the nineties. With both Heaton and Finch also leaving the area around that time...'

Barclay nodded. 'There's a link there.'

'A pretty obvious one.' She looked at the timeline of events scrawled out on the evidence board. 'Something happened around this time. That's clear. But look, Finch left in 1992. A good few years before the others. We find why she left, we might just be a step closer to what's going on here.'

'And the middle fingers?'

De Silva shook her head. 'That's the part I can't figure out. Out of all of this, we know that the middle finger was taken from all victims, but as far as we know, only one victim's family has received it by post.' She took a breath. 'We need to know if the families of *these* victims ever got anything in the post, Barclay. All of you.'

'We'll get on it,' Barclay said. 'There's one more thing.'

De Silva smiled. 'There always is,' she said. 'Go on.'

'Jacob Meeks,' he said simply. 'His name crops up in the investigation notes of each of these three cases.'

'Of course it does,' she said. 'So we'll speak to him today.'

'It might be worth us speaking to the families of these victims, too? Understand why they left the area,' Barclay asked.

'Dredging up stuff from over twenty years ago.' De Silva puffed her cheeks and blew out until her lips smacked together. 'I know we have to do it. Hopefully they'll have good memories.'

'I don't think you could easily forget the death of a loved one,' Barclay said. 'Especially one that died like this.'

The implication in Barclay's words was clear, de Silva thought: *you* wouldn't forget. But see that's the thing. Memory and facts are two distinct things. The facts are cold, they are what they are. But memory is different. It's warmed by emotion, made fluid by time, made inaccurate by our own interpretation of the facts.

The desktop phones rang out in unison. Braxton got to his first. 'Braxton speaking.' He nodded, as though the person on the other end could see him. 'Yes, ma'am.'

Murphy.

'The DSI wants to see you both.'

'Did she say why?'

'She didn't, and I wasn't about to ask her.' Braxton chuckled. 'She scares me, and I don't mind telling you.'

De Silva glanced at Barclay, and she recognised that look in his eyes. The same thought had crossed her own mind.

What now?

Murphy looked like she hadn't slept. Her eyes were pink, almost bloodshot, and the skin around them was puffed and dark. She needed to drag a brush through her hair, but de Silva would keep that to herself.

'Come in, come in.' She was jittering. Her hands moving in quick, nervous motions. A half-empty mug of coffee sat on her desk. The milk had settled in a pale ring on top, but the smell of the coffee permeated the room. 'Sit down.'

'Is everything okay, ma'am?' Barclay frowned as he took in the scene.

'No. Everything is not fine.' She slumped into her office chair, and for a moment de Silva thought she'd see some weakness in her. 'The National Crime Agency have had me running around here, there and everywhere just to accommodate their needs while they're here. I feel like their bloody PA.' She looked at them both, then sat up straight, tucked in her shirt and clasped her hands together. 'They're going to want to speak to you both again,' she said quietly.

'I'm not sure there's anything else I can say,' de Silva said. She knew she sounded combative, unhelpful, but it was also the truth. She'd told them everything she knew. Other than the obvious. Ritchie's attendance at that school didn't mean there was a direct involvement with him and what happened last year. No link between him and Crosby.

She was convinced that, in all their years of friendship, Crosby and Ritchie would have recognised each other. Surely. Their names would have kicked off some memory in each other's minds. She'd met Crosby at work, had known him for years before she even introduced him to Ritchie, and when she did there was no flicker of recognition on their faces. She'd have picked up on it. Wouldn't she?

'Yes,' Murphy said. 'I feel the same about this whole thing. They've looked into the hack, given that the perpetrator of the hack accessed your files specifically.'

Barclay sat up straight to match Murphy. 'Do they think there's a link?'

'Do you not?' Murphy snorted a laugh. 'Come on now. It's already crossed your minds, I know it. And if it hasn't, I'd have to question your current roles.'

De Silva and Barclay exchanged a glance.

'Of course we've thought about it,' de Silva said. 'Did they find anything?'

'No.' She shook her head. 'Unsurprising.'

'I doubt they'd tell us even if they did.' De Silva picked at the cuticle on her thumb. 'I'm still not sure I know why they're here.'

'Yes,' Murphy said. 'Or their reason for being here is becoming less obvious, and of course they don't have to share anything with us. They're not obliged. I hate to ask this,' she said. 'Is there anything either of you have held back on? Something you've not told them.'

'No!' Barclay almost shot out of his chair.

De Silva shook her head.

'Because if there is, I'd hate to be blind-sided. I'm here for you both as much as they think I'm there for them. You both are my primary concern, though. I'll have your back.'

De Silva's chest tightened like a hand had clamped around her lungs. Did she know? Had Murphy guessed that de Silva had been dishonest, that there was some link between her dead husband and the Lamond case?

She'd known all along that the closer she got to answers, the more likely it was that someone would discover that Detective Chief Inspector de Silva's dead husband was connected to Rainford Lane School for Boys.

'De Silva?'

'No.' She said it too quickly, she sounded almost like Barclay had. Defensive. 'No, there's nothing.'

Murphy stared into de Silva's eyes for just a few moments longer than felt comfortable. 'Right,' she said. She opened her top drawer and took out a manila file and slid it across the desk.

De Silva thought that Murphy may be the last person to use a printer in the building, other than Barclay. He liked it in his hands. 'What is it?'

'This came into my email this morning and it's been logged on the PNC and database within the last half hour,' Murphy said. 'Your Jacob Meeks.'

De Silva felt Barclay's eyes burn into the side of her head.

He reached over and grabbed the file. 'That name. Again and again.' Then he opened the file and his eyes went wide.

'You'll be wanting to get down there now, I assume,' Murphy said.

'Yeah,' Barclay said.

He handed the file to de Silva.

A body had been found in a flat early this morning, when blood had leaked through a downstairs neighbour's bathroom ceiling.

The victim had been hit over the head. His limbs and head dismembered from the torso and left in the bath.

The victim's middle finger had been taken.

The victim had been identified as Jacob Meeks.

Twenty-Three

'What do you think this means?' Barclay asked. He had that edge of nervousness, anxiousness in his voice he had whenever something new cropped up.

'I don't know.' De Silva turned onto the main road and put her foot down, slightly above the speed limit. 'It doesn't make sense.'

'It doesn't make sense or we can't make sense of it?' He said it to himself, but de Silva smirked.

'Oh he's getting philosophical: God help us all.'

His face turned pink. 'You know what I mean.'

'I do.' She sighed.

She felt herself drift off. Out of the car. To her interactions with Meeks. Was there something he'd said that could shed a light on why they were on their way to investigate his murder? She couldn't remember anything that stood out.

She swerved a pothole in the road and it brought her back to herself.

'What are you thinking?' Barclay asked.

'I'm not too sure.' She paused. 'The reason he does what he does, our killer I mean, can't be the same as why he's chosen to murder Jacob Meeks, surely? Why him? If they're connected, I mean.'

'Well, we spoke to him about his involvement with the cases we're investigating, and he shows up dead. Not much of a stretch to say they're connected,' Barclay said. 'I noticed that our known victims are of similar ages. And as we know, all of them had moved away from Merseyside in the 1990s. All except for Meeks. He's moved around, but never away. Plus he's a minimum of about twenty to thirty years younger than the previous victims.'

'So why him?' Another pause. 'Did you manage to track down the detectives who took over the case after you were reassigned to the Lamond murders?'

'No,' he said. 'They resigned, I know that. Young to retire. Late thirties, early forties.'

'I'll pay O'Brien a visit. See what he can recall.' She'd intended to see him Friday, but she'd have to change her plans. In truth, she was worried about seeing him. She felt guilty for not reaching out sooner, for being a bad friend to him when he clearly needed her. Needed someone.

Although she didn't hold out much hope for that. If he'd known something, he'd have come forward earlier, given her any key information she could use. Still, a face-to-face conversation might help jog his memory.

O'Brien was getting old, she reasoned with herself, his memory not quite what it once was. The case was only last year, and it was massive for the force, all over the news with lots of media attention. Surely he'd remember.

'That's a good idea,' Barclay said.

De Silva mm-hmm'd. 'I just have this feeling,' she said.

De Silva thought about the moment Murphy had slid the report across her desk from the first responder at Meeks's flat. The panic, the horror, was written there in the black ink of her words.

Bloodied. Hacked. Leaked. Screamed. All past-tense verbs depicting the terror of the moment the first responder discovered Meeks's body.

She glanced at the map on the dashboard screen. They were less than a minute away from their final destination, and the anticipation in the car was thick.

De Silva parked up outside of the police cordon, where passers-by had stopped with their phones out, recording, photographing, posting to socials. She knew it wouldn't be long before the media arrived, swooping in like scavengers.

Area Forensics Manager Brennan approached them, already in his white suit. 'You'll want to suit up.' He pointed at a small white tent next to the main, larger one which covered the entrance to the building. 'I'll catch you inside. Brace yourself.'

De Silva noticed that Brennan locked eyes with Barclay when he said this and as he walked away she laughed.

'Jesus,' Barclay said. 'You faint at a post-mortem just *once*, and nobody forgets.'

De Silva patted him on the shoulder. 'They'll forget. In about ten years.'

'Great.'

'In the meantime, Post-Mortem Princess, we've got some work to do.'

Barclay locked step with her. 'Please don't start calling me that.'

'Oh, I didn't start it.' De Silva tore into a clear plastic bag and slid herself into the suit.

'Well... well, who started it?'

'Snitches get stitches, Barclay. I'm no grass.' She nodded to the suit he held in his big hands. 'Come on, get a move on. I'm not waiting for you.'

'You've got to tell me.'

'Not a chance.'

De Silva was suited up and pulling on the blue shoe covers before Barclay had even opened the bag containing his suit. She rolled her eyes as he climbed into it and pulled it around himself, fastened it tight like a second skin.

As they walked into the tent at the entrance of the building, the world outside fell away. The noise of the street seemed to dull, the seagulls that inhabited areas further in-land every year fell quiet and the rumble of cars from the main road had gone.

De Silva felt that familiar shift within her. Like her skin had hardened, her stomach tensed, her lungs barely moving, heart a dull thump-thump under her rib cage. She'd become a calm, solid thing. Ready for whatever was up those stairs.

'So, you're going to tell me, aren't you?'

'Not now, Barclay, for God's sake.'

They headed for the lift, and found that it had been blocked off, turned into a crime scene all its own. De Silva knew why. The lift would be the quickest route in and out of the building. If the suspect was looking for a speedy escape, this would be it. Inside there could be a shoe print, a piece of fibre or blood from the victim.

De Silva leaned in, looked up into the back corners of the lift and spotted a security camera. *Good.* If he entered or left this way, he'd have been recorded. Hopefully, they'd get a description. Hair colour at least. She'd once witnessed a forensics analyst determine a suspect's shoe size from an image captured on a doorbell camera, based on his perceived height and build in relation to the measurements of a victim's front door.

It could be done.

'Looks like we're taking the stairs,' Barclay said over her shoulder. He took them two at a time and reached the first landing while she was still halfway up the first set.

She made a mental note to start running again. She'd loved it once, but she was younger then. Her body able to cope. Now it ached and begged her to stop.

The fifth-floor landing crawled with people in white suits. In and out. Collecting samples in metal cases, changing out batteries on digital SLRs, or carrying in additional lighting rigs. Despite the activity, the place was almost silent except for the click of cameras and the gentle shush of their crime scene suits as they moved through the flat like spectres.

De Silva heard Brennan now. 'Make sure you go over that bathroom again. I don't want to miss anything.' He walked out into the living room area as de Silva and Barclay walked through. 'There's a lot in there,' he said. 'We're going to be here for some time.'

'As long as everything is catalogued,' de Silva said. 'Will we be in your way if we take a look around?'

'Just don't touch anything. We're still cataloguing.'

De Silva had always been the type of person who needed to touch in order to feel a connection. When she was a kid, she didn't understand why she couldn't touch a painting in a gallery, or run her hands along some long-dead Egyptian's sarcophagus in the World Museum. There was so much information held in brush strokes, in the layers of acrylic paint, in the rough edges of stone, it seemed a shame to her not to experience it all.

But, in the instance of a victim dismembered in his own bathtub, she kept her hands at her sides, though her fingers twitched to experience something other than the thin protective gloves she wore.

She moved to the bookshelves and scanned them quickly. Every book was about some sort of conspiracy, authored by someone who claimed to know some element of truth that the rest of us didn't.

'You know what's weird?' Barclay's voice from behind her.

'Other than this bookshelf?'

'Out here, there are no signs of struggle.'

He was right. Everything was in order and appeared to be in its place. She ran a finger across the shelf in front of her. No dust. Whatever he was, Meeks was a clean man. He liked things in order. The only things out of place were two glasses of water, both full, on the coffee table near the couch.

De Silva slipped into that space where her mind formed pictures and developed them into colour. She imagined Meeks on the couch, reading a book from his shelves. A knock would have come from the door. Maybe he'd buzzed the person up from outside, or maybe they'd tail-gated when someone left or arrived.

Either way, Meeks would have opened the door and let the person in. They'd have talked for a moment, he'd have poured his guest a glass of water and one for himself, then placed them down, on coasters of course, on the coffee table. He'd have known this person, maybe even expected their arrival.

She imagined Meeks excusing himself to go to the bathroom. The killer kicked down the door, splinters flew in the air as Meeks spun around from the sink where he was washing his hands. The killer, to de Silva just a black silhouette, moved quickly. Swung something he'd have brought with him and smacked Meeks in the side of the head.

She took a look underneath the couch, but there was nothing there, just a strand of white string. But there was no dust, no crumbs from dinner last week, nothing he might have dropped and forgotten about.

'There was a corkboard under there,' Brennan said from the bathroom door. 'One of my SOCOs found it. It's been catalogued already, so it's downstairs.'

'What was on it?'

'I didn't see it,' Brennan admitted. 'I'll let you know when we've processed it.'

De Silva nodded. She turned to the desk on the wall near the front door, which looked brand new, as though never used, and in the top drawer she found three packets of antibacterial wipes, only one of which was open.

'I need to see the bathroom now,' she said. At the door she said to Brennan, 'Could I have just a few minutes alone? I promise I'll be quick.'

'Just don't—'

'Touch anything, yeah I know.'

The white suits filed out but Barclay stood in the doorframe, arms folded, and watched.

She took it in. The blood all over the bathroom floor, which had seeped through into the bathroom downstairs. She spotted hair on the edge of the sink, imagined Meeks being hit by the killer, then falling down, his knees having given up, his head bouncing off the edge of the basin. Bloody fingerprints on the base of the otherwise pristine, white plinth. He'd been conscious at some point. Struggled from the floor.

She shuddered as she imagined him still awake, still able to understand that he was in pain, that he would likely die, while the killer went to work on his head or arms. The scene was rushed. There was no attempt to remove the body from where he was killed, to take it somewhere and bury it. Like the others. This felt different to her. Not like the others.

'What're you thinking?' Barclay asked.

'Necessity,' she said. She moved toward the door, slipped off one shoe covering at a time and replaced them with new ones on a table just outside the door.

'You done?' Brennan asked, eager to get back to it.

'Yeah,' she said. 'Thanks.'

'What do you mean, necessity?' Barclay asked.

'This is different,' she said. 'There's no... end to this. It's violent and bloody, and it looks like our other victims, doesn't it? But it's not. His body wasn't taken away and buried somewhere public, and if the killer was disturbed by someone else, then that person would have called the police. But they didn't, because he wasn't. I think he was murdered for another reason.'

Twenty-Four

There was an air of anticipation in the incident room, keen and almost static. Barclay felt it the moment he walked in. He looked around but couldn't see Lawrence. He imagined her now, sitting in one of the break rooms, calling him the Post-Mortem Princess. Laughing about it. With people he didn't know, people who didn't know him.

Paranoia talking. Lawrence was one of the good ones, he knew that.

'Listen up.' De Silva's voice grabbed the detectives' attention. 'Jacob Meeks, thirty-seven years old. His head removed from his body. Middle finger of the right hand taken. We're working on the assumption that it was someone he knew. So far, we know this MO, don't we? Though the killer's "work" was incomplete, we can work under the assumption that this *could* be him.'

Barclay recognised that she had been careful with her language. Assumption. Could be.

De Silva went to the evidence boards. To the other victims, Finch, the man in the woods whose name they didn't yet know. 'The victims get older as the years go on.'

She was right, of course. Finch had been in her sixties when she was murdered. The man in the woods was, according to Carey's estimations, in his mid-thirties to early forties. Heaton, the most recent victim before Meeks, was almost seventy.

'So what're we saying?' O'Connor asked.

'Well,' Barclay chimed in. 'It's either that he doesn't have a victim type at all, and the progression in age is just coincidence, or that as he gets older, he craves an older victim. Something about the years between them? The age gap? But that doesn't explain Meeks.'

'I don't think so,' de Silva said. 'Meeks may have been killed by our suspect. We can't be certain that's what we're dealing with. Not yet.'

Braxton called out, 'If it is the same fella, then why the break in his pattern in terms of age?'

'I don't think Meeks is part of the suspect's pattern. I think he was murdered for some other reason. We know he was investigating these murders, or present shortly after the victims were found.' She turned to face the room then. 'Braxton, O'Connor, I want you looking into Meeks now. Known associates, friends, family. I need you to find any matches between his life and the lives of any of these other victims.'

'Sure,' Braxton said.

Barclay approached de Silva and lowered his tone. 'What do you think is happening here?'

'I'm not sure yet, but I've got this hunch.'

Barclay knew from experience that de Silva's hunches were very rarely wrong. He struggled to peel his eyes away from de Silva's face, her cheeks flushed red with the rush of theory, of investigation.

'What do you need me to do?' Barclay asked.

'Carry on with what you're doing,' she said.

He sat down at his desk and opened his computer. Instead of working, he thought of Nick, the solace he'd found in him, in the bed they'd shared until just two weeks ago. How familiar it had felt, how his husband had touched him just how he liked. But there had been something in Nick's eyes at the moment they both came. Barclay had reflected on it since.

It was a sadness. A regret. Maybe, he supposed, a wish that it had never happened. That a line had been crossed. Nick had read and not replied to Barclay's last message. The *I love you x* sat there in their chat, naked and unacknowledged.

He checked his phone again. Still no reply. He wanted to call Nick, tell him he loved him and hear him say it back. But maybe Nick needed space, time to process that they'd had sex, that he did, in fact, still love Barclay, and what that meant for their separation. For himself, for Barclay. For Sarah. That little life at the centre of it all.

When they'd adopted her, there was no thought that they'd ever separate. It was an impossible scenario they'd laughed off when the social worker had asked about the stability of their relationship. Barclay had been offended, affronted even, but Nick had talked him around.

'It's just her job,' he'd said. 'It's not personal, and no it's not because we're gay. She has to do the right thing for everyone. Us and whoever we get to adopt.'

Barclay went through the process, the whole thing, knowing that he didn't want kids. Still, he went through the motions. Said the right things. Just because it was what Nick wanted. He'd never intended to be a father, he just wanted to live his life. There was damage done to him by his parents, the way he'd been raised, their own divorce. His dad had moved on so quickly with a new family and he'd barely seen him after that.

He didn't want that for any kid.

But when he met her, this shy little dark-haired girl with eyes the colour of melted caramel, something drew him in. He'd wondered what that force was, and finally on her last birthday, when she blew out the candles and said, 'Thank you, Daddy,' and hugged him close, he knew.

It was the need to protect her. To show her that things can last, relationships can endure, love can conquer everything and happiness is as solid as stone.

He'd failed her.

He'd left her.

He didn't fight Nick when he'd wanted him to go.

He should have.

He wondered what she felt, what she thought about the separation, about her daddy no longer being there for breakfast, of sharing a bed with him in a box room at her nanna's house.

He wondered whether she was embarrassed by him. Whether she knew what embarrassment was. Or whether, like he hoped, she loved him anyway.

He had to believe that he and Nick would get back together, where they belonged. Sarah would be happy and safe.

Trust in their reunion was all he had left.

He heard de Silva's voice, clear as day through the fog of his own mind. 'We've got to go,' she said. 'That was Brennan. Wants to see us.'

She had hold of her phone, but Barclay was certain he hadn't heard it ring. He nodded, tried to lift himself from the murk of his own life into the gloom of his work. 'Do you think they've found something?'

De Silva shrugged. 'Most likely.' He followed her out to the lift.

Barclay pressed the button for the ground floor. He checked his watch. 'We should miss the traffic,' he said. 'Shouldn't take us long.'

De Silva jiggled her keys in her pocket. She did that when she wanted to drive. She'd said once, 'You drive like my grandad used to, Barclay,' and that had stuck with him. He didn't think he drove badly, but yes he did stick to the limit, always indicated and never ever touched his phone while he was driving, unless a call came through on the car's screen.

They passed the first five minutes of the drive in silence. Normally, she'd put the radio on to fill the gap in conversation, but she was clearly caught up in her own thoughts, and Barclay was glad of the quiet.

'The middle finger,' she said finally. 'You think it's as Meeks said, a "fuck you"?'

'It could be,' he said. 'We don't know anything for certain.'

'I feel certain, Barclay.'

He nodded. 'Go on...'

'I think the key is in what these people have in common. It's a "fuck you" to them,' she said.

Barclay felt as though she was clearing through her thoughts, trying to organise them out loud, hoping something would click.

'But it's bigger than that,' she continued. 'There are so many of them. A "fuck you" to something they were all a part of. They all shared.'

Barclay had already considered it. 'Yeah, there's a reason they all left Merseyside within a few years of each other.'

'Something they did, maybe,' de Silva said. 'Something they were involved in. Something our killer knew about. Maybe belonged to himself.'

That stuck in Barclay's mind. He'd considered all of this before. It was obvious, almost a foregone conclusion. He hoped that by the time they got back from Brennan's lab, O'Connor, Braxton and the others would have had another break in the case. Something to lead them down an avenue of investigation that didn't feel like just pissing into the wind.

The lab was cold compared to outside. Barclay felt the skin on his arms prick, his chest hair bristle against his T-shirt.

'What have you got for us?' de Silva asked.

Brennan nodded toward his office off the main lab area, where technicians worked away at machines Barclay didn't recognise and frowned at evidence under microscopes.

'Need to be quick,' he said. 'Lots to get through. We'll be working overtime.' He closed the office door and eyed de Silva. There was something nervous about him, something in the way he moved, shoulders hunched, his fingers fidgeting. 'Take a seat.'

De Silva sat first, but Barclay stood near the door. 'What have you got for me?' she asked.

'Size nine shoe prints,' he said. 'The victim was size seven. These are Nike trainers that don't match any in the flat. They belong to someone who was in the flat at the time of the death or shortly after. We know that because the prints were recovered from the blood in the bathroom.'

'We'll do a recce of anyone in the building,' Barclay said. 'Get them to you for comparison.'

'Thank you.'

'We found some hair on the sink, I'm sure you saw that.' He sighed and leaned back in his chair. 'We're confident it belongs to the victim, but we're running DNA comparison to be sure.'

'Anything else?' de Silva asked.

'Some fibres. We're running them now, comparing them to the victim's clothing, anything we found in his washing basket.'

The fibres would less likely belong to clothes folded away in drawers or in his wardrobe, unless he'd done some laundry on the day. Barclay supposed that failing any positive match, that's where they'd test next, to eliminate anything from inside Meeks's flat.

'We found them in the bathroom and also on the couch,' Brennan said.

'Is that it?' de Silva asked, impatience in her voice. 'You could have put all of this in an email, or we'd have read it in your report. Don't tell me you dragged us over here for this.' She laughed, and Barclay thought it was her attempt at trying to take the edge off her comment.

'There is something else.' Brennan avoided de Silva's eyes now. Clasped his fingers together. 'I've not shared this with anyone else yet,' he said. 'But you have to understand that it has to go into my report. I have no choice in that, as you know, and I'm sure you'd want all of the evidence out there so you can catch this bastard.'

De Silva sat up straight. 'What is it?'

'It's... delicate, I suppose. I wanted you to see it before anyone outside of this lab.'

'What is it?' she asked again, that impatience back in her voice.

'But it will be in my report to you, and as you know, Murphy and the Chief Constable are copied in on that. I know the NCA are involved in all of this, and Murphy will ask me to share it with them too.'

'Brennan!'

'Come with me,' he said.

He walked out of his office, held the door open for them and led them through to an area of the lab that was all glass windows. Inside was evidence from Meeks's flat. A rug, the coffee table, two glasses, the books from the shelf that Barclay had seen de Silva studying.

And a corkboard. Brennan stood by it, though it had been turned so that the back faced them.

'What is this?' Barclay asked.

Brennan said, 'This is the board I told you about at Meeks's flat.' He turned it around.

It was a network of maps, photographs, names, all linked together by lines of string, stuck on by tacks. There were newspaper articles, one for each of the victims that they'd found, and some they didn't yet recognise. There was a darker patch, where the sun had not touched the cork in years. 'This here,' Brennan said, pointing at the patch. 'Something was removed from here.'

'By the victim?'

'Can't be sure. Though we did find a tack on the floor.'

'That's not something Meeks would have stood for,' de Silva said. 'Did you see that flat? It was pristine.'

Barclay saw it, and Brennan noticed that he'd spotted it and his face fell. 'De Silva...'

'What?'

'Look.'

She did. She studied the board, her eyes flitting from photograph to name to map. And finally, she settled on it and she barely breathed.

There, on the corkboard, a line running from the photographs and newspaper reports back to one single point. A class photograph from Rainford Lane School for Boys.

And beneath it, a photograph that was unmistakable. Barclay had met him only once, in passing, when he'd picked de Silva up for work because her car was in for its MOT.

Below the picture of the toothy youngster, a name.

Richard de Silva.

Twenty-Five

De Silva hadn't been able to look at him. In truth, he hadn't been able to look at her either, though for different reasons, she assumed.

The car journey back was in complete silence, but inside her mind the noise was unyielding. The constant chatter of her inner critic. It knew the truth of her, that she was a liar, that she'd do anything to protect her dead husband's memory, protect herself, protect her own interests in this case since before the NCA showed up and ruined everything.

She'd dropped him at the OCC, and said, 'I'm going to need to take some time.' She didn't wait for a response, but knew what Barclay must have been thinking. He'd have thought that this would be too much for her. The weight of finding her dead husband's name and school photograph on the corkboard of a murdered internet sleuth would be too much. That, once again, de Silva would retreat back into herself, into the recesses of her grief and possibly into the bottle.

In truth, though it had crossed her mind, she had no desire to do any of that. The guilt was too much. She'd lied to him. Perjured herself to the NCA. Had been dishonest with her superior officer.

The scaffold of her lies, the truth only she knew, would fall and all of this would come crashing down around her. She'd have to tell the truth about her dead husband's connection to Lewis Lamond, to former-DCI Crosby. And now, his link to the case they had started to investigate before Ritchie had even died.

For her, there was only one place she thought to go. Not home, not to the off-licence and the empty, dry end of a bottle of Pinot Grigio and not back into the black of her grief.

—

O'Brien's face dropped when he found de Silva standing on his doorstep. He took her into his arms immediately. 'My God, Win. What's wrong?' There was genuine panic in his voice 'What's happened? Never mind, come in. Come in.' He pulled her inside his house, through to the kitchen and put the kettle on.

'I needed someone to talk to,' she said. Her voice sounded thick with the swell of her guilt, and for the first time since leaving the OCC, she felt the wet warmth of tears on her cheeks.

O'Brien put a steaming mug of tea in front of her, and next to it a glass milk bottle, the kind she hadn't seen since the nineties, when she'd run down to bring it in before anyone else had the chance to. He sat down next to her. 'Now come on, it can't be all that bad. It's not like you've murdered someone. Jesus, Win, tell me you haven't.'

She laughed in spite of herself. 'No,' she said. 'Although I think DSI Murphy may think it's worse.'

O'Brien looked at her side on, eyebrows arched. Expectant. 'Well, what've you done?'

'I lied to Barclay. I lied to Murphy. I've withheld key information about a case from the National Crime Agency.'

O'Brien was silent, his mouth open just slightly. Any further and he'd be able to catch flies. 'So it is as bad as all that. Win, what were you thinking? Were you even thinking?'

'No,' she said. 'No, I don't think I was. Not properly.'

'Talk me through it.'

'You sure?'

'I'm not on the force any more; what're they gonna do, sack me for speaking to a friend?'

'Withhold your pension?'

'They can't do that! Can they do that? You're right, you'd best go.'

De Silva laughed again. O'Brien had that thing about him. He could use humour to diffuse tension; but, she knew from the many times she'd stood in his office, he could give you a bloody good telling-off if he needed to. And, more than anyone she knew, she needed a telling-off the most.

'Last year, when I tendered my resignation.' She took a deep breath. It had been the time she was ready to leave, put police work behind her. 'I was sorting through some of Ritchie's stuff. Found some old school reports, swimming certificates, all of that.'

'So?'

'From Rainford Lane School for Boys.'

O'Brien scanned de Silva's face, though what he was looking for, she didn't know. Her sanity, maybe. 'The same school that Lamond went to,' O'Brien said. He stood now, moved away from the table, one hand at the back of his neck. 'The place that pushed him over the edge.' O'Brien shook his head. 'Jesus, de Silva. Is that why you withdrew your resignation? To try to solve this yourself?'

De Silva looked away from him, ashamed. 'That place pushed Crosby over the edge, too,' she said. 'School mates, remember?'

O'Brien nodded. 'Was there never an inkling that they knew each other?'

'I've thought about it. Tried to replay every interaction I saw them have, and nothing stands out.'

'This is big, Win.' He moved back to the table and drained the tea from his cup. 'You have to go to Murphy with this. If she finds out later…'

'There's something else.'

O'Brien shook his head, took a deep breath, his shoulders squared as though bracing himself. 'Of course there's something else. There's always something else with you.'

'The murders we've been looking into. The man in the woods, the other victims we've found across the country. They're all connected. Somehow: we're not entirely sure how yet.'

'So?'

'So, someone was sure. One of the victims was on his way to figuring it out. Maybe already had done. See, he was an internet sleuth and—'

'He was a what?'

'An armchair detective,' she spat out. 'Anyway, he had this board. He'd connected each of the victims back to Rainford Lane School for Boys.'

His eyebrow arched again. 'That's interesting. Any evidence?'

'Well, no. But we've not had Holden look at his computer yet. It's in a queue.'

'I'd see if he can bump that up the queue. It could be key to your investigation.'

'There's something else.'

'Jesus Christ, Win, will you just spit it all out at once instead of this dramatic drip-feeding.'

'Ritchie was on that board.' Her voice was quiet now. 'That board ties him to the school. The cat's out of the bag, as they say. Everyone will know that Ritchie was somehow related to the school, to Lamond. To Crosby.'

'What was this victim's name?' O'Brien asked. 'The one with this board.'

'Meeks,' de Silva said. 'Jacob Meeks.'

'Meeks,' O'Brien repeated. 'Meeks.' As though searching his mind for recognition of the name. He added, 'I see. And you've come to ask me whether I think you should tell Murphy that you already knew or go on like this is new information to you?'

'No!' She took a breath. 'Yes. I'm an awful person, I know.'

'Awful?' He snorted a laugh. 'You're bloody terrible. De Silva the Diabolical, actually. But my honest advice?'

'Yeah.' She knew what he would say. She knew that no matter what, he would do the right thing. He'd tell her to do the right thing. That was how he was, how he'd always been.

'Keep it to yourself,' he said. 'What will come of you admitting the truth? You'll be booted off the case.'

Oh, she thought. This wasn't what she'd expected from O'Brien. He'd been her mentor throughout her career, he'd always steered her right and she'd always trusted it.

'Preserve your reputation. Move forward from now. This is new to you. Ritchie's connection to this is shocking, it's heart-breaking. And it's a mystery. Do you hear me?'

She heard him loud and clear.

'Now that's out of the way, can we please catch up?' He moved off to the kettle.

'There's just one more thing,' she said.

O'Brien sighed. 'Honestly, this behaviour needs to stop, Win.' He laughed. 'You need to come and see me when you're not about to burn your own house down.'

'The detectives who were assigned to the case me and Barclay started. The man in the woods.'

O'Brien looked down at the floor. 'I told you I can't remember.'

'I know, but we can't find them,' de Silva said. 'Anywhere. Who were they? It would be useful if we could speak to them.'

'It should all be on the record, de Silva, come on. You know that.'

'It isn't,' she said. 'Their names are. But who they are, where they worked, where they went, when they resigned, why they resigned, what they knew about the case. There's nothing there.'

'I don't know what you want me to say.'

'Do you remember anything about them?'

He exhaled through his nose. 'You know, my memory isn't what it was. A few years ago, I'd have had that information stored right up here.' He tapped the side of his head and winked. 'But now, it's all a blur. Like there's a mist.'

That stuck in de Silva's mind like a nail only half-hammered into a piece of wood. It would snag at her, tear her clothes and cut her skin. It was, she remembered with a sinking feeling, how her mother had described how she felt. Before the tests and the doctors and the eventual diagnosis. Before the slow deterioration into what she was now.

A lost mind in the body of her mum.

'That's okay,' de Silva said. If she forced him, it would make him distressed. Cause upset and frustration. Sure, having the information would help, but it wasn't the only thing they had. She made a mental note to check on him every other day. Keep an eye on how he was talking, the things he was talking about, any repetitions or confusion.

She checked her watch. 'I've got time for another brew if you want to put that kettle back on?'

—

De Silva didn't sleep much. The guilt of her lies lay next to her in bed and breathed loudly, letting her know it was still there. Still watching with eyes that shone like burning coals.

About two a.m., she to get out of bed, slide open the patio doors and sit on the tiny balcony overlooking the small park and the fishing lake. From here, she couldn't see the street. She was able to forget that she lived on a new-build estate with hundreds of other people. From here, she was alone.

The air was cold in her lungs and on her skin and she went back inside to pull a throw from the end of the bed to wrap around herself.

Sometime in the early hours, she found herself back in bed, the patio door wide open, the blanket still on the balcony. Her clock said it was 05:18 a.m., and she decided not to fight against her insomnia any more. It would win. It always had.

She turned the temperature on the shower to the lowest setting and stepped in, tried to breathe through the shock and washed herself quickly.

She checked in on Bonnie before she crept downstairs: she was still fast asleep. Her school uniform hung over the banister, just like Laney and de Silva's mum had done when they were young.

She grabbed her portable blender and some fruit from the bowl on the countertop and headed for the car. She liked driving early, when the roads were still quiet, when the eastern sky was lightened with shades of orange and pink even though sunrise wouldn't come for some time and people were still curled up in their beds.

In the incident room, someone had brought in Meeks's evidence board from Brennan's lab. He must have been finished with it. She wanted to go to it. To look at her Ritchie's face when he was just a boy, the face she'd seen so many times in her dreams.

Barclay sat at his desk, his head on his chin, his breathing slow and rhythmic. She almost didn't want to wake him. Almost. She put a hand on his shoulder and squeezed gently.

He started, almost jumped out of the chair, his head whipping around until he caught sight of her. 'De Silva, bloody hell! What're you doing here?'

'Couldn't sleep. What about you?'

Barclay shrugged, wiped at his mouth with his fingers. 'Same. I started looking at that CCTV footage from Meeks's building. Then, guess what? I fell asleep. Not in the comfort of my own bed, but in this place.'

De Silva felt that Barclay had said a lot with that one sentence. 'The footage is back already?'

'I asked them to rush it through, given what's going on.'

'Anything of note?'

'Seriously, what're you doing here?'

'I can't sit at home again, Barclay.' De Silva felt her face burn and knew it was guilt. 'I know it's only a matter of time before Murphy asks me to step back from the case. Professional distance, conflicts of interest and all of that. I want to be here while I can.'

'But he was your husband, de Silva. Tied up in all of this somehow. I never expected, when we were put back on this case, that it would connect back to Rainford Lane. To Lamond.'

'To Crosby,' she said. 'The NCA will come knocking soon, too.'

'Do you think Ritchie knew them? Like they were school mates?'

De Silva fell silent, couldn't look at him. 'It's something I've considered.' Another silence. She hoped that Barclay would read the awkwardness correctly: she didn't want to talk about this.

'Here.' Barclay spun his computer screen around to face de Silva. 'You see him come in in just a second. Takes the lift. Pick him up again outside of Meeks's flat, on the camera in the corridor there.'

De Silva watched. The man was tall. A hoody pulled up, head slightly bowed so that you couldn't make out his face. All in black. Purposefully nondescript. Even his trainers were black, but she couldn't make out the brand. In those shadows, she doubted whether anyone could determine his shoe size.

Barclay skipped ahead and pressed play after forty-seven minutes. The man stepped out of Meeks's flat into the corridor, closed the door behind him and walked back toward the lift. 'He leaves the building straight away. All done. In under an hour, de Silva.'

She found herself nodding. 'Yeah.' She paused. 'We need to get access to Meeks's phone records. See if he was expecting anyone, a delivery. Maybe a message from a friend or a phone call.'

'Already put the request in,' Barclay said. 'Doubt they'll pick it up before nine a.m., though. And even then, God knows how long before we get an answer.'

She mm-hmm'd. 'Do we have a full list of men who went missing in the nineties from the Merseyside area yet?'

'I think O'Connor completed it last night.'

'Good,' she said. 'Let's take a look at it.'

De Silva got to her feet and walked across to Meeks's evidence board. There was a man on it she didn't recognise. Even Charles Heaton had already made the board, linked back with string to Rainford Lane. There were pictures of Crosby and Lamond as kids, she wouldn't have recognised them, but their names were written underneath and pinned to the board.

'These two.' She pointed to one photograph of a boy named Billy Thompson, and then to an older man, a piece of string ran from his photograph to the headline about a man found in the local woods, and a question mark on a post-it next to his face. 'Neither of them are any of the other victims we've found. The younger one, I'd say, a pupil at the school maybe? The question mark, I assume, means Meeks wasn't able to track him. But this older guy, he's the odd one out here.'

'You're thinking he's our man from the woods?' Barclay approached, a tablet in his hands. 'Meeks appeared to think so.'

'We can't rule it out,' she said. 'But we also can't take for granted that Meeks was right.' She stared at the man's photograph, at his name written underneath. 'Bob Brendan,' she said. 'Is he on our list of missing men?'

Barclay swiped his finger on the tablet once, twice. 'Yeah,' he said. 'He's here.'

'Next of kin?'

'Listed as Mary,' he said. 'Mary Newton now, according to McLachlan and O'Connor's research. Remarried ten years ago.'

De Silva reached out and touched Bob Brendan's photograph, it had yellowed and started to stiffen. In the top right corner, the *Liverpool Journal*, dated 3 January 1997.

She stared at him, his balding head, his eyes that were bright even in the chrome blending of black and white.

'Who are you?'

Twenty-Six

Barclay's head bounced against the window as de Silva drove over a pothole. He'd left a round greasy stain on the glass and rubbed at it with his jacket sleeve. He'd not had much sleep, not since the text message came in just after midnight.

> What we did was a mistake. A moment of weakness. I think, for both our sakes, we need to carry on as we were. Let's rearrange dinner this week for another time.

Barclay had hoped that the time they'd spent together would lead to their reconciliation. Their little family of three would be together again. Forever. When he'd read Nick's words, Barclay had felt dirty. Cheap. Like all it was to Nick was a fuck, when it had meant so much more to Barclay.

He had typed and deleted so many words, unsure how Nick would take them. He swung between anger, regret and longing, and that dream of his family being one again took another step back into the shadows. In the end, he decided to leave it, hoped that the words he needed would find him at some point.

He'd lain awake the rest of the morning until his phone pinged again at one minute past four. He had grabbed it, hoping it was Nick. Instead, it was an email from the gym reminding him that his direct debit would come out soon.

In the end, he'd got in his car and headed to the OCC. At least he could do some work in those hours where sleep evaded him.

'That nap in your office chair catching up with you?' De Silva's voice was low, but clear.

He laughed. 'Yeah. Sorry. I'm rubbish company at the moment.'

'You think you're ever good company?'

'I'm the best company there is. You know that.' He laughed, but inside he knew the truth. He'd been sullen, miserable, distant. 'Just... you know, not this week.'

De Silva smiled. 'I'm saying nothing.' She pulled up alongside the kerb of a house with a long front garden. 'This is the one,' she said. 'Mary Newton.' Smoke billowed up from behind the house, light grey and stinking.

'Looks like they're having a barbeque.'

De Silva only glanced at him, her eyes wide, her mouth open, and Barclay knew what had crossed her mind. She was already out of the car, running up the drive, before Barclay had managed to open the passenger door.

Barclay jogged to catch up with her as she slammed her full weight into a side gate which swung on its hinges and clattered against the brick of the house. He followed de Silva around the side and out onto a flagged patio, where a log burner was alive with yellow and orange flames, where smoke unfolded itself and spread into the air.

De Silva screamed, 'Stop what you're doing!'

A woman stood next to two clear plastic boxes. One was completely empty, and she'd made a good start on the second box, all paperwork from what Barclay could tell. The woman screamed at the sudden sight of strangers in her garden. Broke into loud wails that echoed through the garden, reverberated off the fence panels, the colour of oak.

'Mrs Newton?' Barclay asked. He needed to be certain it was her. He took all of her in. She was tall, skinnier than she looked on her driving licence photo and her hair had turned grey in the years since. 'Step back from the fire,' he said. 'Put down the papers.'

De Silva snapped on some gloves and was already rooting through the box of paperwork at Mrs Newton's side. That put Barclay's teeth on edge. Potential evidence needed to be handled with care. She'd jumped straight in and now it could be contaminated.

'What's in the box, Mrs Newton?' He moved toward her, unclipped his cuffs from his belt and fixed them lightly around her wrists. Not usually necessary in these situations, but it would stop her from burning any more potential evidence. She sobbed, and for a moment, Barclay felt bad for her. 'Mrs Newton!'

'I'm sorry,' she managed. 'I'm sorry.'

Barclay manoeuvred her to a small wall on the edge of the patio and sat her down there. He kept an eye on her, but moved closer to de Silva. 'What have we got?'

'VAT receipts, stuff from the Inland Revenue, before it was HMRC, for a business called Rising Stars,' she said over her shoulder. She dug to the bottom of the small box, her watch clicking against the sides, and pulled out a leather-bound volume. She looked up at Barclay then.

'What is it?'

'Don't look in there,' Mrs Newton shouted. 'You're not supposed to look in there.'

De Silva opened the cover. Photographs of a man with hordes of kids. Camping trips, plays in an old assembly hall, him at a piano while kids stood around him, open-mouthed. Singing. 'That's Bob Brendan,' de Silva said.

'That's Rainford Lane School for Boys,' Barclay said. 'Look.'

De Silva turned page after page, scanning the background of each picture. Finally, she came to a newspaper clipping. *Prominent school awarded for changing youth lives.* Barclay felt his stomach lurch.

He turned back to Mary. She'd found something on the floor to focus on, her breathing irregular and catching in her throat. She was somewhere else, had removed herself from the garden, from the fire and the boxes of her husband's life.

—

De Silva turned on the heat in the interview room, higher than it needed to be. It was a trick they used to make the interviewee feel uncomfortable, on edge. More likely to get to the heart of things just to get out of the room.

'Would you like some water before we start?' de Silva asked.

Mary shook her head.

'Okay,' she said. 'And do you prefer Mrs Newton or Mary?'

Mary shrugged.

'I'll call you Mary then,' de Silva said. 'When we arrived at your property, we found you burning paperwork in your garden.'

Mary shrugged again.

De Silva slammed her hand onto the desk; the sound almost made Barclay jump, but he managed to keep his composure. 'This is very serious, Mary. You've chosen not to have a lawyer, but now you need to answer my questions.'

Mary locked eyes with de Silva now, and the two stared. There was a shift in Mary then, a kind of boldness that squared her shoulders and straightened her back.

'We arrived at your property to find you burning paperwork,' de Silva continued.

'That's not illegal,' Mary said.

'Destroying evidence is.'

'Evidence of what?'

'You tell us. We arrived after you'd destroyed a lot of it.'

'Mary, I'd strongly advise you to seek legal representation,' Barclay said. He almost felt bad for her. She was upset, distraught: in one day she'd found out that her husband who'd been missing for decades was, in fact, dead, and had been arrested herself.

'I haven't done anything wrong.' There was something in the way she said 'I'. An inflection or stress that made it clear that she was absolving herself of any wrongdoing, any part in the things that had happened at Rainford Lane School for Boys.

'Why don't you tell us about your husband,' de Silva continued. 'Robert Brendan.'

'Bob,' Mary corrected her. 'What do you want to know? He went missing in '97 and you told me today that you've found him dead. What else is there to say?'

'Not just dead,' Barclay said. 'Murdered.'

She looked at him then, her brown eyes looked almost black. 'Yes, you said.'

'Did Bob work at Rainford Lane School for Boys?'

Mary laughed, a cold sound that came from between her front teeth. 'He ran that godforsaken place. He loved it there. He turned those kids' lives around. He won an award. He dedicated his life to them.'

'Did you and he have children of your own?'

Mary looked away from the detectives. 'No,' she said. '*We* couldn't. *He* couldn't.'

'If I asked you what you burned, would you tell us?' de Silva asked.

Mary was silent for a moment, as though contemplating whether she would or wouldn't. 'I suppose it doesn't matter any more,' she said. 'There were things he asked me to do. In the event that he... you know...'

'Died?'

Mary nodded.

'What did he ask you to do?' Barclay asked.

'There were reports he'd written personally to kids' parents. Invoices from local businesses to the school. Donations. I suppose he didn't want any of that to come out.'

De Silva leaned in. 'Why do you think that was?'

Mary shrugged.

'Are you aware that there are reports of abuse at Rainford Lane? Accusations that the staff were abusing the boys?'

Another silence. Mary looked up at the clock on the wall to her left and watched the seconds tick by. 'You've got to understand what living with him was like. He made me promise. Made me swear.'

'You protected him.' Barclay made no attempt to keep the disdain from his voice.

She looked at him. 'I was his wife.'

'You're not now,' he said.

'You wouldn't understand,' she said. 'You people don't know anything about the work that comes with marriage. Loyalty. Respect. Love.'

Barclay's fists clenched under the coffee-stained table. She knew nothing about his life, about his troubles with Nick. 'What else did he make you do? Other than agree to destroy documentation?'

She looked away again, her jaw clenched, and he could hear her teeth grind. Finally, she took a deep breath and let it out. 'He loved those kids,' she said. 'With all of his heart. Sometimes, that love was mutual. I knew that. I lived with that.'

A knock at the door. O'Connor. He gestured that they should follow him outside. Barclay collected his notepad and pen and followed de Silva into the corridor. He was thankful for the air con out there, blasting down and cooling him, his T-shirt sticking against his wet skin.

'What is it?' de Silva asked.

'The box you brought in,' O'Connor said. He looked de Silva in the eye. 'There were some loose photos in there. Not in the album you found.'

'Of what?'

'Are you sure you want to see these?' He looked at Barclay now.

There it was. That stab of injustice, that Barclay was somehow less capable of handling things just because of his sexuality. 'Yes,' he said.

O'Connor handed them the photographs in a clear plastic bag. 'They're... difficult to look at.'

He wasn't wrong. The photographs showed at least three different young boys. Crying. Distressed. Their backs marked from caning or whipping. Their noses dripping with blood. And naked. All of them were naked.

'Have these been processed?' de Silva asked.

'These ones have.' O'Connor nodded. 'There are a few more being worked on. Fingerprints on every one of them. Some… DNA.'

Barclay closed his eyes. He thought of his daughter, that little girl he'd done his best to protect, and knew now why O'Connor had asked if he was sure he wanted to see them. He turned back into the interview room, de Silva close behind him, and threw the images onto the table.

'Does this look like love?' His voice raised. 'Does this look like something they fucking enjoyed?'

'Why are you showing me this?' Mary turned the images over so she couldn't see them. 'What's wrong with you?'

'Don't you recognise them?' He was pushing her and he knew it. 'They've been sat in with your husband's stuff all this time. Don't tell me you've never seen them before.'

'I haven't.'

'You're lying! You're as complicit in this as he was.' Barclay turned the images right side up. 'Look at them! It's the very least you owe these kids. Look what your husband did to them. What you allowed him to do.'

'Barclay…' De Silva's voice was low, her hand on his arm.

'What he got away with.'

'Except he didn't, did he?' Mary roared, her voice boomed in the tiny room. 'He was killed. Murdered. Buried out there in the woods! Don't you think that's enough? Don't you think he got what he deserved?'

'No,' Barclay said.

'Interview suspended at 10:37 a.m.,' de Silva said. 'O'Connor, could you see this woman back to her cell?'

Barclay turned away in frustration, hadn't realised O'Connor was still there until de Silva said his name. O'Connor moved in, took Mary by her elbow and led her out of the room.

De Silva closed the door behind them, let it slam and stared at Barclay. 'Jesus Christ, Barclay.'

'It's nothing you wouldn't have said.'

'No,' she said. 'You're letting your emotions get the better of you. You can't let them influence your judgement here. If this is too difficult...'

'God, de Silva. We've worked on this case for months. It's not too difficult. It's exactly what I need. But don't tell me not to be angry about a woman covering up her husband's abuse and rape of young boys for decades.'

Silence.

De Silva's phone rang out, and Barclay was thankful for it. She had her eyes on him as she answered without looking at it, put it on speaker phone.

'Win, I think you need to come home.'

Barclay didn't recognise the voice but assumed it was de Silva's sister, Laney. He knew little about her, other than they didn't really get along, but that she was staying in de Silva's house temporarily.

'I'm working, Laney. What's wrong?'

'There are people here.' Her voice was breathy. Urgent. As though she'd been exercising.

'What people?'

'They say they're from the National Crime Agency.' Laney caught her breath. 'They have a warrant to search your house.'

Twenty-Seven

She'd told Barclay to go back to the incident room, to take the lead on the new information, but he'd insisted on coming with her. 'For moral support,' he'd said. She didn't feel like she needed it, she'd understood that when the NCA had gotten involved, she'd have to do something about Ritchie's paperwork. The bits of evidence that had sat in their shared wardrobe all throughout the years of their marriage; the things the NCA wouldn't believe she didn't know anything about.

Last year, when she finally felt ready to move on, to tidy up Ritchie's affairs, to get everything in order, she'd stumbled across school reports, sports certificates and spelling awards from Rainford Lane School for Boys. And, when she'd decided to stay with the police to continue with her own investigation into her husband's time at the school, she knew that there was a possibility that it would all be found out.

So she'd moved that evidence somewhere safe.

A blue Ford sat on her drive, so she parked behind it, blocking it in. She was determined there would be no escape for them. They'd have to answer her questions. When de Silva parked next to the kerb and got out and stepped onto her lawn, she saw Murphy standing at her front door.

'Can you tell me what's going on?' De Silva kept her voice even and flat. 'Where's my sister?'

'Win, I'm here.' Laney stepped out from behind Murphy onto the front path.

'Where's Bonnie?'

'She's fine. She's at school.'

De Silva nodded, and realised that she was thankful for that. She'd have hated Bonnie to see any of this, especially after everything she'd been through with her mum and dad.

'De Silva, I'm sorry about this.' Murphy sounded earnest, her face tight with concern. 'I only heard about it ten minutes before they got here. I came straight out. Tried to call you…'

'I was in an interview.'

Agents Gray and Summers came out of the house, their faces cold and hard as stone. 'It's good that you're here,' Summers said to de Silva.

'How dare you do this without giving me a heads up,' de Silva said. 'You could have asked me.'

'Would you have let us in without a warrant?'

'Not a chance,' de Silva spat. 'If you wanted co-operation, that's out the window. I want you and your people out of my house now before I contact your superior and file a report for harassment.'

'De Silva.' Barclay's tone was one of warning.

Summers smirked. 'We're leaving.'

Murphy asked, 'Did you find anything?'

'There's nothing to find.' De Silva had to fight the urge to return Summers's smile. That smug face, almost a sneer.

Gray looked to Murphy. 'We will need to speak with her again.'

'Her? I'm stood right here!' De Silva took a step toward the agents, but Barclay grabbed her elbow.

Gray looked her up and down. 'I'm assuming that you'll finally want to suspend her now?'

'No,' Murphy said. 'I'm not sure why you would think that.'

Gray blinked. 'She's connected to this case. Theirs is connected to ours. Therefore, I'll be recommending that we should take it on.'

'You can make your recommendations to someone who cares. You don't have the authority to tell me what to do with my officers. And I'll be making a recommendation that you two are taken off this case due to your extreme bias toward DCI de Silva, your unprofessionalism and lack of courtesy in this matter. Now, I'd recommend you get in your car and go back to your hotel and wait to hear from your commanding officer.'

De Silva was as shocked as Summers and Gray looked. She nodded at Murphy, glad that at least someone had her back. She almost felt terrible for lying to her. Murphy had put her neck on the line for de Silva here, and it was all based on a lie. Like so much in de Silva's life.

Barclay's phone rang and he stepped away.

Murphy waited until the NCA agents' car had rounded the corner. 'I'm sorry that this happened, de Silva. I am.'

'It's not your fault, ma'am,' de Silva said.

'Murphy is fine.' She took a step closer. 'I notice they didn't answer my question.'

Did Murphy know that there was something to hide, or was she just covering all of her bases? Could she look into de Silva's eyes and know that she hadn't been forthcoming? 'I'm not sure what you're getting at.'

'I trust that there *was* nothing to find in there,' she said. 'Or anywhere. I believe you when you say that you knew nothing of the link between your husband and this case. I have to trust that. Trust you.'

De Silva nodded, but for a moment she wanted to let it all out. Sit Murphy down at the kitchen table and tell her everything. How she'd learned the awful truth just months before all of this. 'You'd be right. Could you excuse me? I need to see my sister.' De Silva headed for the house.

'De Silva, you're not by the way. Suspended I mean. Believe me, it's been talked about. But I think we have more to gain with you on this case than with you sitting at home twiddling your thumbs, yes?'

'Yes.'

'I know you'll understand when I say this. But this is it, de Silva. I don't want to have to come in and lead on this case. But I will.'

De Silva wanted to say she'd rather be sitting at home twiddling her thumbs than be taken off as lead detective. But what surprised her most was that Murphy hadn't moved her on to another case already. It's what de Silva herself would do. 'Okay.' A rage built inside her, but she knew that the only person she could aim it at was herself. If she'd been honest with Murphy and Barclay from the beginning, they wouldn't be in this position now. Maybe she should have stayed out of it all, followed her instinct and left Merseyside Police behind.

But that wasn't her. Wasn't how she was built. She needed to see this through to the messy, bloody end.

De Silva promised Laney she'd be home from work early, they could take Bonnie to the park and order some dinner from the Chinese take-away on Warrington Road.

By the time she arrived back at the incident room, she found her team had grown quiet. They'd already heard the news. 'All right,' de Silva called. 'I know you'll all have questions about what's happened today. Now's your time to ask them. Then that's it. We focus on this case and we get the job done.'

The team looked at each other and de Silva knew they wanted someone, anyone, to ask the question they all had on their minds.

'I'll go first,' Barclay said. 'We know now that this case has a connection to the school your husband attended as a kid. How important do you think that connection is?'

The other detectives nodded and looked to de Silva for answers she knew she owed them, but she had to play this the right way. Take care in the things she said, speak slowly, steadily, assuredly. She knew that at some point she'd have to tell Barclay what she'd done. But today was not that day.

'Good question,' she said. 'Going on the facts of the case, we know that my husband attended Rainford Lane School for Boys, we know that this school is where Bob Brendan worked and we know that Jacob Meeks's evidence board links Brendan's murder to the other victims who were murdered in similar circumstances.

'We don't know why Richard de Silva was mentioned on the board, but we know that there were other people on there too. Former-DCI Crosby. Lewis Lamond. And there were others we don't recognise – like Billy Thompson. His age puts him in the timeline to have attended Rainford Lane, but we don't know that for certain. That's something we'll need to focus on today.'

'What about the abuse?' Braxton spoke up, his head tilted to the left as he watched her.

She inhaled deeply and let it go. The thought of her Ritchie, her big strong husband having been in that place hurt her. She'd lain awake at night and thought about it, had imagined him in awful scenarios. 'We know that Lewis Lamond spoke of abuse at the school on record. Physical.' She took a breath. 'Sexual. Violent. Whether all of this is connected… Well, I think that seems likely.'

O'Connor now. 'Do we think that Brendan was murdered because of the abuse? Was he an abuser?'

De Silva nodded. 'Good question. We found images among the paperwork that his ex-wife, Mary Newton, attempted to destroy before we arrested her. The images were violent and sexual in nature. Kids.'

The room erupted into protests of disgust. De Silva let it run its course. They were entitled to show their disdain for the extreme behaviour of Brendan and God knows who else at that school.

'So the wife knew all about it?' Lawrence. Her eyes were wide, watery. De Silva knew this case would affect her, but these were the things that needed to be done if she wanted to become a detective.

'Yes,' de Silva said simply.

Silence. De Silva let it ring in the office between them before she pressed on.

'Is there anything else?'

'Did you know?' Barclay again. 'About Ritchie's connection to the case? Before yesterday.'

De Silva looked at him, held his eyes for a few moments longer than necessary and almost crumbled. 'No,' she said.

'Ritchie's connection to this whole thing was just as much of a surprise to me as it was to everyone else.'

Barclay turned his head, and de Silva couldn't read his reaction. She knew, with the sinking feeling of a black weight in her stomach, that he didn't believe her.

The shadows of her memories and her guilt stirred through the stand of trees in her mind that kept them at bay. Kept her safe from having to come to terms with them. But in that moment, she felt the iciness of them get closer, their frigid fingers could almost reach out and touch her.

Sooner or later, she would have to face them.

'Anything else?'

The room was silent.

'Good,' de Silva said. 'Let's get to it. Harris, what's new?'

'We did like you asked,' he said. He turned, grabbed his tablet and scrolled until he found what he was looking for. 'In each case we found, a member of the family, usually the partner, received a finger in the post.'

'Right.' She'd expected this. It was the thing that unified these cases. But still, she couldn't escape the feeling that Meeks's murder felt different. There was something there. Something in the fact that it was unfinished.

This killer took his time dismembering his victims. *But the man in the woods. He wasn't dismembered*. She knew that killers tended to escalate, and she'd already attributed the difference to that. Crime scene reports suggest that he took great care to do it somewhere they'd not be disturbed. Somewhere that could be easily cleaned. So why the difference in Meeks's case? Had he been disturbed? Was that why he hadn't finished his work, hadn't taken Meeks's body and put it somewhere it could be found?

'Split up,' she said. 'Visit each of the victims' families. Barclay and I will call Finch's partner... er...'

'Lucille Rogers,' Lawrence offered.

De Silva nodded. 'Okay, let's get to it. Lawrence, you go with Braxton. We want to ask specifically about involvement at Rainford Lane School for Boys. Volunteer activities or community projects that involve children.' She knew she was teaching her grandmother to suck eggs, but felt the need to say it out loud.

De Silva watched Barclay, busying himself moving things around his desk or to the bin, needlessly, as the others left.

When the door closed, de Silva asked, 'Is there something on your mind, Barclay?'

'Something feels off,' he said.

'This whole thing feels off, I agree.'

'Something's off about you,' he said. 'I know you'll never tell me. I know you don't trust me for some reason. I don't know what I've done to make you feel that way.'

Her heart broke for him. She wanted to cave, wanted to let him know that it had nothing to do with trust. If she told him, she knew that he would have to make a choice: tell Murphy or keep her secret. She couldn't do that to him. This was about protecting his career. His belief, and faith, in the systems and protocols that defined how they did their work. He saw them as protection. De Silva had always thought of them as an inconvenience.

'Barclay...'

He put his hand up. 'No, don't say anything. If you say something other than the truth, I'll know, and I can't deal with any more disappointment. I've booked a meeting room to call Lucille Rogers. Are you ready?'

There was so much de Silva wanted to say. She'd always had this feeling that she wanted to mother Barclay. No, it wasn't that. She wanted to protect him, look out for him, but he was a grown man and didn't need a mother. It was then, in that moment, when Barclay couldn't look at her, when his eyes were downcast, and his mood low, that she thought of him as one of her people.

Family.

'I'll tell you everything, Barclay,' she said. 'I promise.' She put a hand on his shoulder and looked up into his bright eyes. 'There are some things I still need to figure out first. But I do trust you.'

He tried to smile, but she could see in his eyes that he was exhausted. 'Thank you for saying it.'

'Now enough of this mushy bullshit,' she said. 'We've got work to do.'

In the meeting room De Silva dialled Lucille's number into the conference phone sitting on the table. It rang out and for a sinking moment, de Silva thought there would be no answer. Then there was a click. 'Good afternoon, Môr Campsite.'

'Good afternoon,' de Silva said. 'This is Detective Chief Inspector de Silva from Merseyside Police. Is now a good time to talk?'

A long pause. 'I've been expecting your call,' Lucille said. Her accent was thick Welsh, and it made de Silva smile.

De Silva looked at Barclay, who shrugged. 'I'm joined here by Detective Sergeant Barclay.'

'Afternoon,' he said.

'Is this about Margaret?'

'It is,' de Silva said. She waited, to see if Lucille would fill the silence. 'We know she left Bebington in 1992 and moved to Wales. Were you in a relationship at that point?'

'Yes, we were.' There was rustling down the line. Then Lucille grunted, her breathing heavy, then returning to normal. 'She was the love of my life.'

'What made you want to leave the area?'

'We're both from Wales originally,' she said. 'We wanted to go home.'

'But why then?'

'We missed it.'

De Silva glanced again at Barclay. There was a resistance here. Lucille didn't want to talk about the love of her life to two detectives that she didn't know. 'Earlier, you said you'd been expecting our call.'

'There was that murder up in Lancashire, I heard about it on the radio. And that man in Liverpool,' she said. 'The press are likening it to a few other murders that have happened since the 1990s, aren't they? To that man you found in the woods last year. To my Margaret's. After all these years, you've not found the person responsible.'

'Well, that's why we're here,' Barclay said.

'Some things are better off buried,' Lucille said. There was no emotion in her voice now. It was flat, distant. Dismissive.

De Silva needed to push her. 'Did Margaret ever have any involvement with Rainford Lane School for Boys?'

Lucille cleared her throat. 'God, that place. Does it all lead back to that hole, does it?'

'Can I ask what you mean by that?' Barclay scribbled at his notepad.

'That place was evil,' Lucille said. 'I only went there once, but you could feel it in the walls. Coming up through the floor like smoke. It was thick and I said to Marg, "You need to get out of here". She never listened to me. Said I was being silly.'

De Silva leaned in, listening intently, like she used to do at her dad's knee when he told her ghost stories as a kid. The white lady who walked the landing in his mum's old house, in the dead of night, the one he'd seen walk out of their front door and disappear into a bonfire one cold 5 November.

'There's not a day that goes by that I don't think of those boys,' she said. 'So little. So fragile.'

'Is there something you want to say about the treatment of the boys at the school?' De Silva had to play it cool. Not give anything they knew away.

'The people who ran that place,' she said. 'The teachers, the people they had coming in for other stuff... what do they call it now? Extracurricular. They were monsters, and they tore those little boys up.'

'What do you mean?'

Lucille sighed, a long, rasping thing that sounded like she'd held on to it since 1992. 'Will I be in trouble?' she asked. 'For not coming forward sooner with what we knew?'

De Silva shook her head, even though Lucille couldn't see her. 'We just want to find who killed Margaret and the others,' she said. 'That's all.' She knew she could make no guarantees that Lucille would come through this unscathed, not legally, and hoped her words comforted her enough to continue.

'Margaret came home one night. I remember it clearly. The winds had been so high that the cross had fallen off the top of the church. Roof tiles everywhere. And the rain, it whipped down so hard I thought the windows were going to crack. She wasn't going to come home at first, she'd called to say it would be safer to stay. Sometimes they closed the tunnel when the weather was bad.'

De Silva felt a chill run through her body.

'Anyway, she arrived home out of the blue. I'd made some stew for dinner, and was going to freeze the leftovers, when I saw her headlights on the drive. She ran in, and I thought she was just wet at first. She was shaking like she had ice under her skin, and the wet on her face wasn't just from the rain. She sobbed, silently, you know the kind I mean? Where the pain you're feeling is just so much that your body shakes but no sound comes out?

'She couldn't talk at first. I made her a cup of tea, sat her down at the kitchen table, held on to her hand and waited.' Lucille sniffled.

'Are you okay, Lucille?' Barclay asked.

'I'm fine,' she said. 'She told me we needed to pack up some things and we needed to leave. That night. I looked out at the weather: it felt like the dark was growing. Pushing into every corner of the evening, like it was going to come into the house and snuff out the electric. Do you know what I mean?' She didn't wait for a response. 'She ran about the house, putting stuff into her case. I followed her, tried to get to the bottom of it. Finally, when she threw my toothbrush into a bag, I snapped at her.'

Lucille stopped. Another sniffle and a rustle.

'Are you okay to continue?' de Silva asked.

'She told me that she'd seen it for herself,' Lucille said, some strength back in her voice. 'The evil that I'd felt in that place.'

'What do you mean?'

'Do I have to say it?' Lucille sighed. 'Fine. She saw what the boys went through. Had that storm never happened,

Margaret would have left for the day. She taught English. Poetry. Short stories by Poe, *Frankenstein*, all of that. She'd never stayed late before. She always came home and finished any work at the kitchen table.

'But that night, the storm kept her there. Like it was all supposed to happen. Sometimes, God needs you to see the things no one should ever see, doesn't he? Experience it. Live through the worst horrors imaginable.' She cleared the thickness from her throat again. 'She didn't know if they saw her. But she saw them, and it was enough.'

Barclay had put his pen down and was listening. 'Do you know why she didn't report it to the police?'

'I know you won't want to hear this,' Lucille said. 'I know there'll be some police code of silence.' She paused again, and de Silva thought it was more for dramatic effect than anything else. 'That place, that *school*... Well,' she huffed. 'There were police there that night.'

De Silva's breath caught in her throat and Barclay's eyes bulged in their sockets.

'Did she know any names?'

'I didn't ask,' Lucille said.

De Silva's mind raced. It had entered de Silva's head before. An awarded school like Rainford Lane would have been assessed by someone, it would have been under the media spotlight due to the fact that lost boys or those who were always in trouble were sent there to be rehabilitated. There had to be someone protecting it. Social workers. The council. Politicians.

'Detectives?'

Lucille's voice snapped de Silva back to herself. 'Thank you for your time,' de Silva said. 'I appreciate how hard it must have been to go through that with us. We'll call you again if we have any further questions.'

They exchanged goodbyes and de Silva ended the call. 'Fucking hell, Barclay,' she said. 'How far does this thing go?'

'We should report this to the NCA.'

'Not yet,' she said.

'Yes, now,' Barclay said. 'They're looking into Crosby, and Ritchie now, and how all of this links back to Rainford Lane and this bloody app.'

'So are we!'

'They have seniority here,' Barclay said.

'We don't even know who's leading the NCA investigation any more.'

'Then we'll find out.'

'Barclay—'

A knock at the door. A uniformed officer that de Silva didn't recognise walked in, holding a padded manila envelope. 'Sorry to interrupt,' he said. 'Something came for you. It's marked urgent, so I didn't want to leave it in the incident room.'

He handed it to de Silva.

'Thanks, I appreciate it.' She waited for the officer to leave before she continued. 'What are you thinking, Barclay?'

'I'm not sure what to think,' he admitted. 'I think I need time to process it.'

De Silva considered that the writing on the envelope seemed familiar, dismissed it and tore it open. 'I know what you mean. If the others come back with connections to Rainford Lane, I think it's clear what we're dealing with.'

'Targeted murders.' Barclay nodded.

De Silva reached into the envelope. 'Someone with a vendetta—' She felt something hard and cold and unmistakable. 'Oh my God.' She removed her hand instantly and dropped it onto the table.

A finger sat on the table-top. Mottled and discoloured.

'Why do I get all the notes, Barclay?' De Silva asked. 'Surely it's your turn by now.' Last year, during the Lamond case, he'd written specifically to her with threats and vile things.

Barclay closed his mouth, took out his phone and said, 'I'll call Scientific Support.'

De Silva knew without the need of DNA analysis that the finger belonged to Jacob Meeks.

But why has the killer sent it to me?

Twenty-Eight

De Silva was exhausted. She felt the weight of the day in her shoulders and in her legs as she fought not to drag her feet from the car to the front door. She needed a bath, food and her bed. She checked her watch. It was already after eight p.m., and she knew she'd be up and out early in the morning.

They'd compared the X-ray of the body in the woods to the medical records of Bob Brendan and had come up with a match. Dental records were still in the works, but preliminary examination agreed that they were a match too.

It was him. Robert Brendan.

De Silva had sent the finger off for analysis and DNA-matching with Brennan's team, but she already knew whose digit it was. Meeks's. Had to be. The only question was why the killer had sent it to her. She knew from the background check the team had carried out on Meeks that he had no family. No real friends beyond those he knew online. Nothing solid. Nothing physical.

And besides, if the killer gets a thrill from imagining a victim's family receiving a severed finger, imagine the excitement knowing the detective investigating your crimes has opened their post.

Did the killer have some warped idea that sending it to de Silva was the next best thing in the absence of any family? The killer would achieve some amount of thrill from knowing the finger would startle the recipient, no matter who opened the envelope. She wondered whether he pictured her sitting at her desk, crime scene photographs all around her, deep in the shock and terror of his crimes when she received the parcel – whether he imagined her scream at the sight of it, or at least a gasp of horror.

In truth, she'd done neither. It didn't frighten her, and if the killer knew that, he'd try harder next time. That was how he would work. There was no emotion about the victim, no regret, no remorse. But at the thought of someone having received a piece of his handiwork, so to speak, he'd feel an intense hit of pleasure.

She knew from the team's work with the families of all of the victims they had on their evidence board that the envelopes were always addressed to a woman. A wife or a mother. A loved one. She wondered whether there was some sexual element to his actions. Like a flasher gets gratification from the shock he instils in his victims.

True, this was different. More extreme. Violent. But de Silva had that thing that comes with experience, with longevity in a role such as hers. Distance. Some called it professional distance, some called it emotional distance. The crimes of last year were different, where kids were murdered brutally, but in the case of Meeks, she felt almost nothing. Wouldn't allow herself to.

Early in her career, she felt the pain of every death. The agony of every disappearance. The disappointment of every case they were unable to bring in front of the courts or even get through the Crown Prosecution Service. She learned quickly to detach her feelings from the case. It didn't always work, and she knew that one day, she would become too involved. *And*, she thought with a grim realisation, *tomorrow may be that day*. Ritchie was tied up in this, and now everyone knew. She *was* involved, there was no denying that. Emotionally invested.

She had to be.

She quietened her mind, shoved her feelings down into the pit where all of the other things she was only just beginning to work on lived, where they circled around each other like wisps of smoke, waiting to be let loose.

'Wait until you see what I found!' Laney was there at the door. Her face was still bruised, but for the first time since she'd arrived, for the first time since de Silva could remember, Laney's smile beamed across her swollen face.

De Silva panicked for a split second. 'What did you find?' She was grateful she'd removed all of Ritchie's school paperwork somewhere safe. If the glove box of her car could be considered safe. It was safe from the NCA, anyway. For now. 'You been rooting around?'

'Oh no, nothing like that.' Laney waved her hand dismissively and walked through to the kitchen.

De Silva followed her. There was a smell in the air. Meat and tomatoes and spices, and de Silva felt her stomach growl. 'What's for dinner?'

'Look!' Laney stood at the kitchen table, that smile still on her face. Photographs and old leather-bound albums sat there, opened, explored, removed from their plastic protectors and held.

De Silva recognised them instantly. The family photo albums. Pictures of them both as little girls at bath time; their mother, Marie, young and smiling, a glass of something sparkling in a wine glass, her hair permed, dressed in a mint-green frock.

She sat down and tried to take it all in. Their dad, a heavy ginger moustache, sat on a floral couch. His fingers were yellow from tobacco he used to roll himself, and de Silva could almost smell that fruity scent whenever he opened his tobacco tin.

'Jesus, Laney,' she said. 'Where did you find all of these? I thought they were lost.'

'No, not lost.' Laney sat down next to her and held a photograph up. 'Look at this one.' A photograph of a family barbeque, all of the adults standing under a tree, glasses or tins in their hands. 'That's Aunt Alice, isn't it?'

'Yeah, I think so. God, they all look so young.'

'Dinner's almost ready,' Laney said as she stood. 'You keep looking while I finish it off.'

'What is it?'

'I made chilli. Not out of the jar. Mum's recipe.'

Mum's recipe. She always made the tomato sauce from scratch, and de Silva loved the smell as it cooked and filled the house. The same as it filled her home now. It reminded her of her childhood in Kirkby, where all people had were shared recipes and unchanging struggles.

They were happy times.

Happier times.

'Where did you get them?'

'Oh that doesn't matter.'

De Silva scanned the photo of the barbeque again, trying to match the faces with her own hazy memories of that day. 'Come on, tell me.' Then she saw him. O'Brien, in a short-sleeved shirt and matching slacks. Some white leather shoes with tassels on the front. Kath stood next to him, effortlessly beautiful. De Silva couldn't help but smile.

She leaned in closer, and saw a tattoo on his forearm. She'd known the man for years and never noticed the tattoo of a bird there before. Still, he'd always worn longer sleeves. Maybe from the time where visible tattoos were frowned upon in the force.

'No, Laney, I really want to know.'

Laney sighed, heavy and resigned. 'The house.'

'What house?' It clicked in her brain a second later. 'Your house? You've been back home?!' De Silva got up from the table and marched to the cooker.

'Stop it, will you? David wasn't home. I'm fine.'

'Laney, we talked about this.' De Silva tried to keep the edge of frustration from her voice. 'You can't go back home to him. Look what he did to you. Was Bonnie with you?'

'Don't be stupid! She was in school. I just wanted them back before David did something stupid. Burned them or something.'

'But you went alone,' she said. 'He could have come home. He could have hurt you. And all for a bunch of old photographs.'

'They're not just old photographs.' Laney stirred the sauce. 'They're our memories. Mum can't tell us these stories any more, but we can look at all of that and remember it for ourselves.'

De Silva sighed. She understood the sentiment, and the last thing they needed was to fight when they seemed to be making some headway in their relationship at last. 'I know,' she said. 'I get it, and I'm sorry for going on. I'm just worried about you. What if he followed you?'

'I know his car. I was careful.'

De Silva didn't want to get into it with her. She knew that if David didn't want to be seen, he wouldn't be. He could have followed her by taxi or a car he'd borrowed from a friend, or a hired vehicle.

'Don't worry,' Laney said. 'Sit down, dinner's almost ready.'

—

Dinner had been nice. Laney was a good cook, like their mum had been after she'd finally ditched the chip pan. They'd sat and looked at old photographs while they ate and laughed at the time their mum had fallen through a cheap old patio chair. Laney drank from a bottle of Merlot until her lips and teeth turned dark, and de Silva sipped on a steaming black coffee.

She'd felt the pull to pour herself a glass, but knew where that led. Depression, blackouts, the need to punish herself for all of her misgivings. When Laney went to bed, de Silva threw the remnants of the wine down the sink. No temptation.

With a full belly and a heart lifted by their time together, de Silva knew she needed to get some sleep. She closed the blinds and made sure the windows and doors were locked before she climbed the stairs.

In her dreams, like so many she'd had before, she was sitting with Ritchie on the bottom step of the staircase in the house they'd shared together. The one she'd left in the hope the memories wouldn't follow her. Above them, a bloody noose swung from the banister.

She cried. Not from the pain of missing him, not from the guilt of the affair she believed caused his death by suicide, and not from the anger she still harboured toward him for taking his own life. They were tears of frustration.

In her dream, Ritchie wouldn't look at her. She couldn't see his eyes or his face. His shoulders jerked and she knew that he was sobbing, silently. For her part, she couldn't use her voice. It was stuck somewhere in her chest, and wouldn't come out.

A knock came at the door, heavy.

Thump, thump, thump.

She stood and walked to the door and turned back. Ritchie wasn't crying any more. Instead, he was a boy in a school uniform. A grey jumper and forest-green tie. Black trousers and shining leather shoes. He watched her, his tears drying on his face. He stared ahead, as though he didn't see her.

Thump, thump, thump!

De Silva reached out for the door handle, and took one last look back. The boy now hung from the noose, and below him were monsters made from shadows, moaning and reaching for his body.

Thump, thump, thump.

She ran to Ritchie, tried to reach him, as the door caved in. Splinters flew in the air and suddenly a white light filled the space. Intense, blinding. She felt him slip away from her and wondered whether the monsters had won.

When she awoke, she saw light through the edges of the blinds, and somewhere a tap-tap-tap. Her brain was foggy from sleep, her senses dulled, and for a moment she thought she was still dreaming.

It's the security light, she told herself. One of the neighbour's wandering cats had set it off. She closed her eyes and rolled over.

Her door was ajar. She was sure that she'd closed it. Maybe Laney had peeked in to check on her. She thought about getting up, checking the windows and the doors were locked, looking in on Laney and Bonnie, then coming back to bed. But the truth was, the duvet was warm and the weight of it made her feel safe. Secure.

That sound came again. Not a tapping, but something else.

None of the neighbours have a cat.

Her eyes opened.

She climbed out of bed, pushed her feet into her sliders and tip-toed out onto the landing. Across from her own room was where Bonnie slept, the door open just a crack. She looked in on her, and she was flat-out on her back.

De Silva smiled. She'd give anything to have a child's innocence, their lack of worries beyond what was for dinner and the latest toy. But then a sadness overcame her, as heavy as a cowl. Bonnie's home life had been anything but normal, based on what Laney had told her. She didn't know how much Bonnie had seen, whether she'd heard through her bedroom wall all of the awful things that her daddy did to her mummy.

That broke de Silva's heart; but still, they were safe here now. She pulled the door closed slightly and she moved down the corridor to look in on her sister.

Laney slept on her stomach, breathed heavily, and it rattled at the back of her throat. She wasn't sure now which she'd have preferred. Bonnie's innocence or her sister's ability to drink herself into a coma.

That sound again. She couldn't place it.

She closed her sister's bedroom door and peered over the banister into the hall. Nothing stirred or moved, but the sound came again. Her sliders flapped against her soles as she took the stairs.

In the hall, she saw the handle to the front door wiggle. That was it; that was the sound. The hairs on her arms pricked and her mind raced, trying to decide what was best to do next.

Clearly, the obvious thing would be to call the police, but her phone was on the bedside table. Should she call out? Would that startle whoever was there? She looked down at her feet, at the pink sliders there, and knew she wouldn't be able to run if she needed to. She slipped them off.

The handle went upright, back to its normal position, and she watched as a shadow moved around the front door and passed across the bay windows of the living room. She stayed close to the wall and followed it, through to the kitchen. She knew the next logical step would be for him to try the back door.

She thought about running upstairs for her phone, or to shout up for Laney to call the police. Would she hear her? Doubtful in her current state. If she left the kitchen, this person could be inside the house before she even reached her phone. Standing there, in the kitchen, she at least had a chance to fight back.

Then, there he was, stalking past the kitchen window. He was tall, she could tell, but dressed in black, a hood pulled up over his head. She thought of the CCTV footage from Meeks's flat, of the man in black, a hood covering his face, but it couldn't be him. She knew who this was. Knew that it had to be David, that he'd followed Laney here.

She took a step out of the shadows of the kitchen and into the light shining in from the security lamp, as the man in black stepped in front of the window on the top half of the door. They stared at each other and de Silva tried to take it all in. She couldn't see his face still: it was in the shadows of his hood, but on the left side of his hoody was a tiny motif. A moose or a deer, something like that.

If she had her phone, she could have moved quickly and shone her torchlight into his face. But she didn't have her phone. Didn't have anything to protect herself with if he smashed his way in. He cocked his head and de Silva knew he was considering what to do next. She was frozen. Fear had gripped her whole body in icy claws, and she couldn't move. Hardly breathed.

The man lifted his hand to the window and banged so hard on it that a thin line appeared in the glass. Then, he turned away and moved into the shadows at the back of the garden, beyond the glare of the security light.

She wanted to unlock the door, to chase him down; and, if she'd been wearing her shoes, she would have without a thought. It might be reckless to chase down a violent man and tackle him to the ground, but to get him into a cell, to make Laney and Bonnie safe, she would do it without a second thought.

In the morning, she'd have to call for someone to come and fix the window. For a PC to escort Laney and Bonnie to school. They'd have to inform the school of tonight's developments. *Then*, she thought gloomily, *everyone will talk, everyone will make their own versions of what has happened to Laney*. Sometimes the fictions people create to explain the things they have no involvement in are worse than the truth.

De Silva wished she could protect Bonnie and Laney from that. But she couldn't. All she could do was be there for them.

As she started out into the black night, half-frightened that David would return, and half-wishing that he would, she knew they'd need some hard evidence to have him arrested.

It was a good job she'd ordered the security lights with built-in cameras.

Twenty-Nine

Barclay was surprised when he received the call to his work phone. It was already after nine, and he'd settled down for the night, his mother fast asleep in her armchair, the telly still blasting out a rerun of *Heartbeat* from the nineties. He'd left her to it.

'I wanted to apologise,' NCA investigator Ayris had said. 'I know it's late, but could you meet me for a drink? An hour at most, I promise.'

As Barclay got himself dressed, he considered calling de Silva, to see if she'd been invited, or whether it was advisable for Barclay to even go. He decided against it, knowing that she had her young niece staying over.

Barclay drove into the city, parked in the Q-Park at Liverpool ONE, and walked up past the Crown Court, down Castle Street and through to Victoria Street. Barclay loved this part of the city; it was all tall buildings that looked like they were etched in ancient rock, and scrubbed and buffed until they were clean and pale as sand.

Ayris stood outside the door to The Lisbon, and smiled when he saw Barclay approach, that awkward kind of smile you reserve for passing someone in a corridor who you don't know very well.

Barclay had been surprised that Ayris chose The Lisbon, one of the oldest gay pubs in Liverpool, if not the oldest. He wasn't sure whether he'd chosen it because he himself was gay or he'd hoped Barclay might feel more comfortable. In truth, gay bars had never been Barclay's thing. He'd always found them to be too pretentious. Too loud, and hardly felt like the safe space they were supposed to be. Some gay men felt they had the right to touch him when he walked to the bar the last time he'd been here. *Still*, he'd thought, *that doesn't just happen in gay places.*

When Ayris got to the bar, he turned to Barclay and said, 'Thanks for coming.'

Barclay nodded. 'It's fine.' The music wasn't loud, if they sat in a corner somewhere away from everyone else, they'd be able to hear each other in conversation. The place was usually thumping with music, but not that night.

'The drink's on me.'

'I'll just have a lemonade. I'm driving.'

'Sure.' Ayris ordered himself a double gin and handed Barclay his lemonade. 'I'm not driving. Cheers.' He held up his glass, but Barclay just stared.

'What is it you wanted to talk about?'

'Come on, let's sit over there.' Ayris led him over to a corner seat, facing two young lads, painfully thin, playing pool. The balls clack-clacked as they hit each other.

'So... you're married.' It wasn't a question.

'That's none of your business,' Barclay said. He moved his hand from the table, and knew that he was hiding his wedding ring. More than that: what it symbolised. His marriage. His partnership. His Nick. All of it was off the table for conversation. He didn't feel like unpacking his situation with someone from the NCA.

'I'm sorry,' Ayris said. From the crease in his brow and his straight lips, Barclay felt that he genuinely was sorry. 'Sometimes it helps to talk to a relative stranger.'

'No,' Barclay said. 'Thank you.'

He turned away from Ayris then, watched the twinks at the pool table and wished that he'd not come at all. Whatever Ayris had to say, he could have said in email or text. This setting made Barclay nervous as it was, and now with the added pressure of small talk, he wished the earth would open up and devour him.

'I wanted to explain a few things,' Ayris said. 'About our investigation.'

'Other than it's a fuck-up, what else is there to explain?'

'Oh wow, okay!' Ayris laughed. 'I'll take that one on the chin. You're right, it has been a shambles. But I'm in charge now. I'll be here with Grace— er – Fitzgerald.'

'And what makes you think two of you can do a better job than four of you?'

'Summers was in charge. But they've been called back. Fitzy and me, we get along. We know how to talk to people. How to treat them.'

'Fitzgerald didn't seem that way when I met her.'

Ayris laughed. 'Aye, she can be a bit tough, I know. But she's got a good heart; she's by the book.'

'And you aren't?'

'Course I am.' Ayris winked. 'Consummate professional.'

Barclay thought about how Ayris and Fitzgerald were like de Silva and himself. One played by the book and the other clearly didn't and was almost proud of it. Not quite a renegade, but definitely not following any rulebook. He swallowed down his lemonade.

'Are you sure I can't get you a drink? You can leave the car. You could get a taxi.'

'I'm up early for the gym tomorrow, then work.'

'I bet you have a little routine, don't you?' Ayris's eyes sparkled against the dim light of the small booth. 'You get up at five fifteen. You shower and you're out of the door by five forty-five. You drive at the speed limit and arrive at your gym's carpark with one or two minutes spare. You wait until everyone else goes in, maybe there's a bit of rush around six, so you don't have to deal with people pushing past you. Once they're in, you jog in and get to the equipment while other people are chatting or filling up their water bottles. How am I doing so far?'

Barclay closed his mouth. 'I think I will have that drink. And then you can be a little more honest with me.'

Ayris was on his feet already. 'About why I asked you here?'

'No,' he said. 'About these connections between our case and yours.'

Ayris's smile faded just a bit, and Barclay wondered whether he'd crossed a line. Whether Ayris knew he couldn't say anything, and Barclay asking him would put him in an awkward position. 'So, what're you having?'

'Pint of Camden Hells, please.' He told himself that he'd have just one.

As Ayris walked over to the bar, he watched as the two twinks at the pool table checked him out. His jeans were tight, not skinny jeans at all, but they hugged him generously around the bum, around his thighs and calves. His white T-shirt hugged his biceps close too. Barclay could see why people might stare. He was an attractive man, and if he were single—

Well you're not single, so pack it in.

'So,' Ayris sighed as he sat down, passed Barclay his pint, beaded with condensation. 'What is it you want to know?'

'What are you allowed to tell me?'

'Look, I asked you here to apologise. For how this whole thing has been handled. But what can I tell you? Nothing,' Ayris answered, no hint of a smile now. 'But I couldn't deny that face, look at you,' Ayris continued.

Barclay smiled despite himself. 'You're being unprofessional.'

'You haven't seen anything yet.'

Barclay panicked. He didn't know what to do with this. His face burned hot and he worried that Ayris could see him blush. If he did, he didn't say a word.

'The connection you mentioned...' Ayris went on.

'That's right,' Barclay affirmed, his eyes on the pint glass. 'And save the Lamond-Crosby thing. New information only.'

'Speaking of new information,' Ayris said, the playfulness back in his voice. 'De Silva's husband having a link to the case is pretty fucking new. Unless you already knew about it?'

'I didn't, otherwise Murphy would have known. You'd have known.'

'Did de Silva know, do you think?'

Barclay considered this. A few days ago, he'd have said absolutely not, but in the last twenty-four hours, he'd had this feeling he couldn't shake. An unexplainable gut instinct that told him de Silva already knew. 'De Silva's a lot of things. A pain in the arse, I'm sure Murphy would say. But she'd share that information.' Even as he said it, he knew it wasn't true. The question was: how *long* had she known?

Ayris nodded, a slow movement, as though considering Barclay's words. Weighing them up, perhaps against what he already knew of de Silva. 'You want to know about The Woulds app, don't you?'

'Yeah.'

'If I told you what I know about that app, Barclay, I'd have to kill you.'

'Oh, come on!'

'I'm sorry,' he said. 'I can't. Not yet. But what I will tell you is that we want to work with you on this case. You and de Silva.'

'What happened to not being able to deny my face?'

Ayris laughed. 'Aye, you're right.'

Something in the air changed between them. It became still. The music droned on, that song Barclay's mum loved, about men raining from the sky, about getting soaking wet. The game at the pool table continued, clicking and clacking.

Ayris leaned in and Barclay didn't pull away. He didn't think of Nick. He didn't think of their marriage, or the bed they'd shared together. He didn't think of anything beyond that moment.

Their lips touched and for the first time in months, Barclay felt like someone in his life needed him. He felt wanted.

And more than that. Desired.

—

The morning light came through floor-to-ceiling windows that Barclay didn't recognise, and pricked at his eyes like hot needles. He felt an awful dryness in his mouth that he hadn't felt in months. His stomach gurgled, and as his temperature rose, he fought the urge to vomit. He rolled out of the bed and looked around. A lush hotel room with thick carpets, even thicker curtains drawn wide and in the open wardrobe, a small suitcase.

The night came flooding back, hitting hard. The kiss in The Lisbon. The many drinks and kisses that followed. The feel of Ayris's tongue in his mouth. How, when Barclay realised how pissed he was, he just wanted to go home. He'd gotten in a taxi and Ayris had jumped in next to him and given the name of his hotel.

His legs wouldn't hold him upright, so he perched on the edge of the bed, his head spinning. Nick was all he could think about. His smile, his laugh, the way he was with Sarah: silly, fun and comforting. He pictured his husband crying now, as Barclay told him what had happened at the hotel.

There was no one else in the hotel room, not in the shower, or moving around in the bathroom. Ayris had already left. He picked up his phone from the bedside table and found it was dead. Quickly, he reached over to the other side of the bed and plugged it in using a charger he assumed belonged to Ayris.

The remote for the TV was on the floor near his feet, so he turned it on, noted the time was 09:33, turned it off again to save his head from the noise and ran to the bathroom. He showered using toiletries that weren't his own. The scents not his, but not unfamiliar. They were all over him: Ayris on Barclay's skin.

He scrubbed at himself with his nails, as tears slid down his cheeks hotter than the shower water. He knew he'd fucked up. He knew that he'd broken his own heart and Nick's would be next. Their marriage really would be over.

When he did tell Nick, he hoped that Nick would at least listen to him. Could only wish that Nick would be able to see past all of this. But he had told Barclay their having sex the other day was a mistake, had changed the positioning of their relationship again. It had gone from intimate and loving to cold and distant and back again. And now Barclay didn't know where he stood with his husband, other than in a hotel shower washing a stranger off himself.

He barely reached the toilet in time as he threw up all of last night's beer. His heart thundered in his chest and his skin felt cold. He shivered and climbed back under the warm water.

When he'd washed and dressed himself again in last night's outfit, which stank of the pub, he hopped on the train to Speke, as there was no way he was in a fit state to drive, and walked the rest of the way to the OCC. It took him twenty minutes, but the fresh air felt good.

He'd bought a toothbrush, toothpaste and deodorant from a corner shop on the way and went into one of the toilets on the ground floor of the OCC to freshen up. By the time he reached the incident room, he didn't feel as awful. Still, the guilt of the night before lay heavy in the pit of his stomach, and he was certain it would never disappear.

'I've been trying to call you,' de Silva said. Then, when she got a good look at him, she added, 'Jesus, Barclay, you look like boiled shite. Are you unwell?'

'You could say that.'

It dawned on de Silva's face then and Barclay was all too aware that he might smell of alcohol. It would seep out of his skin and mouth, and he wondered whether it would have any effect on de Silva's sobriety.

Something else to feel bad about.

'Where is everyone?'

'I sent them for lunch,' de Silva said.

Barclay hadn't realised he'd been that long. He felt awful for missing the morning. He noticed some black and white footage on de Silva's computer screen. 'What're you looking at?'

'Some cam footage.'

'From where?' He moved closer.

'No, stay where you are. You smell like a Wetherspoons.' She eyed him. 'Are you even fit to work?'

'I'll be fine.' He knew he was lying, that he'd feel like death all day. 'I just need some coffee. What's the footage of?'

'My house. Last night.'

'Is everything okay?'

De Silva skipped the footage on and paused it as a man stood outside a door at what looked like the back of the house. He was tall, his shoulders broad. 'This man tried to get inside my house last night,' she said.

'What the hell?'

'I thought it was my sister's husband last night,' she said. 'While I was waiting for you,' she said, pointedly, 'I asked someone from over the water to bring him in. Turns out he was at his local pub the entire night. In front of dozens of witnesses. All corroborated.' She took a breath. 'But that was last night, and now I'm looking at it...'

'It looks like the man from Meeks's building.'

'It *is* the man from Meeks's building,' de Silva said. She pointed at the screen. 'Look there. See that?' She pointed to the logo embroidered on the man's hoody. 'Last night I thought it was a moose or a deer or something. I cross-referenced it with the footage from Meeks's building, and look.' She brought that footage up, where she'd already stopped it at the right moment.

'A stag.' Barclay's head was swimming. 'So the man who killed Jacob Meeks has tried to get into your home.'

'While my niece was there, Barclay,' she said. 'I've had to request an officer sit outside the house.'

Barclay knew this feeling all too well. Last year, the serial killer Lewis Lamond had made some very specific threats against Sarah on a note that they'd found on de Silva's car, so much so they'd moved her and Nick out to a safe house in Cheshire. Not even Barclay knew where they were. He wondered why the same didn't apply here. Because there was no explicit threat? Maybe. But Barclay couldn't imagine anything more explicit than trying to break into the home of the lead detective in an active multiple-murder investigation.

Did the killer even know that Laney and Bonnie were there?

'I know what you're thinking,' she said. 'They don't have anywhere else to go. They definitely can't go home. There have been no threats made on their lives, so we can't send them to a safe house. We don't know what he'd have done if he got inside. Looked around maybe? Tried to figure me out?'

'Exactly, de Silva.' Barclay tried to keep his voice calm. 'He could have done anything. To anyone.'

'It's the thrill of it,' de Silva said. 'It's just like sending the finger in the post. Attempting to get into my house fulfils something for him, feeds the need for him to feel thrilled. But also in control. He made a choice to come to my house and I had no control over that: he had the control. I've no doubt he'd have gotten in if I hadn't have woken up. That was not in his plan.'

'Who is this man?'

De Silva shrugged. 'Someone who finds excitement beyond his crimes, in doing things that could get him caught. It's a game.'

Barclay closed his eyes tight, and the image of the man in black at de Silva's backdoor was burned onto his eyelids.

'Come on,' she said. 'Let's go and get some coffee. We'll walk down to Mean Bean. You look like you could do with the walk.'

'Yeah,' he said. 'I could do with getting my car later, too.'

'Jesus, Barclay, where did you end up?'

'Trust me when I say that you don't want to know. I can't incriminate you, too.'

She grabbed her coat and threw it over her arm. 'Tell me it wasn't illegal, at least.'

'Definitely illegal in the Middle East.'

De Silva held her hand up. 'I don't want to know any more, thank you.'

'It's for the best.'

They got into the lift and the motion as it elevated them to the ground floor made Barclay's stomach flip. He wasn't entirely convinced a coffee would make him feel any better, but some food might. A little sausage barm with brown sauce would go a long way in reviving him.

He hoped.

A text came through to his work phone from a number he didn't recognise. *This is my personal number, it'd be great to talk. Sorry I had to leave our meeting early.*

Barclay stared at the message, couldn't decide whether to reply or delete it, and then the lift doors opened and he followed de Silva out.

Outside, the fresh air was cool and gentle, and Barclay wished he could just stop walking, close his eyes and let it breeze through his hair.

De Silva's voice broke Barclay's moment. 'What the bloody hell is he up to?'

Barclay's eyes snapped open in time to see what de Silva had focused on. In the far area of the carpark, Braxton leaned into a window, a brown bag in hand, and passed something to the driver. 'Who is that?' He couldn't make out the car's make or model in the glare from the sun.

Then, Braxton headed toward them, a greasy bag filled with spicy-smelling food in his hand.

'You're looking a bit worse for wear, if you don't mind me saying?' He sounded jolly, slapped Barclay on his upper arm.

'I do mind.' Barclay was only half joking.

'We'll be back in about an hour,' de Silva said.

'See you then.' Braxton disappeared inside the building. The stink of his food hung around and Barclay's stomach gurgled.

'Is that...' De Silva squinted her eyes, looked out over the far end of the carpark, where a silver BMW turned onto the main road. 'That's O'Brien's car!'

Barclay looked at her, and knew that his thought was hers too. They'd been here before. Last year, a PC had leaked sensitive information about the Lamond investigation to the press.

'If Braxon's been speaking to O'Brien about this case, we have to be certain, Barclay,' de Silva said.

Barclay knew they could easily check CCTV footage from cameras around the OCC. They'd need to do it in private. He considered asking Lawrence to look into it, but if he'd learned anything from last year, it was not to trust anyone in these situations.

Food will have to wait.

Thirty

De Silva knew the feeling well. The sickness in the pit of the stomach that came not just with excessive drinking, but with the fear of not knowing what you'd done the night before. Or, even worse, knowing *exactly* what you'd done. It sounded to de Silva like Barclay could remember it all, and whatever had happened, he seemed embarrassed. But it wasn't her business to pry.

She'd ordered them both some food online and collected it in under half an hour. In that time, she'd heard Barclay's stomach growl and bubble. He'd inhaled his sausage barm.

They'd found a meeting room to hide away in while they ate, and when they were done, they made their way up to the security office, where Chloe, the OCC's independent security officer, watched multiple screens, internally and externally.

De Silva thought back to her time with Crosby. The man she'd craved more than her own husband, more than anything at times. She wondered whether other officers had ever seen them sneak off somewhere they thought was private. Whether she and Crosby had ever been caught on camera in the throes of their affair.

It had been more than sex to de Silva. She'd thought once that she'd loved him, but when he walked away and went back to his wife, when she'd found out that he was involved with the Lamond murders last year, she had wondered. With her therapist, she came to the somewhat comforting conclusion that she hadn't. That she had been in love with the idea of him. She had loved that he wanted her in ways that her husband hadn't any more. She craved his attention, his affection.

That was all there was to it.

'Nice to see you both,' Chloe said. 'What is it you're looking for?'

Neither of them knew Chloe very well: they'd never really had any need to interact with her in their roles.

'We need to check out some footage from the carpark. The far corner, where the road bends around to the main road.'

'How long ago?'

'Let's say about an hour ago,' Barclay said.

Chloe scanned through the video to an hour earlier and let it play. 'Nothing there.'

'Could you move it forward slowly?'

'Sure.'

Branches on the trees that bordered the carpark swayed in the breeze, moving as though waving for attention. Then, a car pulled in. 'There,' de Silva said. 'Keep it playing.'

The car was silver. A BMW. She recognised the registration and knew it was O'Brien's car. Then, a few minutes later, Braxton climbed out of the car, carrying his lunch and then out of view of that camera.

'So he was with O'Brien,' Barclay said.

'Could you make us a copy of this? Just this section?'

'Sure. I can email it?'

'That would be great.'

They left the security office and headed toward the lift. De Silva's mind felt heavy with worry and with anticipation of the conversation she knew she was going to have with Braxton. With O'Brien too.

He'd retired, sure, but some officers couldn't let go. That was how it went sometimes. They'd spent so much time working the beat or leading investigations that they'd forgotten what it was like to be a normal person. A civilian. Old habits die hard, but it was a habit she knew she was going to have to insist O'Brien broke.

As for Braxton… well, it would likely be a suspension pending investigation; but depending on what he'd shared with their former DSI, it could be a lot worse.

'You okay?' Barclay asked.

'Another leak, Barclay.'

'Potential leak. They might have just been catching up over lunch.'

'He handed O'Brien something,' de Silva said. 'And besides, Braxton brought his lunch back in with him.'

'Coffee then. Tea. A little Diet Coke. It doesn't matter. What matters is the information we have, and that is that Braxton spent some of his lunchtime with O'Brien. That's all we know.'

'And that he—'

Barclay interrupted her. 'And that he handed O'Brien something, yes. Could have been anything!'

She knew he was right, of course. But that instinct in her that Barclay had once said he admired, that O'Brien brought her back into the police for, rang loud and clear. There was more to this situation than just a lunchtime catch-up.

Her phone pinged. An email had come through from an address she didn't recognise.

ProjectRainford@anonomail.com. Her initial thought was that this was some sort of scam or spam, because when she clicked the email, she realised there was no subject. In the body of the email itself, just a mobile phone number and the words *Call me from your Merseyside Police-issued phone number. I won't answer any other call.* She read it over twice, registered the word 'Rainford' in the email address.

As Barclay pressed the button for the lift, de Silva wordlessly handed him her phone. 'Look at the email address.'

He handed her back the phone and stepped into the lift. 'Any ideas? It can't be the man from last night, surely?'

'No,' de Silva agreed. 'That doesn't make sense.' As the doors were about to slide shut, de Silva grabbed them and pushed them back open and stepped out. Barclay followed, his eyes wide, eyebrows arched high, he kept his hand on the door so it couldn't close again. 'I can't call this person from the incident room if Braxton is there,' de Silva said. 'If he's sharing information with O'Brien before I get a chance to speak to them both…'

'Are you going to tell Murphy? About Braxton, I mean.'

'Not yet.' De Silva looked again at the email on her phone, at the phone number, and ominous message. 'Like you said, we're not certain of anything.'

'I booked out Meeting Room Five for the next few hours. Shall we go back there?'

'I'll go,' she said. 'I need you back in the incident room. Keep things moving forward. Get that footage from my cam to the Digital Forensics team. Frame by frame, see if they can detect a face, any distinguishing features, anything that'll help us figure out who this is.'

'De Silva…'

'If one of us isn't back, they'll talk. And if Braxton is leaking information, he'll get twitchy. We've already been gone way too long.'

Barclay checked his watch. 'Fine,' he said. 'But you'll update me before you do anything else, won't you?'

'I promise,' she said. As Barclay stepped back into the lift and the doors closed, de Silva walked toward Meeting Room Five and called the number in the email. The phone was answered before the first ring finished. 'This is DCI de Silva,' she said.

The room was still empty, and she closed the door behind her, then put her phone on speaker mode and sat down. 'Hello.' De Silva hadn't expected to hear a woman's voice. It was soft and light, and sounded nervous. Unsure of itself. 'Thank you for calling me.'

'What *do* I call you?'

A pause. 'That doesn't matter,' the woman said. 'You can call me Breaker.'

'Breaker? A breaker of what?'

A little nervous snigger, and then she said, 'You already know.'

It dawned on de Silva quickly. 'The hack,' she said. 'That was you.'

'In part, yes.'

De Silva analysed the accent. It definitely wasn't local. If she had to place it, she'd say it was from Lancashire.

'Are you still there?'

'I'm here,' de Silva said. 'What can I do for you?' She refused to use the name Breaker. Melodramatic. Like a codename you'd hear in some movie.

'It's what *I* can do for *you*.'

'And what can you do for me?'

'I can tell you why they killed Jacob Meeks.'

Of all the things that had crossed de Silva's mind since she received the email, this was the last thing she'd expected. She took out her personal phone, found the voice memos app and pressed record. 'You know who killed Jacob Meeks?'

'Not who,' Breaker said. 'I said "why".'

'Tell me.'

'Just slow down, de Silva. There are things I—'

'Listen, you contacted me,' de Silva said. The annoyance in her voice obvious. 'If you've got something useful to tell me then say it now, otherwise I've got an investigation to manage.'

Another pause. 'David asked me to send something to the police in case anything ever happened to him.'

'When did he ask you to do this?'

'A long time ago,' she said. 'But that doesn't matter. Time is irrelevant.' There was something in her voice, a thickness that de Silva decided was caused by some emotion. Respect. Love, maybe. 'He was a man dedicated to the truth. He committed his life to helping others – to solving crimes the police couldn't. Or wouldn't.'

'Like the incidents at Rainford Lane School for Boys?'

'His project. His baby,' Breaker said. 'I helped him. At the start, anyway. But he pushed ahead without me. I couldn't keep up. He took it all so personally, because—'

'He attended the school.'

'That's right.'

'What did he find?'

'He pieced it together,' she said. 'I helped him hack some app he'd found on the Dark Web. He knew it was somehow connected to Rainford Lane.'

'Connected how?'

'He wouldn't tell me,' she said. 'There were accounts. Addresses. Phone numbers, email addresses. Card payment information. He put together a list of almost everyone who had a subscription to that app. That's what he asked me to send to the police, and I know you'd spoken to him, so who better?'

De Silva thought on that. 'That's a lot of information,' she said. 'Did he find out what the app is used for?'

'No,' Breaker said. 'The app was taken down before he could do any more. Taken down or moved. That happens a lot on the Dark Web.'

De Silva already knew that from Holden's research.

Meeks's own investigation had gotten further than any team at the police had managed in the decades since the crimes had taken place. Maybe Breaker was right: perhaps Meeks was devoted to the truth.

'Ordinarily I wouldn't trust the police.' Breaker took a breath. 'But this was his wish,' she said. 'And I know your husband was—'

'Don't finish that sentence.'

A pause. Then, de Silva heard Breaker tapping away at a keyboard. 'I'm sending you a document. You can have it checked by your digital team if you like, but I can promise you there are no viruses; this isn't another hack attempt, and I know you won't want to waste any time once you see what's on there.'

Her work phone pinged: another email from the anonymous email address. 'Project Rainford,' she said. 'What is that?'

'It's just what he called his work. I heard an email come through just now, did you receive it?'

'I can see it.' De Silva opened the email and looked at the attachment: RainfordProject.xls. 'It's an Excel file?'

'That's right.'

'You said you knew why Meeks was murdered?'

'It's all right there in that file. Right at your fingertips,' Breaker said. 'He was killed for that information.'

'What do you mean?'

'I'm going to hang up now. This is a pay-as-you-go SIM. Don't try to call it again. If I need you again, I'll contact you.'

The line went dead.

De Silva stared down at the email on her phone. There were three choices: she could go and see Murphy and the NCA with this; she could take it to Holden herself to scan it for viruses or malware; or, she could open it right there and then.

Breaker had told her that there was nothing dangerous attached to the file. But, if de Silva opened it, she'd be taking the word of a self-confessed hacker. The very hacker who'd tried to access hers and Barclay's personal information.

She hovered her thumb over the attachment, took a deep breath and pressed it. Inside the document was a list of names, addresses, payment info and phone numbers, just as Breaker had described.

Her stomach sank as she reached the end of the list. She took out her phone and called Barclay. 'Are you at your desk?'

'Yeah…'

'I need you to go out into the corridor, where no one is around. I'm going to send you an email. I don't want you to take any action yet, do you understand?'

'What's going on?' She heard him moving, the unsteadiness of his breath as he walked.

'Do you understand?' She pressed the forward button on the email. 'This can't get back to Braxton, to anyone just yet. Not until I've had a chance to speak to Murphy myself.'

'I understand,' he said.

'I'll be back soon,' she said. 'Remember, Barclay, no action until I'm back.'

'Where are you going?'

'I'm going to speak to O'Brien,' she said. 'Get this Braxton thing boxed off so we can move on.'

Thirty-One

Clouds had shrouded the sun by the time de Silva reached O'Brien's home on Love Lane. The house was much older than the others across the street, which looked as though they were built in the 1930s.

As she passed by the empty flower bed, an email pinged through from Brennan. It told her that the cuts on the finger she'd received in the post matched those on Meeks's body where his digit had been removed. DNA matching was pending and could take some time with everything else going on. She knew that it would all take time. Just like she'd known the finger was Meeks's without having to send it to the lab.

The only question she couldn't fully answer was why the killer had sent it to her.

She pressed the doorbell and waited, heard O'Brien inside, shuffling about, and eventually he unlocked the door and pulled it open. 'Well,' he said. He reached out and hugged her close. 'This is a pleasant surprise. Come in, come in. I'll put a pot on.'

De Silva followed him into the kitchen and leaned against the counter, watching O'Brien fill up a kettle and find two mugs. 'I'm not here for a social visit, Tom, and I think you know that.'

'What do you mean?'

'Braxton,' she said. 'How long's it been going on?'

'If you're insinuating that Braxton and I are having some clandestine affair, I'm afraid you're barking up the wrong tree.'

'Swerve the jokes, Tom.' There was a sternness to her voice and she kept her eyes on him. He couldn't meet her gaze, and it was then she knew something was wrong. 'Braxton's been feeding you information from the incident room.'

'I don't know what you're—'

'You were seen,' de Silva cut in, her voice softer than she had expected. 'By me and Barclay. Braxton was seen getting out of your car.'

O'Brien poured boiled water into the mugs. 'Just two former colleagues catching up,' he said.

'Do you make a habit of lying about meeting up with friends?' She sighed, could feel the lie festering between them. 'For God's sake, Tom… what did Braxton give you?'

O'Brien sighed. 'Just a little progress report,' he said. 'I was just keeping an eye. It's all there. You can take it!' He pointed to the counter, and de Silva snatched up the thin manila envelope.

'You don't need to keep an eye on me, I know what I'm doing.' She shook her head. 'What did you do with the information he gave to you?'

'Nothing.' He held up his hands in surrender. 'I swear.'

He's lying. 'Then what was going on?'

He handed de Silva a mug of steaming tea and slipped into a seat at the small dining table that had just two chairs. De Silva felt the absence of Kath then. One of those chairs would never be used again.

'I'm lonely,' he said. 'I'm an old man. Past my prime. Over the hill. On the way to the knacker's yard, as my dad would have said.' He looked up at her and said, 'Sit down, Win, you're making me nervous.'

She sat opposite him, felt the mug wobble slightly in her grip as she put it down. 'You're not over any hill, Tom. You're still sharp. Smart. You *chose* to retire.'

'Trust me, there was no choice in what happened.'

That hung in the air between them. He'd retired to care for his wife in her final weeks and de Silva supposed he was right: there hadn't really been a choice for him. It was duty. Responsibility. It was love.

'I knew you'd never tell me anything,' he said. 'I tried with Barclay and he was as tight-mouthed as a duck's arse. Braxton had always been a talker.'

'And now you might have ruined his career.'

'Don't say that.' He looked genuinely concerned for Braxton. 'He showed me nothing but bits. Where you were up to, what you were thinking. The direction you were going in.'

'That's not bits, Tom. That's the whole investigation.'

'You wouldn't begrudge an old man something to keep his mind occupied, would you? That's all it was. A little puzzle for me to chew on.'

De Silva felt that that wasn't all it was. There was something O'Brien wasn't saying. *He can't let go of the job*, she thought. 'Take up Sudoku. Do a wordsearch. Police investigations aren't any of your business any more,' she said. During her leave of absence, she'd felt the sharpness of her mind dull, and so she understood what O'Brien was going through. 'Do I have your word? This stops now.'

O'Brien hung his head then nodded. 'Fine,' he said. 'But this isn't Braxton's fault.'

She wondered what O'Brien had told Braxton to get him to open up. Had he flattered him? Promised to put in a good word with some of his old buddies still on the force? Had O'Brien groomed Braxton the way he had done with de Silva throughout the decades that spanned her career? 'That tea's gone right through me,' de Silva said. 'I'm just going to nip the loo.' As she stood up, O'Brien's phone rang out. She left the envelope Braxton had given to O'Brien on the countertop.

'Well, if you do need a number two, there's air freshener in the cupboard.'

'I don't.'

'No need to feel embarrassed,' he said. 'We all do it.' He answered the phone and de Silva shook her head and went upstairs.

She needed to move quickly. The guest room first, then the master. After snapping on some fresh protective gloves from her pocket, she rooted through drawers filled with underwear, old T-shirts, folded chinos, bed linens.

But she found nothing like what she was looking for. True, she didn't exactly know what it was she thought she might find – but she'd know if she found it.

Before she moved on to the master bedroom, she stopped at the top of the landing, winced at the squeak of a floorboard and listened. He was still on the phone. She could hear him arguing with someone about cancelling a gym membership.

She moved into the master bedroom and knew that she had just seconds before she needed to be back downstairs so she didn't rouse his suspicions. There was nothing out of the ordinary in the wardrobe, or the drawers under the bed, or in the chest of drawers with the small telly on top.

Nothing. She'd been wrong. Breaker's list had to be inaccurate. Some sort of trick. De Silva had been stupid to believe the word of someone who openly called themselves Breaker.

Because of that list, she'd suspected that her friend, her mentor, had had something to do with the terrible events at Rainford Lane School for Boys. She hated herself for it, but knew that if he ever found out, O'Brien would eventually understand. It was a lead, a tenuous and ridiculous one, but a lead that she had to follow through, nonetheless.

She wanted to go downstairs, to come clean, to confess that the real reason she'd come to see him wasn't to challenge him over Braxton, but to find corroborating evidence about his name being on the list Breaker had provided, that O'Brien himself had involvement in this case.

With the weight of her own guilt heavy on her head, de Silva closed the bedroom door and then noticed a string hanging down from the ceiling above her. A loft hatch.

No, this is insane. There's nothing to find.

At the top of the stairs, she stopped and listened. O'Brien was still on the phone.

She had the time.

The string dangled there, an invitation. She pulled it slowly, and a ladder unfolded. She climbed up, and turned her phone to torch mode, the light soft and weak.

The place was standard, really. Boxes filled to the brim with Christmas decorations, tools, old tech. In the corner, an outdated TV that de Silva hadn't seen the likes of since she was a kid.

Then, her torchlight bounced off something in the back corner: it winked at her. She moved closer, careful on the creaking floorboards. A filing cabinet, dented, once pale blue but that paint had begun to flake away.

It had a lock on, and when de Silva pulled at the top drawer, it opened on noisy hinges that squealed like some dying animal. She glanced over her shoulder and waited. She couldn't hear O'Brien talking now, but she was two floors above him.

If I can't hear him, he can't hear me.

She pulled the drawer out to its full extent, slowly so the noise was faint. It was filled with paperwork. De Silva found O'Brien and Kath's marriage certificate, the deeds to their house and old bills that dated as far back as the 1980s.

When she pushed the drawer back in, it only made a tiny whine. Nothing like before. The second drawer was stuck, as though too full. She had to give it a good yank and finally it gave way and opened.

The first thing she saw was a wad of papers, fastened together by black plastic binding combs. She turned it over, saw the title and knew instantly: her fears were true.

The Rainford Project: My Search for the Truth, by Jacob Meeks.

Her mind buzzed, alive with possible explanations as to why something that belonged to Jacob Meeks should be in the loft of a former DSI from Merseyside Police.

Beneath that were old photo albums. Kath and O'Brien's wedding day, trips out with family and friends, pictures with de Silva's dad. She took them out and put them aside, and saw one more, red and leather-bound, at the bottom of the drawer. She lifted it out and into her torchlight, and when she saw the label, her stomach dropped for the second time that day.

It can't be, she thought.

'Oh dear.' O'Brien's voice from behind her was low, menacing, but calm. Her own pulse had beaten in her ears so hard that she hadn't heard him come up the ladder. But when she heard his voice, bile rose from her stomach.

She turned to face him and took a step back, but knew that O'Brien would read that as a weakness, that he himself had the upper hand. She took a step forward again, regaining her ground, held his stare. She was shaking, and hoped to God the loft was dark enough that he wouldn't notice. 'I've called for backup already, Tom. Don't try anything stupid.'

She aimed the torchlight at his feet so she could see where he was, but not blind him. She had to be able to see what he did next.

'You've made no such call.' He sniggered and took a step to his left, covering the ladder down to the landing. 'I've been down there.' He indicated to the hatch in the floor. 'Listening to you snooping around.'

With the phone light illuminating him, she swiped across the screen with her thumb. It was a struggle, holding the volume she'd found in the filing cabinet too. She found the messages screen and quickly typed to Barclay: *Need help. OB's house.*

Luckily, she usually kept her personal phone on silent, so there was no sound when she pressed send. She saw the blue ticks appear and knew that he'd read it. He didn't need to reply. He just needed to take action.

'Move away from the hatch, Tom.' Her voice was even, but inside her senses threatened to overwhelm her, every molecule in her body fired up by the need to get out of there.

'I'm afraid I can't do that, Win, my love.' He paced now, watching her. 'What would your dad say, do you think, seeing us like this now?'

That stung. It would break her dad's heart, she knew. 'Tom, I'm warning you. Move away from the hatch.'

'Oh you're warning me now.' He smiled broadly, and in the semi-dark of the loft, the sight frightened de Silva. 'Put down the manuscript and the photo album and slide them to me.'

'I can't do that.' De Silva took another step forward. To get to the PAVA spray and baton under her coat she'd have to drop everything in her hands, maybe even her phone. He could lunge at her, hit her with something. She could be dead before Barclay arrived.

'Win, please,' he said. 'For God's sake, just put it down.'

She kept the torch on him, watching him, but knelt down and put the manuscript and album down next to her feet.

'Good,' he said. He reached around his back with one hand and drew a steak knife. Within a split second, he lunged at her, and she grabbed the PAVA from her holster. It was too late. He had her around the waist and she was falling backward. She heard a snap and crunch, thought of her bones breaking, and almost choked in a cloud of dust.

O'Brien on top of her, the full weight of him pinioning her down to the ground. At first, she was unsure if he was conscious or not. Then he coughed, and sat up, straddling her chest so that she could barely breathe.

'This isn't how I imagined it ending for you, Win,' he said. 'I'm sorry.' He lifted the knife over his head.

De Silva tightened her grip on the PAVA, lifted it and sprayed into his eyes and mouth. He screamed and rolled away. De Silva took advantage of the situation and got on top of him with all of her weight. She snatched the knife from his loose grip and threw it over her shoulder, somewhere into the shadows of the loft.

Sirens wailed outside, close, and she knew that within a few seconds, the house would be flooded with police officers. Her phone had skidded off, she could see the torchlight illuminating part of the loft in a shaft of white light.

She looked back over her shoulder and on the floor behind her, next to Meeks's manuscript, was the red photo album, which contained some of the most damning evidence.

It was clear that O'Brien knew all about the abuse at Rainford Lane School for Boys. It was clear because he had been there, and that red leather-bound photo album was the proof.

Thirty-Two

Barclay insisted that de Silva see the paramedic who was treating O'Brien's eyes as best she could. 'Just to get checked out,' he'd said. She'd ignored him, as she did whenever he said something she didn't want to hear. He wanted to rage at her. Ask her what she was thinking by instructing him to stay behind at the incident room, to not follow on with backup, when she knew that O'Brien was on that list this person had sent to de Silva. But he knew better.

De Silva was scratched up, her jacket ripped open at the back, covered in dust and cobwebs, but ultimately she was fine.

He watched her then, bathed in the blue lights swirling and pulsing over O'Brien's house and street. The neighbours had stayed at their doorsteps to watch. Only one had their phone in the air, likely recording everything, and de Silva was speaking with Murphy.

Later on, when this had all settled, there would be hell to pay. De Silva hadn't followed proper protocol. She'd opened a suspicious email and an attachment from someone she didn't know. She went off in pursuit of a possible suspect alone. The only thing she'd done right was telling someone, Barclay, where she was going.

But still, he'd done nothing with that information. He hadn't spoken to Murphy as he should have done. De Silva could have been seriously hurt.

Yes, and if we arrived any sooner, de Silva may not have found what she found.

There was merit in her approach, he knew that, but he couldn't justify it. Rules were there to protect them, to govern their actions, to guide them.

He thought of Nick and of Ayris. He was a hypocrite to berate de Silva, even in his head, about not following rules when he'd cheated on his husband.

Vows aren't rules. They're promises. They're the foundation, the least each partner can do for the other.

In the navy, someone had started a rumour that he was a whore. That he'd been overtly sexual with other officers, straight men with families and wives. None of that had been true, but that word stuck to him and stained his skin like muck.

Whore.

That was how he felt right then after this night with Ayris. He needed to speak to Nick and soon. He took out his phone and stared down at Ayris's text one more time. He swiped left and deleted the text message without replying.

'You ready?' De Silva stood in front of him then, looking up at him, her pale skin looked corpse-blue in the lights from the squad cars. 'Could you drive? I'm still feeling a bit shaky. I asked McLachlan to take my car back to the OCC.'

He wasn't sure that he was. 'Yeah,' he said, his voice a whisper. He cleared his throat, swallowed back his own emotions, his own problems which he'd soon have to face. 'Let's get out of here.'

They walked past the ambulance O'Brien was sitting inside, his head tipped back, a paramedic treating him. Outside the ambulance were four uniformed officers. There was no way he could slip out unseen, and Barclay doubted that O'Brien could get very far after his eyes had been doused with de Silva's PAVA spray.

Barclay's car was parked on the other side of the cordon and as they headed toward it, he wondered how de Silva felt, what she was thinking. Knowing that her own husband had attended that school. Had O'Brien abused her husband when he was just a boy?

The only way to get answers would be to question O'Brien himself.

'First things first,' de Silva said. 'We need to get some answers from the NCA. This Ayris fella. I need to know if he knew about O'Brien. If he suspected him in any way.'

She'd read Barclay's mind.

-

Ayris and Fitzgerald had been given a large office on the top floor of the OCC building. Barclay assumed if they were up there, they'd be out of the way, the complete opposite end of the building from de Silva's incident room.

De Silva tucked the two evidence bags containing the manuscript and photo album under her arm as they entered the office without knocking. Ayris got to his feet, his eyes wide and fixed on Barclay. 'Could you at least knock?' He sounded angry.

'We haven't sent for you,' Fitzgerald said.

'Not really the kind of person you send for,' de Silva said. 'I've got some questions for you this time, and I want you to cut the bullshit. We can do it now, or we can do it later when I send for you to come to an interview room downstairs.'

Barclay tried to keep the smirk off his face. He would never have dreamed of speaking to the NCA like this, but it gave him a thrill to watch de Silva go for it.

'All right,' Ayris said. 'Let's all just sit down.'

De Silva stayed where she was, but threw both evidence bags onto the table. 'Answers,' she said. 'Now.'

'What is this?' Ayris held up the manuscript.

'A book,' Barclay said. 'Written by Jacob Meeks. I read some of it and believe me, it's quite a read. It describes his abuse at Rainford Lane School for Boys. In detail.'

Ayris was unmoved, his face a mask of professionalism and distance. 'Does it detail any involvement in the murders you've been investigating?'

'We haven't gotten that far,' de Silva admitted. 'But I do have a theory if you'd like to hear it?'

'De Silva, we're not your enemy,' Fitzgerald said. 'We want to solve this as much as you do.'

'I'm glad you say that.' De Silva reached for the second evidence bag, the photo album, and held it up for them both to see. On the front of the album was written *The Woulds*. 'You can start by sharing what you know about The Woulds app.'

Ayris and Fitzgerald exchanged a look. Barclay felt they were weighing up their options, trying to decide how much they could divulge, what sharing information meant in the light of all the evidence obtained from O'Brien's own loft.

'We know you're upset,' Ayris said. He stepped closer to de Silva. 'We know O'Brien was your mentor.'

He was her friend, Barclay thought. *Her dad's friend, too. He was more than just a mentor.*

'I can't imagine what you're going through,' Ayris said. 'We can't give you all of the answers you want. But this—' Ayris took the photo album from de Silva. 'I think this goes deeper than what we originally thought, and okay. I'll tell you what we know about The Woulds app.'

'Ayris!' Fitzgerald stood up. 'You can't be serious?'

'These two detectives are closer than the NCA has ever been,' Ayris said over his shoulder. 'If we're co-operating, then we're sharing information. I think you might both want to take a seat for this.' Ayris offered de Silva his chair.

Barclay took a spare chair from the corner of the room and glanced at de Silva. Her shoulders had lowered, the frown on her brow had straightened and she sat down at the small office table.

'What is The Woulds?' Barclay asked.

Ayris took a deep breath, closed his eyes and let it go. 'We've been tracking the app as best we could for years. As you know, it's on the Dark Web, so that's made things so much harder. They take it down, it can be gone for days, weeks, even months, or it moves and we have to find it again. But one thing it never, ever does is change its name.'

Barclay thought on that for a moment. To reduce the chances of detection, the logical step would be to rename it over and over again. Then whoever was investigating it would always be on the back foot: their investigation would have to start all over again. 'That doesn't make sense,' he said.

'You're right,' Ayris said. 'Unless the name is so recognisable, so engrained in Dark Web activity, that they don't need to change their name.'

'You think someone's protecting them?' de Silva asked.

'We do.'

De Silva nodded. 'I think one of those people protecting it is O'Brien.'

Ayris looked away, though Barclay couldn't say why. Whether he was sparing de Silva the knowing look on his face or something else. Had the NCA already reached that conclusion?

'What else is there?' Barclay asked.

'The last time it was removed, last year,' Ayris said, 'our digital people managed to get access to it. They downloaded it, using a VPN. The app is sophisticated, smart, really cleverly designed, and when we finally found it on a black-market app site, it was sold in a bundle with an app called In2Web.'

The app he asked me about when we first met.

'In2Web is a virtual private network, a VPN, that allows people to access the internet anonymously,' Ayris explained. 'We tested it, and The Woulds app only works with In2Web, it doesn't work with any other VPN.'

'Hence them being bundled together and sold on the Dark Web,' de Silva said, nodding.

'That's right,' Ayris said. 'When we managed to download The Woulds app, we found that there are two types of membership. One is free, the other is a subscription service.'

'If it's paid for, then there'll be a trace,' de Silva said. 'A paper trail through the subscriber's bank account.'

Barclay nodded. 'That's the list. The one Meeks asked Breaker to send us.'

'Who's Breaker?' Ayris asked.

'You spoke about a theory…' Fitzgerald interrupted.

De Silva nodded. 'I think that Meeks was murdered because of his investigation into the deaths we're looking into. I think after his abuse at that school, he became obsessed with understanding everything he could about it. Tried to make sense of his own history. Our investigation found that every single one of those victims was tied to Rainford Lane in some way. I'm betting Meeks knew that. When those people started to die, he became even more focused on solving it.'

'But who would kill him?' Fitzgerald asked.

De Silva looked down at the table. Barclay felt the change in her. The awkwardness, the unwillingness to say the thing that needed to be said.

'O'Brien,' Barclay said. 'Or at least, he orchestrated it. I bet that book of Meeks's was taken from his apartment by the killer and given to O'Brien.'

'You don't think O'Brien and Meeks's killer are one and the same?' Ayris's interest was piqued now.

'No,' Barclay said. 'The CCTV clearly shows a tall, broad man. That doesn't match O'Brien.'

'He had someone kill Meeks for him,' de Silva said, finally. 'To shut Meeks up. To stop his investigation. To keep the secrets of Rainford Lane School for Boys buried there.'

Ayris nodded.

'And it all comes back to this.' De Silva pointed at the photo album in Ayris's hands. 'To The Woulds.'

'What is it, Ayris?' Barclay asked.

Ayris sighed and said, 'The nearest we can tell is that it's a tracking tool.' He paused, his eyes flitting between Barclay and de Silva and back again. 'It's a social media app where abusers can have access to their victims through paid subscription where they can contact them easily through messaging or calls. Their victims have a free version of the app and can receive incoming messages, calls. Video calls. We believe that sex traffickers use it to identify targets. But above all' – here he held up the photo album – 'just like this album, it's a catalogue.'

Thirty-Three

The heating was on high in Murphy's office, and she and de Silva sat in an awkward silence. Murphy was focused, her eyes staring at her computer screen; de Silva sat with her hands clasped and waited.

'I can't believe what I'm reading here,' Murphy said. 'De Silva, the things you've done.'

De Silva nodded. 'I know.'

'Former-DSI O'Brien may have let this type of behaviour fly, but I won't have it. Not on my team and not in this force. Your actions are a blatant disregard for the protocols and policies we have in place; they exhibit an utter lack of respect for me and my position.'

'I know.'

'Well, I'm glad you know, de Silva, because that means you'll know what's coming next.'

De Silva did. Disciplinary action. Suspension. She'd already had her resignation speech planned, rehearsed and ready to go.

'You're lucky for a few reasons,' Murphy said. 'You're lucky that you weren't injured in the first instance; you're lucky that the file you opened didn't bring down our entire network for a second time; but you're also lucky that your actions have resulted in the arrest of a person involved with one of the most heinous and continued acts of abuse I've ever witnessed in my entire career.'

De Silva hadn't expected that, and hoped the shock on her face was well disguised.

'People have a tendency to remember the mistakes you make, de Silva, you should know that. Whether your methods get results doesn't matter. These rules were put in place for a reason. The evidence you've obtained at O'Brien's residence, though damning, was obtained without a warrant. I don't need to remind you of what that means, do I?'

'No, ma'am.'

'I will take action with you,' she said. 'But not right now. You're too far into this case that I fear removing you would put it into a tailspin. Another thing you're lucky for. But I promise you, de Silva, there will be consequences.'

'I understand.'

'Good,' she said. 'Now, I hear O'Brien has been brought into a holding cell?'

De Silva nodded. 'The hospital cleared him for release a few hours ago. He was brought straight here. I've no doubt the press will have a hold of the story soon.'

'I'll handle the press,' Murphy said. 'Are you up for this? I know O'Brien means a lot to you.'

De Silva was unsure how to answer. Once upon a time, O'Brien had been a father figure to her. Had taught her everything she knew.

Well, not everything.

'I'll ask Barclay to lead the interview.'

'Yes, I think that's the wisest thing you've done this week. Still, I feel uncomfortable with you being present during it. Your being there could have an effect.'

De Silva bit her tongue, thought better of arguing. But she needed to be in that room. She needed to look O'Brien in the eye and hear him answer their questions.

'If I have your assurance that you can remain professional and remove your emotions from the interview, I'll allow you to be present in the room. But under no circumstances are you to interact with former-DSI O'Brien. You can observe, and that's it.'

'Yes, ma'am.'

'One more thing before you go.' Murphy looked back at her screen. 'This thing with Braxton.'

'I've going to place him on leave for now,' De Silva said. 'Things are moving really quickly here, and I don't want to get distracted.'

'You're not concerned he'll speak to the press?'

'No.' De Silva had considered this since she saw Braxton leave O'Brien's car on the CCTV footage. 'I think Braxton has shared information with someone he thought he could trust – a former colleague. I don't think he'd speak to the press.'

'Good. But we need to make sure of that, don't we?'

'Yes, ma'am.'

De Silva had been in that office for a telling-off more times than she could remember, and when she left Murphy, she felt a sadness in her. Murphy and Ayris had been right: O'Brien had been her mentor and more. She didn't understand the things he was involved in, not thoroughly, and she questioned whether she could even get to the bottom of it, whether she had the heart and the stomach for it.

She took the stairs down to the ground floor: she needed the time to get her head straight. How could she look at O'Brien and see not her friend, but the monster he was? How could she hear him answer questions about the awful photographs she found in the red photo album?

She thought she knew now how this all linked together. That each of the victims of the crimes she'd investigated were, in some way, related to Rainford Lane School for Boys. Teachers, volunteers, groundskeepers. They'd run when they'd either discovered the truth of the abuse, or were afraid their involvement would come out and destroy their lives, like they'd destroyed those boys' lives.

They'd paid for their transgressions. If O'Brien knew who had murdered them, de Silva needed to find out. She had to treat him as just some other suspect.

But he isn't just some other suspect.

She questioned whether Murphy was right. De Silva should be nowhere near this and, if she was being truthful, neither should Barclay. It was too late now to have respect for the rules she had flagrantly ignored for all of her career. She'd have to see this one through.

By the time she hit the ground floor, her heart beat hard against her chest and she made a promise to herself that no matter what – as soon as all of this was over – she'd get back to the gym. Back to the levels of fitness she'd maintained before Ritchie.

In the corridor where the interview rooms lined the walls, she found Barclay waiting for her. He seemed nervous and shifted his weight from one foot to the other, a closed casefile in his hand. 'Are you okay?' he asked, as soon as he saw her.

'Just the standard dressing-down, you know.' She doubted very much that Barclay did know what that felt like. 'Is he in there?'

'They're bringing him up now. I've asked Lawrence to sit in with us, I hope that's okay? It'll be good for her.'

De Silva shook her head. 'She can take your lead,' she said. 'I'll be observing. Murphy's orders.'

'Bloody hell.'

'No, she's right.' De Silva pushed open the door to the interview room and found Lawrence sitting at one of the three chairs on the near side of the table. A portly man with thinning hair sat on the other side in a black suit. De Silva had never seen him before, but assumed he was O'Brien's lawyer. He glanced up at her with tired, red eyes and said nothing.

She dragged a chair off into the corner of the small room and waited. Sudden anxiety gripped her, unsure how she should react when O'Brien came into the room. Should she stare or look away? Look ahead and not at him? What was the proper way to act when your friend appeared to be involved something like this? Her stomach churned.

Finally, she heard footsteps out on the corridor, as Harris and O'Connor escorted O'Brien into the room. *Braxton*, she thought, *call him after the interview.* She needed to know whether her assumption about him – that he'd trusted the wrong person – was right or wrong. Still, there would be consequences for him as well as for her.

There always are.

Seeing O'Brien in handcuffs was a sight she struggled with. She found herself watching every movement he made: she couldn't help herself. He sat down next to his lawyer and stared at her. She couldn't read his face. There was nothing there. No emotion.

Barclay sat down next to Lawrence and pressed record on the wall unit. 'This is the interview of Mr Thomas O'Brien by Detective Sergeant Barclay and

Police Constable Lawrence of Merseyside Police. Also present are—'

'Can we just get on with it?' O'Brien said softly. 'This stuff always bored me.'

'—are Detective Chief Inspector de Silva and Mr O'Brien's legal counsel.' He looked at his watch. 'The time is 4:33 p.m.'

'Mr O'Brien, at 1:15 p.m. today, DCI de Silva entered your home and—'

'Without a warrant, I should say,' O'Brien said. He nudged his lawyer and added, 'Write that down, Burt. I know you'll remember, but humour me.'

'From my understanding, Mr O'Brien, DCI de Silva came to speak to you about you gleaning information from a detective sergeant on an active case.' Barclay's voice was even.

O'Brien shrugged. 'I asked questions. I can't control what I was told.'

'But you used that information to your advantage,' Barclay said. 'Didn't you?'

'I'm afraid I've no idea what you're referring to.'

'When DCI de Silva was at your property, she found a manuscript titled *The Rainford Project: My Search for the Truth*, written by Mr Jacob Meeks, a person who was murdered recently in his own home. Also found on your property was a photo album. Can you recall what was inside that photo album, Mr O'Brien?'

'My wedding day? Holidays to Cyprus? There were plenty of albums up there, so who can say?'

'This photo album had the words "The Woulds" written on the front of it. Do those words mean anything to you?'

O'Brien stared at Barclay. 'You know,' he said. 'As an experienced interviewer myself, I find your line of questioning basic. There's no real skill here, is there? Did you even attend the training on suspect interviews, or were you too busy at home playing daddy to your little Sarah?'

De Silva leaned forward, willing Barclay not to react. She could see what O'Brien was doing: playing on Barclay's own weakness – the view he had of himself.

Bastard.

'Could you please answer my basic, unskilled question then? Do the words "The Woulds" mean anything to you?'

'Other than that app you detected last year, no. Remember that investigation? The one you almost buggered up beyond repair? It's a good job de Silva was there. She finally got some work done on it.' He looked at her then. 'Didn't you?'

She sat back in her chair again, wished that the corner would swallow her up. Any care or warmth she had for this man quickly turned stone cold.

'So you know that The Woulds is the name of an app that our Digital Forensics team found on the phone of a victim last year,' Barclay continued. 'You know that it is also a leading area of investigation in a case currently being handled by the National Crime Agency.' Barclay stopped. De Silva knew he was leaving space for O'Brien to fill, but he didn't. 'What would those specific words be doing written on the front cover of a photo album that looks to be from the 1990s, found in your loft?'

'Don't answer that,' Burt said.

O'Brien said nothing.

Barclay opened the casefile on the desk and slid a photograph across the table. 'Do you recognise the tattoo in this photo?'

'Don't answer that,' Burt advised.

'I have one just like it,' O'Brien said.

'This here,' Barclay said. 'This wording. It says "Kath". That was your wife's name, wasn't it?'

'You keep her name out of your mouth.'

'We found this photograph of the tattoo with Kath's name on it inside the album DCI de Silva found in your loft.'

'My client has no further comments,' Burt said. 'I'd like to have a private word with him.'

'You think you've got me,' O'Brien said. 'But the truth is, you've freed me. You've no idea.'

'Don't say anything else, Tom, I'm warning you,' Burt said.

'But once they get their claws into you, that's it,' O'Brien continued, his eyes wild. 'You're theirs.'

'Who are you talking about?' De Silva couldn't help herself.

'Oh she does speak!' O'Brien snarled. 'You think this starts and ends with some school for bad kids in the arse-end of Liverpool? This is bigger than you. Bigger than the force and bigger than the NCA.' He took a breath, steadied himself. 'No, I'm glad it's over. I'm relieved.'

'And I'm relieved Kath wasn't here to see this,' de Silva said. 'Why did you even ask me back last year, O'Brien? Why did you seek me out to look into the deaths of those girls? Kelly Stack and the others?'

'De Silva...' Barclay had turned to her, his voice low with concern and warning.

'This interview is over,' Burt said, standing.

'Goddam it, Burt. Sit the hell down.' He leaned forward, his elbows resting on the table. 'I had no idea these cases were related to Lamond and that school. No idea at all.'

'You must have known,' de Silva said.

'Why must I?'

'Because some of the boys who attended a school you had ties with all came into your life, in one way or another,' de Silva snapped. 'DCI Crosby first. Then Ritchie through me. Then Lamond.'

O'Brien smiled. 'Oh,' he said. 'Oh, do you see, Burt? How clever she is? She gets that from her dad. He was so observant. Sometimes, some would say, a little too observant, but no matter.' He looked to Barclay again. 'My legal counsel would like some time with me now. I'm certain he'll want to get some things in place, you know?' To Burt he said, 'Come on then. Five minutes, then you can get back to your wife and kids.'

Barclay suspended the interview and stopped the recording. He waited for Burt and O'Brien to leave the room, where they were escorted down the corridor by Harris and O'Connor, before he turned to de Silva. 'This isn't what we agreed.'

She put her hands up in surrender. 'I know, I'm sorry. He just… I need answers.'

'We all do,' he said. 'But let me get to them my way.'

A silence passed between them then, in which Lawrence bit at her thumbnail. 'Shall I make us a coffee?' she asked.

'No,' de Silva said. 'I'll do it. You two need to talk about what's next.' She stood and paused at the door. 'Good job, Barclay.' She didn't wait for his response, but walked to the small kitchenette a few doors down.

Quickly, she made some instant coffee in four cups and stuck a teabag into a fifth. She put one sugar into O'Brien's and barely any milk. That was how he liked it, and she made it almost on auto-pilot, despite herself.

She found a tray in the cupboard under the sink, among empty bottles of washing-up liquid and cups stained with coffee. Back in the incident room, she placed three coffees and the tea on the interview table and retreated to her corner.

O'Brien was escorted back into the room alone. 'Where is your legal counsel?' Barclay stood, flapped by this sudden change in strategy.

'I excused him,' O'Brien said. He sat down opposite Barclay and Lawrence and let out a long breath. 'Now we can talk in peace.' He took a sip of his tea and smiled at de Silva. She looked away.

'What do you want to talk to us about?' Barclay asked.

'Incidentally, you'll want to get someone out to Burt's property quick-smart, I'd think. There are things he'll want to put in place. I'm sure he's already made one or two calls. Burt Reeves.'

De Silva was on her feet and at the door, where Harris and O'Connor waited. 'I need you to get a unit out to the home address of Burt Reeves,' she said softly. 'He's just left. Make the call while you tail. And one of you check that list we got from Breaker. See if he's on it.' They nodded and left without another word.

O'Brien sighed, the sound of a man releasing the things that he had held in for too long. 'You know, that man has looked after the interests of the people who run that app more than I ever could.'

'In what ways?' Lawrence asked.

'Be quiet, little one; the grown-ups are talking now,' he said.

'Did you kill Jacob Meeks?'

'No.'

'Was he murdered by someone else under instruction from you?'

That little smile on his face told de Silva that they were on the right track. 'So much has happened, I forget where I'm up to sometimes. I will tell you this, though. My being here. My arrest. It will kickstart a clean-up operation the likes of which you've never seen before.'

'Is that why Meeks is dead?' Barclay asked. 'Part of a clean-up operation? He knew too much, didn't he? Committed it all to the page, and even if he self-published, it'd have still been out there in the world.'

'The clean-up operation started a long time ago,' O'Brien said. He looked at de Silva directly, then. 'Do you still believe your Ritchie killed himself because you were fucking Crosby?'

Thirty-Four

Barclay was on his feet as de Silva got to hers. He half-dragged her out of the room and into the corridor. 'No, de Silva,' he said. 'No. I'm sorry, but I'm going to have to ask you to leave.'

'Not a chance!' De Silva's eyes were wild. 'I need to know what he meant.' She tried to push past him, but Barclay blocked her way.

'I'll let you know what he knows,' he said. 'Trust me.' In truth, Barclay was as rattled as she was and hoped his face didn't betray him. 'Go home,' he said. 'I'll ring you when we're done.'

'Barclay...'

'I mean it, de Silva.' His voice was stern then, strong and commanding. 'Go home.'

She looked into his face with those big blue eyes, deep as an ocean, and in that moment, Barclay saw how frightened she was. Whatever O'Brien meant could impact de Silva's entire life. It could derail her, ricochet her back into the abyss of depression and trauma where she was just last year.

There was so much left to do. The killer was still at large, they didn't fully understand the connection between Ritchie, Lamond, Crosby and the others. They were no closer to rooting out The Woulds. Barclay couldn't afford to lose de Silva now.

'Do you trust me to do this right?' Barclay asked. She nodded. 'Then let me do it.'

'I'll be around,' she said. 'You ring me as soon as it's done.' With that she walked off down the corridor to God knows where. Barclay only wished that she wouldn't end up staring at the bottom of a glass, or worse, a bottle.

He ducked back into the interview room and closed the door. He took in a deep breath to steady his nerves and sat down opposite O'Brien, whose face was expressionless, despite everything. He'd never seen someone look smug without looking happy about it before, but that was exactly what he was reading on O'Brien's face.

'I take it de Silva had to leave.'

'Tell me what you mean by that comment,' Barclay pressed.

O'Brien shrugged.

'Do you have any love for her at all, or was all of that just a lie, too?' Barclay was aware all of this was going to be on the recording of the interview, but he didn't care.

'I care very much for her,' O'Brien said.

'You suggested that Mr de Silva's death by suicide wasn't caused by the issues he and DCI de Silva were facing in their marriage.' His throat felt dry, and he could hear it in the hoarseness of his words. He swallowed down some cold coffee. 'Do you know something about his death?'

'You should read Meeks's manuscript,' O'Brien said. 'I'm certain that it's all in there. Though, I'd read it before de Silva does, if I were you.' He shook his head. 'Tough read,' he said. 'Now. Let's get down to it. You're treading water here, Barclay, in that awkward way you do.'

Barclay shuffled the questions around in his mind, the ones he'd prepared earlier. Sometimes, you have to jump about, be guided by the suspect, then circle back to clarify anything you need.

'Bob Brendan, Margaret Finch, Charles Heaton. Are any of these names familiar to you?' Barclay continued, 'Sharon McEntire, John Abbot, Terry Peters. Were these people part of the "clean-up" you mentioned earlier?'

O'Brien shook his head. 'You're asking all of the wrong questions. Maybe we should let the little one here have a go, eh? Save yourself some embarrassment? Oh don't look at me like that. You always look so sullen. You should get some help. You know, I know a very good therapist who—'

'Were you involved in their deaths, like you were involved in Meeks's?'

'Very tricky.' O'Brien smiled; to Barclay he looked almost amused. 'You'll never find Meeks's killer.'

'Why is that? Because I'm looking at him right now and you'll never admit to it?'

'Because they don't want you to find him. God, *I* don't even know who it was.'

'You make it sound like you're someone of importance to these people.'

O'Brien winked.

'Who are they?'

'They're every parent's worst nightmare. They infiltrate schools, like they did at Rainford Lane. They're at sports practices, they run flute lessons on a Tuesday afternoon, they hold Sunday School events, they whizz around in ice-cream vans selling sugar to little kids.'

'Spare me,' Barclay said.

'And all the while, you've no idea that those little, smiling faces are being assessed. Their family life, their socio-economic status, how likely they are to be immediately missed. Would anyone care if little Billy went missing in the woods?'

Billy, Barclay thought. *I know that name.*

'How long have you been practising that little speech?' Barclay felt pressure in his forehead above his eyebrows and tried to relax his face. He knew he'd be frowning, angry and determined. But the less O'Brien knew about how Barclay was feeling, the better. 'You're the one treading water here.'

Meeks's evidence board. One of the names there had been Billy Thompson. 'You mention Billy,' Barclay said. 'Who is that?'

O'Brien shrugged. 'Just an example,' he said. 'As good a name as any.'

'You say you want to get to it, so let's get to it. Tell me what you know.'

'I'll tell you this,' O'Brien said, twisting in his seat and looking up at the ceiling for a moment. He looked back at Barclay after a few seconds and said, 'There's a difference between revenge and necessity.'

'What does that mean?' Lawrence's voice was so light, almost a whisper. Barclay had forgotten she was even there with him. 'Are you saying some of these murders were revenge and some were necessity?'

De Silva said something similar after Meeks was found dead.

'I'm not sure I'm interested in saying any more on that right now.' O'Brien yawned. 'It's been such a long day.'

'I'll tell you what I think happened,' Barclay said. He cleared his throat. 'You orchestrated the murder of Jacob Meeks because he knew too much about this little operation you're a part of. The killer took the manuscript from Meeks's home and gave it to you for safe keeping. Maybe to destroy it. I think you had some involvement in the murders of Finch, Brendan and the others.'

'You're not forgetting Ritchie de Silva, are you?'

'You want to talk about that now?'

O'Brien shrugged. 'I don't think I've got anything left to lose. Even if you do catch up with Burt and he hasn't made any calls.'

'What are you talking about?'

'It doesn't matter.' He took a breath. 'I knew him as Ricky, all those years ago. I didn't recognise him when de Silva introduced us decades later. How could I?'

'No, how could you remember the faces of all of the boys whose lives you destroyed? I can imagine that's quite a struggle.'

'But then I read Meeks's manuscript, and I connected it all.' O'Brien looked at his nails. 'Besides, Ritchie wasn't one of mine. No, he was someone else's favourite.'

'Whose?'

O'Brien took a swig of his tea, and Barclay thought about how calm O'Brien seemed. How matter-of-factly he was talking about the abuse of little boys. Then O'Brien said, 'He was one of Bob's.'

'Bob Brendan?'

O'Brien nodded. 'It's true, Bob had a few favourites. Like Lewis Lamond.'

Barclay had half-expected his name to crop up during this interview. It was bound to. The little boy they'd abused until he'd cracked. The little boy who'd grown up to commit some of the worst crimes in Merseyside's history. 'Did Kath know that you'd abused children at Rainford Lane?'

O'Brien's eyes were brim-full of tears then. 'Kath knew nothing!' His voice was loud, thick with feeling.

Whatever he was, the monster that, at some point in his life, had begun to act out on his sickening impulses, this much was clear to Barclay: O'Brien had loved his wife.

'Do you think I take pride in it? That this is something I wanted?' Tears fell down O'Brien's face then, thick and heavy, and they tapped onto the table in front of him. 'I wanted a family. Kids of my own with my Kath. I didn't put these desires there.' He pointed at the side of his head. 'Didn't want them. But there they were.'

Barclay's fists clenched, so he moved them under the table. 'What happened?'

'I think it was the power,' he said. 'That feeling of control. Of owning, even though they weren't mine.'

'You felt powerful, in control, possessive, of the boys you abused at Rainford Lane?' Barclay had learned a technique during his therapy sessions: to repeat back the emotions, thoughts and feelings of the person speaking, to prove you're listening. You're understanding.

O'Brien nodded and snivelled through the tears. 'I wanted so badly to stop. I could have thrown that album in the fire, but I didn't. I had to keep it.'

Barclay finally felt like they were getting somewhere, that O'Brien's walls were finally crumbling and caving in. The photos in the album would probably be enough for the Crown Prosecution Service, because O'Brien could clearly be identified by his tattoo, but Barclay wanted him on record. 'Did you abuse them?'

'I did,' he said. 'Of course I did. But I was never alone.'

'Can you give us names?'

Barclay felt Lawrence shift beside him: she was on the edge of her seat, almost leaning over the table.

'My life is forfeit, you know that, don't you?'

'You'll be safe,' Barclay said. 'We can protect you. There are special wings for—'

'For people like me? Like Lewis Lamond? How safe was he? They'll come for me like they came for him.'

Of course, O'Brien was right. Lamond's death in incarceration had never sat right with him or de Silva. That was part of their investigation, and he wondered whether the NCA had looked into that yet. He'd have to find out. That meant speaking with Ayris, and he wasn't sure he was ready for a one-on-one just yet.

When they'd left his office earlier, Ayris had followed Barclay out, waited for de Silva to head down the corridor and said, 'Did you get my text?'

'I got it.' Barclay nodded. 'But I'm not replying. What happened between us was bad. I'm married, and I'd like to stay that way.' He'd walked off then without hearing what Ayris had to say.

'There's no way you can protect me from them.' O'Brien's voice brought Barclay back to the interview room.

'If you tell us who they are, we can do something about it,' Barclay said.

'These people are faceless. They're like spectres now. Everything is online. Everything is anonymous. Sure, there are a few who are out on open chat rooms, scouring for girls and boys; but these people… you've no idea what keeping their secrets means to them.'

'Is Burt Reeves one of them?'

'Only as much as I am,' O'Brien said, wiping his eyes with the back of his hand.

'Will you tell me what you meant about Ritchie de Silva?' Barclay knew he needed to at least get some information: it would be the only thing that would stop de Silva going to O'Brien's cell and beating answers out of him. 'For de Silva's sake.'

O'Brien took in a deep breath through his nose. 'What happened to Ritchie... so tragic. But it was the start of it all. Bob Brendan, he'd lain out under the pines all those years. Decades had passed, and I think everyone just assumed he'd run off. Sure, we held our breaths in case he surfaced and spilled everything. You see, Bob would have had a lot to lose when he disappeared.'

'I'm asking you about Ritchie de Silva, can we stay on topic, please?'

'I'm trying to tell you,' O'Brien said. He wiped at his face again until it was dry, until the tears had gone, and only the pink of his eyes could indicate that he'd expressed any emotion during the interview. 'It's all there in Meeks's manuscript, and I think Ritchie killed himself because he knew the body found in the woods was Bob Brendan.'

'Go on...'

'You see, Ritchie de Silva murdered Bob Brendan.'

Thirty-Five

Wednesday 1 January 1997

Bedtime was never really time for sleep. It was when they would come, literal nightmares crawling down the corridors, monsters and demons of their own making.

There had been some fireworks the night before. For New Year's Eve. We were allowed to go up on the roof to watch them and wait for midnight, and Mrs Jones, the deputy head, made sure we were bundled up against the cold. It was freezing up there, but the fireworks burst all around us, booms and explosions of lights – all the colours I'd forgotten about, the ones I'd not seen since my dad sent me off to Rainford Lane School for Boys. Some of the other boys had called it Painford when I arrived, but they said it only in whispers, careful the teachers didn't hear.

It wasn't long before I learned why. Within just a week of my being there, I came to know the truth of the place. Came to understand why some of the boys called it Painford. Learned to expect the monsters at bedtime.

And on that night, after the fireworks, after the tea party we had, with corned beef and piccalilli sandwiches, cakes, biscuits, jelly and ice cream, when we'd all been returned to our dorms, the monsters came.

I heard doors along the corridor open, and boys whisper, 'No, please,' and I knew that even if I pulled the covers over my head and held my breath, they'd come for me too. I closed my eyes when my door opened, squealing on its hinges like it was in agony. I could tell it was Bob from the way that he breathed. Though, at night he liked to be called something else.

I'd shared my room with an older lad called Ricky back then, but I'll tell you more about him later. I heard Bob say, 'Come on, little Ricky. Time to play.'

He'd always called him 'Little Ricky', even though he was fourteen and big for his age, and I always thought that he could take Bob on if he had to. I suppose, looking back, some people freeze in the face of the abuse like we endured. They can't act.

'Bob, please,' Ricky said. 'I'm tired.'

He slapped Ricky, and I knew without even seeing them that there would be tears on Ricky's face. 'You call me "sir", don't you?' He shook Ricky by the shoulders. 'Don't you?'

'Yes,' Ricky said. 'Sir.'

Hit him back, I begged silently. *Hit him back for all of us.* But he didn't. He got out of his bed and then Bob came over to mine, unsure on his feet, and I could smell the beer on his breath.

'Come on, Daveyboy,' Bob said. 'I'll let you go first tonight. I've cut my nails, see.' He smiled, his teeth yellowing, and held up his fingers for me.

I felt bile rise from my stomach and I could taste the tang of the piccalilli sandwiches at the back of my throat. I got out of bed without saying anything and followed Bob out into the corridor. There were fewer boys out in the corridor that night, all of us bare-footed, in our pyjamas, some of the older ones in just their underwear.

They'd let some sleep on, and I envied them. I recognised the other lads out there, older, around Ricky's age. Micky was the eldest, I think two years older than Ricky, and Tommo was just a few months younger than him, but he was built the same. Tall and broad, even their voices were similar.

In truth, it was hard to tell anyone's age in Painford. It was another aspect of us that didn't seem to matter in that place.

The last two came out of their dorm, followed by the policeman, the one they called The Bear because he was covered in hair, and no one knew his actual name. There was no sort of introduction, no polite hello or handshake, no two-truths-and-a-lie. Matty, a lad of eleven, was already crying, but his dorm-mate, Lewy, made no sound.

I'll tell you more about Lewy later. He has a story all his own. His own quest for a truth.

Afterwards, when Bob had finished with me, we knew to walk down to the shower block, where Mrs Jones turned off the heat and made us shower in what felt like ice water. She would pace up and down, her heels clicking loudly against the tiles and she would call us names. Whores. Sluts. The devil's boys.

She knew what was happening to us. She knew it all and she blamed us, just like the men did.

We walked back to our dorms, dripping and freezing, and I wrapped myself in my thick duvet and knew that in the morning it would smell of damp. I cried from the pain and from the cold, and Ricky sat on the floor next to my bed and held my hand until I finally managed to fall asleep.

I woke up in pain and knew that if I dared look at the sheets, there'd be blood. But that, by then, was not unusual. I heard the squeal of the dorm door and a whispered, 'Fuck!' They'd stopped locking us in weeks ago, I suppose they thought we'd never come out at night unless they were with us. I think they thought we were sufficiently oppressed to do as we were told. For the most part, they were right.

But when I saw Ricky moving in the shadows, his shoes and coat on, his hood pulled over his face, I knew that they'd been wrong.

'Ricky...' I whispered. 'Where are you going?'

'Go back to sleep, Dave.' He hurried back over to my bed. 'Go back to sleep and forget you saw me. I was in my room all night, okay?'

Something was going on and I felt the panic of it, like thunder in my chest. 'But what's happening?'

He sighed. 'We're going to teach Bob a lesson,' he said. 'Now go back to sleep, I'll be back soon.'

He patted my head and turned to leave. I sat up and tried to catch the words in my throat before they came out. I was scared, terrified, of what Ricky meant. But ultimately, I knew that I wanted to be a part of it. 'I'm coming.'

'No you're not,' he said. 'If we get caught, then our lives won't be worth living.'

Something passed between us, something unspoken that we both could say but didn't want to: our lives aren't worth living now.

I was smaller than the other lads, at just ten years old, who was I to think I could help them in whatever they had planned? I'd just get in the way.

I rolled the duvet back, and then cold hit me like a block of ice, then we both saw it: the dark stain of blood on the sheets. In the darkness of the room it appeared almost black. 'I'm coming,' I said.

I was out of my bed and shoving my feet into my battered old trainers, while Ricky searched through his small chest of drawers and pulled out the only other jacket he had with a hood. It was dark blue, the type of coat you'd use for hiking. It was too big for me, and I pulled it on and rolled up the sleeves to my wrists.

We crept out into the corridor, and Ricky pulled the door closed slowly, so the usual squeal was nothing more than a squeak. Out in the corridor, Lewy, Micky and Tommo were waiting, all in equally dark clothing, their faces covered; but I knew it was them from their shoes: as equally destroyed as my own.

'What's he doing here?' Micky bounded up to Ricky, his voice a hiss.

'He has a right to be here, Micky. Come on. Any one of those lads in this dorm does.'

'He'll get in the way,' Lewy mumbled.

'I think we should forget this, lads,' Tommo said. His voice was high for his age, almost effeminate. In the years since this night, Tommo is the only lad I have been unable to find. It's almost like he disappeared.

You'll see why.

'We're doing it,' Micky said. 'He has to know. This can't go on.' He was breathless, his voice rising, and I could see, even in the darkness, that his eyes were shining with tears. 'Think of every lad that's passed through those doors. Every lad that will pass through those doors when we're gone. Think of yourself. The things he's done to you. Tommo, think of how many of his mates he's allowed to—'

'Be quiet, Micky,' Ricky said. 'You'll wake everyone up.'

The lads exchanged looks and a conversation passed between them that I couldn't make sense of back then. But now, looking back, I can see their faces as clear as day. They spoke about their pain, their own truths, their shared histories. I felt that, for them, that night was going to be a beginning.

Looking back, I know now that that night was the start of many things for me. An awakening to the awful things that those in power did to those who were not. They'd take what they wanted and they wouldn't apologise. It was then I realised that authority was never to be trusted.

As I've said already, one of those people in power was a policeman. Sometimes, even he brought friends. They walked those corridors at night and did things to us when they thought no one was watching or listening, when they thought no one cared. We knew they were police because sometimes, when they were done, we'd hear them talking about cases they'd worked on while we trundled off to the shower block. What struck me most about those conversations was how matter-of-fact they were. How it seemed that they'd returned to some normalcy, like they'd just finished their dinner, or had gotten into their pyjamas and sat in front of the telly talking to their wives or girlfriends about their day.

I struggled to keep up with the lads. Their legs were longer and they could sneak easily, whereas my own legs were still small and thin like matchsticks, and I was clumsy on my feet. Ricky saved me from tripping over my own shoes and making a racket more than once.

Bob's bedroom was at the far end of the school, in the west wing where we weren't allowed to set foot. He was the only one who slept on the ground floor, right next to his office, close to a door that led down into the basement where they would take us. Where the clinking and clanking of pipes, the roar of the boiler, would drown out any cries we made.

Back then, I didn't know how Micky knew exactly which room to take us to. There was no plaque on the door that said 'Bob Brendan'. On reflection, I can only guess that Micky was taken there at least once. It's something that didn't occur to me, the adrenaline coursing through my body made everything else seem unimportant.

We arrived, and Micky put his finger to his mouth as he turned the doorknob. The door made no sound as it opened, and when it did, we saw Bob on his back, snoring.

I remember thinking how normal he looked. Just like a man who was asleep, not like the monster that came to me in the dead of the night. On his bedside table was a glass of water. Next to the water was an old-fashioned lamp with the green shade made of glass, the kind you'd find in a library or something. I remember it because it stuck out – everything else was drab, tarnished in some way.

I wondered whether that was the plan: to throw his glass of water over him, startle him and we'd run off back to our dorms.

But that was the notion of a ten-year-old. Naïve. Stupid. Sure, I knew violence, I learned it in the basement of that school, but what happened next I couldn't have even conceived of.

Micky went in first: on the balls of his feet he made no sound, like a leopard stalking its prey. He pounced, jumped on Bob's chest. Bob made an awful sound, a huff which turned into a rattle, the breath heaved out of him, and Micky put his hand over the man's mouth.

Lewy, Tommo and Ricky swooped in, holding down Bob's arms and legs. He struggled under their weight and then, after a moment, he stopped.

'What the fuck are you doing?' he hissed.

'Shh, Bobby Boy,' Micky said. 'If you're quiet, I'll make it quick. Remember that? Remember saying that to me my first night here?'

There was a rage in Micky that I'd never seen before. By day, the teachers were in charge, and at night, Bob and his friends were; but in the early hours of 1997, the night was ours.

'Get back to your room now, you little shit,' Bob said. 'You go back to your room and we'll forget about all of this. But if you don't—'

'Then what?' Micky asked. 'What can you do to us that you haven't already done?'

I watched from the doorway, my head a tangle of thoughts, trying to anticipate what would happen next.

'Lads,' Tommo said. I could hear his upset in the wobble of his voice. 'We've scared him. That's enough, let's go.'

'If we go now,' Lewy said, 'he'll ruin our lives until the day we leave this place. Come on, Tommo, you get that, don't you?'

'No.' Tommo stood up, loosed his grip on Bob's arm and backed away. 'I can't do this.'

Bob took advantage of that, grabbed Micky by the hair and yanked his head back. He cried out in pain and Bob threw him to the floor. He then kicked Ricky in the face and was on his feet quicker than I thought he could ever move. He reached for a switch on the wall and turned on the big light, and that's when he saw me. His eyes flashed and he strode toward me, gripped me by the oversized jacket and lifted me up so that my face was level with his. 'So you think you're going to turn into one of these little fuckers, do you? Well, I'll teach you a lesson.'

I heard the clink of his belt unfastening, a sound I was too familiar with, but Bob's eyes never left mine. I remember how angry he looked, how animal-like: a snarling dog, thirsty for blood and hungry for flesh.

Then there was a sound I'd never heard before. *Thuck.* Bob's eyes went wide, his mouth open, and as his fingers loosened from my coat, I fell to the floor, too frightened to register the pain. In truth, I'd pissed myself, and hoped that none of the lads saw. If they did, no one ever said anything.

As Bob sank to his knees, I saw Ricky there behind him, as shocked and frightened as Bob had looked. I heard the tap-tap-tap before I saw the old lamp in Ricky's hand.

Blood dripped from the brass base onto Bob's rug. And in the silence that followed Bob landing face first, I knew that we were all in deep trouble.

Thirty-Six

Barclay dropped the scanned printouts of Meeks's manuscript and closed his eyes. He couldn't imagine what those boys must have been thinking, the desperation they must have felt. But there it was, a primary source's account of what happened the night Bob Brendan was murdered. Just the truth that O'Brien had said he would find in the pages of Meeks's manuscript.

He was certain that Micky was former-DCI Mike Crosby, that Ricky was Ritchie de Silva, and Lewy was none other than Lewis Lamond, the serial murderer who'd been found hanged in his cell while awaiting trial. And Tommo, of course, was Billy Thompson – the man they had assumed Meeks was unable to track down.

Their man in the woods had been connected to the death of de Silva's husband, to Lewis Lamond and his crimes. He thought back to the time he'd been put on the Lamond killings, when his first victim was found. De Silva had already gone on her leave of absence after Ritchie's death, and O'Brien had called him in to take the lead on the Renshaw girl's disappearance, and though none of them said it out loud, they all knew she would turn up dead.

'What about our guy in the woods?' Barclay had asked O'Brien.

O'Brien waved a hand. 'I've got someone in mind to take over that. Someone who doesn't have your experience, and you know what, Barclay? This is a good opportunity for you. Your own case. Think of that.'

Barclay hadn't had to think about it. He'd moved on to the more high-profile, urgent case and didn't give the man in the woods a second thought until much later. The last he'd heard, two detectives were working the case. That had stuck out as strange to him, but given the force's need for cutbacks due to government funding, it didn't surprise him. Now they couldn't find any trace of those two detectives. They could be missing or worse still, dead.

Who are you to know anything about funding and resource, or the reasons for other officers retiring or quitting?

Still, he beat himself up over it. He was a sergeant with Merseyside Police, and he should have spoken out. He chose not to, and now more people were dead.

The manuscript held answers, he was certain of that. Whether it was all of the answers they needed to resolve the case, he wasn't sure. He knew he needed to speak with de Silva: he'd promised that he would share the information he got.

A clean-up, O'Brien called it. But cleaning up what?

He wondered whether the clean-up in Lamond's case was because he knew about the abuse at Rainford Lane and had brought it up in his interview. That, if the case went to court, it would be a matter of public record that, when the courts heard about it, they'd need to know more. Need to act.

He'd need to listen to the recordings again, but when they'd questioned Lamond about The Woulds app last year, following his capture, he had answered in a way that struck Barclay as odd – particularly his answer to whether he'd heard of it before.

If Barclay remembered correctly, Lamond had shaken his head and answered, 'No, I've never heard of an *app* called The Woulds.' Lamond had deliberately stressed the word 'app', Barclay was certain. Did Lamond, or the other boys, know about the photo album of the same name which contained all of their nightmares, their horrors, the awful things done to them?

They must have done.

He'd get someone to check the recordings to be sure. Harris, maybe. In the meantime, he needed to ring de Silva and arrange to meet.

But first, he'd have to deliver what he knew to DSI Murphy.

—

Barclay came away from his meeting with Murphy uncertain about how she felt. What did she think about the latest update from O'Brien? She'd been left with the copy of the scanned manuscript Barclay had prepared for her.

As he exited the lift on the basement floor and took out his phone to ring de Silva.

He was inside the incident room before de Silva answered. 'Where are you?' she asked.

'The OCC. Where are you?'

'I'm out for a walk,' she said. 'Needed to clear my head.'

'Where? I'll come and meet you.'

She sighed. 'The old runway,' she said. 'I can come back.'

'No, I think it's best we talk outside of the office. Give me five minutes.'

Before he left, he told the others that he'd be nipping out for half an hour. The atmosphere in the room was sour, so much so that Barclay could almost smell it. 'Finish early,' he said. 'A lot has happened. Go home to your families.'

He didn't hang around to see whether they'd take him up on his offer. If they were anything like he was, they'd have ignored him and stayed on. Worked through the case, gone over the transcripts from O'Brien's interview, done whatever they could to keep the case nudging forward that little bit more.

It was only a short drive to the carpark off the Garston Shore Road roundabout. He left his car there, but didn't see de Silva's Kuga parked anywhere and assumed she'd walked.

Bit of a walk. In the car, it was nothing. Still, he made the decision to take the scenic route. There was an alternative path, a road really, that went to the Liverpool Yacht Club, but Barclay wanted some time to think. To put the pieces of information he'd learned in some sort of order.

The footpath to the river was narrow and lined with trees and shrubs. It was the kind of path you'd have to walk down single file if you were with other people. He felt his foot slide, and instantly knew. He lifted up his foot and saw dog shit smeared between the tread of his black New Balance trainers.

He groaned, tried to wipe it off on some grass, but all he managed to do was smear it. He was tempted to go home, to clean it off in the garden with the hosepipe then throw the pair in the wash. But that meant getting in the car with his dirty trainer, fresh and stinking. Maybe the walk would shake it loose.

The path opened up onto another that ran parallel to the river. The tide was in, brown water rising to milk-white peaks in the wind that blew down the estuary toward the yacht club.

To his left, on a field of balding yellow grass, weird for this time of year, a father and his daughter held a kite by its strings and watched it dance in the sky. He could hear the wind beat at it from where he was. There was a constant drone from the Wirral which disturbed the air, but otherwise the place was pretty quiet.

The reeds along the edges of the path were short, but, as with the over-grown nettles, they'd leaned into the path, almost blocking his way forward. He squeezed between them, worried he'd soon be covered in ticks or stung by the tiny hairs on the plants.

He was even more certain that this news would devastate de Silva. That she'd sink lower than she had before, worse than when she'd found Ritchie dead. Her path through life had been like this one: lined with things that can sting and scratch and hurt.

I guess we have that in common.

He wondered whether she would have the strength to come out the other side of all of this. She meant a great deal to him; he cared for her, and that feeling wasn't just the usual bond between colleagues. To Barclay, it was something more.

He realised far too late that he should have gone the other way. Should have taken the easier path. *But*, he thought, *when have you ever done that?*

Nick was the love of his life, and he adored Sarah. That was all there was to it, and he hoped Nick could see that. Ayris was a complication. A means to an end. Just sex. But, in just a few hours of Ayris's company, Barclay had felt things he hadn't felt for years with Nick. Listened to. Understood. Desired.

He turned left at the yacht club, across another path and then onto the runway. De Silva approached from his left, and together they headed down toward the airport. 'You took your bloody time,' she said.

'It's a fair walk from the carpark, I forgot. Where did you park?'

'Just there.' She gestured vaguely over her shoulder. 'Come on then, out with it.'

Barclay needed to buy himself some time. He was most definitely not prepared for this conversation. He doubted that any amount of time would be enough but it had to come from him. He couldn't let her find out by reading it.

'Bit of an odd place to go,' Barclay said. He started to walk down the runway, potholed and broken apart by plants and weeds clawing their way through cracks in the concrete. De Silva walked with him.

'My dad used to bring us down here,' she said. 'When he was teaching me and Laney to ride our bikes. Then, when Ritchie and me started seeing each other properly, we'd come on the bus. Spend the full day here. We brought butties in tinfoil, some bottles of water. We'd walk and—' She stopped herself. 'I've not come here for a trip down memory lane, Barclay. I came here to think. And now you're here. So tell me what you need to tell me.'

Barclay slowed his pace and felt a chill blow across his face. It made him shiver. 'I don't know how to tell you this,' he said.

'Just say it. That's how.'

'I've read part of Meeks's manuscript, and it corroborates what O'Brien told me.'

'What did he tell you?'

'But obviously that doesn't mean it's true.'

'For God's sake, Barclay!'

'The manuscript talks about a particular night at Rainford Lane. De Silva, I think that your Ritchie is in it. Ricky, Meeks calls him. And Crosby, and Lewis Lamond. And Tommo, who I think is that Billy Thompson kid from Meeks's board.' Barclay bit the inside of his cheek and thought, feeling de Silva's anticipation rippling from her. 'Bob Brendan is in it too,' he said. 'The part I read talks about abuse, about how these kids wanted revenge. It's about the night of Brendan's murder. It says that Ritchie was there at the time.'

'Jesus…'

'There was a scuffle. A fight broke out, and Meeks says that Ricky was the one who delivered the blow which—'

'You can say it, Barclay,' de Silva said. 'The blow which killed Brendan?'

Barclay nodded. He wanted to jump in with some positive spin, but there wasn't one.

'I need to read the manuscript, Barclay. Now.'

'I don't have it with me. And anyway, it's hard to read. I'm not sure—'

'I'm not asking.'

'Murphy's read what I read. She doesn't want you to read it. De Silva, I think I agree with her.'

She nodded, and Barclay thought she looked defeated. 'Maybe you're both right. She's asked me to come in "for a detailed conversation".' Here she mimicked Murphy's accent.

'That doesn't sound good,' Barclay said.

'No, it doesn't.'

Silence passed between them and they found themselves at the gate that looked onto old airport hangars. For a moment, they peered through the wire. The main activity of the airport was at the other end, and Barclay wasn't sure what this end of the airport was even used for. Storage maybe, a place to house the old things no longer used, no longer cared about.

The past.

'I don't think it's a coincidence that Ritchie killed himself the day Bob Brendan was found in the woods,' de Silva said.

O'Brien had confirmed as much already, but Barclay was happy that de Silva had arrived at that conclusion herself. If Ritchie had killed Brendan all those years ago, it stood to reason that the discovery of his body could trigger some fight or flight response in Ritchie. It was a shame that he'd taken his own life, rather than come forward with what he knew. De Silva may have been able to help.

But then, if he did, Barclay supposed, O'Brien would have known exactly who he was. *If he didn't already know.* He could see how Ritchie may have felt like there was no other option.

'I haven't been able to stop thinking about him.' Her voice was thick and wobbled, and when Barclay looked at her, he saw tears on her face.

He put a hand on her shoulder, but all he could do right then was listen.

'His sad little face when he came home for summer after his first year in that place,' she continued. 'I should have known. I should have asked him what was going on. Made him answer me.'

'You were a kid yourself, de Silva, for God's sake.'

'His mum though.' She wiped at her face. 'She didn't care. She loved him, but she didn't care that there was something wrong. Even my dad tried to speak to him a few times, but Ritchie would have none of it. He was stubborn even then.'

'You sound alike.'

De Silva laughed despite herself, then her face creased and fresh tears came. 'Oh God, I just keep picturing him there. In that school with those men. The other boys. He must have been so frightened.'

Yes, he must have. 'You didn't know that he went to that school?'

'He never spoke about,' de Silva said. 'Never. Not about friends, school work, what it was like. I had no idea that he was so close to home all that time.'

Barclay nodded. Rainford Lane School for Boys was not far from where de Silva grew up in Kirkby.

'If I'd have known...' De Silva's voice wobbled and she held her breath.

Barclay pulled her close to him then and squeezed. He'd always thought that a hug had healing properties, and he wanted so desperately to heal de Silva from her agony. He'd give anything for her to skip this part.

It was necessary, he knew, to go through the pain of this. Of learning new things about our loved ones, and even worse in her case because she couldn't speak to him, couldn't pick up the phone and share her husband's pain with him.

'I can't help but think,' de Silva said into Barclay's chest, 'whether Ritchie knew who O'Brien was.' She pulled away and wiped her face again.

In Barclay's experience, trauma has a way of burning places, faces, feelings and experiences onto the mind.

Your body has a way of remembering it. Barclay had no doubt that Ritchie would have recognised O'Brien the moment de Silva introduced them; but he wondered whether O'Brien had remembered Ritchie. Whether, at Rainford Lane, Ritchie would have been just one more lad in a sea of many little boys with pale, tear-soaked faces.

'And this Billy Thompson. Was *he* able to shed any light on it?'

'O'Brien?'

'God, I can't even say his name.' She turned away from the gate and headed back down the disused runway as a plane from the airport rumbled behind them and launched itself into the sky.

Barclay thought about that. He had mentioned a Billy going missing, but in passing, as though it was just a story. Barclay said, 'My guess is he won't remember. I doubt he even knew Meeks. Or Crosby until all of that stuff with Lamond last year.'

'Or Ritchie.'

Or Ritchie.

Barclay was unsure what to say next. He wasn't entirely sure what it was that de Silva needed to hear from him. He wanted to give her space to begin working through the fresh grief she was now enduring. The second time she was grieving her dead husband. 'I'm really sorry, Win,' he said, finally.

'We need to find this Billy Thompson person,' de Silva said. 'Get the team on it. They'll need to speak with every single one of the partners of the victims we've found. See if they remember any names. I doubt it, but it's worth a try.'

'What about—' He stopped himself, thought better of it. But if they were questioning the families of the victims who'd received the middle fingers of their loved ones, it stood to reason that they should question everyone.

'What about what?'

He didn't want to say it, but he'd already opened his mouth and now the half-thought festered between them. 'I know you said Ritchie never spoke to you about Rainford Lane. But what about Crosby's wife?'

De Silva stopped dead, her boots scuffing the concrete. 'That's a bloody good thought, Barclay. But I can't go and speak to her. I don't know what she knows about... well, you know. Me being there could mess the whole thing up.'

'Are you going to see Murphy?'

'Not yet,' de Silva said. 'I know she'll boot me from this case now, given everything that's come out. But I'm not ready to give up on it just yet.'

'So what're you going to do?'

'I want to check on the search of Burt Reeves's house,' she said. 'Murphy arranged for a warrant to search the place, and I want to be there.'

'Sounds like a plan.' A quiet passed between them then, a peaceful one.

Then de Silva said, 'Can you smell shit?'

Barclay wanted the runway to open up and swallow him, or for a plane to land on his head. 'I think it's the river,' he said.

—

'I can only imagine what you must have been going through,' Barclay said. In truth, he couldn't imagine it at all.

'It's been hard,' Ann said. Crosby's wife was younger than Crosby had been, or at least looked younger. A good skincare routine maybe, morning and night, with many steps.

She'd made the house lovely. It wasn't big, but it was homely. Comfortable. The kind of place you could easily relax, and it had, what was it Nick called it? Positive vibes.

The living room was bright with natural light which came through the bay windows. The wallpaper, navy-blue stripes with brilliant white, really flattered Ann's plain but lovely style.

'I have to ask, and I know we asked you last year when your husband initially disappeared—'

'I've not heard from him.' She put her mug down on a coaster made from what looked like an olive tree on the white coffee table. 'If I heard from him, I'd call the police. I don't want anything to do with him.'

'And there has been no activity on your bank accounts that could be him?'

'You know the answer to that already.' She sighed. 'But no, and I've moved my money into my own accounts now.'

It was true, they had checked their joint bank accounts, and found one that Crosby had set up two years ago with three thousand pounds in it. Both went untouched.

'I have another question, then I promise I'll leave you alone.'

'Go on...'

'Did he ever mention anyone by the name Tommo or Billy Thompson?'

Ann paused, cocked her head as if trying to recall. 'No, I don't think so.'

Barclay had suspected as much.

'Oh, actually, he did have a friend whose name was Thompson. Not sure on the first name. But he moved away years ago. Canada, I think. Yeah that's right, he and his partner went to Canada.'

'Do you have contact details for him?'

'No,' she said. 'I only met him a handful of times.' She looked down at her mug on the table, steam flowing out in thin wisps. 'You work with Win de Silva, don't you?'

Barclay felt his throat tighten. 'I do, yeah. She's my boss actually.'

'Ah,' Ann said. 'How is she?'

Barclay couldn't give anything away. If he told Ann the truth of how de Silva was, she'd ask questions and that could lead him on to talking about Ritchie. When they'd questioned Ann last year, she'd not known anything about Rainford Lane School for Boys and Barclay was sure she wished she still didn't know anything. Back then, they didn't know Ritchie was also a student there. That, according to Meeks's manuscript, they'd been friends. 'She's fine,' he lied. 'She's doing great.'

'We used to see a lot of each other.' Ann smiled as though remembering something fondly. 'Tell her I was asking about her, won't you?'

'Of course I will,' he said. 'I'd best go. I'll be in touch if we need anything else.'

'I may not be around much longer,' she said. 'I'm planning on moving to Wales to be closer to my parents. I finally managed to get our holiday home on the market: that was in my name. This place is a different matter, of course.'

'You have a holiday home?'

'A cabin,' she said, proud. 'Gorgeous. Up there in Ullswater. My grandfather built it and left it to my dad, but it was too much for him. He switched it over to my name.'

This was new information to Barclay, and he wondered whether it would be new to de Silva, or whether she'd already been there with Crosby. Whether they'd spent lost weekends up there while their respective partners were at home.

He wondered whether that was where Crosby could have been this whole time.

Thirty-Seven

Burt Reeves's property on Runnymede Close was stunning, de Silva thought. A squat house that seemed too close to the ground in comparison to its expanse. He'd been paid well for whatever he did for O'Brien's mates. She shuddered to think, especially as she'd been able to confirm that Burt Reeves was indeed on the list provided by Breaker.

Scientific Support had already gained access to the property, and the street, which was patchy from cracked tarmac and hastily repaired by the council, was cordoned off at either end. People stood there with their dogs, and de Silva imagined that, later, they'd recount the time police invaded the home of the Reeves family.

Murphy had rung de Silva's personal phone three times, and de Silva knew what was coming next. She'd be moved on to another case. But, if she never went to her meeting with Murphy, if she never stayed in the same place for too long, Murphy had no way of tracking her down. That would annoy her beyond belief, de Silva knew, and the knowledge of it made her smile.

De Silva donned the usual crime scene protective suit and walked into the house. She went to the bedroom first out of instinct: if Reeves had run, then the evidence would be right there in the master bedroom. In truth, it would be the lack of things that would be the evidence of his fleeing. The underwear drawer would be ransacked, the family safe open and empty, passports would be gone and his wife may have panicked about which shoes she should pack.

The master bedroom was tidier than de Silva had expected. Off the room were two smaller rooms: an en suite, clean and sparkling, something de Silva's would never be. But then, she couldn't afford cleaners. There were no toothbrushes on the marble countertop where dual sinks were sunk below gold-coloured taps. The other room, bigger than the bathroom, was lined with cupboards, wardrobes, shoe racks. Most of it empty.

That's it then, she thought. *He's gone, and anything he knows has gone with him.* He must have moved quickly.

She was glad that as soon as she'd left Barclay at the interview room with O'Brien earlier, she'd already put in calls to the airports, to Interpol, to the NCA, that a possible suspect was on the loose. They'd find him sooner or later, and there was no way he was getting out of the country unless his family had fake passports.

But how common are they these days?

De Silva didn't actually know the answer to that, but it was worth considering. In one of the cupboards, behind rows of grey suits, the colour of stormy skies, de Silva found the safe, an old-fashioned one, painted black with shining paint. It was open and empty, just as she'd imagined.

Her personal phone rang out from her pocket. Murphy again. She turned the ringer off, leaving it on vibrate. She didn't button the call, because then Murphy would know de Silva was purposefully ignoring her.

The house had been carefully decorated, each piece of furniture or artwork was curated to tie the place together in a theme of gold. Some people thought gold looked cheap, but de Silva had always liked it. Maybe it was Mrs Reeves's own design and if so, she had good taste, in de Silva's opinion. De Silva wondered what Burt must have told her to get her out of the house so quickly.

Or was she in on it?

Nothing would surprise her about this case any more. Crosby, O'Brien, her Ritchie, they'd been tied together for decades, their stories and histories no longer just shapes in the gloom of the pines as she'd imagined her own. When they'd came into contact with each other again, whether O'Brien recognised them or not, Crosby and Ritchie would have recognised him. Their suffering would have come back to them, as fresh as the day it had all started.

Ritchie's suffering was over now, he'd made sure of that himself, but if he'd have come to her back then, they might have been able to end the suffering of countless children through this app.

Still, the question had gripped her since the moment she knew Ritchie was part of that school's haunted history: had Crosby and Ritchie recognised each other when she'd introduced them? She reasoned that they must have done, but had resolved, no, conspired, to keep it to themselves.

Had it been a game to Crosby then, to bed the wife of his childhood friend? Were they even really friends, or had they not just been two kids thrown together by circumstance, by their shared horror?

These were questions she may never get answers to.

Her phone rang again. She was ready to button it until she saw it was Laney. She answered and tucked her phone into the hood of her suit when she heard the screaming of a child in the background. Bonnie.

'Laney?'

Laney sobbed, breathless, her voice hoarse as though she'd been shouting. Or screaming. 'Win, please, he—'

The line went dead. She turned out of the walk-in wardrobe and marched from the house. Outside, she ripped of the protective suit and shouted to the uniformed officers there, while she tried to call Laney again.

'Get on that radio,' she ordered. 'I need officers to 1 Amber Mews. Now!'

Her call to Laney went unanswered. She stuffed her phone into her pocket and ran for her car, as the officers scrambled at their radios to make the order. What had happened to the officer she'd ordered stationed outside of her house, she couldn't guess.

In reality, she should have got in one of the squad cars, blasted the blues and twos, she'd have gotten through the gridlock, bounded through the red lights and made it home in time, but she was already in her car, already speeding out of Runnymede Close.

Her mind raced. Scenarios shifted and twisted and turned in on themselves as she thought of the man who had tried to break into her house. The man who'd been at Meeks's apartment building. The man she had assumed was David before his alibi came back clean.

She put her foot down and swerved through the traffic on Speke Road, she didn't care if she was caught on any camera. She was heading for home – that's where she'd asked backup to meet her – but in reality, she wasn't even sure if that's where Laney was. No time to second guess herself, she had to just keep moving.

There were roadworks near the slip-road onto the M57, and cars sat waiting to move forward, but she bypassed them all on the hard shoulder. Other cars beeped at her in annoyance.

Prescot was just one junction away, maybe a ten- or fifteen-minute drive at the most, but the seconds passed like hours. She tried Laney's phone again and it answered this time. Bonnie was still crying, and she could hear breathing. Erratic and rasping but close to the phone.

'Laney? Laney, can you hear me?'

The breathing slowed, became shallow and stopped.

De Silva slammed the steering wheel hard. 'Laney!' she screamed. Then, slowly at first, the breathing returned. Ragged still, but it was there.

As she rounded the corner onto Amber Mews, the flashing lights of her backup in the rear-view mirror, she didn't know what she was walking into.

She left her car on the drive, keys in the ignition, engine still on, her exhaust spewing smoke. A uniformed officer passed out cold on the driveway. The door was wide open, and from inside, she could hear Bonnie crying.

The little girl, her tiny niece she barely knew, was sitting next to Laney, her hands on her mother's face. Tears had soaked her face, as she looked from de Silva in the doorway to her mum.

De Silva walked in, shaking from top to toe, as she heard car doors slamming shut behind her.

Laney's face was a bloody mess, swollen and cut but as long as that horrendous rattling came out of her mouth, de Silva knew that her sister was alive.

A voice said from the doorway, 'Paramedics are here. Open the door.'

She hadn't remembered closing it, but she was thankful that someone had had the good sense to call for an ambulance, just in case they were needed. She'd find out who later and thank them personally.

'Daddy,' Bonnie sobbed.

Then de Silva knew. She felt it in her like it was something old and stirring: an instinct. She knew, before she even turned, that David would be standing there.

And he was.

His chubby fists were clenched and scratched. There was blood on his face and on his green Hollister T-shirt. His face was so changed, not just lined by the years since she'd last clapped eyes on him, at Laney's wedding, but it was almost animal. Wild.

In that moment, she realised she'd left her baton in her handbag in the car, but underneath her jacket, on her harness, was the PAVA spray. And then she remembered, she'd used it on O'Brien. The thing was probably empty.

As she got to her feet, she grabbed Bonnie by the arm and pushed her into place behind her. De Silva took a step forward, making sure she was between David and the people she cared about.

'The garden's crawling with police, David,' de Silva warned. 'There's no way you're getting away.'

'It's your fault, you know,' he said. He spoke through gritted teeth, and spittle foamed on his lips. 'I didn't have a clue where she was.'

Then it was her fault. In sending someone to question David, de Silva had inadvertently identified that not only was Laney with her sister, but she was in Liverpool. Somehow he'd found them, but de Silva couldn't think about that right then.

'You need to open the door and let the paramedics inside,' de Silva said. She spoke calmly, but her body was rattling with anxiety, with fear. 'I know you don't want this to get any harder. She needs medical attention.'

He tilted his head to look at his wife on the floor. Her breathing was worse, gasping and rattling. 'I was going to let it go. Let her have her little time away, knowing she'd come crawling back on her hands and knees, begging. Like she always does.' Laney's chest rattled. 'But then you sent police to my door,' David continued. 'You got people talking, and then all of a sudden, no one wants to know me. No one wants to drink with me. Because of you and your stinking slut of a sister.'

Pounding at the door now.

'Get the ram!' de Silva shouted.

She heard someone echo her order and within seconds, the pounding at the door grew louder.

At that, David lunged at her but she swooped to the left, grabbed Bonnie and held her in her arms. David hit the floor. She moved quickly, put Bonnie by the window, far enough away from David. Though she screamed, there was nothing else de Silva could do.

David was back on his feet, and de Silva pulled out her PAVA, held it in front of her and hoped it would deter him from taking another step. She didn't know how much was left.

'This stuff hurts, David,' she said. 'Like it really hurts.'

He was too close to Laney now, so she circled and he copied her, moving in an arc away from her, but getting closer to Bonnie.

Bang. Bang. Bang. The door was just seconds away from giving in.

'Why are you doing this, David? She doesn't love you any more.'

'Because she can't ever leave me, and she needs to know that.'

'She already did leave you.'

He roared at that, bared his teeth like a dog and then the door came off its hinges and uniformed officers flooded the living room. David lunged at them, so one of them hit his knee with a baton. He screamed in pain and was down on his knees.

Two paramedics rushed at Laney and de Silva grabbed Bonnie, and as she watched the continued chaos in front of her, she said, 'Shh, baby. Everything's going to be fine now.'

De Silva knew that it was a lie, but sometimes white lies are necessary. A text message pinged on her phone and she checked it. Murphy: *I need to see you. Now.* There was no way she could put it off any longer, but there were other things she needed to do.

Thirty-Eight

De Silva left the hospital two hours later. Laney was going to be fine. Her face was a mess and she had two broken ribs, but David was in custody and he couldn't hurt her again. She'd made sure that two uniformed officers were stationed outside of Laney's room. There was no immediate threat, de Silva knew that, but it would make Laney feel safer, and that, de Silva was shocked to find, comforted her too.

She'd thought of taking Bonnie and staying the night at a hotel while someone fixed the broken window that David had forced his way through. Then, when she found childcare for Bonnie, de Silva could go in and clean up the place.

But Bonnie wanted to stay with her mum, didn't want to leave her side. Laney had said, 'It's fine.' She smiled, but even that seemed to bring her pain. 'I'd like her with me.'

De Silva thought that it would be best for Laney to take time alone. To heal. To process the awful thing that had happened to her, the thing Bonnie had witnessed. But clearly there was a bond between the two of them that transcended trauma and horror: it was a bond that de Silva could never understand.

Her own mum sat in a nursing home, barely remembering to brush her teeth or comb her hair – she had no idea who de Silva was some days. And sometimes, de Silva envied her mum that. She wished on those days where she made the choices no one else would make, when she'd lie to her friends and colleagues and commanding officers, that she didn't know herself either.

'I love you,' de Silva had said. She leaned down and kissed her sister's forehead, and repeated the gesture toward her niece, who seemed so small lying in her mother's arms.

Laney only smiled.

As she drove out of the carpark, she removed the hastily written note from her windscreen – *Merseyside Police officer on duty* – and scrunched it up. She pressed the button on her steering wheel and instructed the car to dial Barclay's number.

'My God, de Silva,' he said. 'Are you sure you're all right?'

'Physically,' she said.

'Is Laney?'

De Silva didn't know whether her sister was okay. She was safe. But safe and okay were two different things. 'I think so,' she said. 'Murphy's breathing down my neck. Wants to meet now, but I'm not sure I can face her.'

'I'm sure she'll understand, won't she?'

De Silva wasn't entirely sure about that one. 'How did it go with Ann?'

He exhaled sharply. 'Do you ever remember her talking about having a holiday home up in the Lake District? Ullswater.'

This was news to de Silva. 'No, I don't.' She was surprised that Ann hadn't mentioned it when they'd interviewed her about Crosby's whereabouts.

'Did… Crosby ever mention it?'

She knew what Barclay was trying to ask. 'I've never been there, Barclay. I didn't know the place existed.'

'I'm sorry to ask.'

She understood why he had to. 'Do we turn it over to the NCA?' he asked. 'We've got enough going on, and Crosby's disappearance is their case, not ours.'

He had a point. She couldn't escape the feeling that there was still something about the NCA investigation that she didn't trust. But, in reality, they had too much to do already. They could be looking for two separate murderers. Meeks's killer, and the one who targeted those who had worked at Rainford Lane in the 1990s.

She felt as though Meeks's murder had been made to look like the others, simply to throw them off the scent. Still, not simply a crime of opportunity or chance. It was planned. It had to be.

If he was murdered because of his manuscript, he would always have ended up dead. One way or another.

'De Silva?'

'I'm here,' she said. 'I was thinking. Do you think Ann knows where Crosby is and has done this whole time?' She looked at her watch. It was getting so late.

Silence. 'I'm not sure,' he said. 'She didn't give that impression. But then she never told us about the holiday home when we first interviewed her. It's her family's home. Not in Crosby's name… it's an easy miss.'

'One we shouldn't have made,' de Silva said. She had to wonder whether the NCA already knew about it, whether they'd already been to scope it out. There was no way to tell, not without asking them outright and drawing unnecessary attention to the fact that they were asking about Crosby rather than focusing on their own case.

But now both cases are related. We have the right to know what they know.

'Let's stall,' she said. 'Just an hour or so. I need time to think. Gather everything up and see what's what. Why don't you head home? Get some rest. There are some things I need to finish then I'll do the same.'

'You're sure?'

'Yeah. I'll see you in the morning.'

Sooner or later, she'd have to return Murphy's call, but first, she needed to do just one more thing.

—

Braxton pulled open his front door and instantly de Silva could smell the stale beer on him. It almost made her stomach churn. His eyes sprang wide when he saw it was her, and he pulled his brown dressing gown tighter across his hairy chest, grey and wiry.

'Ma'am,' he said. He winced, but de Silva waved it off.

'Can I come in?'

He looked back over his shoulder, then turned to her and nodded. 'You'll have to excuse the mess, I've been a bit—'

'You don't need to explain,' she said. 'And I won't keep you long.'

The living room was a mess. On the coffee table was an open box with a half-eaten pizza inside, Hawaiian if she wasn't mistaken. *Pineapple on pizza is a sin.* Flies had started to gather around it, to land and eat and regurgitate and go again. Next to it, empty brown bottles of lager.

'You can sit down,' he said. 'Please. If you like.'

He was nervous. Jittery. Maybe he'd started drinking when she'd asked him to leave, or maybe he was just now sobering up, and the jitters were no more than the post-drink jangles she knew so well. Where your body knows it needs to move, to get going, but it can't quite get there.

She stayed standing as Braxton sat, open-legged, on the couch. 'I wanted to check on you,' she said. 'But I can see how you are.'

'This isn't… it's not something I usually do, but I—' He stopped himself and looked up at her, his eyes wet. 'I'm being sacked, aren't I?'

Now she did sit down, regardless of the pizza crumbs on the couch. 'No,' she said. 'No, you're not at all.' There was much she wanted to say, about her own misguided belief in O'Brien, about their relationship and how, after her dad had passed away, he'd become her father figure. Someone she looked up to.

Instead, she said, 'I don't know why you shared information with O'Brien, going against our policies. Our code. Your team, Braxton. O'Brien isn't one of us any more. Regardless of why or how he left, he made that choice.'

'I know.' He stared at the half-eaten pizza, hardening and stinking in the greasy box. His fists clenched.

'You shared information with a civilian.'

'I know.'

'But I don't think you did it maliciously. I don't think you did it to leak information. I think you did it because O'Brien's your friend.'

He looked at her then, his fists unclenched. 'But what does Murphy think?'

'I'll deal with Murphy,' she said. 'We need you back, Braxton. But do me a favour: take tomorrow. Go the gym, get some fresh air and for God's sake, tidy up.'

Braxton laughed. 'It's a show in here, isn't it?'

Everything is messy right now, de Silva thought. Everything had been upended, had been untethered from the binds that kept all of it together. The savage truth about her husband's school years, the terrible knowledge of her mentor's involvement with child abuse in a closed-down school and the burning throb of living in the present, knowing what she knew, unable to speak with Ritchie, to understand why he did what he did.

'Have you heard about O'Brien?'

He shrugged and nodded. 'Just goes to show, doesn't it? You can't trust anyone because you never really, truly know who someone is. Not properly. You're on chatting terms and next thing you know they're one of Jimmy Savile's lot.'

De Silva wasn't sure what to say. There was truth in his words: we never really know the people in our lives. She thought of her own lies, her own deceit, and whether she should finally come clean, to Barclay at least.

'I can't help but think,' Braxton continued. 'Whether he worked any cases with kids... whether he took advantage, you know?'

De Silva got it. But right then, she couldn't let that thinking in. She didn't have the time, but soon, after all of this was over, she needed to circle back around to it. Address it. Deal with it. Grieve him, too.

'Don't tell me who told you, for the love of God,' she said finally. 'I'm sorry. I know he was a friend to you.'

'And to you,' Braxton said. 'Has he co-operated, at least?'

'He's told us some things, yeah,' she said. 'Look, I'll catch you up properly the day after tomorrow.' She stood up. 'You look after yourself, won't you? Put those bottles in the bin and get on with things. You don't want to end up reliant on that stuff.'

Not like I was.

'Yes, ma'am.'

'And call me "ma'am" one more time, I'll have you tossed in a cell.'

Braxton smiled despite himself. 'Sorry,' he said. 'Let me see you out.'

'I'm fine. You get some rest.'

As she got into her car, her phone buzzed. Brennan. She frowned. It was late and she was tired, and she couldn't think of anything worse than speaking about work. But then, he wouldn't call late without good reason.

'Evening, Brennan.' She started the engine and her call jumped from her phone to the car's speaker system. 'What can I do for you?' She pulled out of Braxton's road and onto the main carriageway toward home.

'I'm so sorry about calling this late, de Silva.' His voice sounded strange, panicked or excited, she couldn't quite tell. 'But we had some results back from the Meeks crime scene.'

'Oh?'

'Yes, and I thought you'd want to know right away.'

Go on then...

'I appreciate that,' she said. 'Thank you.'

'I'll email you a copy of the report over as well, but...' Here he took a long breath and let it out quickly. 'We found some hair that we believe didn't belong to the victim, which I've already ordered testing on, but we do have the results of some blood samples back.'

De Silva had a sense that something was coming. Something big, something that would break the case wide open, and the key to it was found in Brennan's lab.

'One of the blood samples we found belonged to our vic, as expected; but the other...'

'Did you find a match?'

'We did,' he said.

'You know, any new police officer has to submit a DNA sample in the form of a swab,' he said. 'There was a bit of a lag in getting the same from existing police officers, but we got there. As you know.'

She did know. Some officers kicked off about it, though she couldn't really understand their reasoning. Some said it was an invasion of their privacy, some even worried the government would use them for nefarious purposes.

'Well, among that sample was where we had our second hit.'

O'Brien. It had to be him. His involvement in this case was undeniable now, and he had so much to lose that it had to be him who silenced Meeks, despite what he said during his interview.

'It's O'Brien, isn't it?' she asked.

'No,' Brennan said. He took another breath and then paused and de Silva wanted to scream at him to just spit it out.

He said, 'The blood sample matches DNA provided by DCI Michael Crosby.'

Thirty-Nine

Wednesday 1 January 1997

In the quiet that followed the thud of Bob Brendan hitting the carpeted floor, none of us moved. None of us even breathed. We waited, knowing that each of us were waiting for the same thing: for the wind that had clearly been knocked out of him to come rushing back. For him to take breath, ragged and desperate, into his lungs, and to stand up.

He didn't.

Ricky stood over him, the lamp base still in his hand, blood dripping from it. Tommo was right there next to him, his mouth open wide. Then there was panic. Confusion. And within all of that, Micky tried to keep everyone quiet.

'Shh,' Micky said. 'Shut up or someone will hear us.'

Tommo's eyes were red, and he stared at Ricky. I remember wondering whether they even remembered that I was there. 'Is he... dead?'

Ricky knelt down, put his fingers to the side of Bob's neck, like I'd seen them do in films. Ricky's eyes closed, and I knew. In that moment, I think we all knew.

Bob Brendan was dead.

'What do we do?' Tommo's voice was high, frightened. 'What do we do? What do we do?'

'Shut the fuck up,' Micky hissed.

'Shit,' Ricky said. 'I've killed him. I've really fucking killed him. They're going to make our lives hell if we don't go to prison first.'

I remember thinking how calm Lewy seemed. He didn't seem upset, didn't appear to be distressed at all. He looked at Bob's body, cooling on his own rug, and it seemed to me as though he felt nothing. I suppose, looking back, I realise why that might have been. He was unwell even then, as a boy. Finally, he said, 'He deserved it.'

'But I killed him!'

'Ricky, relax.' Micky again. 'We'll deal with it.'

'How?' Ricky's eyes were wild.

'We'll...' Micky looked down at Bob's body and then quickly back to Ricky. He looked at Lewy then, and something passed between them. 'You should get out of here,' he said.

'No way.' Lewy crossed his arms. He wasn't going anywhere.

Micky shook his head, and said, 'We'll get rid of the body.'

Those six words changed all of our lives. They spun us out into different trajectories, and not one of us could have known what would happen when we were grown, when we were men; but that was where it all started. In the room of Bob Brendan, where five kids stood over his body.

We found Bob's car keys on a hook near the door, next to his winter coat: an old and battered navy-blue duffle he wore when he had to go outside into the playground. It had a smell to it, like it had never been washed. Bob himself had a smell to him, not just as he lay still and quiet on the rug, but in life too. There was beer and this almost sawdust body odour that reminded me of the woodwork room.

Lewy was in charge of rolling the rug and carrying it on his shoulder, while the others gripped hold of Bob's body. My part in it was to carry the car keys and to move ahead to the next junction in the corridor to make sure that no one was going to surprise us. Tommo had thrown the old duffle coat over Bob's face, probably so they didn't have to look at him.

His eyes were still open, I remember that, and they stared. The most frightening stare I'd ever seen in my life, like he was looking through you. Through all of us. I wondered whether he was remembering our faces, saving them to his spirit memory, his ghost brain or whatever they have, so that he would know exactly who we were when we came to hell to join him years later.

I remember thinking what hell for us might be like. We had lived it, hadn't we? Sure, I'd been there just weeks, but others had lived under Bob's rule for years. Would our hell be a spiteful repetition of our time at Painford, now that Bob's eyes had remembered our faces?

Maybe when I die, I'll know the answer to that question. But in the meantime, we each of us lived a different hell quite separate from each other. But hell nonetheless.

I moved from corner to corner on tip-toes, and clung to those bloody keys like they meant life or death; and, in a way, they did mean that.

We put Bob in the boot of his own car; Lewy threw the rug on top of him, and we all ran around to the groundskeeper's old shed. He always left it open, but none of us would have dared go near it usually. Micky and Ricky grabbed two spades, though one had a wobbly handle. It would have to do, I supposed.

No one came. No one saw us. No one heard the scream of the car engine as it started, or the rattle it made as we drove down the potholed road that led out onto the Rainford bypass.

'Where the fuck are we going?' Micky was at the wheel, and had stalled the car twice.

'I know where we can go,' Lewy said from the passenger seat. 'I went there once or twice with this girl I knew.'

'Where?' Ricky's voice was deep and he never took his gaze from the dirty window. I don't know what he was looking at it, but he seemed... haunted.

'These woods I know,' Lewy answered. 'Right by the water. Go right here. We need to get onto the M57.'

Years later, when I learned how to drive, I drove that route from Painford to the woods at Freshfields. It's changed a little now, with all the road infrastructure improvements. But I followed it as closely as I could. I travelled there month after month, year in and year out, and never once was I able to find exactly where we'd buried him. Though, I was sure, I'd come close a few times. But, you see, it was dark when we left Painford, and it was dark when we arrived at the woods.

The carpark at Freshfields had no gate on it. There were no lights and especially, back then, no CCTV cameras. You see, the government didn't have the network to spy on its citizens back then, not like it does now. People were free to come and go and do what they wanted. Even if that meant burying a body.

I remember getting out of the car, where we had sat so close to each other, heat radiating off our bodies and into the freezing cold of the carpark. The sea, I didn't know which one then, was somewhere out there, over the sand dunes. If I held my breath, I could hear it hitting the beach.

For a moment, Lewy closed his eyes and listened to it. Just listened, then said, 'I love that sound.'

I wanted to get moving. I was shaking from the cold and the ground felt hard under my feet, and it was then I realised what the older boys were intending to do. It crept up on me like you'd feel a spider in your hair.

All the while, Tommo cried, until Ricky stood in front of him and slapped him hard across the face. 'You stop this,' he said. 'Now!'

Tommo whimpered, but I didn't hear him again the whole night.

We followed the fence for as long as we could and under the trees and the dark seemed to get darker. Somewhere out there, I could hear whispers. A constant chatter. I believe in ghosts, of course I do – I've seen too much not to, and that night I was convinced I could see people out between the trees, just standing there. Watching. I wondered how many of them had been buried beneath the pine trees. How many of them would come to know Bob once he was under that same ground.

We left the fence and walked over the small hills, and I almost tripped over tree roots. There, Micky slammed the blade of his spade into the ground, but it was frozen and the blade didn't go in very far. 'Here,' he said.

I was sent down the hill, close to the path, to make sure nobody came by. From there, I could hear the other lads grunting, could hear Tommo snivelling. But me? I felt nothing about it. The man who had hurt me, badly sometimes, was dead. I wasn't sure if that meant it would all stop. There were other men that could keep the bad things at Painford alive.

When they were done, after what felt like hours stood in the cold, they came to find me. They were hot, sweating, but they were ready to leave. 'Where's Tommo?' I asked.

The others looked to each other, then started whispering Tommo's name into the darkness. He either never heard, or he didn't want to hear. Still, we waited for almost an hour, according to Micky's watch. We searched the hills and pathways and we couldn't find him.

I wondered whether the ghosts of the forest had taken him to be one of their own. Whether that was the price we had to pay for them accepting Bob.

Tommo was gone, and we had to get back before the sun came up, otherwise someone would know what we had done.

As we drove the car out of the carpark and back toward Painford, there was a silence. The others stank of sweat, the way the men did in the basement on the nights they came for us.

'What if Tommo's gone the police?' Ricky asked. 'What if he tells?'

No one answered.

We took the car to a farmer's field just a twenty-minute walk from Painford. Micky wiped down the steering wheel, the door handles, the boot. There was some blood inside, but there was nothing we could do about that. It had dried. And there was the rug of course, and the lamp too. I hadn't seen who had carried it out, but there it was.

Micky wiped that down too.

Lewy took out his lighter and put it against the seats in the front and the back, turned it onto the material that lined the boot. We watched the flames take hold of the car until they roared like they were furious.

Then we left.

As we got onto the bypass and headed back toward Painford, we heard a boom. *The car*, I remember thinking, but no one else spoke.

It was done.

We returned the spades to the groundskeeper's shed and we went to our dorms, and we never spoke of that night again.

In the months and years that followed that night, I always did wonder what happened to Tommo. When the school was finally closed down, I lost track of Micky, Ricky and Lewy too.

I didn't hear about, or from, any of them for a long time.

Forty

Barclay put down his copy of Meeks's manuscript, the damning account of how de Silva's own husband committed murder and conspired with others to conceal it. Still, all they had really was Meeks's word, and he was dead. There was no way he could even corroborate his own story now. There was that hacker that de Silva had spoken to though. Breaker, she called herself. The name made Barclay cringe, but from what de Silva told him, she may have known more.

He was tired, bordering on exhaustion really and even though it was after midnight, he couldn't get comfortable in the tiny bed. The memory of waking up in Ayris's hotel room alone haunted him. He remembered the condom, he recalled the kissing and the moment when they both climaxed and then lay next to each other. He remembered staring at the ceiling after it, feeling sick not from the alcohol, but from his own guilt.

He picked up his phone and texted Nick to see if he was awake, that he really needed to speak to him, and that no, it wasn't about getting back together. Nick read it straight away, started typing, then stopped. Started typing again. Stopped. Then finally, he said, *Come over. Be quiet. Wake up Sarah and I'll kill you.*

There was that sick feeling again. The kind of biliousness that comes with the knowledge that a lie, an untruth, is about to come out. He drove there without the radio on, trying to rehearse what he was going to say, how he was going to say it, but it was useless. There was no way to anticipate what was going to come out of his mouth, or how Nick would react.

Nick was at the doorstep when Barclay arrived, in the fluffy dressing gown Barclay had bought him that time they went to York for a long weekend. They'd stayed right next to the River Ouse, near the Memorial Gardens, but they'd barely left the hotel room the whole time they were there.

That was a long time ago. A different Barclay and a different Nick.

Nick put his finger to his mouth, but gestured that Barclay should follow him inside, to the kitchen. There, Nick had already made two cups of tea.

'Come on then,' he said. 'What couldn't wait until a more social hour?'

Barclay didn't know where to begin. The words turned to ashes in the back of his throat, and he struggled to clear it. He took a sip of the hot tea. 'I'm not sure where to start,' he said. He sat down at the table and felt like it was about to pour out of him: his wrongdoing, his embarrassment.

Nick sank to his knees and looked up at him. 'I know what you're feeling, because I'm feeling it, too,' he said.

Barclay blinked. 'No, no—'

'What I did to you was awful,' he said. 'But I needed space. To think, to figure things out, to see if I still wanted this. Your work... it scares me. It's not just in our house when you talk about it, it was literally almost in our home. That man Lewis Lamond, he could have come here. Could have done something to us. To Sarah.'

Barclay nodded, he knew all of this already. He already knew that Lamond's threats to Sarah last year had rattled Nick, rattled them both. Barclay had apologised over and over, even though, in his heart, he knew that there was nothing he could have done to change what had happened.

'Nick, I need to just get this out.'

'So do I!' Nick dragged a chair over and sat in it, so that he was facing Barclay, and held his hands. 'I made a mistake. Not wanting to be around you, asking you to leave the house. I miss you. The other day, when we... it was the best I'd felt in months.'

'But your text. You said it was a mistake.'

'I panicked,' he said. 'I didn't know if I was ready to talk about trying again. To apologise. To admit that I was wrong all this time. I love you, Ben, and I don't want to be without you.'

Barclay felt bile rise in his throat and he closed his eyes, tried to swallow it down. Here it was, the thing he'd wanted to hear most since he'd left, and he had the opportunity to take it. To forgive himself for what he'd done, to forget about it, to move forward with his family.

'Are you going to say something?' Nick laughed, nervously.

Forgetting. Acting as though nothing had happened with Ayris. Forgiving, whether himself or Nick. These weren't things he could do easily, not while there was something left unspoken. It would eat at him for the rest of their lives.

'I slept with someone.'

For a moment, Nick didn't move. Didn't break eye contact. Didn't react at all. Then, he blinked. He nodded and before Nick spoke his next words, Barclay's heart had already sunk, a storm-battered ship lost to the sea. 'I did too,' Nick said.

Barclay let that sink in. He had slept with someone else, and had tortured himself to distraction. He'd gone over it in his mind, the sex, how much he'd enjoyed it, how disgusted he was with himself afterward, how he'd scrubbed his skin. That Nick had slept with someone too wasn't a cause for celebration; it wasn't something that could unite them and bring them back together.

It was further proof of the reasons they should be apart.

Barclay got to his feet and paced. He wanted to leave, but couldn't. He wanted to hold Nick close to him and tell him that it was okay, but he couldn't do that either.

'Ben, speak to me.'

The thought of someone touching his husband, his Nick, the idea of someone else being inside him. That they'd enjoyed it. Together. Maybe in this house, in their bed. It made his skin crawl, his stomach clench and acid burn at his throat. He knew he was being a hypocrite but in that moment, it didn't matter.

'Who was it?' Barclay's voice was breathy as he stopped pacing. 'Not Stefan?'

'No,' Nick said. 'Just... a random guy from the app.'

He knew what app Nick meant. So ashamed of using it, he couldn't even say its name. Barclay felt that that was somehow worse. That he'd given himself to a stranger, rather than someone he worked with, or a friend. Things could happen in the heat of moments spent with a colleague, a talk with friends could evolve into something more, especially when emotions were raw, when someone was feeling lonely.

They were not accidental, because consent was there. Intent. But they were different to purposefully seeking out a shag on Grindr.

'What about yours?'

Barclay looked away. 'Sort of a colleague. Not someone from work, but someone I've had to work with.'

'Do you want to tell me what happened?'

No. 'Do you want to know?'

'No,' Nick said. 'I don't want to know.' He stood up, and tried to take hold of Barclay's hands again, but Barclay moved away. 'I don't want to know because it doesn't matter. It's happened and it's in the past. Ben, look at me.'

Barclay couldn't.

'You came here to talk to me about getting back together.'

'No, I didn't. I came to tell you what I'd done.' Barclay struggled to keep the volume from his voice. 'I came to tell you what happened and to apologise, because I feel like I've done this terrible, awful thing.'

'All you did was have sex, Ben,' Nick snapped back. 'Both of us did. We were separated, and we're both men. We have needs, and those needs should be satiated.'

A cold way to look at it. Barclay shook his head. 'Did you do it here? In our bed?'

Nick glared. 'No,' he said. 'Look, this doesn't have to mean anything, Ben. We've done it. But what we have between us is love. It's old and it's familiar, and I think we need to find our stride again. I miss you.'

Barclay's face scrunched, and he felt the burn of hot tears on his cheeks. 'I miss you,' he managed. He reached out to Nick and pulled him close. He could smell the familiar floral scent of Nick's shampoo. The citrus fruit aftershave he always sprayed on after his shower, even though he wasn't going anywhere. 'And I love you,' Barclay added.

He could have taken him to bed right then and fallen asleep with his husband in his arms. He could have woken up next to him and surprised Sarah at breakfast. He could have taken her to school. He could come home, finally, to his husband and his daughter after work.

'But I can't do this any more,' Barclay said. 'I love you so much, and this is killing me to say.' He let go of Nick, and saw tears on his face too, glistening in the low light of the kitchen. 'I think we've pushed each other too far away to find our way back.'

Barclay kissed his husband's forehead, the way he had done whenever he said goodbye, or went to work, or to the shop for bread and milk; and he knew it would be the last time his lips would touch Nick's skin.

Barclay's tears dried as he made his way to the incident room. He knew that he should sleep, but his mind wouldn't let that happen. Not now.

The OCC was a strange place in the early hours of the morning. There were footsteps somewhere above him, some officer working a case they couldn't escape from, either that or they were close to making an arrest.

The distraction of work could be good, and if not, then he could lounge in an office chair and hope that sleep came at some point.

The corridor was freezing cold, and he noticed the lights were on in the incident room, the door wide open. He thought of the man who'd tried to break into de Silva's house, of the hacker who called herself Breaker, and if there was anything he was certain he was ready for right then, it was a fight.

When he burst through the door and found de Silva there at her computer, he cocked his head. 'What the hell are you doing here?'

She looked away from her computer. 'Seem to be making a habit of this, don't we,' she said, wearily. 'Anyway, never mind me, what are *you* doing here? And tell me you have coffee.'

'I couldn't sleep. And no, sorry, I don't.'

De Silva frowned. 'Couldn't sleep either,' she said. 'Did Brennan catch you? Murphy?'

'No, not tonight. Why?'

'A sample of blood from the Meeks crime scene.' She stood up. 'Matches Crosby's service personnel DNA swab.'

'You're joking?'

'I wish I was,' she said. 'But the good thing is we have him for this too. The bad thing is that we don't have him at all.'

'Ann Crosby's holiday home seems like a good place to start.'

'I agree,' she said. 'I was just finding it on the maps. Two hours' drive.'

'You weren't thinking about going out there alone, were you?'

'Certainly not.' But there was something in her voice, a forced stiffness that bordered on rehearsal.

'Yes you were. And after last year as well!' He was incredulous. 'You could have got yourself killed. What, do you think because you've known him for years, or that you used to sleep with him, he won't hurt you?'

De Silva looked down and for the first time ever, Barclay thought he caught her blush. 'I'd have called it in,' she said. 'When I arrived. I just feel like I've got a better chance of getting him to talk if I'm alone. If that's even where he is.'

'We don't need a cosy chat, de Silva. We need to bring him in!' He felt anger rise in him, but choked it back, knowing only some of it was for de Silva herself. The rest was for him, for Nick. 'You can't keep doing this.'

'Doing what?'

'Running off and doing your own thing without giving a damn about anyone else.' His voice rose. 'You can't keep lying to my fucking face.' He was into it now, and there was no going back. He had no choice but to ride it out. 'You knew that Ritchie was involved in all of this, didn't you? Before we all found out, I mean. And don't lie to me, de Silva. I can't take it any more.'

De Silva stared at him, her eyes wide and wild, and she bit her lip. 'Yes,' she said. 'I knew about Ritchie.'

'When?'

'Last year.'

'Last year!'

'I found some paperwork of his. Some old school reports, certificates. From Rainford Lane.' She looked away again, rightfully ashamed of herself, Barclay assumed. 'I'd hoped that I could find out what happened to him. Make sense of it all, investigate it in secret.'

He took a breath, ready to snap back, but thought better of it. He spoke softly and through gritted teeth. 'You can't separate work and your life when your life *is* the work.' He took a breath. 'You don't, no, you *won't* play by the rules. You take chances when there are protocols in place to protect us, all of us. You lie to your team. To your friends. And above all, you're bloody horrendous to work with.'

'My God, Barclay, is there *anything* you like about working with me?'

She'd done it. Defused him. He felt his shoulders drop, the muscles in his face soften. 'Not really.' He smirked in spite of himself.

De Silva was frustrating, but he understood her. She took chances because protocols slowed her down. There was no space for empowerment in free-thinking. Her approach to cases was different than what Barclay had seen in his career so far.

'You don't have to come,' she said. 'I'll go alone.'

'As if I'm going to let you go alone.'

'So what are you thinking?' de Silva asked. 'What do you want to do?'

'We inform the NCA,' he said. 'We go with backup.'

'If we go there all guns blazing, and he is there, he'll run,' she said. 'We might never find him again. We could be calling out backup to Cumbria for no reason. How do you think that'll look?'

'A damn sight better than if the front page of the *Liverpool Journal* is about how two Merseyside Police detectives' bodies were found at a lodge in Ullswater.'

Forty-One

De Silva looked at her watch. The sun was still hours away from rising, and the map showed that they were less than ten minutes away from Ann's family's lodge. De Silva thought it best that they take Barclay's car as Crosby would be too familiar with hers. If he were there and he was awake, if he were looking out for someone approaching, he'd be able to spot her white Kuga a mile off.

They'd passed Windermere just a few miles back, and as they turned toward the lodge, the main byways turned into twisting rural narrow roads, and Barclay had to turn on the full beams just to see. All around them were trees and in the darkness you could just about make out hills, and the eerie glow of animals' eyes in fields.

De Silva wished they could get there sooner, but Barclay was right to slow down, to be cautious when driving on unfamiliar roads. *But still*, she thought, *if I were driving, we'd be there by now.*

'I'm still not clear on the plan when we get there,' Barclay said.

'We park a little further down the road. Proceed on foot. We stake the place out.'

'That didn't work out too well for us last time, de Silva.'

'Well, it's different this time,' she said. They were prepared. They were ready for Crosby to be there, ready for him to react violently as he had done at Rainford Lane last year.

There were no other cars on the road, no one staggering home from the pub or a bar, no students thinking they're cool for having a house party and keeping their neighbours awake. It was peaceful and, if de Silva was honest, she envied the people that lived here.

But the city was in her, it was a part of her, and there was no escaping it. If she stood outside, away from the sound of the engine, from Barclay's humming, she wondered what she would hear. Whether she'd hear anything at all, other than the wind cascading down the fells.

She'd been up here before and had always found it to be a magical place, though couldn't say why. Something about its size, the expanse of nothingness. Somewhere, she had thought, she and Ritchie could retire to. But he'd said it would be too isolating, especially in the winter, and everyone would know their business. She had hoped that by the time they'd come to retire, neither of them would have any business worth knowing about.

That the soap opera of her life would have aired its final episode long before retirement.

But that was never meant to be, she reflected gloomily. Her life had been one dramatic incident after another, and she had no handle on it. Her life had spun out of control the moment she slept with Crosby the first time. No, before that, when her dad had died.

Surely that was the start of it all.

And at the centre of all of it were choices she had made. Bad choices. Therapy could only do so much, she'd realised a few weeks into her sessions. There are some things therapy can't fix, some wounds it cannot heal, and even more that the patient doesn't want touched.

But now things were worse than ever. Ritchie was a murderer and so was her lover. Her mentor was an abuser of children – potentially an abuser of Ritchie and Crosby, and she'd not known any of it. Why he'd not spoken to her about the abuse was a question that had haunted de Silva since she found Ritchie's school reports and connected the dots. Of course, that was before she knew that Ritchie had murdered Bob Brendan.

'We're just a few minutes away,' Barclay said.

De Silva had expected the lodge to be on the lake, but when she'd researched it earlier, she'd found that the lake was still a five-minute drive away, that the lodge was on some land off a country lane, all by itself. That surrounding it were tall, old trees, and to access it you had to open a metal gate and drive up a stone driveway, and behind the lodge was a single-track road that led up into the fells.

The car would be too noisy for the stone driveway, and the gate itself might even give them away.

'Pull over here,' she said. 'We'll walk the rest.'

Barclay pulled over into a small lay-by, which may have been a passing place before the road was widened at some point. He switched off the engine and looked at her.

He was waiting for her to do something, say something, take action; she wasn't ready to yet. The roads were dead and the drive passed quicker than she'd anticipated, but she knew she had to get moving. She'd need to keep the element of surprise if Crosby really was here.

People are counting on you to get this right.

She climbed out of the passenger seat and onto the empty road. The stars and moon were covered by thick clouds, and the only light came from a lamp post further down the road.

Barclay took out his phone and turned on the torch, but de Silva shook her head. They'd do this in darkness until they had absolutely no choice.

They started down the road and Barclay said in a low, hushed tone, 'How're you feeling?'

She assumed he meant how she felt about potentially coming face to face with Crosby again. 'I'm not sure,' she said. 'Scared. Nervous.'

Barclay nodded. 'I think I should have stopped for a wee somewhere.'

'Oh for God's sake, Barclay.'

'Sure I can hold it.'

'Well, you'll have to,' she said. 'I'm not listening to you piss on the side of the road. Imagine you got hit by a truck with your pants by your ankles...'

'You know we don't actually drop our pants down when we have a wee, don't you?'

'Of course I know that.'

Up ahead, a path joined the country road, and led up to a gate. In the darkness, it looked white, like it was made of bones instead of metal. She took out her mobile phone and pressed the call button. 'We're about to enter the property now,' she said. 'Are you close?'

Ayris's voice was loud over the thrum of an engine. 'We're about ten minutes out. Is there any sign of him at the property?'

'We can't see yet,' she said. 'We're going to move in for a closer look.'

'De—'

She buttoned the call and turned her phone to vibrate. If he was on the property, there was no way she'd want Ayris calling her to alert him.

'Maybe we should wait for them, de Silva.'

'Yeah, we could do. Or we could sneak past the gate, see if we can see any lights. Any movement.'

'We agreed…'

'No, you said we should bring backup, and we did,' she said. 'Beyond that, I just nodded.'

'Which is an agreement.'

'Well, I'm sorry. But you can wait here if you want. I'm just going to cross the gate. See what I can see.'

'The gate, de Silva. No further on,' he said. 'You see anything, you come back here to me. I'll wait for the backup.'

'I think you're forgetting who's in charge here.' *Barely*, she thought. 'But all right.'

Barclay nodded.

The gate was old, she could see that now she was next to it. The top hinge was corroded, and she had no doubt that if she pushed it open, it would scream like a fox. But she needed to get around it, to get past the trees lining the road and get eyes on the lodge.

She took one look back at Barclay, standing by the side of the road, glancing the way they had come from, and put her foot on the middle bar of the gate. It sagged and groaned under her weight and she froze until it stopped, then cocked her leg over and climbed down the other side.

Rounding the trees, she saw the lodge at the top of a hill, surrounded by oak, alder and birch. All well-established trees, and she wondered how long this lodge had stood in this spot. It seemed to blend in with the hills, the trees, almost like it was a part of the landscape itself. But maybe that was just the low light, a trick of the night time.

It was made from wood, but painted dark, she could tell that much. At the front was a raised decking area with steps up to the house from the side of the hill. There were tall windows, maybe patio doors, but she couldn't tell from this far away.

The tree branches hung over the roof, and it had a certain aesthetic about it. That romantic quality that would make even the shortest weekend getaway perfect. Crosby had never brought her here during their affair, never even mentioned it.

True, their liaisons started out of a need for de Silva to feel attractive again – Ritchie had stopped wanting sex – and de Silva had internalised that. She wasn't sexy, wasn't desirable, wasn't wanted. Crosby filled that gap, and months into it, when the hasty fucks turned into longer trysts, and the sex became more sensual, more caring, de Silva had started to get feelings. By the end of it, when Ritchie had killed himself, she knew that she had fallen in love with Crosby and tortured herself for loving them both.

Was this lodge in the lakes his and Ann's last sanctuary together? Was this where they came to try to reconnect, try to love each other again? Or did Crosby not love de Silva enough to bring her here? She was being ridiculous, pondering the romantic notions of someone she knew to be a vicious killer, and in that moment she realised something about herself.

Despite the things that Ritchie and Crosby had done, there was still that burning desire within de Silva, that need to feel needed.

She saw the flash up ahead before she heard the boom. It came from the decking, she thought, and as she froze at the sight, something whooshed past her face. She felt it more than saw it, it moved that fast, and behind her, tree bark exploded.

Oh my God.

She squatted down and searched for cover, realising what it was, as another flash came from the deck, then the unmistakeable sound of gunfire.

She scrambled forward, found a fallen tree trunk, stripped bare of leaves and branches, and hid behind it. She took out her phone, but Barclay was already calling. She answered and said quietly, 'I'd say he's here.'

'Was that—'

'He's got a gun,' de Silva said. 'Stay where you are, Barclay, no heroics.'

'Fuck!' She could hear the frustration in his voice. 'Are you hurt?'

'No,' she said. 'I need you to ring Ayris, see how far out the team are. I'm safe. I've got cover. Do it now.'

As she ended the call, she knew she was anything but safe. She peered over the top of the trunk, felt the roughness of bark on her hands. Another flash, then the trunk exploded in front of her, splinters and bark flew, but she ducked back down. Wood isn't bullet proof, she knew that. It might slow a bullet down, but ultimately, she couldn't stay there forever. Her only option was to run for the gate and hope he didn't hit her, or try to make it to the lodge itself. See if she could somehow sneak up behind him.

While she thought and her phone buzzed in her hand, Barclay calling, she heard it. The thud of boots on wooden decking, the rustle as they made their way through grass.

He was coming for her.

Forty-Two

Barclay could hear his own heartbeat thundering in his ears, the gush and rush of his own blood as it coursed through him. His head swam, and he felt, for just a moment, unstable on his feet. He bent double, hands on his knees, and breathed in slowly through his mouth, out through his nose. There was no time for this, he needed to be moving, but he had no choice. The panic attacks that had begun when Nick asked him to leave had been hard going, difficult to manage, and even now with his friend's life on the line, he had to take the time.

Finally, when the dizziness subsided, when the abject fear rolled back and his breathing returned to normal, he tried to call de Silva again, but it rang out. He'd heard another gunshot a few seconds ago, but after that... nothing.

He'd told her this was a bad idea, but before they left the OCC, she had insisted the best option was for them to arrive before the Armed Response teams and Ayris. They would approach softly at first.

He couldn't stay and wait and hope that Ayris and the AR team arrived in time to save de Silva. He had to get going. Had to do what he could. He sent his location to Ayris and headed for the gate, ignoring Ayris's call which came through almost instantly.

God, she could already be dead. He might have already killed her.

He vaulted over the gate in one swift motion, landing gently on his feet, and circled around the stand of trees that blocked the view of the lodge from the road. Up ahead, a tree trunk lay across the ground, and he could just about make out someone sitting against it.

De Silva.

He walked across the grass slowly, almost on his tiptoes, to make as little sound as possible. The cold of the night air had crept in and a mist covered the field, swirling about him as he moved. The clouds had begun to clear, and the stars pricked tiny holes in the fabric of the night sky.

Hyper-aware of the sound his shoes made on the grass, he approached the trunk and de Silva slumped against it, still unable to make her out in the darkness. Then, just when he'd almost reached her, she moved, pulled down a hood Barclay didn't remember her wearing and he saw that it wasn't de Silva at all.

Crosby's face was stone and unmoving. He looked sick, thin. Maybe that was what months on the run did to a man. Barclay wouldn't know. But what he did know was that in Crosby's hands was a shotgun, and it was aimed at him.

As he got to his feet, Crosby said, 'How many are coming, and don't lie to me.'

'Where's de Silva?'

'She's alive,' Crosby said. 'How many?!' He poked Barclay with the muzzle of the gun.

'I'm not sure,' Barclay said. In truth, he wasn't sure. 'Armed Response teams. The NCA.'

'How far away are they?'

Barclay had to think quick. He was either asking him this so they could plan an escape, or to understand how much time he had to kill him, and de Silva if he hadn't already, and get away before any backup arrived. 'About half an hour away,' Barclay lied. 'We headed off before they were ready. De Silva's orders.'

Crosby grinned. 'Just like her. Running head-long into stuff she's got no business heading into.'

'Where is she?'

Crosby tilted his head backward. 'She's inside.'

He must have taken her inside quickly. He'd have tied her up so that she couldn't escape, and then come back out to bait Barclay. But he'd have had to have moved fast. *Tricky*. 'We found Meeks's manuscript. We know what Ritchie did. We know about O'Brien. And your involvement with Lamond.'

'Lewy was like a brother to me,' Crosby said. 'What they did to all of us was... But what they did to him. He got the worst of it. What they did to him changed him. None of what he did was his fault.'

'He killed teenage girls, Crosby,' Barclay said. 'No amount of trauma can be blamed for that.'

'Shut up!' Crosby shouted. 'And get your hands up.'

Barclay did as he was told. 'I need to make sure that de Silva is okay,' he said. 'If she is, I'll contact the AR team and ask them to back off. Just put the gun down.'

'They won't make it here in time,' Crosby hissed. 'Get inside the house.' He shifted the gun quickly to show Barclay that he should go on ahead, then pointed it back at him. 'Move!'

Barclay headed toward the house, which was in total darkness still. He hoped that de Silva truly was okay, that she wasn't injured, bleeding out on the floor. He should never have let her go on alone, but did she ever listen to reason?

Never. Crosby had the truth of it.

As he walked up the steps to the top of the deck, he glanced back toward the road. He couldn't hear any sirens, nor see the flash of AR team vehicles.

Just hold on a little longer.

He could turn, grab the gun, maybe get Crosby to fire his shot into the decking. It would take him some time to reload, and Barclay could take that opportunity to get the better of him.

You could. And he could shoot you. You'd die out here.

Barclay knew, when he'd crossed the threshold into the lodge, that the situation had completely changed. There was no element of surprise. Crosby had expected them, had been waiting for them. Had O'Brien tipped him off somehow? Or maybe he'd gotten a message to him via Reeves, his solicitor, the man who seemed to have disappeared.

Then, in the distance, the whirr of sirens. He felt the butt of the gun slam against the back of his head and the floor of the lodge came rushing up to meet him. Crosby shoved Barclay's legs through the door and slammed it shut, bolted it.

The pain pulsed through Barclay's skull like fire, made his vision blurry, the room around him a haze.

'You lying fuck!' Crosby said.

Barclay rolled over onto his back; Crosby's gun was in his face. The flashing blue lights from the road washed over the lodge. Crosby ran to the window and closed the blinds. Barclay took the opportunity to look around, but couldn't see de Silva anywhere.

The swarm in his head began to quieten and subside, and as he got to his feet and took in the living space, he knew for certain that de Silva wasn't there. He bounded over toward Crosby, but he spun around and pointed the gun at him.

Barclay put his hands in the air. 'Where is she, Crosby?'

'I told you,' he said. 'She's alive. Now get back down on the floor.'

'Show me where she is,' Barclay said. 'Show me she's safe and I'll co-operate.' Through a gap in the blinds, Barclay could see the Armed Response team coming over the metal gate from the road.

'You'll co-operate because I'm telling you to!'

'This is Cumbria Police,' a voice boomed, crackling through a microphone. 'Put down your weapon and come out with your arms raised.'

'You're not getting out of this, Crosby,' Barclay said. 'They'll surround the place and move in. The only choice you have now is whether they take you out of here in cuffs or on a stretcher.'

'GET DOWN ON THE FUCKING FLOOR!'

Barclay sank to his knees. 'Tell me where she is.'

'Shut up!'

'If you've hurt her, I swear to God—'

'You swear to God what? I'm the one with the power now. Not you. Not them.' Spittle flew from his mouth as he raged. 'Not Bob fucking Brendan and certainly not O'Brien. You think you found this place by accident?'

Through the pain in his skull, it took a few moments for that to truly click with Barclay.

'I made that happen,' Crosby said.

'Ann,' Barclay said. 'She led us here.'

'Dumb bitch still thinks I love her.'

Barclay had to keep him talking, if only to buy more time for the Armed Response teams and Ayris to come up with some sort of plan. A helicopter thundered through the once peaceful skies outside. 'Don't you?' he asked.

'Not for years.'

'What about de Silva?'

Crosby glared at him; his eyes looked black in the darkness of the lodge, and Barclay couldn't read the emotion on his face.

He tried again. 'Did you kill Jacob Meeks?'

'I didn't kill him,' Crosby said.

'We found DNA putting you at the crime scene, Crosby. We already know that—'

Crosby was in his face then, the shotgun between them. He raged, 'Do you see? It's already started.'

'What has?' Barclay thought back to what O'Brien had said, the clean-up he'd promised would begin. 'What are you saying, Crosby?'

'They're fucking framing me.'

'You're saying that they've framed you for Meeks's murder? Why would they do that?'

'Don't you see, you thick fuck?' He moved away from Barclay then, tears streaming down his face. 'I was told that we'd have a new life. Be able to start again, somewhere new. They have that kind of power, you know? But there was just one thing I needed to do first.'

'What? What did you have to do, Crosby?'

He got a grip of himself then, held back his tears and looked out of the window. 'They're getting closer.'

'What did they ask you to do?'

'I lured you here through Ann,' he said. 'I knew you'd speak to her. Given everything that's happened, it was the logical investigative step to go back to her. Everything was coming apart. None of us knew that Meeks had written everything down.'

The book had been the catalyst for all of this, but they couldn't have known about Meeks's book until after they'd had him killed. 'They had him killed because of his investigation. The work he was doing with his online friends. The internet sleuth people. Then they realised he'd written a book; whoever killed him gave it to O'Brien. He was supposed to burn it,' Crosby said. 'That's what I was told. But he kept it, didn't he?'

Barclay couldn't guess why O'Brien had kept such damning evidence; maybe to recapture the thrill of the things he'd done, or been involved in.

I doubt he'd ever tell us.

'Why don't you tell me more about that night,' Barclay said. 'When Bob Brendan died?'

'That was just the beginning,' Crosby said.

'Do you want to tell me about it?'

'We were The Woulds back then,' Crosby hissed.

Like The Woulds app. Like the photo album de Silva found in O'Brien's loft.

There were tears on Crosby's face now, his voice hoarse. 'The ones who would do as we were told. The ones who wouldn't fight back.'

'Until you did.'

Crosby sat down, made sure the gun was aimed at Barclay and as bright white lights began to shine through the windows of the lodge, he said, 'I always intended for it to stop. I couldn't take it any more. They hurt us so badly.' He looked away for just a moment. 'That night, I knew what I was doing. I told the others we were just going to scare Bob, but I knew what I intended to do. I was going to end it.'

'But Ritchie got there first.'

'He got carried away,' Crosby said, almost defensive. 'Caught up in the moment, in trying to protect Davey Meeks. He was just a kid. Ritchie never intended to kill anyone that night. That's not who he was.'

A voice boomed again, 'If you don't come out with your hands in the air, we will be forced to come inside and we *will* use any force necessary.'

Barclay heard someone shout, 'Are you crazy: there are two officers in there!' It sounded like Ayris.

'You don't know what it was like for us.' Crosby was almost sobbing, and Barclay knew he'd eventually get sloppy, and that could lead to an accident. He needed to be careful.

'Whatever happened to you doesn't excuse Lamond murdering innocent girls; it doesn't legitimise you luring detectives out here for what? To kill us? Kill de Silva?'

'I HAD TO!' he screamed. 'That was their price. If I wanted to have a new life, she had to go.'

'So you chose yourself over the woman you loved.'

'I never loved her,' Crosby said. 'I just had to get close. It was never supposed to get this far. It was all *supposed* to end last year. My plan was to get her good and drunk and fuck her, and then when she was passed out—'

'You were going to make it look like a suicide. Like grief for Ritchie.'

'But she ended it, and I couldn't find a way back in without incriminating myself.'

'You're scum, Crosby. You're worse than the people you work for. They were right about you. You will do as you're told, won't argue back. You're still The Woulds!'

Crosby screamed, raised the gun again, but this time Barclay caught hold of the muzzle and twisted it away from Crosby's body, gripped hold of his left hand and managed to boot him backward.

The gun went off: books on the shelf nearby burst into pulp, and Barclay ducked out of the way, unsure if Crosby still had hold of it.

Crosby was scrambling around in the dark. Barclay reached around, felt his way across the floor, but couldn't find the gun. Then, Crosby was on his feet again and the gun was shoved into Barclay's face. He could feel the heat of the last discharge on his cheek, could smell the smoke of the gunpowder and Crosby quickly reloaded the gun.

'Where is she?'

Crosby grinned. 'She'll be with her husband by now.'

Barclay's heart could have stopped and he wouldn't have noticed. Those words stabbed at him like five knives to the gut and chest. He'd killed her.

Crosby had killed her.

Everything around him fell silent. The sound of the sirens gone, his own breathing was still and he could see Crosby's mouth move, but couldn't hear a word he said.

Then, there was torchlight in the room, focused on and around Crosby. The Armed Response team were here, their faces scrunched up in anger as they bellowed things that Barclay couldn't hear.

Crosby moved as though he was placing the gun on the ground, then suddenly sprang up and fired. An officer went down, and then suddenly the sound of the room came back to Barclay as one single shot hit Crosby in the shoulder. The gun flew from his hand, and he hit the ground as though he'd been smashed into by a train. He screamed in agony.

Barclay was helped up to his feet by some of the AR officers and taken out onto the front lawn, where Ayris and Murphy waited for him. He turned back to look at the lodge and then felt his knees buckle and he went down and vomited onto the grass, thick bile that tasted like acid.

Two paramedics came into the field as Crosby was brought out by three AR officers, their guns slung safely across their backs. Crosby cried out in pain, though to Barclay it sounded distant and tinny.

Somewhere, someone was saying, 'We need to get that cut looked at. It looks nasty.' He looked in the direction of the voice, and Ayris was there, his head tilted, his eyes on Barclay's.

Barclay nodded. At that moment, he wanted to be anywhere else than standing outside that lodge. Every time he blinked, de Silva was etched into his eyelids, the last time he'd seen her: walking away from him toward the gate. Toward her death.

He should have gone with her. Should have been at her side. Together, they might have stopped him before Crosby—

Murphy put a hand on his shoulder. 'De Silva,' she said. 'Where's de Silva?'

Barclay felt as though a stone had lodged in his throat and had swelled, and that the words were stuck behind it. Her husband had died, and now she had followed him to the grave at the hands of her lover – the hands of Ritchie's own friend.

'Barclay, can you hear me?' She looked to Ayris and shook her head. 'I don't think he can hear me.'

'He's in shock,' Ayris said. 'We need to get him to the ambulance.' Ayris led Barclay away, back toward the gate they'd come in from, back to the last point he'd seen de Silva alive. How would he tell Laney? Her niece, Bonnie?

Her mum in the nursing home, would she even remember who she was?

Barclay stopped and looked back to Murphy. She asked, 'Barclay, where is de Silva?'

'She's dead,' Barclay said finally. 'De Silva's dead.'

Forty-Three

The car was warm, not a sticky heat, but the kind that was comforting. A blanket in autumn, an open fire in winter; like when you finally slip out of your boots and let your feet breathe. When you step into a hot bubble bath or stand under the shower, streaming and steaming.

That was how de Silva felt.

She couldn't open her eyes because something was across them, wrapped around her head and tied too tight at the back. It dug into her scalp.

Her tongue was dry and swollen and she could taste the metal tang of blood. She was dizzy, confused, out of it and as hard as she tried, she couldn't focus on anything. Not her own breathing, not the rumble of the car as it sped somewhere and not the words of the man somewhere to her right.

She tried to move, but her hands were fastened together and tied to something solid.

He's driving, she thought. *He's driving and you're in the passenger seat. Come on now, wake up, girl. Get yourself together.*

Her head throbbed, and she could hear it pulsing as much as she felt it. Beneath that, somewhere close, she heard the man's voice again. It was close to her, but it was clipped and strained, like when you've been laughing or crying. Or screaming. It was muffled too, as though the person speaking had something over their mouth.

Still, de Silva couldn't escape the feeling, deep inside her, in her bones, in her blood, in the space between her cells, that she knew the voice.

Ritchie?

When Crosby had hit her with the gun, she'd all but blacked out. She remembered only snatches: being carried away. Seeing Crosby standing by the fallen tree, the gun still in his hands. The musty smell of the lodge. A beige rug with tassels at the foot of a bed. Patio doors and the sound of a car engine.

Then she had completely blacked out.

If Crosby hadn't taken her inside, hadn't carried her to a car at the back of the house, then who—

The voice said, 'Come on. Wake up.'

He tapped her face lightly with the back of his hand, and she could tell they were hairy. They smelled like wood and fire and food.

'Wake up,' the voice said again, muffled. 'For God's sake.'

She heard the brakes squeak, the crunch of tyres on gravel and then the car stopped. Something shifted and a door opened. Not hers. Then, seconds later, it did open, the freezing air hit her hard in the face, like ice.

She heard a snip and her hands were free. He took her by the arm and dragged her out of the car. 'I told him,' he said, 'not to hit you so hard. Take some deep breaths.'

She did. Not because he'd told her to, but because her body needed it. Craved it. When she drew in a deep breath, her chest hurt. She must have injured it somehow. Maybe it was from being carried over this person's shoulder, maybe it was from being slumped over in the passenger seat.

He held on to her arm and said, 'Don't move. We're pretty high up.' There was something in the way he spoke. Not the sound of his voice, because that was still muffled; no, it was the rhythm of his speech, the way his voice rose and fell.

Ritchie, is that you?

He pushed her down to her knees. 'Take the blindfold off,' she said. 'Please.'

'Can't do that.'

'Where are you taking me?'

There was a pause. 'They want you gone. No loose ends.'

'There are people coming,' de Silva said. 'Backup.'

'Oh, they arrived,' he said.

'They'll find us.'

Then de Silva saw it, a tiny sliver of night at the bottom of whatever was across her eyes. If she tilted her head back, she'd know who she was speaking to, but that would be too obvious. She needed to buy herself some time.

'Did you kill those people? Finch, Heaton, the others?'

'Oh, they had to pay!' the man said. 'They were bad. Some of them did bad things to us, and the others... they knew about it and what did they do? They left. Didn't say a word. We could have died for all they cared. Well, fuck them!'

'And Lewis Lamond? Did you kill him?'

'Lewy was my friend,' the man said. 'Whatever he was. Whatever he did. Whatever they drove him to. He was our friend. We didn't kill him.'

We?

'That wasn't part of the deal,' the man continued. He moved just a step: she could hear his shoes crunch on loose stones.

'What deal?'

'The one we made with *them*,' he said. 'Enough talking! We've got to get going.'

'They'll catch you,' de Silva said. 'Whatever you've got planned, they'll get to you.'

'No, they won't,' he said. 'I'm a ghost.'

Those words hung between them for a moment, before the wind blew them away like cobwebs. In that instant, she thought of her Ritchie over the banister.

'Did they kill Lewis Lamond? The ones behind The Woulds?'

The man took in a sharp breath through his nose. 'They're cleaning everything up. You, the NCA, you've exposed them too much, and now… well, now they have to protect themselves. We drew you out here just so we could kill you. You and your buddy.'

'Even if we died, there's still traces of them. Of you.' She hissed at a pain in her chest. 'Reports. Evidence. DNA.'

'Yeah,' he said, and she could hear the sneer in his voice. 'For now.'

Of course, she thought, *if they had the power to get to Lewis Lamond in jail, they could easily make evidence disappear. Like O'Brien had done with those two detective constables…*

'Everything and everyone can be erased,' he said.

She tilted her head just a little, was able to see the tops of trees as they sloped down toward a lake. The only sound was the wind that howled around them, and beneath that, the man's breathing.

'Ritchie,' she said, her voice quiet, almost lost to the wind. 'Is that you?'

There was quiet then, except for the rush of the current from the lake. Then, he laughed. He pulled off her blindfold, and as her eyes adjusted, she looked up at the man, a balaclava over his face. But his build, his hands, his eyes.
Ritchie.

Then, he slipped off the balaclava, dropped it at her feet. 'Your husband is dead,' he said.

It was true, he looked so much like her Ritchie, even sounded like him. But it wasn't him. There was something in the shape of his nose, the roundness of his chin, now that she could see his face, that reminded her of the little boy on Meeks's evidence board.

'Billy Thompson,' she said.

He took out a pair of hand pruners from his pocket and touched her face. 'Who do you think I should send your finger to?' he asked. 'Your sister hates you, your mum doesn't even know who you are. Your dad's dead, your lover fucked you just to get close to you. He used you, Win, and your husband? What a goddam coward.' He grinned at her. 'Who's left to love poor Winifred de Silva now?'

She lunged at him then, shouldered him with such force that they both went over the edge of the fell. Her world turned upside down, and she couldn't focus. They were tumbling and then she heard him scream.

The wind huffed out of her body as she slammed into something hard, and as she struggled to get her breath back, she found herself up against a rock. She managed to get to her feet; the pain in her chest was raw, agonising.

He was on his feet now and he was coming at her, limping. A branch pierced his thigh. De Silva scrambled up the fellside, clawing for purchase on rocks and sods of earth. She needed to get to the car, needed to get somewhere safe to call Barclay and tell him where she was.

The top of the hill seemed so far away, seemed an insurmountable peak she'd never be able to manage and as she looked back over her shoulder, he was there, right behind her, despite the branch in his leg.

She turned and kicked out, managed to boot him in the face and he slipped down the hill. De Silva moved quickly: that move had bought her seconds and in this situation, time was precious.

The car, a battered red Mondeo, was in view now, the doors open, the engine still idling. She slammed the passenger door closed and limped around to the driver's side. She closed the door, put the car into gear and was about to take her foot off the clutch when—

The window shattered. He reached in and grabbed her right hand. The car stalled and she tried to take her hand back from him, but his grip was like a vice. 'I'll take it,' he hissed. 'Like I took the others. Took Bob's.'

He managed to force her middle finger in between the pruners and slammed them shut. The pain turned her vision white. She felt dizzy. Sick, like she was going to pass out. As he opened the door, she managed to restart the engine and get the car into gear. It lurched forward as he shoved at her, but it was too late.

The car had stalled again, and as he pushed her over to the passenger seat and climbed in, the pain gripped her properly. She looked down at her hand, gushing with blood, her middle finger missing, and screamed in agony.

'We'd best get going,' he said. 'We're still a bit away.'

She reached inside her jacket for the PAVA spray from her harness, but as she pressed the button, it only hissed. It was empty since she'd arrested David.

Thompson laughed at her, knocked the can out of her hands and backhanded her across the face. She fell against the door and the car skidded as they sped off. She could feel from the motion and the way her stomach flipped that they were going down, and fast.

Her heart was slowing. She felt hot and light-headed. She needed to make a move now, before she passed out; before he achieved whatever he had planned for her; but the pain was agonising. She moved quickly, but it felt like slow motion.

She pulled the steering wheel toward her. The engine revved. The world spun. Tree trunks were in the sky, and the stars were on the ground, and flip and flip and twist and turn.

Crunch.

She could smell smoke and blood and diesel. She could hear her own breathing, ragged and quick. She looked through the windscreen, cracked into the outline of a spider's web, and she knew she was trapped. To her left was a tree, and the car door a wreck. Her leg was cut badly, and the pain from her hand and forehead was almost too much to bear. She could feel something warm slipping down her face and knew she was bleeding from there, too. She wanted to go to sleep.

Across from her, in the driver's seat, he sat there, his face turned away from her, as though looking out at the woods they now found themselves in.

Her whole body ached, but she had to move. Had to get out of the car and ring for help.

As she sat forward, her chest throbbed. *A broken rib*, she thought. *Must be.* Still, she moved. Slowly. She put two fingers from her left hand to his neck and found a pulse, still strong despite the crash and the blood that seeped out of deep cuts in his left arm and neck.

She needed to get out of the car. The door was busted, and the gap between the tree and her window wasn't big enough to squeeze through. She shifted her weight and leaned across him toward the window he'd smashed just moments ago. He could wake up at any moment if he wasn't already conscious. He could grab her. Finish her off.

Still, she pulled herself across him, the pain in her leg and hand making her moan and wince. She was just seconds from being free of the car when she felt his grip on her ankle. He looked at her with angry eyes, almost wolf-like in the darkness.

There wasn't much strength left in her, but she mustered it and pulled her aching leg through the window. He tried to open the door to come after her, but it wouldn't budge and de Silva was thankful.

'You fucking bitch!' he screamed at her. He was moving, heaving himself up toward the window.

De Silva reached for a rock on the ground, flew toward him and smacked him with it. When he slumped forward, his eyes still on her, she unclipped the cuffs from her harness and slammed one end onto the steering wheel, the other onto his wrist. 'Don't go anywhere,' she said.

He screamed. He howled. She was a bitch, a whore, all of the things men call women who have overcome them. Bettered them. The things they think still hurt.

She found it hard to put weight onto her left leg, and she was losing blood all too quickly from her missing finger, but de Silva climbed the side of the hill they'd tumbled down again, clinging to trees and branches for support. Finally, at the top, breathless and in agony, in the distance she saw the swirl of blue emergency vehicle lights. Of police. Her people. Her safety.

Her personal phone was busted, cracked and unusable. She searched her pockets for her work phone. That screen was cracked, and had been for well over a year; she'd never had it fixed, but when she touched it, the screen lit up.

She found Barclay's number and pressed dial. It barely rang once before he answered, his voice thick.

'De Silva, where are you? Crosby said you were dead; we couldn't find... are you all right?'

De Silva looked over her shoulder, but couldn't make out the car below the horizon of the hill she'd managed to climb. 'I'm going to send you my location. I need help. An ambulance for me, and for Billy.'

'Billy Thompson?' Barclay paused. 'Jesus, de Silva. What the hell is going on?'

She pinged her location to Barclay's phone. 'Just get someone here.'

De Silva could hear Barclay climbing into a car, saying to someone, 'I need paramedics following me. Now.' His engine came to life. 'I'm on my way, de Silva. Just hold on.'

Her leg ached, her chest throbbed and her arms were weak. She dropped her phone and the light from it went out. De Silva's last thought, before her world turned black once more, was the hope that the thing hadn't, finally, died.

Forty-Four

Six months later

De Silva found herself in her old house, the one she had shared with Ritchie. The one where she'd found him slung over the banister. She'd wished that when she had moved house, the memories of that awful night would stay there; but that hadn't happened. The memories haunted her.

She sat on the bottom step of the staircase, where she'd been in so many dreams before. Next to her, Ritchie was a little boy. The boy she'd met and loved and played with when they were kids in Kirkby. Above them, a noose swung from the banister, and blood drip-dripped from it onto the tiled floor.

The little boy Ritchie wouldn't look at her; he'd turned to face the wall. He was crying, his sobs were loud and pulled at her heart. There was a need in her to comfort him, to protect him, but she knew that it was too late. There were no words she could say that would solve what he had gone through.

Thump, thump, thump from the front door.

She stood and walked to the door, put her hand on the handle and turned back to the stairs. The little boy wasn't crying any more, but stared at her with big, watery eyes.

Above him, adult Ritchie twisted on rope. His face was bulging and purple and unrecognisable. Below him, the shadow monsters moaned and reached for his feet with claws and teeth.

Thump, thump, thump!

She wanted to run back to the little boy, to hold him close and tell him that things didn't have to be this way.

Thump, thump, thump.

But she stayed where she was and turned the handle. Light flooded into the hallway and in front of her stood Ritchie, a ligature mark around his neck. His skin pale. He stepped in, his face twisted and menacing and he walked toward the younger version of himself.

She wanted to go back, to save little Ritchie from himself, but instead she turned away from them, stepped into the light and—

The alarm on her phone rang out loudly, but her eyes opened gently and she rose for the day. She stretched and felt the pain in her finger like a hot knife. The surgery had been a success, and although she'd never regain full functionality, the surgeons were pleased with her progress after months of physical therapy.

She moved to the bathroom, turned on the shower, then stood in front of the mirror and brushed her teeth. She looked down at her right hand, the scar there was a constant reminder of that night, though it had started to fade.

After her shower, she dressed quickly. She wanted to be early, not on time, but ahead of schedule. She wanted the time to prepare for what she was going to say. What she was going to hear.

She wanted it out of the way as soon as possible, but what then? She'd have nothing to do but think about it.

There were still six weeks left of her suspension. Despite everything she'd been through, Murphy hadn't let her poor judgement go unpunished.

The waiting room in the visitors' centre was cold, but de Silva welcomed it. She'd thought ahead, based on her experience of visitors' centres in the past, and put on a thick jacket. Whether she shivered from the cold or from adrenaline coursing through her, she didn't want Crosby to see it.

When finally, an hour later, she sat opposite him, he was handcuffed to the leg of an old metal table; paint had chipped off and people had etched their names and dates of their visits. A record of visitors of the incarcerated.

'Here she is,' Crosby said. 'My lover.'

His face was exactly how it looked that night in Cumbria, how it had looked last year at Rainford Lane, though somewhat skinnier. Paler. They'd thought that Lamond had help from someone, possibly a police officer. She'd never imagined it would have been Crosby. When she looked at his face, she felt that flip in her stomach she'd always felt when she saw him. She pushed it down with the other emotions she didn't want to feel again, deep in the pit of her heart where the bad things lived.

'Wasn't sure I'd ever see you again.'

'I wasn't sure I wanted to see you,' she said.

He looked down, away from her, the way he did when he was guilty of something. And he was guilty.

'Why did you?'

'I needed answers.'

'I told Barclay everything that night at the lodge,' Crosby said. 'He can tell you.'

'I know what you told him,' she said. 'But I needed to hear it from you.'

'Hear what from me?'

'That what we had… that it meant nothing to you.'

He sniggered. 'Jesus, look at you. So desperate for validation.'

'This isn't about validation,' she said. 'This is about closure.'

He blinked at her. 'I see. And this will give you closure, will it? Well fuck you.' He spat on the table in front of her. 'Then again, we already played that game, didn't we? And I was the best you've ever had, admit it.'

She shook her head. 'You had me fooled. I saw genuine concern in you for the cases you worked on, for the girls that Lewis Lamond murdered last year, but all of that was a lie, wasn't it?'

He shrugged. 'I didn't know it was him at first. But he came to me after the second one hit the news. Told me everything. I just had to keep up appearances.'

'You disgust me.'

'You think I enjoyed fucking you behind Ritchie's back? Think I enjoyed it at all? Look at you. Look at the *state* of you. One little flirt and you had your legs spread like warm butter.'

She closed her eyes and in that moment she wished she'd never come to see him.

'And yet it was me that finished it,' she said. 'That must have really hurt. I didn't want you any more; but I suppose you could always go back to your wife.'

'She never stopped wanting me.'

'And now she's sat in a jail cell.' De Silva smiled. 'Just like you. Jailbird man and wife.'

'At least she's alive,' he said, his lips curling back over his teeth. 'Didn't kill herself like some pussy.'

She knew now that Ritchie had killed himself because Bob's body had been discovered, because he was so frightened that someone would find out that he'd been the one who had killed Bob Brendan. That hurt her heart more than anything. She thought of him hanging from the banister, of walking in on him there.

'You tried to cover up Brendan's murder,' she said. 'You failed. You tried to shield Lamond from us. From me. You failed at that too. You manipulated me, and your wife, to meet your own ends.'

'I didn't fail there.'

'She's awaiting trial,' de Silva said. 'I'd say that's another fail. Your friend Billy murdered all of those people. The people who'd abused him or who knew about it and kept quiet. Now he's in prison too. You were sat in that lodge for months like Brokeback fucking Mountain, and we got you. *I* got you.'

'What's your point?'

'You, Billy, your wife, O'Brien. You're all in the exact same place where Lamond was.'

Crosby's eyes narrowed. 'I'll go into protection. These people aren't playing. They're serious. This isn't some little photo album from a school in the arse-end of Liverpool. Not just some app. It's bigger than that. An industry. It's money. They'll do anything to protect that.'

'I wonder how that'll end for all of you.'

'Don't mistake me, bitch. When they're done with us, they'll come for you.'

She stood up and looked down on him. 'I hope they don't come for you, whoever you think is out there. I hope you stay in here and rot for what you've done.'

Crosby smiled. 'I know you do.'

'The man at my house,' de Silva said. 'Was that you?'

He shook his head. 'Tommo,' he said. 'You had evidence that Ritchie was associated with that school. We make that disappear and then…'

'You'd make me disappear too?'

He stared.

'When I introduced you to Ritchie… you already knew him. And he knew you.'

Crosby nodded.

'And O'Brien?'

'We both did,' Crosby said. 'Me and Ritchie. O'Brien didn't know us, but me and Ritchie: we knew.'

De Silva nodded. That was it. That was all she needed to know. The elaborate scheme, though she now knew the reasons, was all still beyond her comprehension.

They did what they did. That's that.

When she got back to the car, the tears fell, and she thought about her old house, the bedroom where she'd spent so much time drinking, or vomiting, or hungover. She remembered how she felt the shadows of her grief all around her, how she'd felt them with her everywhere she went, even in the pines at Freshfields.

She couldn't live with the shadows any more, she knew that. She had to find her way forward. Find her way out of the woods of her own memories, her own grief, to see what lay beyond.

She had to find her way back to herself.

As she drove home, her mind turned to O'Brien. To the man she'd loved and respected, how she felt he had manipulated her. Groomed her. They'd finally tracked down the two detectives he'd put on the case of the man in the woods when she'd taken her leave of absence. One was missing and the other had died in a freak car accident on the M62.

He'd done that, she knew. He'd used them for appearances' sake and as they circled the truth of it all, he'd had them killed. Made them disappear. O'Brien had refused to see her, and so one question went unanswered: how did he know, then, that the body in the woods belonged to Bob Brendan?

She may never know the answer. There were many things she may never know the full answer to, and that was something she was going to have to live with. But, if Crosby's claims that the people behind The Woulds app were cleaning house, she had the grim feeling that she may not have to live with not knowing for very long.

Forty-Five

Barclay put the roller on the paint tray when the doorbell rang. His stomach grumbled at the thought of food. He'd been working so hard all day and needed the break.

The delivery driver handed him a white plastic bag, and Barclay could smell the Thai spices through it. 'Thanks, mate,' he said as he closed the door. He walked through to the kitchen, old and battered and not to his taste just yet, and found a plate in a cardboard box marked *DINNER PLATES*, in large black letters.

He poured the pad thai onto the plate and tucked in straight away. Sarah's room had been finished last week, and she'd already had her first sleep-over last night. They'd watched two movies; she'd fallen asleep ten minutes into the second one, and he'd tucked her into bed. He watched her for just a few minutes longer, and marvelled at how peaceful she seemed, how untouched by the troubles of the world.

He envied her that and loved her for it at the same time.

The living room was shaping up. He stood, plate in hand, and looked at his own handiwork. He loved the crispness of the freshly painted white walls, how clean they felt, but around the fireplace, he needed a splash of colour. He'd chosen a deep sage that added warmth, but was neutral enough to go with most furnishings.

For now, the place smelled like paint, like newness, freshness, and since he'd moved in and started work, he'd not experienced a single panic attack.

He'd start on the kitchen next, but the whole thing needed ripping out. It would be a building site for weeks on end, and the thought of it made him feel sick. Still, he had his own house now and wasn't sleeping in a single bed in his childhood bedroom.

The kitchen would be costly, but it needed doing. The cupboards were so bad the doors were coming off their hinges. It was a safety concern really, and Sarah couldn't go out there unsupervised: Barclay would never allow it, not with how it was.

He'd spoken to Nick a few times, but only ever about Sarah's care, and about the mortgage on their old home. Nick had agreed to sell up, that they'd split the money and he'd find somewhere new to live, somewhere he could afford on his own. They'd been civil, courteous, co-operative, and Barclay was thankful for that. There'd been no talk of them getting back together.

Barclay was exhausted. He'd taken the week off to finish the living room, stairs and landing, and he was almost there with it, though his body ached. He'd thought about inviting de Silva around to see it, to have some pizza and zero per cent beer, to get her out of her house, out of her headspace. But he didn't think she'd want to.

Besides, Bonnie and Laney were still staying at de Silva's while Laney secured herself a new place to live. Last he heard, she was ready to start packing.

Ayris had stayed in Liverpool, and there was no sign he was going back to London just yet. There were still things for the NCA to do. Crosby, Ritchie, O'Brien, they were only small parts of their case. The Woulds app was still unsolved, and this clean-up operation O'Brien spoke about: well, it concerned them. It concerned Barclay and de Silva too.

He picked up his plate and moved to the couch, sat down to survey his work again and felt something dig into his back. He pulled out Sarah's tablet from beneath a cushion. She must have left it when he took her home that morning. He'd have to drive it round first thing, or there would be murder come breakfast time. She liked to sit and watch a Spider-Man cartoon while her cereal turned to slop in her bowl. It was gross, but it was how she was.

He put his dinner aside, opened the tablet and grinned at her wallpaper: a picture of her, Nick and Barclay. It was taken last year at Princess Park, when he and Nick were still pretending things were fine, and Sarah was oblivious.

He scrolled to the left, saw all of the games she liked to play, Disney+ and YouTube for Kids, too. Then there it was.

His breath caught in his throat.

A brown outline of a bear's head, and at either side of it, two green pine trees. Beneath it were two words.

The Woulds.

Acknowledgements

Wow, book two already! It's been quite a whirlwind writing *Better Off Dead*, and I'm truly thankful for everyone who has shown me support throughout this process, and while *Black Water Rising* was being released. I'm going to keep the acknowledgements shorter this time, I promise!

Particular thanks go to Chris McDonald and the team at Serenity Booksellers – Stockport Noir is fantastic, to Bob McDevitt, Dawn Geddes, Lin Anderson and team at Bloody Scotland, and Marc Dunleavy and the team at Theakston Old Peculier Crime Writing Festival for taking a chance on a debut author. Your support is greatly appreciated, and I'll not forget that. Thanks to The Curious Cat Bookshop and Liverpool's Waterstones for your support, and to Pritchards of Crosby for providing the goods at the *Black Water Rising* book launch.

To my wonderful team: the patient Hattie Grünewald and the incomparable Rhian Parry from The Blair Partnership; and to Louise Cullen, Alicia Pountney, and the always-on-it Kate Shepherd – I'm sorry for all of the last-minute emails, stressing over small details, for the many mini-heart attacks I've given myself. You handle everything so brilliantly and with care.

To the other editors who've worked on this book and done amazing work in making me look like I know what I'm doing: thank you to Radhika Sonagra, Catriona Camacho and Becca Allen.

Emma Carey, you continue to be my ride-or-die when it comes to knowing what I'm trying to achieve, and for talking sense into me when it's needed.

Sarah Maclennan, my good, kind, and brilliant friend – I know you've always got my back, and I appreciate you for it.

To all of my friends (particularly The Tripod) and my family, and to Matt – thanks for your unwavering support in all of this. Love and appreciate you all so much.

Finally, thank you to every person who has picked up *Black Water Rising* and *Better Off Dead* (and hopefully took it to the till with you!), your support means so much.

I hope you've enjoyed *Better Off Dead*, and my advice to you would be: prepare yourself for book three.